Centauria — The Ancient Realm

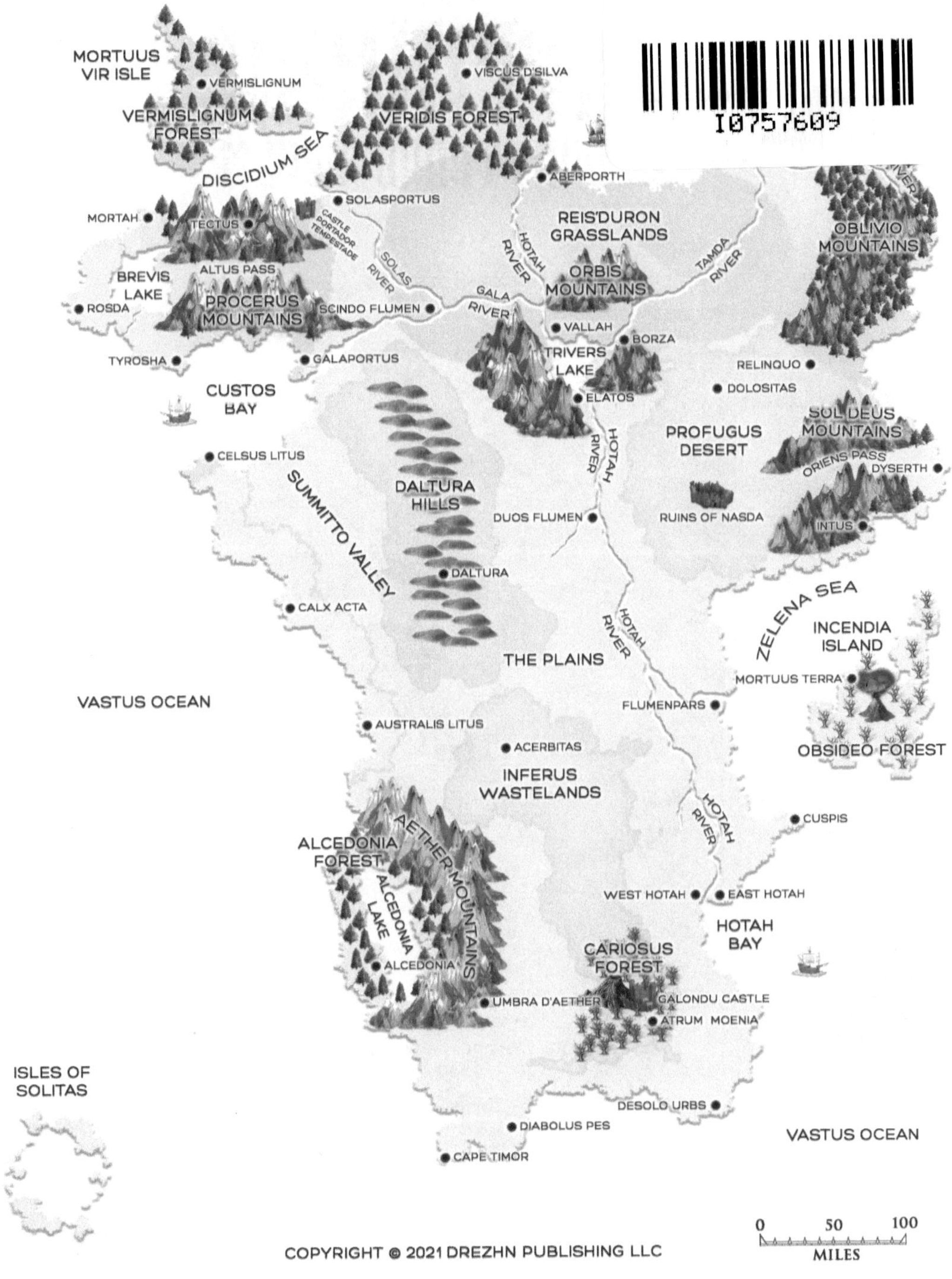

COPYRIGHT © 2021 DREZHN PUBLISHING LLC

CENTAURIA
THE SHATTERED REALM

PROPAD DEEP

TRUE HEIR

BOOK FOUR OF THE DARK HEART CHRONICLES

DREZHN

PUBLISHING

TRUE HEIR

Published by Drezhn Publishing LLC
PO BOX 67458
Albuquerque, NM 87193-7458

Print Edition - December 2021
Version 1.3 – June 2023

Cover design by Drezhn Publishing LLC
Cover illustration by Jonathan Myers

HARDBACK (DUST JACKET) ISBN: 978-1-947328-57-0
HARDBACK (CASE LAMINATE) ISBN: 978-1-947328-77-8
PAPERBACK ISBN: 978-1-947328-56-3

READ *SCOURGE* FOR FREE

Do Eshtak's tattoos hold the key to the between?

danielkuhnley.com/become-a-conqueror

Sign up and read *Scourge*, A World Of Centauria Novella. Be the **FIRST** to get sneak peeks at my upcoming novels and the chance to win **FREE** stuff, like signed books.

Never use persuasion magic on a powerful wizard.

That was Emorith's hardest lesson to learn. Right from that fateful moment, Magus forced her to use her manipulative sorcery to further his evil purposes. She regretted everything he put her through with one exception: their son Illian. Him, she loved with all her heart.

Magus demanded she cast an apocalyptic curse and destroy an unsuspecting city. She steeled herself to refuse him... but then he threatened the life of her beloved child.

With Illian's life on the line, what choice did she have? She wanted to protect the city and its citizens, but her son would always come first. No, there must be another way. Will she be able to thwart Magus and save them all in time? Or is their fate already sealed?

Scourge is a prequel novella to *The Dragon's Stone*, the first book in *The Dark Heart Chronicles* epic dragon fantasy series. If you like thrilling adventures and terrifying magic, then you'll love Daniel Kuhnley's enthralling tale.

BOOKS BY DANIEL KUHNLEY

EPIC DRAGON FANTASY

<u>The Dark Heart Chronicles</u>
*†The Dragon's Stone
*Reborn
*Rended Souls
True Heir

Scourge (novella)

SUPERNATURAL SERIAL KILLER

<u>Alice Bergman Novels</u>
*Birth Of A Killer (novella)
*The Braille Killer
*The Night Mauler
*The Chrono Slasher

CHRISTIAN YA SCI-FI/FANTASY

<u>VR Academy</u>
Kiara Kole And The Key Of Truth

* - Also available as an audiobook
† - Previously released as Dark Lament

Visit Daniel's website to find these books and more!
danielkuhnley.com

To my wife, Marsha. This book would not exist if it wasn't for your love and encouragement. You pushed me and helped me every step of the way, never letting me give up even when I felt there was no way I could ever finish the series. After fifteen years, I've finally proven you right. It is done!

To my Lord and Savior, Jesus Christ. Your light led me through the darkest days. I am forever yours.

THE DARK HEART CHRONICLES

TRUE HEIR

· 4 ·

DANIEL KUHNLEY

CHAPTER ONE

ittle dragon.

Those two words, forever seared into the forefront of her mind, drove Aria's fury. Two words tied to the only two people she loved in the world.

Little dragon.

Pravus's last words to her. The cause of Alderan's death. Fuel for her rage.

Little dragon.

Night cloaked the dark plains below as she and Cinolth flew toward the last place the little dragon had been spotted. Nothing would stand in the way of her hunting down the traitorous dragon and ripping the scales from its hide. As they drew near their destination, lightning flashed, revealing a scene below that her mind worked hard to process: a standoff.

The flash had been just that, but the image burned in her mind. Two dozen orcs, weapons drawn, surrounded four gnolls. Rage swelled in her chest and burst from her lips in a roar that rivaled that of Cinolth. It took every bit of will power to keep herself from calling down lightning from the heavens and destroying them all. Had she not known Karraar to be among them, she never would've held back.

Cinolth's voice entered her mind. *"I'll burn them alive."*

"No," she fired back. *"They might have information about the little dragon."*

A cloud of sulfuric smoke billowed from Cinolth's nostrils and swept past Aria, stinging her eyes. *"Extract the information, and then I'll eat them all. I could use a satisfying meal."*

"Until they've outlived their usefulness, I want them kept alive."

"A pack of ferzh would better serve you. These beasts live without thought of anything beyond themselves and their own survival. I assure you

that they cannot be controlled."

"And yet Pravus controlled them," she bit back.

"Do not fool yourself. Pravus bound them to himself and to each other with blood mezhik."

Aria snarled. *"Then I'll do the same."*

Cinolth's head jerked around. One of his red, serpentine eyes met her gaze. Fiery ash spewed from his mouth. "No!"

Rage simmered on the tip of Aria's tongue. "Give me one good reason."

Cinolth straightened and flew faster. *"Blood bonds weaken the spirit and lessen the strength of a wizard. Why do you think Pravus grew so weak and fell so easily?"*

As she reflected over the past year, she couldn't deny what Cinolth claimed. The man who rescued her from Portador Tempestade certainly wasn't the man who fought on the battlefield. She recalled how weak he'd grown when she first arrived at Galondu Castle. He had blamed it on the distance he'd teleported, an undeniable fact given what she now knew, but his full strength never returned as it should have. The only event that had occurred between those two events was the blood bond Pravus made with the zhebəllin.

Cinolth's head bobbed. *"Now you understand."*

"Wouldn't it still be a good idea? I could create blood bonds with every species of evolved creatures and control them all."

"Orcs, gnolls, zhebəllin, and other fallen races are susceptible to such blood oaths, but no higher races are. You are still naive and have much to learn."

"Don't you dare—" Cinolth swooped down and settled on the ground with a thud, jerking Aria forward and disrupting her thought.

The orcs and gnolls turned in their direction, weapons poised for an attack. Mezhik crackled at Aria's fingertips as she slid off the side of Cinolth's neck. She landed hard on the ground, jarring the bones from her feet all the way up through her spine. With a touch of mezhik, she cast her pain away.

Using mindspeak, she said to Cinolth, *"I'll handle this. Go find yourself some food."*

Cinolth didn't respond but took to the air, nearly knocking her off her feet. She knew he did it on purpose, but she had more important business than scolding him. Besides, it wouldn't do her a fat bit of good. Instead, she conjured a ball of light and stalked forward through the wet, waist-high, golden grass. Her fingertips stroked the stalks as she walked, reminding her of Red's corn patch back in Viscus D'Silva. She touched her stomach and smiled.

You'll live far better than I ever did, blood of my blood.

One of the orcs—a massive beast of muscles and veins—positioned himself in her path. Several fox hides, soaked with rain and covered in dried blood, draped around his thick neck. A golden ring hung from the cartilage between the nostrils of his porcine nose, and blue eyes glared from beneath ridges of fiery-red eyebrows. A mace rested atop his left shoulder.

The monster snarled and slurred his words. "Ah, yes, the famed dragon rider and recent widow. Assumed you'd be older—" He wet his lower tusks with a grayish-brown tongue. "—but you're good on the eyes… for a human. Think I might make a trophy out of you." Some of the other orcs roared with laughter.

"Enough," she growled. "You will bow when in my presence."

The beast laughed, yet his hand tightened around the handle of his mace. "Orcs bow to no one but our master, Zin."

Aria balled her right hand, and a purple, sparkling glow enveloped her fist. She yanked her arm down by her side. The orc groaned and dropped to his knees; his height now matched hers.

Several of the other orcs drew closer. One of them roared and launched himself at her. With a flick of the wrist, she released a burst of mezhik into the ground. A seven-foot-long spike of pure granite shot up through the grass and impaled the beast mid torso.

Blood gushed from the wound and ran down the length of the spike. The orc sputtered blood and wheezed one final breath before his yellow eyes dulled and he fell limp. The other orcs quickly backed off.

Not as stupid as I thought.

She turned her attention back to the first orc and moved within inches of his face. "What's your name, foul beast?"

The orc fought to stand back up, but Aria kept the air around him weighed down with a thousand pounds of force. It took a good minute for him to realize that struggling was futile. Finally, he relaxed and said, "Murtag." His breath reeked of sewage.

Aria retreated several paces, swiping at the air in front of her nose. She coughed. "You will address me as your queen. Am I clear?"

"As glass."

She squeezed her fist tighter, dropping Murtag to his hands and knees. "Did you not just hear what I commanded of you?"

Murtag nodded. "Yes."

"Address me properly, or I'll remove your head from your shoulders and mount it on one of the walls in my castle."

Murtag's face nearly touched the ground. "Yes… my queen," he grunted.

"There you go." She withdrew some of her mezhik, lessening the force driving him toward the ground. "That wasn't so hard, was it?"

Murtag rose back up on his knees. "No, my queen."

"Good." She eyed the other orcs and the four gnolls. Each of them failed to meet her glare. "From this point forward, all of you will set aside your differences and work together in service to me. If any of you are caught fighting, you will be put to death. Both parties, no matter who started it. If this isn't something you feel can be achieved, let me know now. I'll be happy to end your lives right here."

"No, my queen," each muttered.

"Very well." Aria moved around Murtag, keeping the pressure on his shoulders. The others backed away, and she strode toward the four gnolls.

Karraar, her indebted slave, bowed low as she approached. "My queen."

The others mimicked him, albeit with what she perceived as a touch of reluctance. Her rage flared but remained within her control. She would deal with the three of them later. Right now, she needed answers.

"Rise." The four beasts straightened, each towering over her by a good two feet. She scanned her surroundings but failed to see the reason Karraar had requested her presence. "What's the meaning of this? Where is the dragon?" Mezhik crackled just beneath her skin, begging to be released. "Did you request my assistance to save your own hide?"

"Never, my queen. Please, follow me." Karraar turned and led her a dozen paces south where the grass lay splayed on the ground for a good, long stretch. The other gnolls remained behind with the orcs. "This is where the beast crashed down. It slid to a stop at the far end over there."

Her eyes followed the conjured light as it swept across the area.

No little dragon.

She walked over to the far end of the damaged area and knelt to examine the grass. Many of the stalks were charred, and dried blood spattered the surrounding foliage. A single claw mark pressed into an exposed patch of wet dirt.

Aria stood and faced Karraar. "And then it took off again?"

Karraar joined her. "Yes, but only for a short stretch." He led her farther south until they reached another spot. "It crashed again right here."

A three-foot diameter of smashed grass. But still no dragon. "Help me understand why I'm still not seeing a dragon. What the gods happened?"

Karraar scowled at the ground, then nodded. "I think you'll want to hear the story first-hand." He signaled one of the other gnolls.

A gangly beast with brownish-orange fur and mismatched eyes—one a deep amber and the other a yellowish white—joined them. Bloodstains painted his leather armor, and a deep, puss-filled gash ran crosswise along the right side of his neck and down into his collarbone. He favored the shoulder, his arm hanging limp at his side.

Karraar pushed him forward. "Tell our queen what happened, Durqel."

Durqel picked at the wound on his neck and kept glancing back at the other two gnolls as he spoke. "The others think I'm crazy, but I know what I saw. Gods be my witness." Although gruff like Karraar's, Durqel's voice came out several octaves higher and a bit faster. Almost slurred. "When I moved in for the kill, the beast struck me with one of its claws. Quick as a flash." He pointed at his neck. "Right here. Never felt anything so painful. Surprised me. And I don't surprise easy. Ask Karraar."

Karraar gave Durqel a curt nod. "I can confirm that. Durqel may not look like much, but there's no one I'd rather have fighting at my side. That is, of course, other than you, my queen."

Aria ignored the complement and the reeking stench that permeated the air. "And then what happened?"

"Gods be my witness—" Durqel's eyes shifted about as he hunched down half a foot. "—the dragon changed into a man right before my eyes. I admit it left me stunned. Wasn't expecting a man. Didn't even know dragons could shift."

A shifting dragon, or a man?

Aria frowned, the tale perplexing. "What did the man look like, and what happened to him? Where did he go?"

Durqel shrugged and licked his wound with a long, pink-spotted, gray tongue. His face contorted, and then he spat something greenish brown on the ground. "Sorry about that." He shook his head, then continued, "It happened so fast. An instant if not quicker. Can't recall his face. The lot of you all look the same, you know. Anyway, he stood. Back to me. Tall for your kind. Stepped away from me and poof!" He raised his hands and spread his fingers wide.

Aria's mind searched for explanation but came up short. "Poof?"

"Yeah, just that. There one moment and disappeared the next. Mezhik, you ask me." Durqel cocked his head and stared up at the dark sky. "Do dragons have mezhik?" He glanced over his shoulder in the direction Cinolth had flown off. "Never met one personally. Not entirely sure I'd want to. They would be much scarier if they did have mezhik."

She eyed Durqel. "You're sure of what you saw?" He nodded wildly.

"Durqel is good for his word." Karraar bent down and pointed at a spot on the ground. "Here's your proof."

Her gaze followed the path of Karraar's outstretched finger. Plain as day sat a single footprint wedged between flattened stalks of grass. Large for a human yet too small for a giant. The five toes ruled out orcs and ogres, each having six toes per foot.

Aria touched Durqel's arm, her fingers twitching with mezhik. The beast flinched, and his eyes doubled in size, but he didn't pull away. She had half a mind to drain the life from his bones for allowing the little dragon to escape. However, another beast loyal to her might prove useful in the future.

The stench of Durqel's breath churned her stomach when he exhaled. Rotting flesh and decades' worth of unscrubbed filth—far worse than that of Murtag's breath. She glanced down at her flat belly, knowing the pregnancy heightened her sense of smell.

You will be worth it all, my love.

Swallowing back revulsion, Aria focused on Durqel's eyes. They jittered within their deep-set sockets. An involuntary reaction to something she knew well not long ago: fear. Once, she would've pitied a beast like him, but now it only made her loathe him more.

An intolerable weakness.

One thought would end his life. Mezhik danced across her fingertips. Intoxicated her with its touch. Soon, she would give in to it, but not just yet.

Aria set her jaw and spoke through clenched teeth. "Now's the time for you to really think about what you saw, Durqel."

His eyes focused on her hand, his pupils dilated. "I told you all I know. I swear it." Somehow, the beast managed to make himself smell even worse as renewed sweat glistened through his fur and ran between his eyes.

Aria recalled a book in Pravus's library that spoke of wizards with the gift to view memories of those they touched: *Fizärd Mämärä*. She didn't know of any, but Wizard Wrik might.

Thinking of the giant man eased the pain of her losses just a little, and she wondered if news of Alderan and Pravus had reached his ears. It likely hadn't, given the timing. But how would he react to it? The man worked for Pravus, but the two of them were always at each other's throats. Still, Wrik displayed a fondness for Alderan. Then again, it could've been all for show for her benefit.

She pushed Wizard Wrik and everything else from her mind. It would all have to wait. Right now, she must focus.

Durqel's coarse, grimy fur stuck to her fingertips when she pulled her hand away from his arm. She wiped her fingers on her trousers but knew a thorough scrubbing and a long soak with perfumes would be required to eradicate Durqel's stench from her skin. Moreover, the trousers she wore would receive no such treatment. They would face the flames as soon as she reached Galondu Castle.

Aria turned to Karraar. "Escort Durqel to Galondu Castle and personally assure that he's provided with the *finest* amenities. I must speak with him on this matter again."

Karraar bowed low, a grin upon his muzzle. "I understand, my queen. I assure you he will *not* lack of want."

"Good." She withdrew her mezhik and flexed her hand. A few dozen yards away, Murtag rose to his feet.

After signaling the other two gnolls, Karraar and Durqel dropped on all fours and headed south across The Plains.

Aria reached out to Cinolth with her mind. *"Come for me."*

She returned to the group of orcs and laid out her demands of them. "The lot of you will camp here for a fortnight. If anything returns to this area, you will capture it and bring it to me, understood?"

The orcs looked to their leader, Murtag. He nodded, and then they all said, "Yes, my queen."

"And where will we find you, my queen?" Murtag said.

Aria pointed behind herself. "Galondu Castle, to the south."

"I know of it." Murtag dipped his head ever so slightly. "It will be as you've commanded."

Pravus had relished power, and now she understood why. Every command she uttered built upon the last, compounding her confidence. And each command carried out added to her power. Soon, she would be unstoppable.

"Good."

Cinolth landed close by, driving the orcs backward. She smiled as she returned to Cinolth and mounted him. The air cracked like a whip beneath Cinolth's great wings as he lifted them off the ground and carried them high into the sky.

A ferocious army of clouds gathered around them, tall with thunder and black with rain. Reminded her of home. She missed the days spent on the porch back in Viscus D'Silva, rocking in her chair, listening to the pouring rain, and jumping with every flash of lightning and rumble of thunder. Although it hadn't been that long ago, the memories felt like another life. One she dreamt up but never actually lived.

Perhaps it was.

She mindspoke to Cinolth. *"Where are we headed?"*

"To the wall outside Duos Flumen. The gateway needs to be reactivated so that our armies can travel freely."

Had her mind not been occupied with death and a little dragon, she would've suggested such a plan. *"Good."*

A few minutes later, Cinolth spoke to her again. *"And what did your dogs have to say about our little dragon?"*

A crack of thunder shook the air and opened the heavens once more. Drenching rain fell hard, pummeling her face. Cold. Wet. Perfect. She held onto Cinolth's neck with her legs and leaned back against him. *"Can dragons wield mezhik?"*

"Yes, but the gift is extremely rare."

She opened her mouth and swallowed down the raindrops. *"And can they shift?"*

"Not without assistance."

Assistance?

Her mind drew a blank. *"What do you mean by that?"*

"A dragon would need an object imbued with mezhik, like a necklace or ring. Only the most powerful and skilled of mages could create such an object. Therefore, the dragon would need assistance."

"According to one of my dogs as you call them, our little dragon shifted into a man and then teleported away."

"Then our little dragon is no dragon at all."

Aria sat up straight.

A man then…

The thought pumped her heart harder. Leaning forward, she rested against Cinolth's hot neck. Steam rose off her face as she allowed her mind to wrap itself around her newfound knowledge. Every wizard she knew had been accounted for on the battlefield, so who was this dragon man? Why did they kill Alderan?

An impossible thought struck her. A vile, evil thought she dared not nurture. She pushed it from her mind, but it crept back in and dug its claws deep into her mind. No matter what she did, she couldn't shake it. If she couldn't shake it, she must deal with it. So, she did.

How did Alderan wind up behind me when he'd been fighting Cinolth?

She swallowed hard, forcing her mind to think through the painful process.

Did he try to kill me?

Nausea grabbed her stomach and wrung it like a wet rag. A mournful groan slipped through her parted lips.

Alderan? My own brother?

Tears burned her eyes and sorrow tore at her heart. Yet truth didn't ring with those thoughts. How could it?

Alderan would never have betrayed me.

No… he must've saved my life. But from who?

If it was a dragon that had attacked her and not a man, as Cinolth claimed, where had it come from? Why target her? A single, simple answer popped into her mind: *because of Cinolth.*

What other explanation could there be?

None.

Killing her would kill Cinolth, too. But how had the little dragon known?

"Somehow, it must've been you," she said aloud.

"I am the dragon man?" Cinolth scoffed.

"No, but you're the cause of my brother's death. You took him from me. You're the one who brought the little dragon into my life. You killed them both."

Cinolth lurched back, folded his wings against his body, and twisted his head around to face her. The wind and rain whipped around them as they started to plummet toward the ground. *"Explain yourself before we crash into the earth."*

"You told me the other dragons hated you and kicked you out of the Valley of Dragons. I'm certain they're aware of your return. They must be the ones who sent the little dragon to kill me. Therefore, it's your fault. Alderan's dead because of you. Admit it."

"As I explained before, a gift such as wielding mezhik is rare for dragons. So rare that only one dragon alive has that power. You must understand that only three dragons in the history of Centauria have ever possessed such a gift. So, trust me when I tell you that the little dragon was no dragon at all."

"Trust you! How could I ever do so after what you did to Pravus? You impaled him with your tail and bit him in half!" She raised her arms, used her mezhik to gather energy from the raging storm, and drove lightning through the back of Cinolth's skull. It did nothing to him, and she knew it wouldn't, but the act made her feel marginally better.

"Enough," growled Cinolth.

He spread his wings wide about thirty meters above the ground. His entire body jerked back as his mighty wings caught wind once more with a wicked *thwack*. Aria's face slammed against the back of Cinolth's neck, narrowly missing one of his spikes. Pain blistered from her left cheek, and a coppery taste filled her mouth.

She pushed herself upright and spat blood into the wind. Her tongue confirmed two loose teeth and a gash on the inside of her cheek. She'd suffered far worse at the hands of evil men. Unlike then, she now possessed the ability to heal herself. Purplish-white tendrils rose from her fingertips and flowed into her cheek. The pain faded as the wound closed.

A cancerous silence grew between them as they glided across the late evening sky. The rain continued to fall in sheets, but they'd outflown the lightning and thunder. At least that which existed outside of her mind. Within her mind, the storm raged with violence unmatched by anything the gods could conjure. She would never forgive Cinolth.

Ten minutes later, Cinolth's voice broke into her mind. *"As soon as you take up the throne, you must make several decrees. First, anyone who defies your rule will be dipped in tar and chained to poles outside the castle gates where they will serve as human torches to light the night. Second, anyone who comes forward with verifiable knowledge of Cyrus's whereabouts will be given a position in your courts. Furthermore, I will send my army across the Ancient Realm and raze any town or city that tries to prevent them from flushing out those who escaped from the Three Kingdoms. Lastly, we will sail the oceans until we capture Princess Zelanora. She must be executed in public so that your rule cannot be challenged."*

Rage nearly blinded Aria. It took every bit of concentration to continue holding on. She breathed deep and said nothing.

"Good. Allow your hate for me to build. It will soon prove useful."

Knowing her thoughts were not hers alone, Aria focused on the dark clouds above them and cleared her mind of everything but her three loves. She mindspoke to Cinolth through their connection. *"A grand funeral for*

Pravus and Alderan must be held. The realm will know how much I loved them and the lengths I'll go to avenge their deaths. After that, we will announce the coming of an heir."

"For Pravus, yes, but there will be no funeral for your brother."

Aria beat Cinolth's neck with her fist until his scales slickened with her blood. "I am your master! You will not deny me!"

"Do not fool yourself. You are master of nothing. Not even your own mind or the mezhik you possess. Once you've rested, you'll come to your senses and understand why what you want cannot be so."

"Mark my words, dragon. After we vanquish our last enemy, I'll find a way to rip the beating heart from your chest."

Cinolth laughed in her mind. *"I look forward to that day."*

As do I.

As they flew south, the gigantic wall that wizards Mutius and Bardaric built rose out of the night, its rocky surface slickened with recent rain and highlighted by moonlight. Cinolth landed near its center, and Aria leapt to the ground. Her boots sank several inches into the sticky mud.

"I must hunt," Cinolth said.

Aria ripped her boots away from the mud's grasp and stalked forward. "I will not wait for you."

"So be it." Cinolth beat his wings and took to the sky, nearly blowing her over in the process. She had no doubt he did it on purpose.

She shrugged away her wrath as best she could and reached out to Karraar with her mind. Given the great distance that separated them, she expected the attempt to fail, yet somehow, they connected. *"Head toward my location. The gateway will be functional by the time you arrive. It will save days from your journey."*

"Yes, my queen," Karraar replied.

Aria severed the connection with Karraar and focused her mind on both the great wall before her and on its twin just north of Galondu Castle. Only one of the one hundred virtual ropes had been severed between the two walls after her army had passed through the gateway. It would be trivial for her to make the connection again and re-enable the gateway.

Within her mind, she located the missing connection between the two walls and strung the virtual rope between them. The effort, far greater than she'd imagined, stole the strength from her legs and took her to her knees.

As before, a brilliant light shone from the wall but didn't sting her eyes or blind her. Heat blasted her and the wall quaked as the rock transformed into magma and the magma into black glass. The heat faded, and the wall's surface shimmered, rocked, and swirled. An image formed beyond the violent surface: Galondu Castle.

She forced herself back to her feet but struggled to pull her boots from the mud. The castle swayed before her, and her vision spotted with darkness. The world tilted sideways, and the muddy ground rushed toward her, but then something caught her from behind and yanked her back to her feet just before she plunged into the mud face-first.

Weak with grief and fatigue, Aria collapsed into strong arms. "I've got you, my queen."

Pravus?

The world slipped away from her.

CHAPTER TWO

Jagger stood atop Obitus Ridge, her mauve tunic billowing at her back. A lavish, bluish-purple garment dressed the skies overhead, adorned with wisps of fiery clouds. A sight fit for kings and queens but rarely witnessed by anyone but those of her kind. After all, few outsiders had traveled to Reothadh in the last several centuries. The ones who dared do so left the world without a trace.

The last of the evening sunrays fought to warm her back and neck, but the bitter, biting wind matched their strength. The battle between the two foes would soon be over as dusk marched up the far ridge from the west. To her, a native of Reothadh, neither cold nor heat bore consequence. With skin as thick and as tough as dragon scales, she rarely gave notice to either.

Yet today, her skin prickled. For certain, it wasn't the cold that gave rise to the gooseflesh on her arms and neck. Nor was it borne of impending danger or certain doom. Perhaps it rose with an awareness of wonder and awe. Better yet, she sensed that it prickled with anticipation.

Jagger's eyes narrowed and her brow furrowed as she peered across the darkening chasm and scanned the eastern face of the western ridge. All looked as it had before. She squinted, hoping to glimpse something she'd missed, but nothing revealed itself. "Anticipation of what?"

Three-thousand feet below lay Zimska Vala, a forgotten village nestled within the circular ridges that formed the tail of the Zmaj Mountains. The only place she'd ever known.

Home.

Jagger gazed down at the dimly lit, snow-covered vale. To the untrained eye, Zimska Vala appeared calm and serene. A simple place where one might find kindness, warmth, and shelter no matter one's past or future. Perhaps even love. But her eyes knew better. Knew what darkness lay beneath its placid white surface. Yes, she knew the hearts of her people.

Dark as my skin and as cold as winter's peak.

The thought startled her. Gave her pause as she swallowed hard. Words hissed from her lips in a vaporous cloud, "Is that really what I think of them? Of us?"

How could she not? History didn't lie.

To the north, snow crunched beneath heavy feet. The tell-tale jangle of copper coins accompanied the crunch. The noise drove her dark thoughts to the back of her mind; deep into the shadows where they could grow without notice. Unchecked. She need not look to verify Grimbold, her father and fellow flamewatcher, approached.

An assassin he's not.

Jagger smiled to herself. "Evening, brother."

They were all brothers and sisters while on watch, and it'd taken her several months to get used to such terms with respect to Grimbold, her father. She guessed he might've had a tough time calling her sister at first, too. Although he never voiced it if he had. Now, after twelve long years, it came more naturally to her lips than "father" did.

Grimbold stopped next to her, matching her height shoulder-to-shoulder, but only because of the uneven ground. Had it been flat, he would eclipse her by a good hand's length. Perhaps a bit more.

"Sister." His baritone voice rumbled in her ears. "I assure you that the noise I make when I approach benefits you."

Jagger shook her head and let out a soft snort as she eyed Grimbold. "How do you do it?"

Black whiskers glistened on the man's cheek for just a moment as the last remnants of sunlight caught their wiry ends before fading away. Had it not been for his trimmed beard, a feature attainable only by those in their clan who eclipsed sixty years, she never would've guessed his age. His face featured no wrinkles, not even around his beautiful, sapphire eyes.

His mouth curled upward on one side as he turned and faced her. "And what is it you think I do?"

Heat flushed her cheeks even as the words spilled over the edge of her lip. "You read minds."

Grimbold chuckled. "Were that the case, I'm certain we'd be having a very different conversation."

"Then what?" As usual, he didn't answer, so she probed further. "Tell me your secret."

"There is nothing…" His voice trailed off and his eyes grew wide as his gaze broke from hers and moved toward the south.

She turned, her mouth open with words that teetered on the tip of her tongue. It took but a moment for her to locate the source that had silenced him, and it drove away the need for words. A fair distance down the steep, snowy slope, a faint light emanated. Anticipation consumed her once more.

"Auh!" She reached over and took Grimbold's hand as tears formed in the corners of her eyes. "It… can't be, can it?"

Grimbold squeezed her hand but attempted no reply. A sideways glance at the man sucked the breath from her lungs. Tears streaked his face and hung in his beard even as the smile he wore broadened. Never in her life had she witnessed her father cry, and the sight of those tears drove ones of her own down the sides of her face. Yes, she found her answer. The source of her anticipation.

The Cave of Rebirth.

Her skin prickled once again. Grimbold turned to leave, but Jagger held fast to his hand. "Wait…"

He faced her again, his brow furrowed. "For what?"

"I…" She what? Had a feeling that something was different? Not as it should be?

Grimbold glanced back toward the cave. "We must go tell the others." His stare hardened as his focus returned to her. "Now."

Jagger clung to him and wiped her face with her other hand. "No one else can know. At least not yet."

"What?" His tone cut into her like a jagged rock. He shook his head. "No, no, no." Grimbold pointed at the southern slope. "That light is what we've been waiting for. Nearly a century, Jagger. Do you hear me?"

"Yes, but—"

"This moment defines my entire existence. *Our* existence."

"I know it does, but…" She couldn't look him in the eye any longer.

"But what?" He stamped his foot in the snow. "How can you stand there and tell me that no one else can know? They have every right to. It's our duty to inform the clan. You know that."

Jagger released his hand and knelt on one knee. She closed her eyes and shoved her hands deep into the snow. The ground hummed and tickled her fingertips as she reached toward the cave with her mind. "Can you not feel it? Something is different."

"Different how?"

She opened her eyes and motioned with her head. "Join me. Feel for yourself."

Grimbold glowered at her. "I'm not like you. I don't sense things the way you do." His expression soured further. "And neither should you."

Sometimes, Grimbold's stubbornness nibbled her nerves. This was one of those times. "You can, but you choose not to."

Grimbold scoffed. "And why would I do that?"

"I don't know. Maybe you're scared of what might happen. What you might feel."

"Pfft." He crossed his arms and returned to the question at hand. "So then, what's different?"

Jagger closed her eyes again as the past flooded her mind and pulled her into its tempest. She was much younger. Just a girl. The adults in the village were meeting to discuss some matter concerning the loss of livestock. The subject insignificant, she and the other children engaged in a game of hide-and-find. Soon, she found herself wandering through the home of Bannok, one of the elders. She shouldn't have been there. Knew it was wrong even as she scoured the three-room house without thought as to what she might be looking for. The home proved far larger and more decadent than the single room shack she shared with her father. Yet it felt far less inviting.

Just as she was about to leave, something caught her eye. Buried in the corner of the main room behind a stout wooden desk, she discovered an ancient scroll. Unrolled on the desk, she couldn't decipher the cryptic symbols scrawled upon its surface. Still, because of the way her mind had always worked, she committed every detail—right down to the last dot and curve—to memory.

Time moved forward within her mind. Several years later. Elder Bannok stood before her and a few others and taught them how to read and write what he called "the ancient language." Days later, memories of the scroll returned to her. Its cryptic symbols filled her head and morphed into discernible words. The prophetic words spoke of future events, but their meaning remained incomprehensible.

Jagger's eyes snapped open to the present. Arteries jerked in her neck as the words leapt from the scroll within her mind, alive with meaning. Pulse racing, she pulled her hands from the snow and stood. She looked Grimbold in the eye. "Gwendor isn't the one who comes through the fire." Excitement trilled her voice.

Fear crept into Grimbold's features and lifted his voice an octave. "You can't possibly know that."

She scowled at him. "Yes, I can, and I do."

He scowled back. "And *how* do you know?"

Jagger closed her eyes for a moment. Focused on the Cave of Rebirth and how it had felt. "Because the one coming possesses… *mezhik.*"

"Mezhik!" The blood drained from Grimbold's face, and he swayed on wobbly legs. She caught him as he collapsed onto his knees and pulled him into her arms.

Her fingers kneaded the thick, coarse hair on the back of his head. "Now you understand why we can tell no one?"

He leaned back, stared her in the eye, then nodded. "If what you feel is correct, and something has changed, the elders will blame us just because we witnessed it, and they'll kill us both."

She scowled at the darkened sky as though it had somehow become the enemy and not her clan. "That's right."

Grimbold sighed. "But I thought we awaited Gwendor's return." He stood and stepped over to the edge of the ridge. His hand raked into his hair and stopped at the crown of his head. "How can this be?"

"It's simple." She rose. "Gwendor must be dead."

Grimbold turned back, his features twisted with confusion. "Yes, but that's when he returns to us. It has always been this way. Unless…" His eyes narrowed for a moment and then grew wide.

She nodded. "Yes, brother. He gave his life to another… or someone stole it from him."

"Gods…" Grimbold pulled on his beard.

"So, you believe me now?"

He ignored her question and turned back toward the vale. "We must reach the cave before the next watch and seal off its opening before anyone else sees the light and discovers the truth."

Jagger nodded. "I know." Despite a sense of urgency, she stood there, her eyes locked on the faint light as her mind warred over what came next.

Grimbold kissed the top of her head. "We must go. The Cave of Rebirth awaits, and the night won't last forever."

"Yes."

Chills swept through her in waves as she reached beneath her tunic and fished out a short, wooden whistle that hung from her neck by a strip of leather. Grimbold retrieved his own whistle—one identical to hers apart from the name carved into its underside. Each name matched that of the ferzh the whistle would summon. Jagger's whistle bore the name Eis and Grimbold's Rauch.

Together, they blew them. No detectable noise ushered from the whistles, but each offered a unique tune audible to just a single creature. Within twenty seconds, the two wolf-like beasts appeared on the ridge with them.

Rauch, the male ferzh, stood several inches taller than Eis and had broader shoulders. Perfect for carrying someone Grimbold's size. Rauch's dark-gray and black fur blended with the shadows, and his haunting, yellow eyes displayed wisdom gained only with age. Lean and muscular, he ruled the surrounding snow-capped mountains and every creature within them.

Eis was unlike any other ferzh Jagger had ever seen. Her thick, white fur shone in the pale light, and her icy-green eyes displayed a kindness unheard of among her species. Jagger had never laid eyes upon a more beautiful creature.

She and Jagger were perfect companions. The two of them loved each other, not as master and slave but as two sisters transcending species. The clan envied the unbreakable bond they shared.

Grimbold mounted Rauch, leaned over Rauch's haunches, then grabbed two fistfuls of Rauch's thick mane. A wicked smile twisted Grimbold's face when he looked back at Jagger. "To the light!" He and Rauch plunged over the edge of the ridge and vanished from Jagger's view.

Jagger climbed onto Eis's back and twisted her fingers into Eis's luxurious fur. The beast looked back at her and growled low, signaling her desire to chase after Rauch. Jagger smiled as she leaned forward and tucked herself against Eis.

"I know," Jagger said through mindspeak. *"You don't ever want to get left behind."* Stomach aflutter, she held on tight, took a deep breath, and said, *"Go."*

Without hesitation, Eis lunged forward and descended the steep slope, carrying Jagger toward a future she couldn't begin to fathom.

CHAPTER THREE

Nardus sat at one of the large tables in the Great Library with Theyn, Zerenity, Wrik, Rakzar, Urza, Ridan, Bakkan, and Gnaud, yet his mind kept returning to the battlefield. To Shardan. Shardan's death. Sacrifice.

No matter how he looked at it, he failed to make sense of what went wrong. Shardan wore the amulet Nardus had given him. It should've protected him from the little dragon's fire just as it had from Cinolth's flames.

So why didn't it?

He turned to Gnaud. "Shardan wore Magus's amulet. How could he have died?"

Gnaud cocked his head. "Are you referring to the red, teardrop-shaped amulet with black wings?"

"The very one," Nardus said.

"*Drezhn Herţ.*" Gnaud nodded thoughtfully. "I was under the impression it had been lost to the ages."

The crypt and a multitude of spiders crawled into Nardus's mind. He shook them off and clenched his fist. "It was until I yanked it off the corpse of Magus Carac in *Ţämbaḻl dhef Däd Dhä.*"

"Oh my!" Gnaud grabbed his own face and pulled on his long whiskers. "Such a dark picture I'd rather not have painted in my mind."

"Perhaps the amulet lost its enchantment." Wrik's tone made it seem as though he might know more than he offered. But then again, how could he? He hadn't been on the battlefield.

But he knows prophecy.

Nardus didn't know Wrik very well at all, but the big man had helped him save Gnaud and get Theyn's shifting under control. So, why would he hold back vital information about the nature of Shardan's death, especially given the relationship he seemed to have had with Shardan?

He wouldn't.

They were all under great duress because of Cinolth. Therefore, none of them likely sounded like themselves. So, he let it pass.

"Maybe, but I don't think so." Nardus scowled at the book lying before him. "I'm certain something else must've happened. I'm just not seeing what it is right now." He sighed. "I won't rest until I figure it out."

Theyn placed her hand on his leg beneath the table. "Neither will I."

"You both need to let it go and focus on the present," Wrik said. "Otherwise, we have no chance of defeating Cinolth."

Wrik had no family. No son. He couldn't possibly understand. Even so, Wrik was right. Nardus knew it but still wanted to rip the man's head off for saying it.

But what would figuring it out accomplish? Even if he discovered what happened to Shardan, it wouldn't bring Shardan back. Nothing would.

"You're right." He swallowed his anger and turned his attention to the book laid open before him. *The Banishment of Light.* Its thin, translucent pages were worn with age. Unlike most books of history, this one didn't focus around the events of an age or a specific ruler. Instead, it focused on a single subject: Hemär Dhef Əllíṭ.

Had Nardus known of the book's existence a thousand years ago, Centauria's history would've been much different. The situation they now faced likely never would've happened. Even though he possessed the ability to slow down time, he couldn't turn it back or move it forward. As far as he knew, no one in the history of the world ever could. But if it were possible for him to do so, would he? The Cyrus side of him wouldn't hesitate, but he was no longer one man or of one mind.

None of my children would exist.

The question persisted in the back of his mind as he focused on the ancient text before him. He peered up at the others and waited for their conversations to cease. Once they did, he said, "Listen to this." His finger scanned the words as he read aloud, "ʕätūr himself forged *Hemär Dhef Əllíṭ* with his own hands deep within the core of the planet."

"The Hammer of Light?" Ridan said.

Nardus confirmed with a nod, then said, "You know the ancient language?"

Ridan glared at Nardus. "Are ya surprised of this because I'm female, because I'm dwarven, or both?"

"Both," Urza confirmed. "But especially because you're a dwarf."

Ridan rose from her chair. "Ya think I can't take ya?"

Click-click!

Silver flashed with light as Urza twirled her knives. "I'll carve you up like a roasted boar before you take another breath."

Nardus was about to intervene when he caught motion out of the corner of his eye. Zerenity's hand moved ever slightly in a circular motion.

What are you up to?

The scent of lavender blossomed in the room as long stems topped with purple flowers grew right out of the tabletop. As tensions eased, the flowers withered.

Well done, Zerenity.

Ridan eased back into her chair. "As I was about to say, how does one forge a weapon made of light?"

Zerenity leaned over the table, her silver locks dragging across it. "The weapon isn't made of light but possesses the light of Ɂäṭūr himself."

"That's ridiculous." Urza twirled her knives one last time and sheathed them. "The gods don't exist."

Theyn bared her teeth. "Speak for yourself, *Ʊnbäəlläfär*. Zhedäɂ Ɂʊn has protected me my entire life." Claws dug into Nardus's leg.

Nardus winced. "Theyn, my leg." She ripped her hand away without as much as a glance. Five spots darkened with fresh blood on his trousers.

"The sun god?" Urza growled with laughter. "She's no more real than Ɂin, the moon god."

Ridan leapt upon the table. Daggers flew from her eyes, and she seethed. "Say one more thing against the gods, and I'll show ya their wrath!" Bakkan rose from beneath the table and made his presence known with a deep, guttural growl.

Urza's knives twirled in her hands again. "They don't—"

Nardus slammed his fist down on the table and stood. "Enough!"

The room fell silent as Ridan returned to her chair. Urza backed off a little slower than previously. Bakkan held his ground between Ridan and Urza, his hackles raised and froth hanging from his jowls.

Nardus glared at each of them in turn before speaking again. "Our backs are against the wall, and we choose to fight amongst ourselves? No!" He smacked the table again. "This isn't the time. In fact, there is no time where fighting between us serves a purpose."

"He's right," Rakzar said. "The odds are already against us. Let's not make them worse. We must work together, or all will be lost. Everyone needs to sit down and listen to what the man has to say."

"Oh my, yes." The little gordak peered up at Nardus and smiled. "Please, do continue."

Nardus took a deep breath as he sat back down. After locating his previous place in the text, he read aloud, "Once completed, Ƨäṭūr presented the mighty hammer as a gift to Dredge Marlocke, the first ruler of not just the Ancient Realm but all Centauria."

Zerenity's eyebrows rose. "He ruled all nine realms?"

"Remember, this was thousands of years ago." Wrik's golden eyes gleamed behind thick spectacles. "At that time, only one realm existed in the world." He drew his hands together and formed a circle with his forefingers and thumbs.

"Yes, yes. One realm." Gnaud removed his spectacles and began cleaning them with his shirt. "Well before the cartographers' maps were ever used."

Ridan cocked her head. "What's the cartographers' maps?"

Nardus sighed heavily. "Not that your question is invalid, Ridan, but time is short, and we need to focus. May I continue, and this time without interruption?"

Everyone agreed with a curt nod, except Rayah. She sat alone at another table with her back to the group. Nardus understood her pain all too well and didn't blame her for not participating in the discussion. If not for the urgency of their situation, he would've done just the same.

When the time is right, I will mourn for you, my son.

Swallowing his own pain, Nardus began reading again, "A prophet himself, Dredge Marlocke prophesied that the hammer would never be used as a weapon of war but would serve just one purpose: to destroy the dark heart. Because of this prediction, he had the hammer placed in a secret vault and the vault sealed with mezhik wards that could only be broken once the dark heart revealed itself to the world."

Cinolth The Dark.

He scanned the rest of the page with his finger and then flipped to the next page before reading further. "During the Great War, Magus Carac located the vault and found a way to circumvent the wards protecting it. He took the hammer and tried using every kind of mezhik in existence to destroy it, but the hammer proved indestructible. Once he realized the task futile, Magus sent his most loyal servant, Verin, to hide the hammer deep within the Quietus Forest. No one ever saw the hammer again, nor did anyone ever hear from Verin again after that day."

Nardus sat back in his chair and ran his fingers through his hair. They needed the hammer to destroy Cinolth's heart and rid Centauria of him once and for all. However, many more obstacles still stood in their way before the hammer would prove useful. Without Shardan's bow to pierce Cinolth's scales, they had little chance of defeating the dragon. But even that obstacle wasn't the first they must tackle. The list seemed endless. The more he thought about their odds, the more the fire in his gut dwindled.

What chance do we have of winning?

Rakzar's claws clicked against the tabletop. "Isn't the Quietus Forest—"

"Haunted?" said Urza.

Rakzar growled. "That's not what I was going to say. Everyone knows there's no such thing as ghosts."

"Really?" Urza crossed her arms. "How about you tell that to your friend Amicus."

"He was a figment of my imagination, not a ghost."

Urza shrugged. "Are they not one and the same?"

"Forest giants live there." Everyone turned and watched Rayah approach the table. "That's what Rakzar was going to say."

Zerenity smiled as she placed her arm around Rayah's shoulders. "The giants might be big, but they lack smarts and often turn against each other during confrontation. They present a minor problem compared to fizbärz."

Ridan's forehead scrunched. "And what are those?"

"Evil little creatures that buzz in your ears and chant lullabies that put you in a trance and make you forget everything you've ever known, including yourself." Wrik grinned, his teeth gleaming in the light. "Once they've captured you, they starve you to death and then feed you to their pet foxes. After the foxes rip the flesh from your bones, the fiƨbärz devour your bones with their sharp, little teeth."

Gnaud jumped to his feet atop the table, launching his spectacles right out of his hand. "Dear Ƨäṭūr!"

Theyn leapt from her chair, snatched Gnaud's spectacles out of the air, and landed right back where she'd started. She handed Gnaud the spectacles. "You should be a little more careful with those, little guy."

"Thank you." Gnaud inspected his spectacles and gave them one last rub before shoving them back on his face.

Urza stood, towering over the table. She spread her arms wide. "What's the point of all this?"

"Hope." Zerenity stood and began circling the table. "Planning and moving forward gives us hope of restoring order and peace to our world. Without hope, we're all lost."

Nardus stared at the book until the letters began jumbling together.

Have I lost all hope?

"Hope is all that holds back the eternal darkness." Wrik turned to Nardus. "So, what is your plan to keep hope alive and restore peace in Centauria, Cyrus?"

Cyrus. The name carried with it connotations Nardus could never live up to and a burden he dare not bear. "Don't call me by that name. I'll never be him again."

Wrik's gaze hardened, along with his tone. "We are beyond such pettiness, especially from you. Without Cyrus, the prophetic branch we travel down ends in darkness, despair, and death. I for one am not willing to continue the journey without hope. You deny us Cyrus, and you deny us the hope we need. You deny us life." He pointed a finger at Nardus. "You must set aside everything you've known and suffered as Nardus, or it will all have been for nothing. Cyrus is the one we need right now." He sighed. "Surely you can see that."

Cyrus...

Nardus lowered his head. "What you're asking of me..."

Theyn leaned over and wrapped her arms around Nardus's neck. "Wrik is right. You must embrace all that once was and set aside all that is. I know you hate mezhik, but it's the only thing that will save us."

"You saw me on that battlefield," Nardus said. "I did everything within my power to win, but it made no difference. We failed to destroy Cinolth, and Shardan died because of it."

Theyn stroked his back. "No, my love, you held back, and I understand why. It was the thought of losing your daughter again. Any father would've done the same. Pravus held so much power over you because of the bond he shared with her, but that's no longer an issue. We can save her *and* defeat Cinolth. I'm certain of it."

Nardus breathed deep. Theyn and Wrik were not wrong, but he still didn't like it. Giving himself over to Cyrus drove fear into his heart. The man held no affinity for anyone but Ɂäţūr and would pursue justice without remorse.

If I do this, how will I assure Shanara's safety? Will I ever find myself again?

"*We are one,*" the voice of Cyrus said within his mind. "*It is the only way.*"

Is it?

"You did hold back, Nardus, but it isn't where we failed," Zerenity said. "We all held back for one reason or another, but that isn't the root of our failure. No, I'll tell you what it was. We entered the battlefield without a thought toward Ɂäţūr and the strength we wield through him. How can we win if we stand alone? The darkness nearly consumed us, and I fear it will if we make the same mistake again."

To his surprise, neither Theyn nor Ridan nor Urza raised objection to what Zerenity said. He would have if he'd formulated a valid argument. But he didn't. As much as he hated the thought of it, he knew the only chance they had of survival lied in the hands of Cyrus.

And Ɂäţūr.

Nardus resolved himself to do what must be done. He pulled Theyn close and kissed the top of her head. Even after fighting a war, her hair still smelled of flowers. How incredible she was. He leaned down and whispered in her ear, "Once this is over, come find me in the darkness the way I found you."

Theyn looked up, and her eyes met his. Beautiful, yellow eyes.

She smiled, baring her fangs. "No matter how far gone or how deeply buried, we will always find each other. Having said that, you will not need finding the way I did."

He snorted. "I wish I shared your confidence."

She kissed him deep, and the world dissolved around them for just a moment. It was exactly what he needed.

"We share everything, my love," she said.

Nardus and Theyn touched foreheads briefly, and then he closed his eyes and let go of everything.

† † †

Theyn pulled away from Nardus and stared at his chiseled face and unwieldy beard. So much had changed since she first saw him standing in the lava fields back on Incendia Island. Even then, she knew she'd be with him, but she'd never expected him to love her, too. Despite Shaul's death and the way she manipulated Nardus on the ship, she would change nothing.

A reason for everything, Zhedäz 2ʊn.

Nardus opened his eyes, and his irises transitioned from brown to yellow in an instant. "Auh!" Theyn jerked back, not expecting a physical change when Nardus gave himself over to Cyrus.

The others in the room must've missed the transition as none of them reacted to it. At least not audibly as she had. However, none of them missed the thousands of beard hairs that fell from Nardus's face and disintegrated into nothing.

"Now that's a cool trick," said Ridan.

When Theyn glanced back at the others, she noticed that even Wrik and Zerenity looked awestruck by the strange phenomenon, Wrik's eyes wide behind his spectacles and Zerenity's lips parted. Then, starting at his neck, Nardus's clothing began changing. His tattered, blood-soaked, white shirt morphed into the makings of dark blue robes. His worn trousers carried the transition all the way down to his leather boots, and the boots repaired themselves and transitioned from brown to black.

"It is done." Even the pitch and tone of Nardus's voice had changed.

No, not Nardus but Cyrus.

Theyn sensed the change between her and Cyrus, and fear struck her heart as she realized what it might mean. With the bond severed, would she be able to keep the beast within herself at bay, or would she lose control again?

Zhedäɜ ɞn, protect me from myself.

"Rid yourself of such foolishness. You know how to control your gift."

Theyn didn't expect or like the foreign connection with Cyrus's mind, and she certainly didn't like his tone. Furthermore, she still didn't see her condition as a gift, and the memory of Berggren's scarred chest would never let her. But none of that mattered as much as what just occurred with Nardus.

How deep did the transition go? Will I ever feel Nardus's mind again?

The thoughts paralyzed her.

† † †

Wrik sat back in his chair and crossed his arms over his chest as he eyed Cyrus. Had it not been for his own extensive research and love of prophecy, Pravus never would've aspired to take over the world. Nor would Pravus have found the cave in the Aether Mountains where Ūrdär Dhef ɜäfn Dhä rested. In truth, nothing would be as it were now if not for him. Thankfully, no one would ever know the role he played in all of it now that Pravus resided in Ef Demd Dhä. Still, it sickened him when he thought about it too much.

Despite orchestrating the events leading up to that moment, never in all his years would he have thought he'd be sitting across the table from a legend of history. Cyrus Nithik, arguably the greatest mage to have ever lived. Wrik couldn't hold back a smile.

Cyrus scowled at him from across the table. "This is not the time for amusement."

"I agree." Wrik straightened but couldn't rid himself of the smile. "In fact, I was just thinking about our next move."

"There's only one path forward." Cyrus stood and eyed the others. "We must raise Nasduron."

"Level it?" Rakzar stood, knocking over his chair in the process. "Aren't we in Nasduron now?"

Wrik chuckled. "That's—"

"Oh, my!" The color drained from Gnaud's face, leaving his pink skin ashen. "That would be absolute madness! Do you not remember why Nasduron was hidden in the first place?"

"Of course I do, Gnaud, and I understand the threat remains, but what choice do we have?"

Gnaud looked around the Great Library, his eyes wide behind his spectacles. "Every protective ward placed around the Great Library and the city beyond these walls would need to be broken to achieve such a feat. Not only that, but the knowledge and artifacts hidden here would likely be destroyed."

Cyrus gestured toward a set of bookshelves with his hand. "I don't give two stones about any of this stuff right now." The table rattled beneath his fist when he struck it. "The only matter of concern is preventing Aria and Cinolth from destroying the world, and we can't do that from beneath the ocean."

Rakzar's eyes widened. "Beneath the ocean?"

"You're safe," Urza assured him. She peered up at Cyrus. "We are safe, right?"

Wrik chuckled again even as his mind returned to the Valley of Dragons and the shade who ripped the life from his bones. Chills consumed him. In truth, none of them would ever be safe as long as Cinolth and Aria lived.

Zerenity eyed Wrik when she responded to Urza. "I assure you that no one will drown."

Wrik didn't like the way that woman looked at him, and he had a sinking feeling she knew more about him than she should. For the sake of everyone, he hoped she wouldn't become a problem. His plate was full enough already.

He pushed his spectacles farther up the slope of his nose and set his mind on the issue at hand. "Why can't you just step back into the world as usual?"

Cyrus shook his head. "That's not possible. The mezhik can only take a person back to the place where they came from. Unlike you, the rest of us traveled here via Sarai, an ancient transport born of mezhik. Because of this—"

"You'd simply stay right here," Wrik finished.

"Precisely." Cyrus rubbed his left bicep, the memory from Nardus's life obviously still with him.

Ridan shoved her chair away from the table and stood. She raised a hand. "Hold up just a minute. Are ya saying we're *trapped* here?"

Cyrus glared daggers at the young dwarf. "Unless you can swim several miles without taking a breath, yes."

Ridan returned his glare with a defiant one of her own. Her voice shook with fury. "Ya did this to me! Ya stole me away and prevented me from avenging Normak's death. I don't even know ya, and I hate ya. May the gods spit on yar grave!"

In a blink, Ridan launched herself off the edge of her chair and landed atop the table just before lunging at Cyrus. Cyrus made no attempt to move, but he didn't need to. The dwarf froze in the air, mid-attack.

Ridan struggled to free herself from the invisible force that held her. "Let. Me. Go."

Wrik approved of the girl's moxie.

"I understand your wrath, but I assure you that it's misguided." Cyrus stepped closer to Ridan. "I did not take your friend's life, but I did save yours. That beast would've ripped you apart because you fought with rage and heart but not with your head." He tapped the side of her head.

"Ya know nothing," said Ridan through gritted teeth. Already her fury waned.

Cyrus smiled at her. "You will have another chance to avenge your friend. Direct your energy there." Ridan flew back across the table and landed back in her chair. She exhaled loudly.

Wrik stood and paced. "Now that we have that issue settled, what is the plan?"

Unlike Nardus, Cyrus spoke with authority. "Zerenity and I will begin taking down the wards that hold this place beneath the water. Theyn, Urza, Ridan, Rakzar, and Bakkan will assist in dispatching anything that tries to prevent us from completing our tasks. Gnaud, you will gather supplies for our journey once we reach the surface." He turned to Wrik. "You will find a way to get us off this island once we reach the surface."

"Yes…" Wrik rubbed his head. "But by then, it might be too late."

"Why?" asked Urza.

Zerenity held up a finger. "Yes, of course. When the island rises, it will displace so much water that it will most definitely create huge tidal waves. No matter how far we are from the mainland, an event like that will not go unnoticed. Aria and Cinolth will be upon us before we have a chance to react." She turned and gazed at Wrik with knowing eyes. "But you have a solution, don't you?"

Wrik did have an answer, but how could she have known? He massaged the back of his neck. "Yes, I believe I do."

Cyrus shook his head. "I know what you're thinking, but Morcinda's halfway across the world right now. Even if we contacted her and she immediately came to our rescue… not even she could prevent waves like the ones that will be generated."

Wrik frowned. "I'm unfamiliar with this Morcinda, but I do know King Forlin."

"The *äəllf äkfeţik*?" Cyrus's eyes flashed like lightning. "That man is both a coward and a backstabber. He'll never lift a finger to help us."

"Perhaps not—" Zerenity winked at Wrik. "—but it's not the king who will aid us, is it?"

Wrik's skin crawled.

Her knowledge is unknowable.

He tried to shake off the fear the woman instilled in him, but it only grew. What else would she prove to know of him?

"Trust me, Cyrus. You will have your wave breakers and transportation." Wrik sat back down.

"Good." Cyrus turned to the others. "I'm aware of the sacrifices we've all made up to this point, and I truly appreciate everything you've all done. I'm also aware of the toll this war has taken on us all. You will quickly see that we still have many tough days ahead of us. Knowing this, none of us will live up to expectations without food and rest, so let's head to the kitchens and then turn in for the evening."

"What about me?" Rayah wiped tears from her eyes. "You didn't give me anything to do."

Cyrus flashed the girl a grim smile. "Mourn for my son while you still can. Another battle lies ahead of us, and we'll need you to be ready."

Gnaud somersaulted off the table and pulled on Cyrus's robes. "Cyrus, we need to talk about this. I don't think you understand the repercussions of what you're about to attempt."

"You're wrong, Gnaud. I fully understand what this means for Nasduron, and I share your concerns. However, the entire Ancient Realm is under attack right now. Soon, Cinolth will take his war to the corners of Centauria. We can't just sit back and let it all burn. The people need us. Cinolth must be stopped."

"As does Aria," Ridan retorted.

Cyrus glared at the young dwarf. "Stopping him will free her from his control."

Sounds like Nardus still has a hold on him.

Ridan stood tall. "Maybe so, but stopping her will free us all."

The more she talked, the more Wrik liked the girl. He knew little of the dwarven clans other than what he'd read in books: superior craftsmanship in weapons and armor, fighting skills that rivaled the best elvish warriors, and attitude that preceded them for days. She embodied the third effortlessly. The only other thing he knew about her was that she'd lost someone close to her.

Haven't we all?

Wrik crossed his arms. "Either way, we must act."

† † †

After the others headed to the kitchens, Rayah found a quiet corner and settled down on the cool stone floor. No matter how hard she tried to get the picture out of her mind, her thoughts returned to Alderan and his charred body. To his last thoughts sent to her.

Every breath she took racked her with guilt. Guilt of being alive to breathe when he'd never take a breath again. The single job she swore to do was protect him, and she not only failed it but failed miserably.

Ȝäṭūr, why did you take him from me? We had our entire future ahead of us, and you ripped it all away. Why? Why do you hate me so much? Am I undeserving of happiness?

She buried her head between her knees and sobbed and choked down air she no longer wanted to breathe. Prayed for death to unite her with Alderan again. But then a thought struck her. Drove cold fear so deep within her mind she thought she'd shake to death.

"This is all my fault, isn't it?" She sobbed. "My hate for Aria killed Alderan."

"No, Rayah."

Rayah startled and knocked her head against the wall. Pain stabbed through her left temple, but she deserved it. She wiped her eyes on her dress and peered up at the tall, dark-skinned man. "Wizard Wrik? I thought you went to the kitchens with the others."

Wrik crouched next to Rayah. "I was just about to go join the others when I heard you sobbing."

She wiped her eyes again, but fresh tears surfaced. "Forget about me. I'm not worthy of your time."

"Never. Everyone has worth." He groaned as he slid down the wall and settled on the floor next to her with his knees raised. "You might not know me, but I know a good deal about you. Alderan always lit up when he spoke of you. His expressions and words left no doubt as to the magnitude of love he held for you."

In Rayah's mind, Aria stood over Alderan's dead body with a snarl across her face. "I don't doubt that he loved me, but he obviously loved her more."

"We both know that's not true."

Rayah balled her fists. "Yes, it is. He left me to save her."

"You mustn't think of it like that." He tapped his knee with a finger. "This is what you need to remember. Had you been the one in danger and not Aria, Alderan would've sacrificed his life to save yours."

Her nails dug into her palms. Sought blood but failed to produce any. "But I'm the one he left behind, and my heart will never mend."

Wrik leaned his head back and gazed toward the high ceiling. "Time will lessen the pain, but I do understand the pain you're experiencing." After a few moments, his gaze fell upon her once again. "I lost someone once, too."

Blurry eyes left Wrik's face fragmented. "But you moved on?" She sniffed and wiped her face again.

"I did, and so can you." A faint, genuine smile curved his lips upward but did nothing to ease the pain strangling her heart.

The world blurred once more. "I'm happy for you, but moving on isn't possible for me."

"When it comes to love and matters of the heart, anything is possible." Wrik retrieved a yellow kerchief from within his robes and offered it to her.

Rayah stared at the yellow square of fabric but didn't accept it. "No, you don't understand. I bonded with Alderan, and now my heart and soul are tied to his for eternity."

He placed the kerchief on top of her folded hands. "It feels that way now, but you will see—"

"Ugh!" Rayah wadded up the kerchief and threw it. "Stop trying to be nice to me! You don't understand me, and you never will."

With a gentle nod, Wrik said, "You're right, but I'm willing to try."

She crossed her arms and huffed. "Don't bother. As I said, I'm not worth it."

"Look, Alderan was my friend, too." He rubbed his bald head. "Help me understand. Why will you never love again?"

Rayah glared at Wrik, but the longer she held his gaze the harder it became to continue fueling her rage. Finally, she caved. "As I'm sure you're aware, I'm a dryte." Tears streamed down her cheeks again, and her gaze fell to her hands. "The easiest way to describe the way our relationships work is to think about the way a ferzh imprints on its master. A single bond for life. For whatever reason, Ƨäṭūr chose to create us this way, too. He made it impossible for us to love twice."

Wrik's nostrils flared as he exhaled. "Wow. I had no idea. I'm... sorry." Sincerity laced his words and eased her pain ever so slightly.

"Thank you." Rayah dabbed her eyes and wiped her face with the ends of her dress. "It doesn't matter, though. Even if it were possible, I'd never want to love anyone else but him."

"Listen..." Wrik's demeanor shifted, his brow furrowed and his gaze cold as steel. He leaned close and whispered, "When the chance presents itself, I will not hesitate to end Aria's life."

A horde of moths stirred in the pit of Rayah's stomach. Over and again, she'd plotted Aria's demise in her head, but to hear the words come straight from someone else's mouth left her speechless. Chills raced down her arms and legs, and not in a good way. Within her heart she knew Alderan would never forgive her if she played a part in Aria's demise.

But you're dead, Alderan.

Tears filled her eyes. She blinked them back. Unless provoked, she wouldn't kill Aria, but would she stop someone else from doing so? A hint of rage flared within her heart once again.

She took you from me, Alderan. If she were to die, how could it not make me happy? The world would be a better place without her and the evil she spreads.

But Ɂäţūr would not condone it, no matter how evil Aria might be. She knew that. Rayah set her jaw.

But I'm not Ɂäţūr.

She searched Wrik's eyes. Soft, golden pools laced with pent-up rage. He hid it well. "I won't stop you, but don't do it for me." Even to her ears, her words dripped with desperation.

"Once, I thought I might love her, but then she stabbed me in the back and tried to have me killed."

He loved her?

Wrik's gaze hardened, and his hand became a fist. "By the gods, I swear I'll choke the life from her with my bare hands."

Rayah gulped. The last thing she wanted was to incite Wrik further or somehow turn his wrath upon her. She nodded, unsure of how else to respond to the man.

Wrik pulled himself up off the floor, dusted off his backside, and smoothed the wrinkles from his robes. He reached out, and the yellow kerchief shot up from the floor and into his open hand. "This kerchief is not something one would call ordinary. It will never soil no matter how it's used. Consider it a gift." He tossed it into her lap, nodded curtly, and walked off.

Rayah stared at the kerchief and then at the spot where Wrik had stood.

Her head spun with emotions beyond her control, and her heart ached for Alderan. But loss wasn't what kept her rooted to the floor. What anchored her to the foundation of the Great Library. No, love and loss wielded no such power. However, guilt did. Guilt weighed her down and turned her stomach inside-out. She snatched the kerchief up and clutched it in her fist. It trembled with each heartbeat.

She looked up. Stared through the vaulted ceiling.

Ҫätūr, what have I done?

CHAPTER FOUR

Savric stood at the bow of the ship, his heart as dark as the black waters that stretched into infinity. Even with the help of Morcinda's water capabilities, sailing across the Gelu Ocean would take at least another day. Another day on a ship with a girl who'd just lost everything. He understood Zelanora's pain far better than he wanted to, loss a large factor throughout his life.

In truth, he lamented over Centauria with every waking moment but wore a brave face for Zelanora. After his failure with Aria, he promised himself that he'd be the rock she needed, no matter the cost. He also prayed that Zerenity and Qotan would survive and that he would reunite with them again one day, but even he had doubts.

With the losses of King Zaridus and Prince Rictar, Princess Zelanora remained the lone heir to the throne. The true heir. Because of this fact, she'd never be safe as long as Cinolth lived and manipulated Aria.

Despite what Savric witnessed in Vallah, he would never give up hope for Aria. A daughter to him in spirit, she was worth saving, and he would do everything in his power to make sure she was given the opportunity if that time came. He'd read many tomes pertaining to the history of Cinolth and the control the wicked dragon held over Magus. Because of that knowledge, he harbored no doubt as to the influence Cinolth possessed over Aria. He'd witnessed her heart and the innocence she possessed not yet a year ago at the café in Daltura.

Every bone in his body itched with regret for not rescuing her from Pravus that day. Had he done so, the world would be in a much better state. For all his meddling, he'd achieved nothing.

Zelanora leaned against the ship's railing on the lower deck. Savric descended the stairs and approached her. Words failed to reach his lips despite knowing she needed comfort. Instead, he slipped his arm around her back and pulled her close. She lay her head against his chest and sobbed quietly.

Sorrow poured forth from her and into him, filling his eyes with tears. Try as he might, no amount of determination or simple wishing prevented those tears from slipping down his cheeks. Two warm streaks against the abrasive winds of the vast ocean.

"Little one." It was all he could muster without losing himself in the moment. Besides, no words would heal her heart or bring comfort to her. Only time would lessen the pain.

She wrapped her arm around his waist and held fast. "What am I supposed to do, Master Savric? How am I supposed to move forward? Everyone I've ever loved has been taken from me." Her voice cracked.

"One day at a time. It will never be painless, but it will get easier. You will see. For now, focus on what lies ahead."

"And what is that? It feels like we're doing the wrong thing. Why are we running and not fighting? Did my father and brother die for nothing?"

"Never." Savric kissed the top of her head. "They died saving you and countless others."

"To what end?" She pulled away and stared up at him. The pain in her eyes tore at his soul. "What kind of life can I ever hope to have now? I'll never be free to live without fear. They'll never stop hunting me." Her hand tightened around the rail. "You should've let me stay and fight. At least I would've died with honor."

He placed his hand over hers on the railing. Both of them stared at it for several moments. Finally, he said, "Honor does not reside in needless death."

Zelanora pulled her hand from beneath his and raised her arms. "Isn't all death needless?"

The girl had a point, and Savric harbored no real answer. "Feathers," he gruffed.

"Feathers is right!" She stamped her foot. "Go tell Morcinda to turn this ship around."

Savric leaned over the railing. The dark waters churned with fury and crashed against the side of the ship as they jetted through them. Such violent seas would've torn any other ship apart, but their vessel traversed them as though they skated across a smooth plane of ice.

Your gift is truly amazing, Morcinda.

Savric cleared his throat. "I am sorry, Zelanora, but our course is set. Let us see where it leads us before we entertain rash decisions based purely on emotion and without sound logic."

She grabbed his arm and pulled him back around to face her. Fury flashed in her eyes. "You're a traitor to my father and to me. You had no right to take me from my home."

Savric sighed. "I understand your anger, and you have every right to feel the way you do, but the focus of it lies in the wrong place. Search your heart, and you will find that I serve the interests of both you and your father. I vowed to protect you from our mutual enemies and deliver you to a woman named Korin in the Shattered Realm. As a man of honor, I gave your father my word."

Zelanora glared at him. "Do not force me down this path based on false pretense."

The accusation slugged Savric right in the gut. "Feathers, girl! What category of false pretense do you charge me with?"

"You claim to have my best interest at heart, but the only thing you've accomplished here is treason." She threw her head back. "Ugh! Can you not see it through those old eyes of yours? You've kidnapped your queen."

Savric took a deep breath and reminded himself that she spoke out of pain more than anything else. "I assure you that I have accomplished nothing of the sort. I act solely on the request of King Zaridus."

"You know as well as I that his request died with him. You are captive of no such obligation."

Savric raised an eyebrow. "Am I not? What value does my word hold if it can be so easily broken?"

She glared at him. "What use is my status as queen if everyone refuses to obey my commands?"

"As of this moment, you are a queen without a kingdom." He chuckled despite himself. "However, I do concede that royal blood flows through your veins, but you must remember that it also spills just as easily as the blood of anyone else. In fact, one might argue that your blood spills far easier than that of a commoner such as myself. You must also remember that your throne has been contested." He shook his head. "No, overthrown. You have no standing army. Therefore, you have no kingdom to rule. Furthermore, a wicked dragon controls the realm."

"I don't care." Zelanora scowled and crossed her arms. "Turn this ship around, or I'll jump overboard and swim back to my kingdom."

She and Aria must be kindred spirits.

Morcinda appeared at Zelanora's side, her blue hair glistening in the pale moonlight. "I see you're working your charm on the girl, as usual."

"Bugger bees!" Savric pointed a finger at Morcinda. "Do not start in on me as well, woman. I have no mind to tolerate it."

"Sounds like you have no mind at all," Morcinda quipped.

Savric opened his mouth to fire something witty back but quickly recognized how similar her words were to something Qotan would've said to him. Instead, he chuckled.

I long to see you again, brother, whether it be in this life or the next.

Zelanora faced Morcinda, her nostrils flared. "I demand you turn this ship around."

"Oh, I see." Morcinda grinned wickedly. "And what is it you think you'd accomplish by returning to your fallen kingdom?"

"The people must know I haven't abandoned them."

"To what end? Another short-lived war where you're left hanging by your neck from some rampart or lying dead in some field? If this is what you strive to accomplish, perhaps you should jump overboard."

Zelanora glared at them both, her hands balled into fists at her sides. "You think you know everything!"

"An impossibility," Savric muttered.

"You're not helping," Morcinda snapped. Savric had no argument. She continued, "What I do know is that a dead queen is no good to anyone. Are you aware that Savric warned your father to prepare for war well before the attack on the Three Kingdoms occurred? Had your father listened, the outcome would've been the same. No one could've known the strength of the enemy. However, we do now."

Zelanora grabbed the sides of her head. "Exactly my point! We must return and defend the Ancient Realm."

"And how will you do that?" Morcinda said. "How will you face an ancient dragon and his mind-controlled army? Are you willing to sacrifice all those people? I doubt it, but even if you are, how do you plan on defeating him?"

"I don't know." Tears rolled down Zelanora's cheeks. "I don't have answers, but I can't sail away and do nothing."

"We are far from doing nothing," Savric said. "The Shattered Realm approaches, and we will find this Korin."

"For what purpose?" Zelanora dabbed her eyes with her cloak as she continued, "Did my father bother to tell you who this woman is or why we should seek her out?"

"Alas, he did not, but that does not make it the wrong thing to do."

"And what if we can't find her or we find out that she's already dead or worse?"

Savric cocked his head. "Worse than dead?" His mind immediately jumped to Qotan once again, but this time regret filled his heart. "If our quest for this woman fails, we will seek another route. However, we must not abandon this one without understanding its purpose."

"Savric's right," Morcinda said. "No matter what lies at the end of our journey, we must take the time to gather our wits and understand what steps can be taken to get us where we need to be. Running head-first toward death will accomplish just one thing: dying."

Zelanora raised her arms. "Ugh! Fine, but when we do reach the end of this journey, our paths will split."

Savric grimaced. "If that is what you wish, we will adhere to it, but please make no decisions until we reach that point."

"My mind is already set." Zelanora turned and stormed away.

Morcinda leaned against the railing and smiled. "I think I like her. She's got a strong spirit."

"Feathers," Savric muttered.

"Now that she's out of earshot, tell me what you know of the Shattered Realm and this Korin woman?"

Savric eyed Morcinda for several moments. "As I told Zelanora, I am privy to no secret knowledge. Due to perilous circumstances, King Zaridus had no time to explain why we must find this woman, but he was insistent that we did. My gut says our path remains true."

Morcinda smiled wryly. "Does it?"

"Well, yes, but that is not all it speaks of." Savric chuckled. "It has also informed me that supper came and went hours ago."

"Ah, yes. For a moment, I feared the loud groans might originate from the belly of my ship and not from your belly. I'm relieved to receive your confirmation."

Savric chuckled again. "Affirmative."

Morcinda pointed toward her quarters. "Knowing your grave condition, I prepared a bowl of sailor's porridge. It awaits you inside."

"Sailor's porridge, you say?" Savric licked his lips, and his stomach rumbled like distant thunder. "Biscuits, too, perhaps?"

"On the high seas?" She scoffed. "The best I can offer you is a lump of stale bread."

"Thank you, Morcinda. That will do right fine." He headed straight for her quarters without another word. As he always said, world problems could never be solved on an empty stomach. In fact, little could ever be accomplished without proper nutrition.

A few spoonfuls into his meal, Morcinda entered the quarters. Her sorrowful expression and slow pace toward the table drove back his hunger. He stood, pulse elevated.

She pulled out the bench on the other side of the table and sat down. Her eyes met his. "Take a seat, Savric."

Knees weakened by the tremor in her voice, Savric couldn't have stayed upright if he'd wanted to. He swallowed hard. "Zelanora did not… follow through, did she?" The girl plunged over the side of the ship in his mind.

"For you, I fear the news far worse." Morcinda slid a leather-bound book across the table.

Savric stared at the book. At ʔäəll Dhef ʔäfn Dhä on its cover. His stomach twisted and churned, and sweat formed on his brow and dampened his palms. Fear ate at his core as he stretched his palm over the book.

"In allit Hiz." The book's golden clasp fell open. He opened the book and retrieved the fountain pen from within its pouch on the inside cover. His gaze met Morcinda's. Her blue eyes crushed his soul with sorrow.

A single tap on the first page with the pen's tip brought forth a message. Savric hesitated, knowing he could never unread whatever text lay on the page. With a deep breath, he set the pen down on the table and read the single line of text: *"Shardan is dead. -Nardus"*

Savric slumped over the book and wept.

† † †

Zelanora lay on a small cot in one of the rooms beneath the lower deck of the ship. Her heart bled within her chest, pierced with arrows of sorrow. Never had she felt so shattered. Had she been alone, the sorrow would've consumed her, but she wasn't. To be certain, no one else occupied the sparsely furnished room, but at the moment, neither did she. At least not mentally.

A special coin lay within her clutched fist. Activated with her mezhik, it had opened a doorway to the past. *Her* past. As long as she possessed the coin, she'd never be alone. The memory always began at the exact same moment…

Knock, knock, knock!

Zelanora leapt off her bed, ran over to the bedroom door, and threw it open. Her mother, Queen Lanara, stood in the hallway, a smile upon her lips. The first time the event occurred, Zelanora hadn't noticed her mother's swollen, red eyes. Now, it's all she could see. Had she known then that it would be the last time she would ever see her mother alive, she might've said or done something different. But she had only been six years old. How much can a child possibly understand about the world and its inherent wickedness at such an age?

Zelanora led her mother over to a small table and sat her down in a chair five sizes too small. Her mother laughed, as she always did. A sweet melody to anyone's ear. Zelanora served make believe tea and biscuits to her mother, her dog Baxter, and three corn dolls her brother had made for her. The two of them spoke of castles and princes for what felt like hours before her mother finally rolled out of the chair and settled on the edge of

Zelanora's bed.

Her mother patted the bed. Zelanora ran over and her mother lifted her up onto it. As always, her mother smelled of spring flowers. She breathed deep, relishing the aroma. Then, her mother pulled a golden coin out of her pocket, but it was no ordinary coin. The coins used in the Ancient Realm bore the head of her father, King Zaridus, on one side and a small map depicting the Three Kingdoms on the other side. However, this coin had neither mark. Instead, one side featured a dragon clutching an egg and the other side a mark just like the one she now had on the inside of her left wrist. The mark of a wizard.

Fizärd Mämärä.

As the memory faded, Zelanora opened her tear-filled eyes. The small room came into focus after she blinked the tears away. "I still miss you so much, Mother."

How would she ever come to terms with the deaths of her father and brother when she still hadn't gotten over the loss of her mother so long ago?

Zelanora returned the coin to the secret pouch she wore beneath her shirt. Then, she rolled onto her side and pulled her knees to her chest.

Ƨätūr, help me.

Chapter Five

Aria awoke in bed with a chill in her bones. She lay there for several moments with her arms wrapped around herself, admiring the pale moonlight that shone through the sheer curtains and bathed the floor in its pale light. One of the many gifts bestowed upon the world by Ƨäţūr. The thought made her smile.

She rolled over and reached for Pravus, but he wasn't there. In fact, the covers on his side of the bed lay cold and undisturbed.

He never came to bed?

Pravus worked hard, sometimes late into the night. A few times, he'd fallen asleep at the table in the war room. He'd likely done so again.

Most nights, she didn't mind sleeping alone, but tonight she needed him. With reluctance, she shed her covers and swung her feet off the side of the bed. The cold floor met her bare toes first, but that wasn't what sent chills up her spine and her pulse racing. Her legs wobbled under her own weight, and she had to grab the edge of the mattress to keep herself upright.

Aria stared at her legs. "What's wrong with you?"

A throbbing pain filled the space behind her eyes. Intensified with each heartbeat. She dropped to her knees and clambered toward the chamber pot. Bile spewed from her lips before she reached the pot and splattered across the floor. The stench of it brought forth even more.

Once she felt certain she'd purged the last of it, she pulled herself back up onto the bed and lay back. After a few minutes of rest, the shaking within her bones and the twisting of her gut subsided. However, the throbbing remained behind her eyes, albeit far less intense than before.

With caution, she rose again. This time, her legs shook just a little. What she needed now was something to fill her newly emptied stomach. She sidestepped the mess she made on the floor and walked over to the washing basin. After flushing her face with cold water and rinsing the bitter taste from her mouth, she donned a long silk robe and rolled on a pair of thick wool socks that reached past her calves. A pair of mint leaves freshened her mouth and breath as she slipped out of the room.

Credan sat in a chair on the opposite side of the hallway just outside her door, his head lolled to one side. He'd obviously been there all night, but why? Had she been sick earlier as well and Pravus had asked him to keep an eye on her? Perhaps she suffered from some contagion. It would explain why Pravus hadn't accompanied her to bed and also her bout of sickness.

Aria nudged the man with her foot. "Master Credan?"

Credan snorted and jerked his head upright. His spectacles teetered on one ear. "Oh, uh, yes." He cleared his throat. "Queen Rosai." He scrambled to stand and fix his spectacles simultaneously. It took two tries to accomplish each. "You're awake."

"I am." She smiled and folded her hands behind her back. "Please summon one of the bedchamber servants to come clean at once."

"Yes, of course." He frowned, his head lowered. Only his eyes rose to meet her gaze. "Forgive me for being forward, my queen, but do you think it wise to be up just now?"

Aria looked down at herself. "Am I not in control of my faculties?"

"Yes, and I apologize if I made implications to the contrary, but you're still very pale."

"I believe the sickness is behind me now. Hence the reason I require a bedchamber servant."

Credan nodded. "Yes, yes. Of course. I will fetch someone at once."

"Good." She looked to the left and then the right. The entire corridor stood empty. "Point me in the direction of my husband. I have need for him."

Credan's eyes bulged through his spectacles, and his face turned a pasty white. "My… my queen?"

She waved her hand dismissively. "You need not put on a performance for me. It's no secret that he requires the services of other women from time to time, Credan, so snap out of it. The entire castle knows."

"I… You…" Sweat trickled down Credan's bald head.

"Honestly, I don't know what's gotten into you tonight. Perhaps you've now fallen ill." Aria waved her hand again. "Forget I asked about Pravus. I'll find him myself." She turned and strolled down the corridor.

† † †

After summoning one of the bedchamber servants to attend to Queen Rosai's quarters, Credan headed toward the southern ramparts of the castle. Never in his life had he felt more fearful than right then. The entire journey up through the castle, he worked to wrap his mind around his encounter with Queen Rosai and how he would approach the glaring issue with Cinolth. Given the opportunity, he would've brought the issue to Wizard Wrik and not Cinolth, but Wrik seemed to be absent from the castle.

A perfect storm.

Credan sighed, knowing the disdain and temper Cinolth exhibited toward every human, Aria included. The impending conversation with Cinolth might prove to be the last one he'd ever have. If so, Lord Rosai would berate him in the afterlife. That is if one existed. Fear of the unknown burrowed beneath his skin and gnawed on his bones.

Does anything come after death?

He'd never thoroughly contemplated such a thought. Everything he was and stood for revolved around Lord Rosai. It always had. No one understood him the way Lord Rosai had, and he'd always be indebted for the kindness Lord Rosai showed him while the two of them were in Fekɛzhn dhä Räd.

"At least most of the time," he muttered.

Credan wiped mist from his eyes and stepped out onto the southern rampart. The bitter wind nipped at his bald head only a moment before he forced it from his mind. His only chance of surviving the encounter relied on absolute focus.

Stick with the facts. Do not embellish.

His heart hammered against his ribcage as his gaze targeted the hulking beast who stood a hundred yards ahead. Had it not been for the promise he'd made to Lord Rosai to protect Queen Rosai at all costs, he would've retreated. Even so, he almost did when Cinolth's gaze met his.

Unyielding pain burst from within Credan's mind. Lit every nerve with fire. Drove him to his knees. Stone against bone. He fought with all his strength just to stay upright and keep himself from falling on his face.

Cinolth's voice filled Credan's head and reverberated down through his jaw. *"That's better."*

Never had Credan experienced so much pain and darkness through a mind connection. Only fear remained within him, everything else lost in a black quicksand that threatened to consume him unto death.

The rampart trembled as Cinolth approached. Credan could do nothing but close his eyes and wait.

"You've come to sacrifice yourself in my service?" Cinolth said through mindspeak.

Credan's lips and jaws failed him. *"No!"* he yelled within his mind.

A hot wind laced with sulfur and ash rippled Credan's skin. "Then what? Why have you disturbed me?" The dragon's harsh voice vibrated his chest.

Credan forced his eyes back open. Focused on a single, red, serpentine eye. Mere inches from his face. "Auh!" He jerked back and nearly fell over.

"Answer me before my patience withers," Cinolth said.

"I... I..." Credan took a deep breath and focused his gaze on a pebble that lay between his knees. "It's Queen Rosai. Something's wrong with her."

"She grieves."

"Yes, but it's more than that. She... She..."

"Spit it out, old man."

Credan met Cinolth's gaze. "She's acting as though Lord Rosai still lives."

Cinolth's nostrils flared. Plumes of smoke rose from them. "And you're certain of this?"

The pain eased from Credan's mind as the darkness retreated. "She searches the castle for him as we speak."

Cinolth latched onto one of the large parapet stones with his claws and ripped it from its place. With a loud roar, he crushed the stone, reducing it to a pile of rubble.

Credan trembled but didn't move. "What should we do?"

"Summon Reubane at once."

"Reubane?" Credan swallowed hard as the blood drained from his face. "What could he possibly do for her?"

"It doesn't concern you."

Credan composed himself and nodded. "As you say. It will take some time to locate him, though."

"Two days. Fail, and I will pick my teeth with your bones even as you draw your last breath." Cinolth spread his wings and leapt over the rampart parapet. The air cracked as his wings gathered wind beneath them and carried him deep into the night.

Credan picked himself up and dusted off his robes. The pile of rubble Cinolth left behind conjured waves of gooseflesh. The small bumps crawled across his skin. He shuddered. "That could've been me."

He coughed then adjusted his collar, its presence around his neck suddenly far too constrictive. Locating Reubane wouldn't be an issue. However, releasing him from his cell deep beneath the castle would be. Doing so would require a wizard, and Credan was fresh out of wizards at the moment.

CHAPTER SIX

The tunnel entrance to the Cave of Rebirth stood before Jagger, a crag carved out of the limestone, granite, and black clay wall. Warmth radiated from within, melting the snow around the opening. A narrow stream of water, born of the runoff, trickled back inside. Had it not been for the stream, she never would've noticed the tunnel's slight downward slope.

A faint light emanated from the entrance and set the drifted snow aglow all around Jagger. Grimbold stood behind her, his hand clasped over her left shoulder but without conviction. Still, she didn't move. Found it hard to breathe. Reverence ensnared her.

Over the years, she'd stood in this very spot at least a hundred times, each time imagining what it would be like when Gwendor returned to them. Never had she stepped foot inside the tunnel let alone the cave, though. No one but the elders were allowed inside the sacred place. Crossing the threshold would've earned her a severe beating and a night in the pit.

Just the thought of the pit rippled her flesh and left her cold. A hole in the center of Zimska Vala several hundred feet deep and black as death itself. Those who spent time down there never came back up the same, if at all. No one in the village slept the nights the pit lay occupied except perhaps those born deaf. The single time it'd happened during her life, she had nightmares for weeks. Sometimes, late at night, she swore she still heard agonizing wails and screams of torture echoing up from the pit.

Grimbold might suffer the same fate because of her, but nothing could be done about it. Still, the thought sickened her.

Concentrate on the present. Welcome the spirit. The flamewalker.

Eis stood at her side, ears alert and hackles raised. Jagger rubbed Eis beneath her chin. *"We must do this,"* she mindspoke to Eis. *"It's the only way to save our people. Our world."*

Eis sniffed the air and growled deep in her chest. Images of fire and water bombarded Jagger's mind, each coming from Eis. Even though Eis understood every word Jagger spoke, her ability to communicate back came only through images.

"Everything will be okay." Jagger hardly believed the words herself.

Grimbold's hand slipped from Jagger's shoulder as she moved forward and entered the tunnel. She expected to feel some sort of sensation like a bubble bursting or a slight resistance when she crossed the threshold, but none came. In fact, the only perceivable difference was the temperature. It rose significantly.

Ahead a dozen paces, the narrow tunnel angled to the right. It's where the light emanated from. Closer inspection of the tunnel walls revealed something unexpected: polished rocks. Dozens of them embedded in the walls. Light reflected off them and multiplied as it volleyed back and forth through the tunnel and toward the opening.

Just beyond its right angle, the tunnel opened into a large, circular cave. Immediately, Jagger took notice of the grayish-beige sand that covered the floor. Somehow, the sand itself flickered like millions of tiny candles—the source of light that filled the cave. She'd never seen anything like it before.

This is the Cave of Rebirth.

The weight of the moment—the cave and its significance—would never be lost on her.

A haven for our god.

Jagger stood there for several moments, spine tingling as she held her breath in awe. Few ever stood where she did now. She looked down at her feet. Six long toes of dark olive hung over the front edge of each of her sandals and dug into the sand.

Should I have removed my sandals before entering?

No sign had been posted in the tunnel, and the book never specified a proper method of entering the cave. Still, unease crept into her bones.

Relax, Jagger.

She exhaled then took in the rest of her surroundings.

At the center of the cave sat a pit filled with ashes, smoldering as though it had just lost the last of its flames moments before she'd entered. Thirteen flat stones, each indistinguishable from its neighbor, interlocked and encircled the fire pit.

Dozens of symbols, carved into the stone, littered the cave walls. She recognized just a few of them, but the predominant symbol straight ahead of her was unmistakable: fire. Its three flames, bound at their base, branched out like a three-tailed fox. A mural of a bird far more beautiful than any she'd ever seen rose out of and above the fire symbol. It featured fiery red and orange feathers, wings that stretched across the wall five feet in either direction, a long narrow tail split into five at its end, piercing golden eyes, a beak sharp enough to pierce the strongest armor, and talons so devilishly long they could still a beating heart no matter how deep it might lie within one's chest.

The flamewalker.

As she looked around, she spotted two archways that led beyond the cave. One to the left and one to the right. The left held a passage that led farther beneath the mountain and faded into darkness. The right opened to a smaller, sparsely furnished cave. Spiderwebs caked in dust but devoid of actual spiders draped from its entrance like a set of rotted curtains. She ducked beneath the webs and gave the cave a quick inspection. A makeshift bed of broken straw browned with age lay against the far wall. A rusted chamber pot lay on its side next to the bed. Diminished flint rocks sat next to a single torch that looked like it might turn to ash if disturbed.

How long has this place been abandoned?

She knew the answer. No one ever occupied the Cave of Rebirth unless the flamewalker was about to arrive.

And I will meet him.

Jagger returned to the main cave to find Eis staring at the fire pit, her hackles still raised. A low growl rose from Eis's throat and reverberated off the walls and low ceiling. Images of fire and death pummeled Jagger's mind.

Jagger hugged Eis's neck and stroked the underside of her soft chin. "Everything will be okay. I promise." Her shaky voice failed to imbue the confidence she sought, but it must've helped a little because the grim images she received from Eis slowed in frequency.

"Well?" Grimbold shouted from the tunnel entrance.

She'd half-forgotten he'd come with her. "Come see for yourself."

A few seconds later, Grimbold entered the large cave, Rauch right on his heels. Grimbold's narrow eyes grew wide as he surveyed the cave. "By the gods…"

As though sparked by his words, the ashes in the pit burst into flames. Eis, Rauch, and Grimbold retreated, but Jagger drew closer and stared into the purple and blue flames. She didn't want to miss a single moment.

One by one, the tops of the flat stones surrounding the pit began glowing reddish orange, like lava. Once glowing, their differences became apparent. Each held a unique symbol. One resembled fire, matching that of the symbol on the wall. She recognized the other twelve symbols as well. Each represented a month in the ancient calendar. Each a god. From what she understood of the legends, none of those gods were worthy of praise or honor, each evil in their own way. The answer as to why the calendar commemorated them lay beyond her grasp.

The flames continued to grow with every passing moment, roaring ever louder as they filled the entire pit and lapped at the ceiling above. Jagger stepped back, awestruck.

Something grabbed her elbow. Ripped the breath from her lungs. She looked back and into Grimbold's tear-filled eyes.

He smiled, but the sadness in his eyes couldn't be hidden. "Come, Jagger. The entrance must be sealed before the others see its light."

Jagger nodded. "I know. It will take us both to seal it."

"Yes, one of us on the outside and one on the inside."

Jagger's heart thundered. "What?"

His brow furrowed. "Gwendor or not, someone must be here to welcome the flamewalker."

"Maybe I was wrong. Maybe I didn't really feel anything." She knew it wasn't true, but she couldn't stand the thought of being without her father. "We should just go tell the elders and let them deal with it."

"No, Jagger." Grimbold sighed. "I feel it, too. Something is different."

"Maybe we're both wrong. Neither of us has experienced the flamewalker's return, nor have we ever experienced what mezhik feels like."

"Agreed, but I know you've read the prophecies. So have I. Denying it will not change anything."

She grabbed his hand. "Then we should both stay."

Grimbold squeezed her hand. "You know that's not possible, Jagger."

"I do?" Her mind knew the truth even if her heart wasn't willing to admit it.

"Yes. You will stay and welcome the flamewalker. I will face the clan."

"Once they realize what's happened, they will mark you as a traitor and banish you to the pit!"

"Perhaps, but no other choice remains."

"No, Father! I'm not prepared to welcome the flamewalker."

"You are, and you will. No one else knows more about it than you. You've read the book, and I know how your mind works. You've memorized every last word of it. More than a thousand pages." He smiled faintly. "You were born to do this."

The truth of his words stung. She lunged forward and buried her head in his chest. "I cannot lose you!"

He held her tight. "Like your mother, I will always be with you."

Jagger sobbed. "Will I ever be able to return to the vale?"

He kissed the top of her head. "No. You must find a way to leave Reothadh." He pulled back, wiped away tears that hung from his beard, then smiled. "You're so much like your mother. She'd be so proud of the woman you've become."

Jagger smiled as a tear rolled down her cheek. "And of the father you've been to me."

He kissed the top of her head then released her. "I love you, my precious daughter."

"And I you."

Terror gnawed the insides of her bones as she glanced back at the chamber. She knew nothing beyond the vale. Knew nothing apart from her clan and the love of her father. How would she survive outside? Beyond Reothadh? As far as she knew, no one ever left the vale's security. If they had, none ever returned.

Tears fell from her eyes as a tightness she'd never experienced before grabbed her chest and squeezed it until she could scarcely breathe.

"Father…" she managed. No more words would come forth.

He wiped tears from her cheeks with his thumbs. "I know, my beautiful daughter, but there's no time. The light from the chamber exceeds my expectations a thousandfold, and the others will surely be coming. The cave must be sealed."

She nodded, her words a tangled mess in the back of her throat.

At the outside tunnel entrance, Grimbold knelt and withdrew two green crystals from his shoulder pack.

Blasting crystals.

Jagger had never understood why he always carried them with him, but now it made perfect sense. A faint smile curled the ends of her lips.

I knew he must have the gift. How else would he have known to keep the crystals with him?

When used in pairs, the crystals could generate a concussive force strong enough to crack the earth or bring down the side of a mountain. The latter being exactly what they needed.

Grimbold rose and handed her one of the crystals. Her hand trembled, but not from its weight or the vibrations emitted from it. As much as her hand trembled, it paled in comparison with her legs. Her knees knocked together, and she fought with every breath just to keep herself from collapsing into a useless pile of flesh.

Rauch padded outside and disappeared into the shadows. Grimbold followed, stopping about ten feet from the outside entrance. He turned and faced Jagger, his face skewed with agony. Based on how twisted her insides felt, hers must've looked the same.

Everything within her begged for her to drop the crystal and run into Grimbold's arms, but the fire that burned back in the Cave of Rebirth called to her as well. A destiny she could not run from. Instead, she took several backward steps, her tear-filled gaze never breaking from his.

"Grimbold!" someone shouted. He glanced to his right.

Jagger didn't understand how anyone could've arrived so quickly. They needed more time. *She* needed more time.

"Father!" She reached out toward him.

Grimbold turned back and gripped his crystal with both hands. She did the same, her heart pounding.

"Now!" he yelled.

They broke their crystals in two, and the entire mountain quaked. Mimicked her heart. Her soul.

Then, a jagged square of blinding light burst from nothing an equal distance between them. The light expanded upward, downward, and out to the sides, ripping right through the tunnel and forming a plane of green light. The ground shook, taking Jagger to her knees, but she kept her eyes focused on her father. On his eyes. The tears falling from them.

Silver flashed.

Grimbold staggered to his left.

Dropped to his knees.

Clutched an arrow protruding from his side.

Ripped it out.

Crimson soiled his shirt.

She couldn't look away.

His lips moved.

She knew the words.

Never wanted them to be the last.

I love you.

Boom!

The sound rippled the air. Crashed in her ears.

She fought her way back to her feet.

Lunged forward.

But her body flew backward.

Head cracked against the back tunnel wall.

Dazed her but didn't knock her out.

It would take a much stronger blow to rattle her thick skull.

She scrambled to get her footing again even as she hit the ground.

Then, the outside world disappeared in a thunderous storm of debris. She shielded her eyes with her arm. Pulled her tunic around and covered her nose and mouth.

More thunder followed. Blinding dirt. Then silence. At least from what lay before her.

To her right, inside the Cave of Rebirth, the fire groaned and roared with life.

She released her tunic and closed her eyes. Focused on the one thing that drove her.

Grimbold. Fellow flamewatcher. Father.

No!

She couldn't allow herself to think about him right now. Doing so would immobilize her. Prevent her from fulfilling the destiny burning in her heart. She must welcome the flamewalker.

She pushed Grimbold, the silver arrow, and his crimson-soaked shirt into a small wooden box within her mind. Closed the lid. Set the lock through the latch and pushed it shut. Shoved the box into a dark corner. Prayed it would stay shut. At least long enough for her to do what needed to be done.

Then, something wet yet gritty like sand raked the side of her face. Her eyes sprang open.

Eis!

In her moment of despair, she'd forgotten Grimbold hadn't left her alone. Reaching up, she pulled Eis's muzzle against her cheek. *"Everything will be okay."* She repeated the words in her mind as much for herself as she did for Eis.

After a few more seconds of hesitation, Jagger pulled herself up from the ground, dusted herself off, then staggered into the Cave of Rebirth. She released the clasp that fastened her tunic around her neck and shrugged the tunic off her shoulders. Then, she removed her sandals. Hot sand squished between her toes as she walked over to the circle of stones.

Dropping to her knees, she gazed into the flames. They roared with fury. A drezhn's wrath. The sound pierced her ears. Thought she might go deaf. She covered her ears with her hands, but the roar only grew with intensity. Vibrated her chest.

Eis backed herself out of the cave, tail tucked between her legs. Jagger didn't blame her. She would've done the same, given a choice.

Black smoke began bellowing from the flames, blackening the ceiling and filling the cave with its toxicity. One drawn breath set Jagger's lungs afire. Consumed her from the inside out. The pain spread from her lungs like wildfire, her blood turned to magma in her veins. She screamed without sound. Drew breaths of pure fire and spewed flames when she exhaled.

Something's wrong!

How had she been so naive to think she could welcome the flamewalker? She was nothing. No one. Untrained. Unworthy. Death would be her reward.

Then, her mind snapped back to the book. A thousand pages of instruction. Every last word ingrained into her mind. Sure, she hadn't trained for this moment, but no one in the clan knew more than her about it, not even the elders.

You can do this, Jagger.

Words from the book filled her head. Spoke of separation of mind and body. The only viable path to survival and welcoming the flamewalker. She recited the words. Allowed them to wash over her. Consume her.

Without thought, her body lifted off the ground. Arms spread wide. Head back. Eyes focused on the ceiling. Mouth agape.

An energy she could only describe as mezhik built in her chest and exploded outward, rippling down through her toes and fingers. Raising every hair on her body.

The fire within her lungs dissipated. Magma ceased to flow through her veins. She looked down only to see herself still on her knees in front of the fire, engulfed in flames yet somehow still alive. No recollection remained of the physical pain inflicted upon her.

A separation of body and mind.

She'd thought the separation to be figurative, but there was no denying the truth within her mind. As she thought about it, she realized that sight and sound were the only senses she detected.

Jagger stood and began scrawling patterns in the sand with her foot. No, not just patterns but ancient runes. As she completed each one, it burst into flames and turned the surrounding sand into glass. She drew five runes in all, surrounding the circle of stones.

Even though the book never explained the meaning of the runes, Jagger understood. A rune for each of the four seasons and a final rune representing the flame of everlasting fire.

Jagger gasped as all her senses returned to her. Sweat poured from her pores, the fire within her quenched. Fatigue plagued every muscle in her body, yet somehow, she remained upright. Alert.

All at once, the flames within the pit died out, and the roar ceased. The smoke in the room dissipated, and the flat stones lost their fiery glow. All but the fire symbol—the one with the three flames. Each of the five runes flickered, and then their flames snuffed out, too.

Jagger's pulse raced as time marched forward without change.

Did I forget a step?

She rifled through the pages of the book within her mind, frantically searching for an answer.

Nothing! I forgot nothing, so what's wrong?

An image burst into Jagger's mind: stirring ash. She turned to see Eis staring at her from afar. Always watchful.

"Thank you," Jagger said, then turned her gaze on the fire pit.

Indeed, the ashes stirred and began to swirl in the air, forming a small cyclone. Some of the ashes remained gray, but others glowed orange and red. It reminded her of fall. Gusting winds stirring up fallen leaves.

At the center of the cyclone, the ashes began clumping together. At first, they looked just like clods of gray clay, but then they began to take shape as though some invisible artist molded them with their hands. Jagger fought off the sting in her eyes, refusing to blink even once for fear of missing a single detail.

A round ball elongated. Stretched into a chin. Jaw lines drew back from the chin. Cheek bones rose, and a humanoid nose formed.

Jagger glanced over at the mural on the wall and gasped. Whatever came through the flames looked nothing like the drawing.

You're no mighty bird.

Her heart hammered as she continued watching the ashes pull together and sculpt themselves. Two holes became nostrils. Lips plumped. Deep eye sockets burrowed into the skull beneath a rigid brow. Ears flapped out just as eyes formed within the sockets. Strands of hair separated themselves from the top of the skull and flowed down to broad shoulders. Muscles grew out of the forming arms and puffed up the chest. Every last detail, right down to the ridges on its toenails, blossomed before Jagger's eyes.

She swallowed hard as understanding of what she saw came to her. A male, formed of ash, stood lifeless in the coals. She'd never seen a human in person but had no doubt as to what stood before her. According to the elders of her village, humans were barbaric beings who lacked the knowledge and skills her clan possessed. They also lacked the ogre blood that flowed within her veins. Half human and half ogre, her race was superior in every way. At least that's what she'd been taught, and she had little reason to question the elders, especially given the circumstances.

In an instant, flames engulfed the body.

"Auh!" Jagger stumbled backward.

The ashen body blackened as the flames continued to burn. Then, molten fissures opened down the length of the human form. Green eyes opened. Blinked away flecks of ash before focusing on her. A hand, blackened with soot, reached out of the flames.

Jaws separated as his lips parted. A croaking moan from a throat likely drier than any desert she could ever imagine ushered from them. "Help me."

Jagger's heart hammered. She hadn't expected him to speak her language. Thoughts swirled in her mind, mimicking the cyclone of ash and fire surrounding him.

What if his hand burns me? What if he tries to pull me into the flames and kill me?

Her mind pulled her back into the night. To the top of the ridge. There, she remembered what she'd felt.

Anticipation.

She stared at the outstretched hand before her.

Could my people be wrong about humans?

His gaze met hers. Sorrow and pain poured from his eyes. "Please."

This is your destiny, Jagger. Do not be afraid.

She exhaled, stepped forward, and took the flamewalker's hand.

The air crackled with red lightning, and then the cyclone of ash exploded outward, extinguishing the flames and knocking Jagger flat on her back. The sand ceased to glow, throwing the cave into complete darkness.

A significant weight piled upon Jagger's legs and lower torso. The flamewalker must've fallen with her.

Jagger tried to sit up, but her strength waned. She panted like a ferzh, unable to manage a deep breath. Finally, she lay still and focused on the darkness.

At first, she heard nothing but her own heart pounding in her ears, but then a shallow, ragged breath broke through the silence. Then, several more.

The flamewalker lives.

What was she supposed to do now? What could she do?

Then, a memory sparked. Page 847 of the manual. The flamewalker would require water to survive the first day. Failure to provide it would extinguish the flamewalker's life.

If she thought he was a threat, she needn't do anything but wait for him to die. It would solve many issues. However, her heart would never let her. The thought of watching anything die when she had a chance to save it left her stomach in knots. Threat or not, she'd never allow it. The only reasons she'd ever kill anything would be for food or self-preservation.

A renewed energy pumped through Jagger's veins, giving her the strength she needed to sit up. With a grunt, she gently eased the young man up and pulled her feet from beneath him.

She sat there for several minutes and pondered her next move, but a solution failed to present itself. "Where am I supposed to find water in a cave?"

A shallow stream of crystal blue water appeared in Jagger's mind. She searched the darkness but couldn't locate Eis's glowing eyes. "Where will I find this stream?"

An archway flashed in her mind. The one she hadn't explored. "Yes, of course."

Jagger stood, lifted the flamewalker over her shoulder, then stuck out her hand and waited. Eis came to her side, and she grabbed a tuft of the ferzh's mane. "Lead me."

CHAPTER SEVEN

Berggren sat on the floor with a bowl of steamed oats and honey. Not his usual breakfast, but the choices were slim in the stronghold. To put it bluntly, there were no other options for breakfast. Niesha sat next to him, her bowl already half empty. She scooped up a spoonful of oats and then turned her spoon over and watched them plop back into the bowl.

"Remind me again how long we're gonna squat in this dump?" Niesha said.

Berggren shoved a spoonful of oats into his mouth and chewed slowly. "As long as it takes."

Niesha huffed. "As long as what takes?"

Berggren waved his hand around. "This thing we're a part of. War or revolution or whatever you wanna call it."

"Wow, you sure have a way of boosting my confidence, big man. Be as vague as possible and avoid the question." She poked at her oats. "You certainly nailed it."

As rotten as she was at times, Berggren couldn't imagine life without Niesha. She, along with Theyn, were the two reasons he fought to not just survive but live.

He tousled her hair. "The question's unanswerable. Better?"

She pushed his hand away and scowled at him. "Forever. That's the word you're trying to grasp, right?"

"That's not what I said." Berggren took another bite of his oats and smiled.

She's just like Theyn.

Niesha sighed. "Right, but nothing's ever what you actually say. Am I wrong?"

"What you are is a smart mouth."

"So, I am right."

Calen walked over and joined them on the floor. "Right about what?"

Eshtak twirled toward them with a steaming bowl in his hands. "Hot, hot, hot, hot, hot!"

"We're stuck here," Niesha said. "Forever." She drew the word out.

"Forever's a really long time," Calen said. "Like practically forever."

"Eshtak loves forever." He plopped down and buried his face in his bowl.

Niesha giggled. "Yeah, like how long Berggren's been alive."

"I'm sitting right here," Berggren said.

Calen snorted. "He might not be as old—"

"Zhebəllin!" came a shout from tunnel three.

The tunnels that led into the main room of the stronghold weren't actually marked with numbers, but it's how Berggren kept a mental track of where each one led. Tunnel three connected the stronghold to Elatos.

The entire room erupted with panic. Same as it had the day they'd arrived. Perhaps a bit worse.

"Damn," Berggren muttered, rising to his feet and discarding his half-eaten bowl of oats on the floor. "How did they manage to burrow through the collapsed tunnel so quickly?"

A man named Hardin emerged from tunnel three, his eyes wide with fright. Somehow, his voice managed to carry over all the shouting and crying. "We need something to reinforce the door!"

Berggren remembered inspecting all four tunnel doors the night they'd arrived. Each was made of pure gray steel—the best money could buy—and more than a foot thick. Each door must've weighed several thousand pounds. A breach had seemed impossible.

Unless they have a wizard with them.

The thought churned his stomach for several reasons. First, it brought back memories of Joriah and the ultimate sacrifice he made while aiding their escape from West Hotah. Second and far more important, they'd be defenseless against a powerful wizard seeing as how they lacked one of their own.

Berggren climbed onto the makeshift stage at the front of the room and addressed the Three Kingdoms survivors. "Citizens of Vallah, Elatos, and

Borza, we must come to our senses. None of us will survive if we continue to panic every time an issue arises."

"And just who do you think you are?" someone shouted. "You're not from around here and certainly not one of us."

Thank the gods for that.

"That's true." Berggren clasped his hands behind his back. "I've never resided in the Three Kingdoms, nor have I ever pledged fealty to any king or ruler, but both those facts remain irrelevant to the current situation we face. For the time being, I'm the man in charge."

"Why should any of us follow you?" another said.

"Answer's simple. I think on my feet and can survive just about anything." He thought about lifting his shirt and showing the people the scars left by Theyn but decided against it. Instead, he continued, "Not only for that reason, but also because the greatest mage that has ever lived put me in charge of this stronghold. If you've got a problem with me, you can take it up with him when he returns."

"We don't believe in mezhik, wizards, or mages," a woman yelled.

A man raised his fist and shook it. "King Zaridus would never stand for this!"

"King Zaridus is dead," Berggren bellowed. "It'd do you all good to remember that."

Calen climbed onto the makeshift stage and pulled on Berggren's sleeve. Berggren leaned down, and Calen spoke into his ear, "Maybe you should stop explaining why you should be the one to tell them what needs to be done and just do it. Save the day, and their trust in you will begin to grow."

Berggren laughed and tousled Calen's hair. "Spoken like a true leader, my young friend." Calen beamed up at him.

Berggren addressed the mob again, "Anyone wants to help, follow me."

"Eshtak helps big friend!"

Berggren jumped off the makeshift stage and pushed his way through the crowd. Calen, Niesha, and Eshtak fell in right on his heels. Several others joined them, too, including one of the men who'd just spoken out against Berggren.

When they reached the tunnel three door, Berggren immediately saw the problem: the gray steel glowed an angry red at the center of the door.

Not good.

During the stronghold's construction, many precautions had been taken to ensure the safety of those seeking refuge within its granite walls, including the addition of what Berggren called a peep hole in each of the doors. He didn't quite understand how the peep holes worked since the hole was undetectable from the other side of the door, but it made no difference. He knew how to use it. A quick peek through the hole confirmed Hardin's claim of zhebəllin.

"Damn."

The little bastards had somehow found a way to build a bonfire inside the tunnel. The zhebəllin used the fire to create smelt and the smelt to melt a hole in the center of the door. To their credit, the plan was ingenious.

The radiating heat slickened the top of Berggren's head with sweat and made it itch something fierce. He scratched it, then wiped it with his sleeve, but the heat brought the sweat right back. Turning to those who'd followed him, he said, "We need to collapse part of this tunnel and pile the rubble against the door."

"They're zhebəllin, for the love of the gods," said the man who'd opposed Berggren. "They eat rock for breakfast like we eat oats."

Berggren already hated the man. "Got a better idea, smart man? Let's hear it."

"Just ignore Mortis," Hardin said. "He never has anything positive to add to a conversation."

Mortis glared at both men but kept his mouth shut.

Calen stepped forward. "I saw some pickaxes and a couple of wheelbarrows back in one of the supply rooms."

Berggren grinned. The boy reminded him of Shaul. "Show me."

Berggren and several others followed Calen back to the main supply room, grabbed everything that looked like it might be useful for chipping and hauling rock, and then headed back up tunnel three. In the ten minutes it took to grab the tools, their situation had worsened. Not only did the center of the door glow red, but it bulged a little now, too.

"Damn!" Berggren grabbed a pickaxe and began chipping away at the tunnel wall about fifteen feet back from the door. Another man and two women joined in. Calen, Niesha, and Eshtak piled the chipped rock into the wheelbarrows, and Hardin and a few others took turns hauling the rock up to the door and dumping it.

Mortis remained immobile, his arms crossed over his chest and a sour expression on his chinless face. "You're wasting your time and endangering us all."

Rage consumed Berggren. He threw down his pickaxe and marched right up to Mortis. "One more word out of you, and I swear I'll knock you flat on the ground."

Mortis, a man half Berggren's size, cowered. His face turned several shades whiter in an instant, and his beady brownish-yellow eyes bulged. "Lay a finger on—"

Berggren punched Mortis square in the face. Mortis staggered backward several steps and then fell on his butt. Blood gushed from Mortis's nose and soiled his tan shirt.

Mortis held his nose and tilted his head back. "Mark my words, Berggren. You'll regret this, and sooner than you think."

"Already regret not knocking you out." Berggren spat at the man's feet, then walked over and picked up his discarded pickaxe. "Show's over, people. Let's get back to work and seal off this door before we have a horde of unwelcome guests to contend with."

Everyone set to work again. After a few minutes, Berggren glanced over his shoulder. Mortis was gone.

First smart thing he's done.

Chapter Eight

Cyrus led the others toward Sionis, an ancient temple that stood at the precise center of Nasduron. From there, he would show them what they'd need to accomplish in order to raise Nasduron from the depths of the ocean.

Ahead, the white stone temple rose more than ninety feet above the cobblestone streets. It easily stood thirty feet taller than any other building in Nasduron and could be seen from almost any point in the city. Unlike every other temple and shrine built in Centauria, Sionis honored Ɔäʈūr, the one true God.

Once they reached the temple, it took them another thirty minutes to climb up to its highest accessible point, a six-sided terrace that surrounded the temple's iconic ivory steeple.

Zerenity leaned over the three-and-a-half-foot-tall stone parapet that encaged the terrace. "I know we're miles beneath the ocean, yet the conjured sky seems so real. I feel as though I could reach out and touch Ɔäʈūr's hand from here."

"Once upon a time, you could have," Cyrus said. "However, Ɔäʈūr no longer visits this place."

Zerenity faced him and cocked her head. "Doesn't he? Am I mistaken about the ancient Scriptures speaking of his omnipresence?"

Cyrus scowled at the woman. "If he is indeed everywhere at once, he must hide in the shadows, for I do not see him."

"The Father of Light hiding in the shadows?" Zerenity guffawed. "An impossibility. I assure you that we do not speak of the same God."

"You're both wrong," Theyn said. "Zhedäɔ Ɔʊn is the one we should look to when it comes to light."

"Enough with the gods and goddesses," Urza thundered. "Why did you bring us up here?"

Ridan, her face ashen, braced herself against the inner terrace wall and held onto Bakkan's mane. "To die."

"That is not true. You're up here to gain understanding of the trials that lie ahead." Cyrus pointed toward a massive spire that rose out of the south. "There are five more monolithic spires just like that one which define the city perimeter. Each spire is built of crystal and stone and is likely protected with rune mezhik, wards, and spell webs. In addition to those safeguards, I'm certain we'll discover traps and unnatural beasts protecting their cores. Attention to detail must be maintained throughout the spire. Traps will likely be triggered by almost any means thinkable. We must disable every last one of them."

"The dwarf's right," Rakzar said. "We *will* die."

Zerenity's hands rose to her hips. "You cannot be serious, Cyrus. What you're asking us to do teeters between madness and impossibility."

Cyrus nodded. "It does, and that's not the worst of it."

Urza scoffed. "Oh, it gets better? Can't wait to hear this."

Cyrus continued, "The spirit of an ancient wizard protects each spire as well. In all, we must defeat seven wizards to—"

"Seven?" Zerenity's eyes narrowed. "You said there are six spires, not seven."

"I did, and there are. However, once the first six spires have been disabled, we must fight the keeper of this temple, too."

Zerenity gasped. "Fight ʔäṭūr? You *are* mad!"

"The seventh wizard," Urza said, flatly, "not your false god."

Rakzar snarled. "You might as well ask us to sprout wings, take a leap off this temple, and fly like a dryte."

Cyrus sighed. "Look, I don't like this any more than the rest of you, but we have no choice. It's the only way to return Nasduron to the surface from within and the only way to leave this place."

"And how many wizards and mages did it take to construct these spires and wards and traps?" Urza said.

Cyrus shrugged. "Hundreds. Perhaps more."

Zerenity crossed her arms. "And you think one mage and one *Fizärd*

Näíʈezhär can undo it all?"

"No, but we must try," Cyrus said.

Ridan closed her eyes. "It's suicide."

Ɛäʈūr, why have you surrounded me with so many doubters?

Cyrus eyed each of them, then said, "We do nothing, and the world burns."

"Yes, I understand, but sending us to our deaths will change nothing." Zerenity looked to the south. "We must find another solution."

Ridan seethed, her face red with fury. "Ya brought us here to die!" She shoved off the wall and launched herself at Cyrus, hitting him square in the chest with her shoulder.

Her weight—far greater than he would've ever imagined—took him by surprise. He stumbled backward. The parapet caught him just below the waist, and Ridan's extra weight carried them right over its edge.

"Nardus!" Theyn yelled.

Wind stormed past as the two of them plummeted toward the cobblestone street below.

Ridan didn't scream. Didn't fight the fall. A stone gargoyle toppled from the top of a building.

Cyrus grabbed Ridan's arm and pulled her to him. She didn't resist as he held her against his chest. Glass eyes filled with unwept tears met his gaze.

In that moment, he remembered a truth he'd somehow forgotten.

I'm not the only one suffering from loss and despair.

He smoothed back Ridan's windswept hair as they continued their brisk descent. "I'm sorry for your loss, little one."

Tears fell from her eyes. Blew back into her hair. "And I'm sorry I killed us both."

Cyrus laughed. "Not this day."

Using mezhik, he commanded the air beneath them to thicken until they slowed to a stop less than a foot from the cobblestone street. He released his hold on the air and they dropped the last several inches. He grunted and pushed Ridan off his chest.

By the time he sat up, Theyn had arrived in her shifted form. She pounced on Ridan and pinned her to the ground, claws extended and teeth bared. A low growl emanated from her chest.

"Theyn, let her go," Cyrus said.

Her response came through mindspeak. *"She tried to kill you! Again!"*

Zerenity arrived in a whirlwind a moment later. "Is everyone alright?"

"We will be." Cyrus got on his hands and knees and crawled over to Ridan and Theyn. He lifted Theyn's chin and forced her to look him in the eye.

"What?" she growled in Cyrus's mind. Her claws retracted.

"I love you," he said to Theyn through mindspeak.

Theyn leapt off Ridan and tackled Cyrus to the ground. *"Don't you ever do that again."* She licked his lips and then kissed him as she shifted back into her human form.

Despite himself, Cyrus held Theyn close for several moments. He couldn't deny the love Nardus held for the shifter. And, if he were honest with himself, the love he felt for her, too. With reluctance, he pushed Theyn off himself and stood.

She will be my death.

Once Rakzar and Urza arrived, Cyrus addressed them all. "There are several things I'd like to say to all of you. First, I'm glad you're all on my side. Each of you brings a unique skill to our cause, and I'm honored to call you allies. Second, I regret bringing you to this place without giving you a choice.

"In the heat of the moment, I couldn't think of a better place to hide from Aria and Cinolth and regroup. Yes, I knew Sarai was dying, but my mind was focused on our survival and the loss of my son. I had no thought as to how we would leave this place without her. I beg your forgiveness."

Theyn opened her mouth to say something, but Cyrus cut her off with a raised finger. He continued, "Last but not least, it's time we get to work. Those spires will not take themselves down, and the world is running out of time."

After reaching the first spire, Cyrus and Zerenity began identifying the multitude of runes and wards protecting it. Each ward was conjured from light mezhik, and Cyrus took note when Zerenity's ability to manipulate nature proved useless against them. Thankfully, he managed to break all thirteen of them in under ten minutes and with relative ease.

He didn't fault the woman for her failure, but it didn't bode well for the group's success. If he wound up having to do everything mezhik related, taking down the six towers and the final temple would take them many days. Perhaps a week or more depending on how draining the process proved for him. Mage or not, he was still human and had limits of his own.

Cyrus eyed the inky black doorway they'd opened into the spire and grimaced. It reminded him of Zhäíţfäí Fäíţ₂ far beneath Mortuus Terra. The last thing he wanted to do was face another demon. He took a breath, then gritted his teeth. "Follow me."

Entering the spire, the seven of them quickly discovered a short pedestal with a circular indention about four inches in circumference and half an inch deep. Three jagged lines separated the hollow circle into parts. Just beyond the pedestal lay three paths separated by stone walls, each leading into a labyrinth of dark corridors.

Words written in ancient Centaurian arced around the outside of the circle. Zerenity translated them for the others. "Three paths. Three challenges. Three pieces of one. Joined, the phase will open." She peered up at Cyrus. "The phase?"

Cyrus scowled and nodded. "An ancient term used to describe a plane of existence conjured with mezhik. They named it the phase because it exists outside of the constructs of time. Within the phase, we will face a wizard spirit who guards this spire. In essence, the wizard still lives and breathes within the phase even though he or she gave their life conjuring it."

Rakzar stared at the pedestal and growled. "You're certain there's no other way out of here?"

"Were there another way, we'd be pursuing it," Zerenity said.

Ridan said, "There are marks on the walls at each entrance."

"Good observation." Zerenity examined each one. "We have three symbols: a book, crossed swords, and some sort of sunburst."

"The three pillars." Cyrus examined each one himself. "Knowledge, might, and mezhik." He spat on the ground, then winced. "Enough."

Urza peered at the ground where Cyrus had spat. "What was that about?"

Cyrus eyed Urza. "Old habits die hard."

Theyn chuckled. She obviously knew Nardus well.

"Look," Cyrus said. "I know none of you want to be separated from the others, but we all know exploring this place as one large group will take more time than we have allowance for. Every moment spent in Nasduron costs many of those in the Ancient Realm their lives. We must split up."

"Agreed," Zerenity said. "Point us in the direction you want us to take, and we'll be off."

"Rakzar and Urza, you'll take the path to the right with the crossed swords. Zerenity, Ridan, and Bakkan, your path lies straight ahead with the book of knowledge. Theyn, you're with me to the left. We'll handle the mezhik." He spat again and sighed heavily.

Let me do my job without interruption, Nardus.

"All of you, remember what's at stake. Be safe. Be brave." Cyrus's eyes flashed with lightning. "But most importantly, do not fail to retrieve your piece of the circle."

"We won't fail," Rakzar said. He and Urza drew their weapons and headed to the right without another word.

Zerenity conjured a ball of green light and smiled at Ridan. "Shall we?"

Ridan clutched a spear in her left hand. Even though she sat on her familiar's back, she still came up an inch or so shy of Zerenity's height. "Lead the way." The two of them headed down the central path.

With a nod, Cyrus turned and headed down the path of mezhik with Theyn at his side.

Ɂäţūr, guide us and protect us all.

CHAPTER NINE

After the others headed into the heart of Nasduron, Wrik set his mind on the task ahead and what it might entail. Once he returned to The Plains, what would he find awaiting him? If Aria were smart, and he knew her to be, she'd have left some of her soldiers in the spot where he'd crashed.

As concerning as that was, what concerned him more was the question as to what type of soldiers she'd left. Aria now controlled the whole of the Ancient Realm, including the gnolls, orcs, giants, zhebəllin, and many other detestable creatures. And that didn't even include Cinolth's mind-controlled army. No matter what awaited him, what chance of survival did he have?

Little to none, but I have no choice.

Even though Aria had started their feud, he was the one responsible for his current predicament. He should've finished her off when he'd had the chance. Then again, he might not have survived if he'd stuck around and finished the job.

Wrik gathered supplies from within the storehouses of The Great Library, including a few bottled spells that might come in handy, an old, chinked sword that looked as though it might've belonged to a zhebəllin, and several throwing knives. Once he obtained everything he could think of needing, he returned to the library and stood at its center.

Would he ever return? He had his doubts. The thought of death didn't scare him, but he desperately wanted to see how every prophecy unfolded. Tracking the progress of certain paths fascinated him. When one path proved successful, new branches always grew.

He unsheathed the one-handed sword and wielded it. With any luck, he'd survive another day.

Gnaud bounded off a chair and landed on top of the table next to Wrik. "Oh, my! Off to slay a dragon?" Mischief gleamed in his eyes.

Wrik pushed his spectacles up his nose. "Were it that simple, I'd cut off Cinolth's head myself."

"I know you have a long journey ahead and an extraordinary task to complete, so I won't keep you. Good luck, and be careful, my friend."

"Thank you, Gnaud. Our time together has enlightened my life."

"If I didn't know better, it sounds like you're saying goodbye."

Wrik didn't reply because there was nothing more to be said. Instead, he focused his mind on The Plains. He always found it difficult to gauge how much time had passed when he visited Nasduron, so he never knew what time of day it would be once he returned to whence he'd come.

Only one way to find out.

After one final look around, Wrik took a deep breath and stepped out of the library and back into the middle of The Plains. Relief washed over him when he found that the sun had yet risen in the west. However, his relief fizzled as his eyes adjusted to the predawn haze and his nose picked up on a horrendous smell he knew quite well. As luck would have it, he stood right smack in the middle of an orc camp. Based on the number of tents, there were likely at least a dozen of them. Perhaps many more.

This ought to be interesting.

He knelt in the hollow of the tall grass, trying to figure out what his best move would be. One option would be to teleport some distance from there, but he wouldn't have any idea of what or who might greet him there. With his luck thus far, the situation would likely prove more dire than a band of orcs. Not only would it be risky, doing so would sap his energy and leave him more vulnerable than he already was.

Another option presented itself when he stuck his hand in his pocket and touched the dragon ring lying at its bottom. Temptation swept through his mind, urging him to put it back on. He almost did without thinking about it but caught himself just before it slipped around his finger. Donning the ring would likely worsen the situation. For all he knew, Aria might've instructed the orcs to attack and kill any dragon they found.

No, he must lean on his strengths. As a wizard of prophecy and master of words, his best option would be to engage the orcs in conversation and rely on their stupidity to gain the upper hand. Likely, he would trick them into fighting amongst themselves and easily escape without lifting the sword he gripped.

Wrik sucked in a long breath, then stood tall. "Hey, have any of you seen the rest of the army? I seem to have gotten separated from my group." The words had sounded better in his head.

"Make a move, and I'll bury my mace in the back of your skull." The thick, guttural voice came from behind Wrik and chilled him to the bone.

Wrik chanced it and turned around, but not quickly enough. The wicked beast shoved a silver collar right through his neck. He swallowed hard despite feeling nothing as the zäbräzär slid on. The churning mezhik within himself disappeared in an instant, leaving him empty.

So, this is what it feels like to be ordinary. Ghastly.

"Drop your weapons, and step back." Snot hung from the beast's nose and swung in a counterclockwise circle when it spoke. "Slowly."

"Yes, of course." Wrik dropped the sword first. In all honesty, it didn't feel comfortable in his hand anyway. The knives clanked against the sword and tumbled to a stop a few inches away.

Those could've come in handy.

He eyed the wretched beast. "You should know that this situation we find ourselves in far surpasses your understanding. Obviously, some sort of error has occurred on your part."

The orc grinned. Or at least that's what Wrik assumed happened when the orc's ugly face contorted and its lip curled upward. "The error lies with you, wizard, not me. My orders were very clear. Capture and escort anything and anyone back to Galondu Castle."

"Galondu Castle?" Wrik exhaled loudly. "Oh, good. In fact, that's perfect. I was about to head there myself. You'll save me the trouble of going it alone."

The orc stepped closer. Got right in Wrik's face. "You must think my kind foolish, but I assure you that we're far more cunning than you might think. I'd go as far as to say we're far smarter than the lot of you worthless humans."

Wrik raised his arms. "Whoa. Far be it from me to judge an entire race based on an encounter with a single member. Especially a race I know so little about."

"Goro, Bog. Bind this wizard's hands and feet." The orc walked over to one of the tents and disappeared inside.

"Do you think it necessary?" Wrik said to the nearest orc. He assumed it to be Goro. "I assure you that Galondu Castle *is* my destination."

The orc snarled and turned to its counterpart. "You know, Bog, there's nothing in this world I hate more than a talking human."

"What about gnolls?" Bog said. "Thought you loathed them most."

"Right." Goro picked his nose and then wiped his bloody finger on his loincloth. "Talking humans are the second thing I hate most."

Bog bound Wrik's wrists and ankles with crude shackles and fetters. The shackles dug into his wrists and tore through his skin. As rusted as they were, he could only imagine the infection they might induce.

Gods, what have I gotten myself into?

"All I ask is for a moment—"

Splintering pain erupted across the back of Wrik's skull. His vision blurred and dimmed as the world tumbled forward. Stalks of grass bent around him, chaffing and gouging his neck and cheeks. The wet ground rose to meet him and smacked him square in the face.

Wrik grunted and groaned. The shackles kept his arms pinned beneath him. He struggled to turn his head away from the muck just enough to breathe.

Another jarring blow. This time to the side of his head. Piercing pain shot through his entire body and then dissipated in an instant. The cold ground and the smells of rain, damp grass, and wet orc faded. Then, the darkness consumed him.

CHAPTER TEN

S avric rolled over in his bed and stared right into the eyes of Morcinda. A scowl distorted her otherwise pleasant features. He grunted as he pulled himself into a sitting position. "Did I get up to nefarious dealings while asleep?"

Morcinda shook her head. "No, but you'd sleep through a hurricane if I let you, wouldn't you?"

"Perhaps." He slipped on his boots and reached for Qotan's staff. "Have I missed a significant event?"

"You're on the verge of it." She turned to leave.

His stomach rumbled, and he chuckled. "Breakfast, is it?"

Turning back, she shook her head again. "Is food all you think about?"

Savric shrugged. "Only when I am famished."

"When are you not?" She left the room.

He rose and followed her out. "Pray tell, Morcinda. The verge of what?"

"An imminent attack." On deck, she untethered several ropes. Weighted bags sailed down from above with a *zing*, collapsing the sails and slowing the ship.

Savric tailed her as she climbed the stairs to the upper deck. "If we are indeed about to be attacked, then why are you slowing us down? Your ship is by far the quickest vessel on water."

"Yes, and in most circumstances, we'd outrun the attack, but we're in a situation now that can only be resolved with a show of might."

Zelanora joined them on the upper deck. "What's happening?"

Morcinda handed Zelanora a spyglass. "See for yourself."

After several moments, Zelanora gasped. "Half a dozen ships are headed straight for us."

"Yes, and did you get a good look at the flags they're flying?" Morcinda said.

Zelanora looked through the spyglass again. "I see… black flags… um… is that what I think it is?"

Morcinda pulled the ship around to face the oncoming vessels. "The head of a blue dog with a silver scarf wrapped around its brow?"

"Yes," Zelanora said.

"Seahounds." Savric pulled on his beard. "They rarely travel far from land, so why are they out here on the open ocean?"

Zelanora returned the spyglass to Morcinda and stared out at the horizon. "We're closer to the Shattered Realm than you think. In case you didn't know it, you've been asleep for the past seven hours."

Savric grunted. "Well, that confirms I am short on sleep by several hours." He placed his hand above his eyes to block the light as he searched the seas. "How long do we have before the seahounds are upon us?"

"At their rate of travel, I'd say about twenty minutes." Morcinda looped a rope around one of the spokes of the ship's wheel, virtually locking it in place. "Now, we need a plan."

Decades ago, Savric and Qotan had sailed to the Shattered Realm to find a special plant known to only grow on the northern slopes of the Vetiti Mountains. They never did locate the elusive plant, but they did face a vessel full of seahounds in the process. Thanks to Qotan and his ability to negotiate his way out of certain death, they'd narrowly escaped with their lives.

Now, they didn't have time to deal with such fiends, especially given the precious cargo they carried. Savric chuckled to himself. Princess Zelanora would fume if she heard him refer to her as precious cargo. As dangerous as seahounds could be for a man, it paled when compared to the ferocity with which they hunted women. Especially if word got out about Princess Zelanora being on board. Seahounds were known to prey on women.

Savric chuckled again.

They have likely never faced women like Morcinda and Zelanora.

The two women proved to be not only hardheaded but also strong willed. Both possessed wits and smarts far greater than any woman Savric knew, save Zerenity. He had little doubt they'd hold their own against the seahounds. His own strength and stamina worried him, though.

The greatest concern he had revolved around their detection. With Morcinda's ability to manipulate water, her ship always sailed faster than the wind and virtually free of detection. So, how had the seahounds detected, tracked, and pursued them with such speed?

Something must be wrong.

Savric eyed the two women who flanked him. Had one of the two betrayed them? If so, how and why? What purpose would it serve? Better yet, who would it serve? Aria and Cinolth? Or Diᴣäfär himself?

Savric shook the thoughts from his head.

Both women are trustworthy.

What that did leave him with was the notion that the seahounds were sent after them by Cinolth and Aria. In truth, that made the most sense by far. Only Ʒätūr knew how far Cinolth's scales had spread when he cursed the world. He'd never contemplated them spreading beyond the Ancient Realm, but mezhik curses tended to work in mysterious and unbelievable ways. Plus, logically speaking, it made the most sense.

Morcinda scowled at Savric. "Well?"

He blinked several times. "Did I miss something?"

"We need a plan, and quick," Morcinda said.

"Yes, of course." Savric pulled on his beard. "We must keep in mind that there are likely humans on those ships, too."

"Seahounds work with no one."

"Under normal circumstances, I would agree, but we live in dangerous and uncertain times. We have no idea how widespread Cinolth's influence is."

"Ah, yes. Mind-controlled slaves." Morcinda scanned the waters with her spyglass again. "Unless my eyes deceive me, you're absolutely right. So, what should we do about it?"

"I think we should try and outmaneuver the ships and then outrun them," Zelanora said.

"You must not realize how fast seahounds are in open waters." Morcinda collapsed her spyglass and hung it from a hook on her belt. "They propel their vessels via manual power and can keep pace with a ship as fast as mine for great distances. Given that there are at least six ships of them, I'm certain we'd fail to outmaneuver and outrun them."

Zelanora's grip on the railing tightened, turning her knuckles white. "What are we supposed to do then almighty queen of the ocean? Just give up?"

"Never." A plan began forming in Savric's mind.

"How about we stop and wait for them to approach," Zelanora said. "Then, we negotiate."

Savric and Morcinda both looked at Zelanora. Morcinda said, "You realize that these creatures do not negotiate, right? They'll defile us, devour us, and then destroy my ship. I certainly will not stand for it."

Zelanora glared at Morcinda. "You're quick to knock down my ideas, yet I've heard nothing from you. What's your great idea?"

"We will face them one at a time if possible and subdue their ships. It's the only possible solution other than complete annihilation."

"And how do you suppose we go about attacking just one of them when the others are closing in on our location just as quickly?"

"I'll create walls of water and resistance to block the other ships while we face the first one."

"If you spend your energy trying to prevent five ships from reaching us, you will be useless in the fight," Savric said. "Without you, we fail."

Zelanora stamped her foot. "Then what?"

Savric twisted several strands of his beard between his finger and thumb. "The three of us will need to work together and fast." He turned to Zelanora. "Combining our mezhik with Morcinda's water skills might prove to be a formidable force the seahounds cannot overcome."

"I'm not sure I understand. How do we combine mezhik?"

"Think of it like a recipe."

Morcinda shook her head and chuckled. "Always about food with you."

Savric ignored Morcinda and continued, "Flour and water do little together other than make a mess, but if you add a bit of salt and lard to the mix, you end up with something far more interesting. With a touch of fire, you've created something delicious."

Boom! Boom!

Smoke rose from two of the approaching ships.

Zelanora gasped. "Forward-facing cannons?"

Boom! Boom! Boom!

Morcinda leaned against the ship's railing and raised her arms in the air. A massive wall of water dozens of feet thick rose thirty feet above the deck and moved toward the oncoming ships. "That'll stop the cannonballs but not the ships. Perhaps the two of you can light them up with wizard's fire."

"One or two ships, for certain, but not six." Savric groaned. "Neither of us has that kind of strength."

Zelanora huffed. "I've never even conjured a fireball before. And, as far as I know, I can only touch an object and see its history and sometimes its future."

Savric reached over and gave the girl's shoulder a squeeze. "You are far more capable than you know. When the time arises, do everything I ask of you, and we will be fine."

The first ship crashed through the water wall and headed straight for them. Morcinda erected another water wall and the ship crashed through it, too. But the walls did their intended job, and the vessel slowed to a crawl. A second ship appeared behind the first. The last four wouldn't be far behind.

Morcinda glanced at Savric. "What now?"

Savric scowled at the approaching vessels, now only fifty yards away. "We allow them to board your ship."

"Are you mad!"

"Trust me. I have a plan, and it does not involve food." He winked at Morcinda, but she clearly didn't find it amusing.

† † †

Zelanora didn't understand Master Savric's plan. What good could come out of allowing the seahounds to board Morcinda's ship?

None.

She wanted to strangle the old man, but then she caught sight of the creature helming the enemy vessel. It was much more beautiful than she'd expected it to be. In truth, she'd envisioned them to look much like the wild dogs she'd seen throughout the Ancient Realm—mangy, matted, and all around filthy. However, this seahound had big gray eyes set deep within a luscious coat of thick blue fur. Not a bright blue hue but a shade more akin to the sky at dusk. And its shorter snout reminded her more of a fox than a dog or wolf.

Judging by the height of the vessel's wheel against its chest, the seahound stood about five and a half feet tall. Identical to the dog on the black flag, the seahound wore a silver scarf tied around its head. However, from those she could see, none of the others wore a scarf.

He must be their captain.

The captain dressed in loose clothing—black trousers and an off-white sleeveless shirt that showed off the beast's furry, muscular arms. A gray sash wrapped the seahound's waist and provided a place to attach the leather scabbard and short sword that hung from it.

Zelanora watched the first ship turn ninety degrees as it came alongside Morcinda's ship. A dozen ropes with sharp metal hooks twirled and then sailed across the gap between the two ships. One of the hooks flew right at her.

"Auh!" Zelanora jumped back a good foot, narrowly escaping her thigh being skewered by the hook. It thudded onto the deck right at her feet and scraped along the wood planks before gaining purchase along the ship's rail. The other hooks staked out similar claims.

A cohesive unit, the seahounds worked seemingly without effort as they pulled the two ships toward each other, narrowing the gap further. Somehow, they managed to pull it off in under a minute. Three planks, side-by-side, slid across the gap and joined the two ships. One of the seadogs jumped up onto the planks and drove nails into each of their ends, securing them to both ships.

At some point, the captain of the first seahound vessel had abandoned his post at the helm and made his way down to the makeshift bridge. The rest of the seahounds gathered behind their captain. A quick glance verified that the other five vessels surrounded them.

We're trapped.

With no one there to protect, all Zelanora could think about was her inability to fight. The more she thought about it, the more she understood how absurd her demands to return to the Three Kingdoms had been. She'd become something she'd vowed never to be. A spoiled princess.

No more.

Zelanora took a half step back and partially hid herself behind Master Savric's bellowing robes. "Tell me what to do, and I'll do it without question."

Master Savric nodded but said nothing as the seahound captain made his way across the newly constructed bridge between the two ships.

Morcinda nudged Master Savric. "Now would be a good time to execute your plan."

Master Savric gripped his staff with his left hand. "Patience, my dear."

"Concentrate on the ivory handle of Morcinda's dagger."

Zelanora startled when Master Savric's voice entered her mind. She'd never experienced anything quite like it. Thinking back to when she was a child, she remembered hearing someone talk about the way wizards could communicate without speaking aloud. They'd called it mindspeak. Had they not been in imminent danger, she would've asked Master Savric to show her more. Right then, she only needed to know how to respond.

The seahound captain hopped down from the makeshift bridge. "Greetings, humans." The quality of its voice was far smoother than she would've imagined, and its accent was unlike any she'd heard before. A strange mix of mainlander and beacher.

Morcinda stepped forward, her palm resting on the hilt of her dagger. "Do I look human to you, dog?"

Zelanora's palms began to sweat. "What now?" she whispered.

"Relax," Master Savric said through mindspeak. *"Allow your mind to take in every word I utter and every detail I give you. Take the information and picture it as though it were a memory of recent events. Make it feel personal."*

"I'll try."

Morcinda and the seahound continued to exchange words, but Zelanora closed her eyes and tuned them out, keeping her mind focused on everything Master Savric said to her.

"Months ago, the seahound fleet was sixteen ships strong, but they made the mistake of attacking this same vessel. Morcinda, armed with nothing but her ivory-handled dagger, took out ten of their ships, killing everyone aboard each of them by slitting their throats."

Zelanora allowed the words to take shape within her mind. She pictured the attack and Morcinda's response. By the end of the battle, blood covered Morcinda from head to toe, yet none of it was hers. She didn't suffer a single scratch. The remaining seahounds retreated and vowed to sail wide of her vessel if their paths ever crossed again.

"Ready?" Master Savric said within Zelanora's mind.

Zelanora had no idea what she was supposed to be ready for, but the last thing she wanted to do was fail Master Savric. "I think so." She opened her eyes.

"Good." Master Savric winked at her and then stepped forward as he addressed the seahound captain. "Pardon the interruption, but it seems as though you have failed to adhere to the rules set forth upon your last encounter with this woman."

The seahound captain cocked his head. "I've never laid eyes on this woman in my life, nor have I seen this vessel."

"No? Then perhaps you will remember the dagger that slew the crews of ten of your ships." He gestured with his head. "Go ahead, Morcinda. Show the beast your dagger." Morcinda frowned at Master Savric but did as he requested.

The seahound captain squinted at Master Savric. "What are you playing at, old fool?"

"Perhaps you suppressed the memory because it pains you. Take your time and search your memories. Do so, and it will come back to you." Master Savric reached back. *"Take my hand and show me,"* he said to Zelanora through mindspeak.

Zelanora grabbed hold of Master Savric's hand. "Now what?"

"Reach within yourself and touch your mezhik. Once you feel it, think about the memory and imagine it as a stream. Let that stream flow through you and into me. Do this, and I will take care of the rest."

"Enough of this nonsense." The seahound captain drew his sword. "Fall on your knees and accept your fate."

Warmth like sunshine on a winter's day welled within Zelanora as she drew upon her mezhik. Every time she touched it, she wondered how anyone ever thought of it as evil. To her, it was an inward expression of the love she shared with Ɂäţūr.

A dozen more seahounds joined their captain, each brandishing some sort of pointed weapon.

Morcinda snarled, "Remove yourselves from my vessel at once, and I'll spare your lives."

The seahound captain pointed his sword at Morcinda and grinned. "No suppression of memory would've taken a woman as brash as you from my mind. It'll be a pleasure licking your blood from my blade."

A flowing stream.

Zelanora willed her mezhik to flow through her. Master Savric's hand grew warm, but the sensation faded after a few seconds. She released his hand. "I can't do this."

"You can, and you must. Fail, and we die this day."

Metal clashed as the seahound captain and Morcinda exchanged blows. Another of the seahounds rushed forward and swung his weapon straight at Master Savric's head. Master Savric didn't flinch as the sword came around. Zelanora cried out and cringed, but the weapon failed to connect. Not only did it fail to connect, but it shattered just an inch from Master Savric's neck. A bright light flashed and the seahound staggered backward, stunned both from the jarring blow and the loss of his weapon.

Master Savric turned and winked at Zelanora. *"A light shield."* He proffered his hand once again. *"I have faith in you, Zelanora. You can do this."*

In that moment, Master Savric reminded her of her father. He'd told her the same thing quite often through the years. She took Master Savric's hand again.

Morcinda leapt backward and yelled something in a language Zelanora didn't understand. What she did understand was the meaning of the large drops of blood on the ship's deck. Morcinda's shirt bloomed red on her left side.

Zelanora took a deep breath, closed her eyes, and gave in to her mezhik. This time, she allowed it to flow freely. As she did, she recalled the false memory of Morcinda.

Grunts, clashes of metal, and cries surrounded her. She forced them from her mind as Master Savric's hand warmed in hers.

Master Savric gasped. *"Dear 2äţūr, your mind is a beautiful creation,"* he said through mindspeak.

The stream of mezhik reversed course and began flowing back into her. At first, it was only hers, but then she felt his, too. Rapid. Hot. Breathtaking.

"Open your eyes, Zelanora."

She complied. More than just a few drops of blood splattered the deck. Two seahounds lay in pools of blood, neither the captain. He stood over Morcinda, blade at her throat.

"No!" Zelanora lunged forward, but Master Savric pulled her back, his hand still clutching hers.

A brilliant ring of pure light shot outward. All the seahounds staggered backward a step, including the captain.

"It is done." He released Zelanora's hand and fell to one knee. "Pray that it worked."

Zelanora rushed over to Morcinda and helped her to her feet. Morcinda clutched her side but still grasped her dagger.

Master Savric's voice entered her mind once again. *"Are you weak?"*

Zelanora gave herself a quick assessment. "I don't think so."

"Then heal her."

She'd never heard Master Savric's voice sound so frail. It scared her, but seeing the excessive amount of blood covering Morcinda's blouse and trousers scared her more. With each passing moment, Morcinda's weight against her increased.

All the seahounds staggered around, seemingly confused. Many of them held their heads.

Zelanora had never attempted to heal anyone before. In fact, she didn't know she possessed the ability to do so.

Morcinda collapsed, and her dagger flew out of her hand and skidded across the deck. It came to a rest at the foot of the seahound captain. The beast just stared at it.

"Heal her, or she dies."

Anger grew within her. How had she lived without preparation? Knowing she was different, why hadn't she sought out a teacher? The answer lay in the ice-cold blue eyes of her father. It sickened her to think about what'd become of her mother, especially given the fact that her father had a hand in it. His reaction to her revealing her abilities made it even worse.

Did he stop loving me in that moment?

Zelanora knew it to be a lie, but the thought still hurt. She pushed it aside and knelt next to Morcinda. The sight of blood didn't sicken her, but she still had no desire to touch it.

How else can I heal her if I refuse to touch the wound?

She cringed when her fingers touched the warm, sticky liquid oozing from Morcinda's side. Morcinda groaned but otherwise lay still.

Don't think about it, Zel. Just do it.

The seahound captain sheathed his sword and reached for Morcinda's dagger. The dagger twitched. Slid a few inches then stopped.

Zelanora reached within and emptied her mezhik into Morcinda's wound until everything doubled through her eyes. Darkness crept into the corners of her vision. She tried to blink it away, but the darkness only grew. Next to her, Morcinda rose to her feet, dagger in hand.

How did she get the dagger?

Morcinda cried out. A banshee. She pointed her dagger at the seahound captain. "Leave this place now, or I will hunt your kind until none remain."

The seahound captain stuck two fingers in his mouth and whistled. Those on Morcinda's ship retreated across the makeshift bridge, taking their dead with them. Once they removed the planks and cut the lines tying the two ships together, the six ships sailed away.

Morcinda turned and stared at Savric and Zelanora. "The two of you make an interesting team. Even though I'm positive I never faced the seahounds before and certainly didn't take out ten of their ships with nothing but my dagger, my mind still pictures it like any other memory." She cocked her head. "How did you accomplish this?"

Zelanora took a deep breath then exhaled it forcefully. "I created the false memory, and Master Savric distributed it with his light mezhik."

"And how long will it last?"

Zelanora shrugged. "I'm not sure."

Morcinda bent down and retrieved a rolled-up piece of parchment. One of the seahounds must've dropped it. She unrolled it, and her expression darkened.

She eyed Zelanora. "Appears you're a wanted woman. Head only."

Zelanora lay back on the deck and closed her eyes.

Ꙅäṭūr, help me.

CHAPTER ELEVEN

Aria hardly touched her breakfast. It wasn't because the toast was slightly burned or that the yolks of the eggs were still cold. It wasn't even because the fruit had yet to ripen. No, the reason for her loss of appetite was far graver. Today, she would bury the man she both loved and loathed. Well, bury wasn't an accurate word for what would become of Pravus. Because of the grim nature of his death, she'd ordered his body burned to ash and placed inside a clay urn.

She cared nothing about traditions or the fact that Pravus was technically never a king. After everything he accomplished, he deserved to rest in the Hall of Kings alongside his father, Pugnus Rosai. Besides, who would ever oppose her and live to tell of it?

No one.

When she returned to her bedchambers, Brema awaited her. The girl wore a faint smile, yet her eyes carried within them a deep sorrow. Aria wondered how well Brema had known Pravus and if Brema had lain with him in the past. From what she'd come to understand, Pravus had no discretion nor preference when it came to the women he slept with. For him, the interactions were little more than a release.

Until he met me.

Aria tried picturing the way Pravus had looked the first time they'd met inside Master Dragnus's study, but the only thing she could see was his broken body on the battlefield. Drained of blood. Head punctured. Chewed in two.

She leaned over and dispensed her breakfast into the chamber pot next to her bed. Brema, ever gracious, held her hair back for her. Yes, thinking about Pravus's horrific demise left her stomach uneasy, but it wasn't the cause of her nausea. No matter what remedies she tried, her pregnancy got the better of her every morning. Thank the gods she didn't suffer from it all day. If she had, she might've killed someone out of spite, the likely candidate Brema just based on proximity.

She liked the girl well enough, but one often hurts those closest to them. Brema had attended to her from the very first day she'd arrived at Galondu castle, and they had become as close as two people with such disparity in station could ever hope to be. Had Aria not risen to power, the two of them might've become great friends. Even so, they'd always been friendly with each other.

She's my servant, not a friend.

Once Aria situated herself in front of the mirror, Brema began brushing out the tangles in her hair. She would've done it herself, but Brema possessed a gentleness that couldn't be matched.

Aria sighed as she gazed upon herself in the mirror, knowing the day would bring with it more pain than relief. Despite her lackluster mood, she forced herself to smile at her own reflection.

But the reflection betrayed her.

Marred her.

Brought back her past.

The Aria she'd left behind when Pravus had fixed her.

Heart racing, she blinked several times, but the reflection refused to change. Refused to display her true self. Instead, it produced a broken young woman. Pale, splotchy skin. Misaligned teeth. Chipped and cracked.

She leaned closer. Touched the mirror. Then her lips. Ran her tongue across the tops of jagged teeth.

Her stomach churned. Threatened to purge what remained of its contents.

What's wrong with me?

"Are you feeling well, Mistress Aria?"

Aria met Brema's gaze in the mirror for an instant before refocusing on herself. Unlike moments before, the mirror reflected the way she knew herself to be. Perfect teeth. Radiant complexion. Flawless, save her many scars. Those she collected and cherished more than treasure.

She touched her belly and closed her eyes. Intoxicating mezhik leeched from her fingers and penetrated her dress. Sank into her skin. An image of her baby formed in her mind. So small. Delicate. Precious.

Is this your doing, little one?

A smile touched her lips once again.

"Mistress Aria?"

Aria's eyes shot open, and her nostrils flared as she exhaled.

Mistress Aria.

It would take effort beyond measure to retrain the girl to address her as queen, and she frankly didn't have the patience or desire, so she left her frustration unspoken. "Well enough, given my current state." She stroked her belly. "I'll relish the day I can keep my breakfast down."

Brema nodded as she began braiding Aria's hair. "Yes, mistress, but your morning sickness isn't what I was referring to."

Anger rose into Aria's throat. "Then what?"

Brema's hands began to tremble. Aria felt the vibrations through her hair. "Master Credan said you were… unwell last night."

"Did he?"

"Yes, mistress."

Aria turned and faced the girl. Brema's pale skin had become pasty white, and she breathed far heavier than she normally did. Aria's throat tightened. "I never left my bed last night, so what would give him the impression I was *unwell*?"

"He said… he said…" Brema swallowed hard and lowered her head toward the floor. Her lower lip trembled.

"Tell me, Brema. His exact words." She took Brema's hands and shook them until the girl finally looked at her again. "Whatever it is, I will not be angry with you."

"You woke in the middle of the night with fever and sickness." Tears streaked down her cheeks. "He said you exited your bedchamber and sought Lord Pravus as though he were still alive."

Smack!

Brema staggered backward, her hand cupped over her left cheek. Aria's hand stung. It took several moments for her to realize what had happened. What she'd done. She had promised the girl she wouldn't become angry, but the girl's words caught her by surprise.

Why would Credan make up such a lie? Does he seek my throne?

Aria rose from her seat. Brema cowered next to the bed. When she reached for Brema's hand, the girl flinched. She exhaled loudly. "Pull yourself together, Brema. You're not ignorant, so I'm sure you understand why I struck you."

Brema nodded, took a deep breath, then wiped her face on her unflattering, drab dress. "I offended you, Mistress Aria, and I am sorry. You have every right to punish me as you see fit. My existence in this world is to attend to and please you in everything I do. Nothing more and nothing less. I've failed you."

"You did, and now you've paid for it. See that it doesn't happen again." Aria waved her hand. "We will speak of this no more." She turned and sat back down in front of the mirror. "Now, do your job and make me beautiful. I have a funeral to attend."

"Yes, mistress."

A few hours later, Aria met Credan in the corridor. The man looked nothing of his usual self, his eyes haggard and cavernous, his shoulders rolled forward, and his back hunched over. The difference between his bow and him standing upright was nearly undetectable, save the slight bend in his neck.

"My queen, you are well beyond radiant."

She continued down the corridor toward the massive doors that led into the atrium. "And you look worse than death itself."

Credan did his best to keep up with her. "I've not slept."

"Too busy spreading lies of my condition, I suppose." The jab felt good. Taking his life would satisfy even more.

Credan gasped. "My queen? I assure you I would never do anything of the sort."

She stopped and glared at him. Intoxicating mezhik swelled at her fingertips. One touch, and his life would be forfeit. "And yet you confide in my bedchamber servant that you've witnessed me traversing the corridors in search of my dead husband."

Credan stared at her hand. Swallowed hard. "I will admit that I did as you say, but it wasn't a lie. As always, I am your humble servant. I only shared my concerns with Brema because she knows you far better than anyone. You took me off guard when you asked me to direct you toward Lord Rosai last night. What was I to do? You were obviously beside yourself. Fevered perhaps. I'm certain your lapse in memory must've been triggered by the energy you exerted while reactivating the gateway. That, plus your loss and your pregnancy. Your brother..." Credan wiped the top of his head with a kerchief. "For all of it, I am deeply sorry."

"Oh, I'm sure you are."

Aria lowered her black veil and pulled the massive doors open using her mezhik. As she stepped into the atrium, the heads of the people turned in her direction, their eyes upon her. Never had she felt so much power. She strode through the crowd, her long train of black lace dragging behind her. Even with short notice, every dignitary had come. She knew they would, for none of them could resist a chance to gloat over the death of a ruler. After all, were they not superior to Pravus simply because they outlived him? Perhaps, but they would meet their demise soon enough. She'd see to it herself.

Given the sheer size of the atrium, its fullness surprised her. The crowd surpassed that of the one that gathered when Pravus had given his speech before they went to war.

Impressive.

At the center of the atrium stood a pedestal made of obsidian with veins of red gold. Atop the pedestal sat an urn painted black with gold pinstripes. It matched the robes Pravus wore. Aria fought back tears as she approached the pedestal. She ground her teeth and drove her nails into her palms.

The people will not see my weakness.

Reaching out with her mind, she searched for Cinolth but couldn't feel his presence. She'd expected as much given his disdain for Pravus. More than likely, he didn't want to experience her grief and pain either. His presence would've detracted from the weight of the event anyway. Plus, she hated him.

Credan stepped past her and stood next to the pedestal. "Lords, ladies, honored guests, we are gathered here to honor and remember the life of

Lord Rosai, king of the Ancient Realm."

Many of the guests cheered, but others sneered. Far more than Aria would've liked. She kept a mental note of each, vowing to disembowel them at a more appropriate time.

Credan continued, but Aria couldn't keep her mind focused. She'd expected Wizard Wrik to perform the ceremony, yet he seemed to be absent altogether. Where could he possibly be on such a momentous occasion? She needed him, the last of her friends.

He'd better be dead.

The thought startled her. Shook her to the core. The last thing she wanted was another death of someone she cared about. The more she pondered it, the worse she felt. Everyone close to her always died. First her mother, Gretchen. Then her *real* father, Red. Vonah and Amicus. Pravus. Alderan. The last name nearly drove her to her knees.

Alderan. My brother. My better half. Why did you die for me?

In an instant, Aria stood atop the southern ramparts of the castle. The wind whipped around her and lifted the train of her dress into the air. She groaned and cried out from her soul, not with words but with rage. Sorrow. Love.

With raised arms, she shouted at the sky, vowing to never love anyone again, not even the child she carried in her womb. "By the gods, let it be so!"

She collapsed into a heap and sobbed.

As she lay there, the world felt as though it were slipping away from her. She began to wonder what purpose she served. Why did it matter whether she lived or died? Yes, Nardus still breathed air, but Cinolth would see to his death no matter how long it took. Pravus wanted to rule the world, not her, and Cinolth wanted to destroy it. Yet deep within she knew it was a lie. Her lust for power grew with each sunrise, and the attention she'd received when she stepped into the atrium had left her breathless and in need of more.

"I am more than the girl from Viscus D'Silva." She rose to her knees. "I am more than the wife of a fallen king." On her feet, she climbed onto the parapet and stood with her feet spread and her arms raised. "I am Aria Rosai, Queen of Centauria!"

CHAPTER TWELVE

Rayah walked through the large wooden doors that led out of the Great Library and onto the cobblestone paved streets of Nasduron. Had it been any other city in Centauria, the streets would've been bustling with activity, but these streets stood empty. Not just empty but abandoned.

The way she understood it, everyone but Gnaud had been forced to leave Nasduron when they sank it to the bottom of the ocean, but she wasn't entirely certain as to the exact reason. Many thoughts came to mind, most surrounding a fear that she and the others would soon die if they didn't succeed in taking down the spires.

Stop thinking like that.

Prominent structures lined the road, each with architecture as unique as the stars in the heavens. It made sense given that Nasduron was once the center of Centauria and the place where every culture and people were represented by a coalition of leaders. A global counsel of sorts.

As strange as the empty streets felt, nothing could've prepared her for the bubbled sky hanging over the city. Even though she knew she stood in a sunken city below the ocean, her mind never really registered or comprehended what that entailed. Yes, the yellowish-white ambient light simulated sunlight, but it didn't carry with it the same qualities of true sunlight. No real warmth came from it, and it didn't emit the same smell, either. Many people would argue that sunlight possessed no scent at all, but she knew better. She'd always enjoyed the freshness of a sunny summer day. Not only did the light not smell as it should, but it also failed to take away the gloom that enveloped her. True sunlight could brighten the darkest of moods.

Not even sunlight would lessen my sorrow.

Rayah continued along the cobblestone street for about a mile before the structures lessened in grandeur. Still, they put to shame any structures she'd seen across the Ancient Realm, each built with hewn stone and fine woods. Farther down the road, she came upon a circular structure constructed of flawless emerald stones and crystals of the purest white interwoven into a magnificent hexagonal pattern. The structure rose out of the ground like a castle spire, piercing the bubbled sky. Keeping her distance, she walked its circumference—a good four hundred paces by her measure—but found no discernible entrance.

As she approached the structure, its immediate surface began glowing with the same yellow hue as the sky in a shape similar to her own. Perhaps a reflection of her aura, but she couldn't be sure. The light brightened in the spots where her hands and face came closest to its surface.

A faint humming noise tickled her ears and grew louder as she drew nearer to it. The hairs on her arms stood on end, not out of fright or chills but from some sort of static energy emitted from the structure. She reached out and touched it. It touched her back. Or more like kicked her square in the chest. Threw her backward a good dozen feet. She slid to a stop on the cobblestone.

Rayah didn't scream and couldn't have done so even if she'd wanted to, the blow knocking the wind from her lungs. She inhaled a deep breath and sat up. Fire erupted across her elbows and on the palms of her hands. "Ouch!"

Bits of dust and cobblestone stuck to her freshly frayed skin. Thankfully, the wounds weren't deep, but they'd certainly need a good cleaning and dressing.

The structure remained unchanged. Taunted her. Left her feeling foolish. No explanation for her blatant lack of caution existed. She chided herself.

Live for Alderan. Fight for justice. Fight for freedom. Don't let his death be meaningless.

On the ground next to her, she noticed one of the cobblestones had some sort of mark etched into it. A circle filled with wavy lines.

Rayah traced the circle with her finger, and it began to glow with a purple hue. Five feet to her right, another cobblestone lit up. Farther still, another one.

Wings aflutter, she rose off the ground and flew over to the second cobblestone. It held the same mark as the first. The next one did, too. Each led to the discovery of another. As she followed them, more became visible.

A secret path, but to where?

After losing track of time at some point, she now found herself standing before a gray stone building. Three steps led up to two wooden doors embellished with ornate ironwork. The door on the left depicted the face of a woman. The woman's closed eyes and drooping features signified great sorrow, a state Rayah knew too well. The other door depicted the face of a man. Eyes wide, cheekbones raised, lips parted in a smile. He was either happy, joyful, or gleeful, but she didn't know which. No matter the emotion, the contrast between his face and that of the woman's was stark.

A metal sign hung above the doors. She could almost make out some of the words, but they weren't written in the common language. From what she could recall, the lettering matched some of the books Alderan had been reading when he was helping Zerenity research a cure for what they thought at the time was a disease. Now that she knew the truth and origination of those viperous vines, she wished it had been a disease. In a way, it kind of was.

Although the depictions on the doors failed to spell it out, she assumed the building must be some sort of temple. But as to the dedication of it to which false god or gods, she didn't know. The answer likely stared her in the face in the form of the sign written in ancient Centaurian.

You would've known what it said, Alderan.

She wiped a rogue tear from her cheek and stepped up to the doors. After more than a thousand years without use, she expected the doors to resist when she pushed on them. However, to her surprise, they swung into the building with little effort, as though they'd just been oiled that morning.

Fighting a tinge of reluctance, Rayah stepped across the threshold and into the large building. Dozens of marble benches lined either side of the square-shaped, dark-gray stone tiles that formed the central aisle leading toward the front of the massive room. Straight ahead rose a platform constructed out of a bleached wood with streaks of amber. Staircases consisting of the same wood as the platform curved up to meet the platform on its left and right sides. Thick, royal blue curtains hung from the ceiling on copper rods that stretched the width of the platform. The curtains were drawn to either side and held open with golden corded rope.

Seven white crystal chandeliers, each at least a dozen feet in diameter and far more glorious than those in the Great Library, hung from the vaulted ceiling and provided exceptional light to the entire room. Unlike any she'd seen before, the chandelier light didn't come from a multitude of flickering candles but from the crystals themselves. Brilliant, perfect light.

Rayah had seen a place like this once before in Aberporth, albeit nowhere near as grand or of such scale. "This is no temple but a performance hall."

Each step she took down the stone aisle reverberated off the walls and high ceiling. The building's architecture lent itself to carrying voices and instruments from the stage, filling every nook, cranny, and corner of the room with beautiful sounds.

Rayah closed her eyes and imagined the room filled with people, music, and flowers. But not just any music. In her mind, stringed instruments carried her down an aisle littered with flower petals. Tears streaked down her cheeks.

A place like this would've made for the best wedding, Alderan.

She dropped to her knees in the middle of the aisle and wept without restraint.

Why did you leave me?

Through her eyelids came a brilliant, purple light. It filled her vision and mind. When she opened her eyes, she saw that the light emanated from a two-foot diameter circle on the flat stone right in front of her. Blue, crystal-clear water gathered within the circle like a small pond.

Rayah reached out and dipped her finger in the water. A wave of energy expanded outward, passing right through her as it swept across the entire room. The seven crystal chandeliers turned black in an instant, casting the room into darkness. Only the purple light from the circle remained.

Just when Rayah thought nothing else would happen, the tile in front of the one with the circle dropped about eight inches. Then the next one beyond it dropped eight inches plus eight more. This continued until twelve tiles had dropped down, forming steps. The blue water receded into the stone, and the purple ring of light faded, replaced by a brilliant, blue light that rose from the stairwell.

Rayah wiped her eyes, stood, and stared down at the open stairwell. Fear and awe dominated her mind. She didn't understand what the symbol on the cobblestones meant, nor did she know why they led her there or where the stairwell would take her, but none of it mattered. Without Alderan at her side to protect, love, and cherish, her life lacked meaning. And without meaning, fear held no sway over her. No matter how deep it dug its hooks into her mind, fear could not restrain her. And so, it didn't.

The first step toward the unknown proved difficult, but then she took another. Soon, she found herself standing on the last step of an impossibly deep stairwell. Looking back up, she couldn't locate the opening.

Rayah swallowed hard as she descended the last step. Twenty paces ahead stood a massive archway dozens of feet wide and tall. Hundreds of symbols were chiseled into the stones that formed it. She recognized several of them, including ones Alderan bore on the insides of his wrists. Writing in the ancient language had been etched into the stone floor just in front of the archway. Perhaps some sort of inscription or warning, but she couldn't be certain.

Within the confines of the archway stood a wall of water. Its brilliant blue surface rippled and undulated. Even at a distance of twenty paces, invisible bolts of energy pricked her skin. She knew the feeling well.

Mezhik.

Silence engulfed her as her mind worked to understand the structure that stood before her. "Dear Ӡäțūr… What is this place, and why have you led me here?"

CHAPTER THIRTEEN

Zerenity stood before a red door with Ridan and Bakkan at her side. The ball of green light she'd conjured earlier lit the wooden sign that hung from the door. The sign contained just a single word, written in the ancient language. She read its translation aloud, "Conjuncture."

Ridan scowled at the sign. "What's that supposed to mean?"

"In the simplest of terms, it's the point of no return."

"If we cannot return from there, why would we enter?"

"I believe what it means is that once we pass through the doorway we cannot turn back. Instead, we must face and defeat whomever or whatever awaits us on the other side."

"And what do ya think that might be?"

"We are on the path of knowledge. Your guess is as good as mine."

Ridan glanced back the way they'd come. "We will never leave this place if we fail."

"Agreed." Zerenity reached for the handle, but the red door opened of its own volition, groaning as it eased inward.

Through the door lived impenetrable darkness, yet it wasn't alone. A familiar presence sent gooseflesh crawling up Zerenity's legs and arms, but she couldn't place it. Ridan and Bakkan entered the void ahead of her, and the darkness swallowed them. The moment she stepped through the doorway, her green ball of light fizzled then winked out. Then, the door slammed shut.

Zerenity tried conjuring another ball of light, but nothing happened. She swallowed hard, her mezhik inaccessible.

A swirling, iridescent vortex appeared about twenty paces ahead. The air sizzled and the room shook with thunderous booms as bolts of blue, green, red, and purple lightning arced outward from the vortex. The hairs on

Zerenity's arms and nape stood on end, energized by the energy in the air. At the center of the swirling vortex stood a figure swathed in a black cloak with its hood drawn low. Had it not been for the vortex and lightning, the two-foot-tall figure might've appeared less ominous.

Beams of white light shot straight down from the ceiling in the space between her and the vortex, creating two cylindrical columns. "Step into the light," the figure said.

Ridan and Zerenity locked eyes for a moment before stepping into the columns of light. The lightning ceased, but the vortex continued to churn around the cloaked figure.

The figure extended its arms, palms up. A glowing blue symbol appeared above each of its outstretched hands. "Which is the strongest?"

The symbol to Zerenity's left depicted what looked like a brain and the one to her right a flexed arm. Zerenity looked over at Ridan. "Which do you believe is stronger? Wisdom or might?"

Ridan studied each symbol for several seconds and frowned. "It depends. How can we make such a decision when we know nothing about the context of the question? Might can move rock easier than wisdom but doesn't always win a war."

"Yes, that's true," Zerenity said. "However, you can be the most brilliant strategist and still lose a war because you lack the strength to fight it. Also, wisdom can be used to make the moving of rock easier."

"Like creating a lever with a smaller rock and a pole or tree branch," Ridan said.

Zerenity smiled. "You're a clever young woman."

Ridan huffed. "Tell that to Torbrek Stonebreaker. He seems to think I'm only good for completing physical tasks, and by that, I mean the ones performed beneath the bed covers."

"Some men never see past our skin."

"I know, but Normak did." Ridan shuddered and looked away, wiping her face with her shoulder in the process. Zerenity pretended she hadn't noticed.

"Strongest?" the figure repeated.

Zerenity crossed her arms. "Wisdom and might complement each other and are of equal strength."

The symbols disappeared, and the figure lowered his arms. "Good." Then, an hourglass filled with amber sand appeared in front of the figure and hovered in the air. "Fail to unlock the chest before the last grain falls, and your souls will be trapped in here forever."

The figure and the two columns of light faded, and then an ambient light filled the large room. A silver chest with a golden lid rose out of the ground beneath the hourglass. Then, sand began filtering down into the lower portion of the hourglass.

Ridan peered up at Zerenity. "Now what?"

Zerenity looked around the room. "We put our heads together and find the key."

† † †

Rakzar led Urza deep into the dimly lit labyrinth. After a time, the stone floors transitioned to a heavy, deep sand. The outer stone walls remained, but shorter walls made of a thick, tangled briar with shiny, leathery leaves and thorns thick at their bases and several inches long rose out of the ground.

"I'm not liking this," Urza said.

Rakzar growled deep. "Neither am I."

As the path widened ahead, strange footprints in the sand drew Rakzar's attention. Urza must've noticed them too, her knives no longer twirling in her palms but gripped tightly.

Light grew out of the darkness far overhead. A massive metal chandelier hung from the black ceiling without rope or chain. Twelve torches burned bright from sconces around its circumference. Four thick, metal chains stretched taut attached the chandelier to four smaller wooden chandeliers, each held up with chains of their own. The additional chandeliers each held six additional torches. The torchlight gave definition to the space, highlighting the outer stone walls and the shorter walls of briar surrounding him and Urza.

"Looks like we've come to the end of the path."

A sound akin to wind through the trees rose and built into a frenzy.

Urza slowed. "What's making that noise?"

Rakzar detected no accompanying breeze or movement, but they didn't have to wait long for an answer. The briar vines scraped against themselves and shuddered. Then, they ripped apart and twisted back together, forming dozens of humanoid shapes with razor-sharp teeth and claws made of thorns. Groaning and howling, their thick vines ground together as they stalked toward Rakzar and Urza.

Rakzar surveyed the area. "We're surrounded."

"I can see that." Urza sheathed her knives. "Give me one of your axes, or we're not getting out of here alive."

"Aye." Rakzar tossed her one of his axes. "Time ta chop some wood."

Urza shook her head. "I can't believe you just said that."

Rakzar growled with laughter. "Thought I'd channel my inner Normak."

"Don't ever do that again."

Urza lunged forward and engaged the first of the briar beasts. One swift swing decapitated the creature, but it didn't go down. Instead, a new head grew out of the stump left behind by the first one. Rakzar achieved the same result with the briar beast he attacked.

The two of them fought to keep the prickly beasts at bay, but they'd soon run out of stamina and be overrun if they didn't find a solution to killing the beasts.

† † †

Theyn walked alongside Cyrus as they traversed the labyrinth. No matter what angle she stared at the man from, she detected no trace of Nardus. The transformation fascinated and terrified her. Based on some of Cyrus's mannerisms and actions, she knew Nardus lingered just below the surface. This thought terrified her as well.

What if Cyrus must do something Nardus would never do? Is he strong enough to fend off Nardus?

With any luck, they'd never have to find out.

"Why did you choose me and not Zerenity for this challenge? She's a sorceress."

Cyrus continued forward, his eyes constantly scanning the path ahead. "Yes, and perhaps it would've been the wiser choice. However, we were and are pressed for time, and arguing with you about the splitting of our group would've wasted precious time we could ill afford and would've resulted in the same outcome. As you know, you're stubborn and determined to always be at Nardus's side, even when he isn't present."

Even though it was true, Theyn didn't like hearing it. Plus, she loathed his condescending tone. Had Cyrus been the man she'd met out in the lava fields, she never would've fallen for him.

Cyrus stopped and held out his arm. "Something lies in our path ahead."

Theyn had better eyesight than anyone she'd ever met, yet she saw nothing but an infinite stretch of path ahead. As confident as she was in her vision, she trusted the man, especially given his grim tone. "Show me."

"I too see nothing, yet I feel its presence. What we face lies beyond the veil of this reality." He cocked his head and looked down at her. "Perhaps you were the wiser choice to accompany me after all."

Cyrus lowered both arms to his sides. Infinitely bright light formed in the palms of his hands, each taking the shape of a lightning bolt. "Not sure what we'll face ahead, but you'll probably want to shift before we do."

"Right."

Theyn reached within herself and summoned the beast. Each time she made the shift, it became easier. Now, the process took a mere moment.

"Lead the way," she said through mindspeak.

Cyrus nodded, then charged forward. She followed close, right up until the walls shuddered and crackled with energy. She slid to a stop, but Cyrus pressed on. The sound of shattering glass swept through the passage, and Cyrus vanished.

"Nardus!"

Theyn surged forward. The walls of reality bent around her. Stretched with great resistance until it finally burst. The sound of shattering glass filled her ears again, and the passage vanished.

† † †

Ridan stared at the large, multi-layered cypher wheel embedded in the floor. Bakkan had uncovered part of it while digging around, and she and Zerenity uncovered the rest of it. Its four golden rings surrounded a silver center disc, and each moved independently of the other. The center disc had a single black symbol etched into it: a star within another star. Each of the three inner rings contained a single black arrow that pointed toward the outer ring. She had no clue as to how the thirty-six black symbols on the outer ring related to the archaic symbol on the center disc or where the three arrows should point.

To complicate matters further, they'd already lost nearly a quarter of the sand in the hourglass. Ridan sat back on her feet and sighed. "How are we supposed to figure this out?"

Zerenity rubbed her chin as she circled Ridan and the cypher wheel. "I've dabbled a bit with potions over the years, but these symbols are different than any I've seen."

Each of the symbols on the outer ring contained a circle with lines, arcs, dots, and other circles within them. A few had additional circles or squiggly lines attached to the right side of the outer circle.

Ridan turned the innermost ring clockwise until the arrow pointed to the left. "How about we just select three of the symbols and see what happens?"

Zerenity stopped across from Ridan and knelt. Her eyes studied the symbols. "That sounds dangerous."

Ridan glanced back at the hourglass. Now, nearly a third of the sand had fallen. "Then what do ya suggest?"

"Admittedly, I'm at a loss."

Ridan turned the other two inner rings until the three arrows pointed left, right, and down. Nothing happened. She tried many other positions, but none seemed to trigger any reaction.

"We're doomed." Ridan smacked the center disc on the cypher wheel.

The three symbols on the outer ring that corresponded to the arrows turned white, and then the two stars on the center disc did as well. Ridan and Zerenity glanced at each other and then watched the center disc. The two stars flashed white and then turned solid red. The entire room quaked for several seconds, and then all the symbols turned black again.

Zerenity's eyes grew wide, and she gasped. "That's definitely not good."

Ridan turned around. The hourglass was now three-quarters gone.

Gods... This is all my fault.

† † †

Urza grunted as she continued swinging her axe. "Remember the reaper wolves we faced in Nasda?"

"Yeah." Rakzar swung his axe and retreated right into a fistful of thorns. He yelped like a pup.

Urza knew his thick hide prevented the thorns from penetrating very deep into his thigh, but the twisted look on his face gave her a clue as to how painful it still was.

"What about them?" Rakzar said through gritted teeth.

Urza dodged a jab and chopped off the briar beast's arms. "Maybe we should try using blood again."

"Good timing," Rakzar said. "I've got a fresh supply."

"Hang on." Urza spun with her axe, chopping at and tossing several briar beasts to the side.

Once she achieved a small reprieve from them, Rakzar quickly smeared blood onto the edges of his double-edged axe. Ever quicker, the fallen briar beasts regrew limbs and heads. If her plan didn't work, she didn't know what they'd do.

With a loud roar, Rakzar surged forward into the pack of briar beasts with his bloodied axe swinging. Urza stood back and watched.

This better work, or we're dead.

† † †

Cyrus stood on a snowy mountain pass. Lightning flashed overhead and thunder rolled across the blackened sky as heavy snow continued falling. Theyn entered the plane of existence and stood at his side, no longer in her shifted form. A familiarity Cyrus could not place hung within his mind.

"I know this place." Theyn walked ahead. A mighty wind kicked up, and she disappeared into the blinding snow.

"Theyn!" Cyrus shouted.

In that moment, he realized it wasn't Cyrus in control anymore. Somehow, Nardus had pushed Cyrus aside. Then, understanding washed over him as a trail of blood appeared in the snow.

Theyn's vision of us...

Around the bend, he'd find Theyn skewered by Cinolth's claw. Dread rose from the pit of his stomach as he reached over his shoulder and drew Brinzhär Dädh. The mighty sword, imbued with mezhik, slid from its scabbard with a ring of metal. Its power surged into his hands, up his arms, and into his head.

This will not be our end, Theyn!

With a mighty battle cry, Nardus charged into the flurry of snow.

† † †

Zerenity paced until she wore a path in the dirt. Just a handful of grains remained in the hourglass. Once time expired, so would they. She'd searched every dark corner of her mind for answers to the symbols but found nothing of use.

Ridan still sat next to the wheel cypher, her eyes closed. She'd been humming the same tune for the last ten minutes. Zerenity didn't recognize it but knew it to be an old dwarven song based on its melody. Made sense, given Ridan's heritage.

Zerenity sat down next to Ridan and placed her hand on Ridan's shoulder. "We're almost out of time. Wish we had a weapon or some explosive powder to blow the chest up."

Ridan's eyes snapped open. Her brow wrinkled and a strange grin on her lips. "Ya are a genius, Zerenity!"

Zerenity frowned. "Am I, darling? How so?"

"I kept thinking I'd seen those symbols before, but I couldn't remember where it was." She bit her lip and leaned over the cypher. "I spent a lot of time in weapons storage and in the forges. One of the walls had a chart of symbols hanging on it. Recipes for alchemy." She pointed at the center disc. "This symbol represents an explosion."

Zerenity cocked her head and eyed the star within a star. Now that Ridan had pointed it out, it looked like nothing else. "You're right."

"Yes, and there are three elements needed to create one." Ridan pointed at one of the symbols on the outer ring. A solid black circle. "Carbon."

Zerenity turned the inner ring until the arrow pointed at the carbon symbol.

Ridan pointed at another symbol. It had a vertical line all the way through its center and two perpendicular lines that didn't quite touch the edges of the circle. "Sulfur."

Zerenity positioned the second ring to point at the sulfur symbol. "And the last?"

"Potassium nitrate." Ridan moved the last ring until its arrow faced a circle with three horizontal lines drawn through it. The center line extended through the right side of the circle and forked into three lines. The middle line had a small circle of its own on its right end.

Ridan moved her hand over the central disc. Zerenity reached out and grabbed Ridan's wrist. "Are you sure about this?"

Ridan glanced back toward the hourglass. "We don't have time not to be."

Zerenity released Ridan's hand as the last grain of sand began to fall from the hourglass. Ridan's fist slammed the center disc. The three symbols on the outer ring turned white, just as they had the first time. Then, the explosion symbol turned white.

The final grain splashed down in the hourglass, and the room quaked as it had before.

We're too late!

Bakkan knocked Ridan right into Zerenity and pounced on top of them both.

The hourglass exploded, blasting the room with sand and shattering the vortex.

Darkness swallowed the room.

† † †

"Stop!" Urza said. "The blood's making things worse!"

Worse?

Rakzar didn't understand why Urza had yelled at him to stop until he turned around and faced his bloody path of destruction. Only it wasn't a path of destruction at all. Instead, the chopped-up group of briar beasts began consuming each other until just three remained. Three hulking beasts that stood as tall as he did.

"Damn." Rakzar growled. "Now—"

From the corner of his eye, Rakzar spotted something on the far wall that gleamed in the torchlight. His eye ran the length of it, right up to a pulley anchored in the ceiling. It was a chain, and that chain held up one of the smaller wooden chandeliers. A quick check confirmed there were three more chains.

Five massive needles punctured his left shoulder. Sank deep into his flesh. Struck bone. Rakzar roared and staggered backward, but the needles remained in his shoulder and scratched against his bone.

The massive briar beast smiled wickedly and drove its other fist of needles into Rakzar's other shoulder. Rakzar's axe slid out of his hand and sank into the thick sand.

A flash of steel severed the beast's arms at the elbows.

Rakzar could scarcely breathe through the pain. He tried to lift one of his arms to remove the needles from his other arm, but agony blossomed in his shoulder until he couldn't take it.

Urza grabbed both severed arms and yanked them free of Rakzar. Fire raged in his shoulders and pain shot up through the sides of his neck and into his ears. His vision blackened and his legs became unstable, but it lasted just a few seconds before the pain subsided into a dull throb.

Urza continued to fight off the three briar beasts while Rakzar recovered his senses. She didn't move as fast as he knew she could. Soon, she'd be spent of energy. He reached down and picked up his axe. The weight of it made his shoulder throb even more. He gritted his teeth and joined Urza in the fray.

The more they chopped, the bigger the beasts grew. A glint of metal drew Rakzar's mind back to the chains he'd seen before being skewered by the beast.

Rakzar ducked beneath a swipe from one of the briar beasts and buried his axe into its thick leg. He tried wrenching the axe out, but the beast took another swing at him, and he had to abandon it.

"Damn!" He retreated toward Urza and pointed at one of the stone walls. "We need to release those chains!"

Urza nodded, took one last swipe at the closest briar beast to her, then bolted toward the far wall. Rakzar ran the opposite direction. Ten feet from the wall where one of the chains was tethered, something caught his foot. As soft as the sand was, it still knocked the breath out of him when he hit it. Sand raked against his snout and the side of his face as he slid several feet before stopping. Sand filled his mouth and scraped along the back of his throat when he took a breath, but he didn't have time to rectify it. Instead, he rolled to the side, narrowly escaping the briar beast's trunk of an arm as it slammed into the sand with a thud just inches from his head.

Scrambling to his feet, Rakzar launched himself toward the wall and the tethered chain.

The briar beast swung at him again. Connected with the wall. Dragged its arm across it.

Crack!

Branches exploded from the briar beast's arm. Wooden projectiles flew everywhere.

Rakzar covered his face as tiny slivers of wood pricked his hide.

Clank! Clank! Clank! Clank!

The chain ratcheted up through the pulley. The briar beast must've knocked it loose from its tether.

Rakzar spat sand from his mouth as he ran toward the second chain. A quick glance backward confirmed the briar beast lumbered after him, its arm still slowly growing back.

† † †

At first, Theyn didn't understand why she felt so strange, but then she noticed how peculiar her shadow looked in the snow. Far larger than it should've been, it resembled neither her human form nor her cat form. She looked down at what should've been a human hand but found it covered in black scales. Razor-sharp claws tipped her elongated fingers. Glancing over her shoulder, she found a black, leathery wing attached to her shoulder blade. A long, spiked tail whipped the ground behind her.

It was then she heard the cry. Realized she clutched something in her other hand.

A woman.

No, not just any woman but one who looked just like her.

Smelled like her.

An impostor.

Rage drove Theyn's claw right through the impostor's spine and out her abdomen.

The snow turned crimson. Pooled beneath the impostor.

Out of the blinding snow came Nardus, sword in hand.

In an instant, Theyn remembered the vision. The pain and suffering they'd shared. Yet this wasn't the last vision she'd had with Nardus. No, this was the false vision conjured by Cinolth's dark heart. So, why were they here now?

Nardus paused once his gaze met the impostor's slumped form. He dropped his sword. Fell to his knees. "Theyn!"

Theyn didn't understand what was happening. Why she'd become the dragon. What purpose did it serve? How would it earn them their piece of the circle?

She shook the impostor from her claw and roared. "Stand up and face me." The wicked voice was not her own, nor were the words.

It's an illusion.

Even though she recognized it, Nardus seemed to be lost within it.

Nardus stood, picked up his sword, and faced her. "I know how this ends." He glanced down at the impostor then stalked closer. "One of us must die."

Theyn groaned and shouted at Nardus with her mind. *"It's me, my love!"* Her words fell into a void.

"Your sword cannot penetrate my scales," the dragon growled.

Nardus turned the sword on himself. Held the blade to his belly with the hilt to the ground. "It doesn't need to."

Theyn's dragon form lunged at Nardus. At first, she wanted what the dragon wanted: to stop Nardus from killing himself. But then, understanding washed over her. Nardus must've known it was an illusion, too. At the last moment, Theyn regained control and threw herself to the side. The blade plunged into Nardus's gut, and then the world shattered like glass.

† † †

If she'd finally met death, Ridan wasn't impressed. As far as she could tell, nothing had changed. She still felt the same as she had moments before the explosion, save the crushing weight on top of her back. At first, she thought it was the darkness, but then the weight lifted.

Thank the gods.

A wet nose pressed into the side of her face. She giggled. "Bakkan!"

Zerenity groaned underneath her. Ridan sat up and then noticed a faint red glow beneath the sand and dirt. She quickly brushed it away, revealing the cypher's center disc.

"Press it again," Zerenity said, sitting up.

Ridan did, and it made a clicking noise. Then, it rose several inches and swung to the side, revealing a hidden chamber. She reached in and retrieved a silver key. Ambient light filled the room once again, and a beam of light shone down on the silver chest.

Ridan unlocked the chest with the silver key and opened it. One part of the circle lay inside. She retrieved it and held it up.

Zerenity hugged Ridan from behind and kissed her cheek. "Well done, darling. Well done."

Wonderful yet painful memories of her mother filled Ridan's head. She wiped her cheek and glared daggers at the woman. "Never do that again."

† † †

Screech!

Glinting metal.

Rakzar hit the ground and rolled, but not quick enough.

Thwack!

Searing pain blossomed across the fronts of his legs as one of the thick chains whipped him and ripped into his hide.

Thwack! Thwack! Screech! Clunk!

Two more chains hit the sand. Overhead, the metal chandelier hung crooked, three of its four supporting wooden chandeliers freed from their tethers. Debris rained down from the dark ceiling.

Rakzar couldn't believe it. Urza had done her job while fighting off two briar beasts.

What's my problem?

He scrambled on all fours and raced toward the final chain. Urza did the same, but she wouldn't outrun the briar beast right on her tail.

Instinct told him to abandon the chain and go for Urza, but doing so would likely cost them both their lives. It would also doom the others. He fought the urge to save her and kept running toward the chain instead.

Rakzar knew the moment Urza went down. Felt her cry deep within his chest even before the sound registered in his ears. A flaming dagger.

Zäṭūr, save her!

He lunged for the last chain. Wrapped his hands around it. Victory grasped, he yanked with all his might.

Nothing happened. The taut chain could not be budged with the extra weight it held.

"No!"

Pounding sand. Close. At least one of the briar beasts approached.

Rakzar had nowhere to go but up, so he started climbing the chain.

The blow jarred him. Rattled the chain. Shook the world. Yet somehow, he managed to hang on.

He climbed without effort. Flew high into the air before realizing he hadn't climbed at all. A twisted link hung just inches below his hands. The beast must've broken the chain.

The ceiling and the pulley fast approached. He needed to exit the ride, but there was nowhere to go but down. Thirty feet and rising.

He kicked. Swung. Released.

Arms flailing, he willed himself toward the stone wall. Smacked against it. Dug his claws into the stone. Started sliding down the wall.

Crash!

All five chandeliers hit the ground. Kicked up a storm of dust. Torchlight dimmed. Faded altogether until only darkness remained.

Stone filed down Rakzar's claws until nothing remained of them. Tore into his flesh until he couldn't hang on anymore. He free-fell. Hit the ground, but not as hard as he thought he would.

As the dust began to settle, Rakzar pulled himself to his feet. His vision was superior to that of humans, but he still needed some sort of light source to see. None existed, so he prayed the briar beasts had the same limitation.

Then, something peculiar happened: one of the torches re-lit itself. Light swept through the room, and Rakzar found himself staring into the eyes of one of the briar beasts.

The beast opened its thorny, branch-filled mouth and roared but failed to produce a sound.

Rakzar dove between the beast's legs and took off toward the one thing he hoped would save him—the torch. He didn't chance a look back as he sprinted toward the mound of twisted metal, wood, and chains.

Hope swelled in his chest as he clambered up the debris and snatched the torch from its holder.

Needled claws dug into his forearm and yanked him into the air. Somehow, he held onto the torch.

The briar beast reared back its other arm, ready to apply the final blow.

Rakzar fought through the pain as he forced his wrist to turn downward. The flame touched the briar beast's arm and immediately caught fire. The fire raged and consumed the entire briar beast before it had a chance to react. Rakzar dropped back to the ground as the beast turned to ash and fell into a pile.

After making quick work of the other two briar beasts, he located Urza. She lay face-down beneath one of the wooden chandeliers. Blood pooled in the sand around her. Numb to his pain, Rakzar lifted the edge of the chandelier and flipped it to the side.

He knelt next to Urza and turned her over onto her back. "Urza, can you hear me?"

Blood oozed from several wounds on her sides. Her eyelids fluttered, then she opened her eyes. "Did we... win?"

The weakness in her voice wrecked him. "Yes. Thank Ɂäṭūr, yes."

Urza tried to sit up but couldn't. Rakzar pulled her into his arms and stood on shaky legs. "I've got you."

"And the... piece?" Urza managed.

Rakzar had completely forgotten about the wretched piece. "I don't give a damn about the stupid piece of circle." He looked around. "For all I know, we haven't even finished the challenge."

Urza held her left side—the wounds on that side more severe. "While fighting the briar beasts—" She took a deep breath. "—I noticed something glowing red attached to the center of the metal chandelier."

Fighting just one of the briar beasts, Rakzar hadn't had time to notice anything. He couldn't comprehend how she'd managed to do so while fighting two of the beasts. "And you think it's the piece we're looking for."

Rakzar carried Urza over to the mound of twisted metal and laid her in the sand. He climbed the mound and began sifting through the rubble created when part of the ceiling collapsed when the chandeliers fell. It took a few minutes to locate the center of the chandelier and dig the glowing piece of stone out. Two crossed swords were etched into its smooth surface.

"You were right, Urza." He stuffed the stone into one of the pouches on his belt and climbed down from the mound.

Urza lay still. Her chest failed to rise, and no breath escaped through her mouth or nostrils. "Urza!" She didn't stir. Rakzar scooped her into his arms and ran.

† † †

Cyrus groaned as he lay on the firm ground, clutching his stomach where he'd stabbed himself with the sword. He held no doubts as to the events being an illusion, yet the pain remained with him. A sticky resistance pulled at the skin of his palm when he moved his hand away from his stomach. Blood glued his shirt to his skin and oozed from the sword-width gash in his shirt.

He sat up, wheezing with each breath. "Am I still in the illusion?"

The dim light revealed stone walls that flanked him. They looked like the same labyrinth walls as before, but he couldn't be certain.

A low moan sounded behind him.

"Theyn?"

No response.

Pain radiated outward from the wound as he pulled himself to his feet. The wall steadied him, but weakness grew in his legs, tingling and trembling as though they might buckle under his weight. He doubled over and clutched his stomach again, the pain overwhelming. His entire body teetered on the edge of collapse, yet somehow, he found the strength to force himself upright.

Behind him, Theyn lay on the ground next to the back wall of the labyrinth passage. He hobbled over to her and knelt, nearly falling on top of her in the process. A large lump protruded from the left side of her head. She must've hit it on the wall somehow.

Cyrus placed his hand on Theyn's head and called upon his mezhik, but it refused to come forth. "Damn this place."

Theyn's eyelids fluttered, and she groaned again.

"Can you hear me, Theyn?"

Theyn squeezed her eyes tight. "Yes, and there's no need to yell." She reached up and massaged the lump on her head. "I don't know what happened, but my head feels like it might burst."

Cyrus sat back and leaned against the wall. "The illusion was something more."

After a few minutes, she finally opened her eyes and sat up. She stared straight ahead. "I was the dragon."

"Yes, I know."

Her beautiful eyes finally met his. "How?"

"No matter how strong an illusion, your eyes resisted." He offered her a weak smile, but it faded quickly, the pain in his stomach too intense to maintain it. Theyn failed to notice.

"And you were yourself?" she said.

Cyrus closed his eyes and put pressure on his wound. "Yes."

"Then why was I the dragon?"

"To throw me off."

"And I was supposed to think you were me."

"I believe so, yes."

Her hand found his, and she wove her fingers into his. "If I'd killed you, we would've died."

"Yes—" A wave of pain contracted his muscles and took his breath.

"Cyrus?" She crawled over to him and pulled his hand away from his stomach. "Zhedäɜ ʒʊn! You're bleeding."

Cyrus gritted his teeth. "A small flesh wound."

"I'm not blind." She touched it gently. "Can you not heal it?"

"For some reason, I cannot access my mezhik."

"I don't understand."

"Neither do I." When he opened his eyes, he noticed a protrusion from the wall where Theyn had leaned against it. It glowed softly with a yellow hue. Cyrus lifted his arm, and it shook profusely. His pain intensified when he extended his finger, but he refused to allow it to control him. "I think we've found what we came here for."

Theyn turned around and removed the protrusion from the wall. She held it up. "We have one part of the circle."

"Pray the others found success as well."

† † †

By the time Cyrus and Theyn made it back to the labyrinth entrance, the others were already there. Urza lay on the floor with Zerenity kneeling over her. Rakzar, Ridan, and Bakkan stood to the side, watching.

Cyrus knelt on the other side of Urza. Her sides were matted with blood. He looked up at Rakzar. "What happened?"

"Briar beasts." Rakzar's arms were covered in blood.

Cyrus couldn't tell if it was Rakzar's blood or Urza's. He met Zerenity's gaze. "Why didn't you heal her?"

"My mezhik refuses to work."

"As does mine." Cyrus growled. "Damn this wretched place."

"What if we exit the spire?" Ridan said. "Maybe it's preventing your mezhik from working."

Cyrus sighed. "I think you might be correct." He stood with Theyn's assistance. "We have nothing to lose by testing it."

Rakzar lifted Urza into his arms, and the others followed him out of the spire. Still, Cyrus and Zerenity failed to access their mezhik.

Zerenity stared at her hands. "I don't understand it."

"I've heard of this kind of mezhik before. It works like a virus." Pain shot through Cyrus's stomach again in waves. He took a deep breath, then continued, "Once it mixes with your blood, it blocks you from using mezhik."

"For how long?" Rakzar said.

"Minutes. Hours. Days." Cyrus shrugged. "I have no idea."

"We need to get Urza back to the Great Library so that Gnaud can help patch her wounds," Zerenity said. "Otherwise, she will likely die."

Cyrus pushed the pain into the back of his mind and straightened. "Yes, but first I need the other two pieces of the circle."

"It can wait," Theyn growled. "You need attention, too."

Cyrus glared at her. "I'm fine."

"Says the man who can barely stand on his own two feet without grimacing." She grabbed his arm. "We're all going back."

He seethed. "This is not a matter of discussion." Turning to the others, he said, "Hand me your pieces."

Rakzar and Ridan produced their pieces of the circle and handed them to Cyrus, but Theyn refused. "I go where you go."

Cyrus didn't have the time or strength to argue with her. "Fine." He turned and faced the spire. Facing a wizard spirit might cost him everything, especially wounded and without mezhik, but he had no other option. "Come on, Theyn. We will meet the rest of you back at the Great Library."

"Wait!" Gnaud's high-pitched voice rang in Cyrus's ears.

Cyrus turned around and watched the little gordak bound toward him and the others. "This had better be good, Gnaud. Theyn and I are about to enter the phase and face the first wizard spirit."

"Dear Ɂäʈūr! You cannot do that!" Gnaud skidded to a halt in front of Cyrus, his chest heaving.

Cyrus scowled at Gnaud. "Why?"

"After you left this morning, I recalled reading a book several centuries ago about how the spires were constructed. After rifling through countless books across numerous shelves, I finally found the book again."

Cyrus held his stomach. Felt fresh blood. "And what did the book say?"

"Even if you enter the phase and defeat the wizard spirit, you will certainly die."

"And what makes you think that?" Cyrus said.

"Oh my! It isn't my thinking but what the book says." Gnaud wiped sweat from his furry forehead. "Once the wizard spirit is defeated, the spire will disintegrate, and the entire section of city will be crushed by water."

"I'll create an air bubble to protect us."

Gnaud shook his head. "It's not possible. Not only will you be outside the protective barrier that surrounds Nasduron, but you'll also be without mezhik. Therefore, you will drown."

"He's already without mezhik," Theyn said.

Cyrus glared daggers at her. "We can swim to the surface."

"No, that would be impossible, too," Gnaud said. "As you know, Nasduron lies miles beneath the Vastus Ocean. You would run out of oxygen far before reaching the surface."

Cyrus knew Gnaud was right. He spat on the ground and raked his fingers through his hair. "Damn you, Gnaud."

Gnaud grabbed his chest. "Oh, my! I am merely the messenger."

Cyrus sighed. "Yes, I know. I didn't mean that." He scowled. "The spires were never made to be taken down, were they?"

Gnaud shook his head. "Never."

He turned and addressed the others, "I know we can find another way out of Nasduron if we put our heads together again."

Ridan mounted Bakkan. "To what end? Ya said destroying the spires was our best and only chance."

"It was, and I admit I'm uncertain as to what we can do now."

Ridan lowered her spear and pointed it at Cyrus. "Tell me why I shouldn't run ya through."

Rakzar arm-blocked Ridan. "Easy, Ridan. We're all friends here."

"Are we?" She glowered at Rakzar. "What do we really know about this man?"

"He's the White Knight's father, and he saved our lives," Rakzar said. "Had he not brought us here, we'd be dead."

Ridan scoffed. "Yar recollection of events certainly differs from mine. I was about to avenge my friend when that golden sludge ripped me from the battlefield and nearly drown me."

"Perhaps it does, but I'm not wrong," Rakzar said. "He made a mistake, just like we've all done before. I spent months trying to kill his son."

Lightning surged in Cyrus's eyes. "You did *what*?"

"Am I the only one *not* on the verge of trying to kill someone?" Zerenity sighed.

Cyrus glared daggers at Zerenity. "You had your chance to kill me already, woman."

Zerenity raised her arms. "Let's all just take a few moments to breathe before one of us does something we'll regret."

Theyn stepped between Cyrus and Rakzar. "Zerenity's right. We're all wound with tension."

"Precisely." Zerenity twisted a strand of hair around her finger. "We cannot undo what's been done, so let's put the past where it belongs and move forward. Agreed?" Everyone nodded their agreement. "Good. Now, let's get back to the Great Library and tend to the wounded before we *do* lose someone."

CHAPTER FOURTEEN

Jagger awoke to the sound of groaning. She opened her eyes and stared up at an unfamiliar sight: a field of glowing, bluish-white stalactites. It took a few moments for her mind to recall where she lay.

The cavern beyond the Cave of Rebirth!

It'd taken a sizable portion of the day to reach this place, especially given her fatigue. Under normal circumstances, she would've ridden Eis, but the tunnels proved far too narrow and the ceilings too low to do so safely. Plus, she'd had the flamewalker to contend with. No amount of shaking roused him from sleep, so she'd carried him the entire way. Thankfully, he'd come through the flames fully clothed. Had he not, she might've left him there.

Jagger wondered how long she'd been lying there, but without daylight or stars to rely on, she had no sense of how much time had passed. That was until she tried to move. Stiff joints and a dull throb at the back of her head indicated it'd been at least a few hours. Given how tired she'd been before, it was more likely several hours. And those were hours she could ill afford to waste.

Undoubtedly, the village had already dispatched hunters to track them beyond the vale. Living in such a small, secluded village, she knew them all. A vicious lot not to be crossed. They would hunt her and the flamewalker relentlessly until they captured the flamewalker, and they wouldn't hesitate to take her life in the process.

And I will not hesitate to take theirs, either.

The young man who lay beside her—the flamewalker—groaned again. From what she could discern, he wasn't under duress, but his feverish skin still burned with fire. She smoothed back strands of blackened hair from his face and watched him for a few moments.

Perhaps he's dreaming.

Eis lay on the ground a good distance from them with her head resting on her front paws. However, she wasn't asleep, her gaze trained on the flamewalker. Based on the redness of Eis's eyes, Jagger doubted the poor beast had slept at all.

Jagger sat up and stared at her surroundings. Stalagmites and stalactites of blue limestone jutted up from the rock floor and hung down from the cavern ceiling, giving the cavern a look of some sort of giant mouth with dozens of rows of teeth. It reminded her of the stories Grimbold told her when she was a child. Stories of nasty creatures he called drezhn. At one time, they ruled the world. And, according to the prophetic scroll she'd stumbled upon in Elder Bannok's house, the drezhn would rule Centauria again.

She eyed the flamewalker. "Unless you're the one who has come to stop them." He groaned but didn't wake.

Jagger rose, grabbed the strip of cloth she'd cut from the bottom of her tunic earlier, and walked over to the small stream of water that snaked its way through the cavern. She knelt and stared at her own reflection. The blue water added an unwelcomed tint to her skin, turning it from a soft olive to a brackish brown.

An ugly corpse.

After dipping the cloth in the icy water, she returned to the flamewalker's side and knelt over him. Jagger held the cloth a few inches above the flamewalker's lips and squeezed several droplets of water from it. The droplets splattered when they hit his lips, leaving his skin splotched. She hoped some of it had penetrated his lips, but she couldn't be sure. As gently as possible, she began wiping the young man's brow with the cloth. The gray soot came off easily enough, but his skin remained red and hot.

Once she'd wiped off his neck, she moved to his arms. The young man wasn't scrawny per se, but certainly no warrior, especially not like those of her kind. In fact, he failed to meet her expectations as to what a flamewalker should look like. Then again, what had she expected? The book spoke only of a mighty bird returning from the flames, not of a human.

Jagger re-wet the cloth in the stream and then wiped his forehead again. Even with red skin, the flamewalker possessed a rugged handsomeness she couldn't deny. For a human, of course.

Do all humans look like him?

A hand grabbed Jagger's wrist. "Auh!" She jerked her arm away and retreated.

† † †

The young man peered into the darkness, his heart racing. "Hello?" His voice cracked, his throat parched. He lay there for several seconds, awaiting a response, but received only silence. "I know someone's there."

A low growl sounded from his right. He reached out but grasped nothing. It took effort to sit up, his stomach muscles all but spent. He exhaled, but the soreness remained.

Two icy green orbs floated several feet above his head, well beyond his reach. The proper response to such a visual should've been terror, yet he experienced none. In fact, he detected only calmness within himself.

He stared at the two orbs. "Where am I, and who are you?"

"Reothadh." The strange yet distinctly female voice came from the opposite direction of the two orbs. "My name is Jagger."

He turned his head to the right, but darkness obscured everything. "And what is Reothadh? A city?"

"No." The female named Jagger elaborated no further.

The young man probed the darkness. "I know I'm not blind, yet I can see nothing but those two green orbs."

"You see Eis," Jagger said.

"Yes, of course. They are eyes, but to whom do they belong?"

"Not eyes but Eis." Jagger sounded out each letter, "Eee. Eye. Esss. She's a ferzh and my sister."

"Ferzh?" It took his brain a few moments to form a picture. "You mean as in the large, wolf-like creature ferzh?"

The ferzh growled low. The hairs on his arms responded by standing on end.

"She understands you," Jagger said. "Best you watch what you say."

He sat up straighter and looked in the direction of the floating orbs. "I'm sorry, Eis. I meant no offense. It's just that I've never seen or met a ferzh before." He scratched his head. "At least not one I can remember."

"She forgives you, flamewalker."

Flamewalker?

He'd never heard the term before. "Why did you call me that?"

"Because it is *what* you are," Jagger said. "You were born of the flames and walked out of them. So, tell me, flamewalker. *Who* are you?"

Born of the flames?

Jagger's explanation left him with more questions and no answer. Nothing she said made sense, but her question stunned him. Until that moment, he hadn't given a single thought toward himself.

Who am I?

He searched his mind for answers. "I… don't know." Admitting it scared him enough, but the implications left him terrified. "If you don't know who I am either then why am I here? And why are we sitting in the dark?"

"We sit in a cavern beyond the Cave of Rebirth. As I said, you were born of the flames."

"I don't understand what that means. Am I not from this place you call Reothadh?"

"You are not one of us," Jagger said.

From her tone, he gathered she might've meant more than her words expressed. He pushed for further explanation. "One of your people?"

"Yes, but it's more than that. You are not one of our *kind*."

He hung on her last word. Tossed it about within his head. Although he remembered nothing of his life, he knew his own nature. "If you're not human, then what are you?"

"As a people cutoff from the rest of the world, we rely on the knowledge given to us by our elders. As such, they horde it, keep it secret, and lock it away for what they deem our own safety."

"I'm sorry."

"Don't be. I am not one to follow rules that make no sense. As such, I know the blood that runs through my veins. A halfbreed. Part human and part ogre."

Halfbreed.

He'd never heard the term before, nor had he ever heard of someone being part human and part something else. He wondered what she might look like. "Oh."

The young man licked his lips. They tasted of ash. He spat several times, but the taste lingered on his tongue. He reached up to wipe his lips with his hand but stopped. The scent of smoke permeated his skin.

Flamewalker.

Maybe Jagger hadn't lied about his origins after all. Then again, what reason would she have to do so? Yet he still found it impossible to wrap his head around the idea of a person emerging from the flames.

Who am I really?

"If I came to this place you call the Cave of Rebirth through the flames of a fire, then why were you here? Were you waiting for me?"

"Yes."

"Why? How did you know I was coming?"

"I am what my clan calls a flamewatcher. We've been awaiting your arrival for nearly a century."

"A century?" The young man scoffed. "You expect me to believe you've been sitting here all this time?"

"Don't be absurd. I am one of several. We do not watch from within the cave but from the ridge that surrounds the vale where our village lies."

"Fine, but why? How did you know I would eventually arrive here?"

"Prophecy and history. The welfare and future of my clan lies with the flamewalker."

"Why? What is it you expect me to do or provide?"

"Gwendor has been our flamewalker for millennia. When he returns to us through the flames, his ashes melt the snow in the vale and fertilize our land. The crops grow strong for a decade, providing us with food that lasts until he returns again. He should've come back decades ago. Because he hasn't, our clan has dwindled in size, our food sources limited to what we can hunt and fish. You should've been him, yet you're not."

"You're certain of it?"

"I am. Gwendor isn't a human but a rare bird. One so rare that another has never been seen before."

"Then how did I come through the flames?"

"There is only one explanation. You must've killed Gwendor."

The young man's stomach churned. "I can't remember who I am, but I'm certain I'm no killer."

"Time will reveal the truth," Jagger said. "Come, I will lead you to the water where you can bathe yourself."

A large hand—far larger than his own—grabbed his wrist and pulled him to his feet. Unlike him, she possessed a thumb and five fingers, and her skin didn't feel like his. It wasn't rough or callused but somehow felt thicker. Reminiscent of an animal hide yet smooth to the touch.

"Thank you."

Jagger placed his hand on her forearm and began leading him through the darkness. Although he could still see nothing, he deduced a few things about her. Based on the angle of his arm, she stood several inches taller than him. She also wore some sort of cloak or covering that likely hid her muscular form. The other thing he noticed about her was the grace with which she walked. Her footfall didn't smack against the solid surface the way his boots did. Either she wore no shoes at all, or she wore something lighter than boots. Eis must've gone ahead of them because he heard no ticking of claws on the ground.

The farther they went, the more his mind wrapped itself in knots.

Will I ever remember who I am? If so, will I remember being a killer?

† † †

Jagger took the flamewalker's clothes and washed them farther downstream while he bathed. When she returned, he sat next to the water with his knees drawn to his chest. She handed him his clothes and turned her back to him while he dressed.

Admittedly, she found him fascinating. Not because he was a flamewalker or because he had no memory but because he was human. If all humans were like him, why did her clan fear them so much? She also couldn't help but wonder if he really could wield mezhik as she'd sensed before entering the Cave of Rebirth. If so, what would it be like to witness it? The thought frightened her almost as much as it excited her.

The flamewalker pushed his hair behind his ears. "Now what?"

She looked to Eis who snorted. "We find the exit to these caves and take you somewhere safe."

The young man frowned. "Are we not safe in Reothadh?"

"My people hunt us. It's only a matter of time before they gain access to the caves if they haven't already. If we're found, they'll kill us both."

"We're being hunted? Why? Is it because of me and this Gwendor?"

Even in the dim blue light, Jagger noticed the young man's face pale.

"Yes, but not just because of you. My father and I made a choice when the Cave of Rebirth came alive last night."

"What do you mean?" he said.

"Sometimes, I sense things others cannot. Last night was one of those times. Somehow, I knew Gwendor wasn't returning to us. I also knew that the elders would be furious when they found out. They would've blamed me and my father for Gwendor's death. Because you returned in his place, they would've killed you on the spot and drained your blood into a bowl. Then, either I or my father would've been sacrificed over the flames of the fire within the Cave of Rebirth to appease our winged god, Gwendor. Once the flames consumed the sacrifice, your blood would be spread over the coals. Doing all this would resurrect Gwendor from the ashes and give life to our village once again."

The flamewalker sighed. "I'm not sure what to say."

"Say nothing. You might've had no choice in what happened, and it doesn't matter right now. We need to go before they find us."

"And how can I trust that you're telling me the truth? How do I know you're not leading me to my death right now? What if you're the one who killed this Gwendor, or what if he doesn't even exist?"

Jagger growled. "I've sacrificed everything for you."

"You say that, but how can I be certain?"

"You can't." She balled her fist. "You must make your choice right now, flamewalker. Choose to trust me and what I've told you, or find your own way."

"You would leave me here in the dark?"

"It's not what I desire, but I will not force you to come with me."

"Then I choose to stay with you, but that doesn't mean I trust you."

"I understand, and I hope time changes your mind, flamewalker. Now, we must go." Jagger mounted Eis, grabbed the young man's hand, and hauled him up behind her. She peered over her shoulder. "Hold on to my waist and don't let go no matter what."

The young man nodded then slid his hands around her, weaving his fingers together. "I'm ready."

Eis needed no prompt. She dashed ahead, carrying them toward what Jagger hoped was freedom.

About an hour later, light shone up ahead. Jagger leaned forward over Eis's haunches. "Once we've cleared the caves, we'll head for the coast."

Images of Grimbold and Rauch filled Jagger's mind. Tears rushed to her eyes, and she fought to hold them back. "I understand, but we cannot go back."

"Go back?" the flamewalker said. "You're communicating with Eis?"

"Yes. She wants to go back for my father and her mate, but it cannot be." Jagger wiped her eyes on her tunic. "My father helped us escape, so I'm certain he's already dead."

"Ugh. This is my fault, too, isn't it?"

"No. We made our choices well before you entered our world. It must be this way."

Crimson stained snow. Grimbold on his knees. Jagger shuddered, unable to shake the image from her mind.

"If there's a chance of saving him, shouldn't we try?" the flamewalker said.

"And if we die, what was the point of all this?"

Eis carried them through a narrow opening in the rock, rounded a massive boulder that hid the tunnel entrance, and skidded to a halt. The flamewalker's hands slipped from around Jagger's waist, and he tumbled across the snow-covered ground several times before coming to a rest face down. Blood spatter marred the pristinely white snow. Unable to believe her eyes, Jagger froze. Her heart hammered against her ribcage.

"Well, well, well. What do we have here, Tubrok?" The massive male known as Suuval dismounted from his ferzh named Tier and rolled the flamewalker over with his bare foot. Blood seeped from a large gash across the flamewalker's left temple.

Tubrok sat atop Toter. His eyes narrowed as his gaze shifted from Jagger to the flamewalker. He sniffed the air and snarled. "A human."

Suuval scowled as he drew his weapon. A long, curved blade. Sunlight glinted off it. "You know our laws, Jagger. We cannot let him live."

Jagger unsheathed her own weapons—two long-bladed daggers—and leapt from Eis's back, landing a few arm lengths from Suuval. "You'll have to kill me first."

Eis joined Jagger, her hackles raised and teeth bared. She growled low.

Suuval laughed. "And keep you from watching Grimbold face the pit? I think not."

Jagger's heart raced.

He's still alive!

Tubrok dismounted. His weapon matched that of Suuval's but featured a brown hilt instead of Suuval's red one. The color difference determined rank amongst the hunters, red signifying the highest. Tubrok would make no move without Suuval's command. She could use that knowledge to her advantage, but how?

Tier and Toter circled, jowls dripping with saliva.

Suuval pointed his weapon at her. "Drop your weapon, Jagger, and I swear no harm will come to you or Eis."

Jagger inched forward. "You're a liar, Suuval. I'm well versed in our laws, especially those pertaining to harboring outsiders. Particularly humans. I drop my weapon, and you'll run me through."

Suuval clicked his tongue twice. Having read every book available to her, she understood the signal. Understood the way hunters in her clan fought.

Dirty.

Given the situation, she must fight dirty, too.

Tubrok came at Jagger, weapon swinging, but she'd anticipated the attack. She dropped and rolled right at Tubrok's legs. The fiend had no time to adjust his swing, his blade slicing the air a foot above her head as she rolled onto her knees.

Tubrok raised his weapon again, but not before her two blades found purchase on the insides of his thighs, slicing right through his tough skin and deep into his flesh as she moved between his legs. Blood gushed from the wounds like geysers, spraying her and the ground.

Tubrok's grip failed, and his weapon fell to the ground. He roared as he dropped to his knees and grabbed his bloody groin.

Jagger wiped her eyes then stood behind Tubrok and kicked him in the back. Tubrok fell face-first into the snow and jerked a few times before going still.

Suuval clapped with one hand against his other wrist while he held his blade above the flamewalker's chest. "Well done, flamewatcher, but you're far too slow."

Tier had Eis pinned to the ground, and Toter held Eis's neck in its jaws.

"Surrender your weapons," Suuval said, "and Eis won't suffer."

Jagger hadn't thought far enough ahead, and now nothing would save Eis or the flamewalker. She bit back tears.

What've I done?

† † †

The young man opened his eyes and found himself staring up at a large, shirtless male with olive green skin. A necklace of bones hung from the male's neck, and black paint marked the male's cheeks and forehead. Despite the frigid air and snow-covered ground, the male's chest glistened with sweat.

The male glared down at him. "Oh, good. I was afraid you'd miss your own death."

"Leave him alone, Suuval!"

The young man recognized the female voice to be that of Jagger, but he never would've pictured her to look the way she did when he turned his head toward her. She held two daggers in her hands, both slick with blood. In fact, blood covered a good portion of her dark trousers and shirt. Unlike the male she called Suuval, her forehead didn't slope back nearly as much, and her dark purple hair complemented her olive skin far better than Suuval's oily, brown hair did his skin. Purple irises gave her an ethereal appearance. Had she not been covered in so much blood, he imagined she would be quite striking.

"He dies now!" Suuval held his weapon with both hands and plunged it right at the young man's chest.

The young man reacted without thinking, grabbing the blade between his hands.

The blade cut into his palms as it slid downward, but the pain he expected to feel didn't register. Instead, his hands started tingling. Not a tingle akin to them waking up after being asleep but something different. More intense. The tingle didn't come from the blade, nor did it come from his hands. It arose from a place far deeper within him. Within his very soul.

He gave into it. Allowed it to bubble up and intensify.

Suuval stared down at him, brown eyes wide. He must've felt it, too.

The blade ceased its downward plunge inches from the young man's chest. Vibrated with an intensity that left his hands numb.

A moment later, a thousand stars burst upward and outward from the blade.

No, not stars but tiny shards of shiny metal.

Just as quickly as the event had started, the tingling faded.

The blade between the young man and Suuval no longer existed.

A red hilt tumbled from Suuval's hands. Landed in the snow next to the young man with a soft thud.

Suuval staggered backward several steps and grabbed at his throat.

Dark blood drooled from the corners of Suuval's mouth as he gasped for air but found none.

Jagger and the young man locked eyes for a few moments. Her gaping mouth said it all. She dashed to the left as he lay there a few seconds more.

Suuval fell as he arose. Conquered and conqueror. He stood over the male and watched the light fade from the male's eyes. Although Suuval earned his fate, sorrow befell the young man.

He wiped tears from his eyes, then stared at his hands. He'd watched the blade cut into his flesh, yet no wounds remained.

How is that possible?

The young man understood nothing of what had transpired, and his head pulsed with pain. His fingers met a sticky, sore spot on his left temple and came away with blood. It must be the reason he remembered nothing after tumbling from Eis's back. So why had his hands healed and not his head?

What's happening to me?

Jagger returned to his side, fresh blood on her blades. Eis joined them. A mighty ferzh with thick white fur. He'd never seen such a beautiful creature in all his life, at least none he could remember in the last twenty minutes of his short life in the light.

She wiped her blades on her trousers then returned them to their sheathes. "You stand there as if this world is still ordinary. Did you not just see what happened? You shattered a blade with your hands. You wielded mezhik!"

Mezhik…

He stared at his hands, perplexed and awed.

Who am I?

"You're definitely the one." She smiled then mounted Eis.

He frowned. "The one what?"

"The one I knew you would be." She proffered her hand. "In time, you'll understand."

He took her hand and she hoisted him up behind her as if he weighed nothing at all. Then, they took off toward a wintery mountain trail.

He looked back. "I thought we were heading toward the coast."

"We were, but Eis is right. We must know my father's fate."

"You know we might not survive another attack, right?"

"Maybe not, but you've brought me hope, flamewalker. It's far more than what I had two days ago."

What happened to me two days ago? Why can't I remember?

Another thought struck a chord in his heart. Drove fear into his mind like a spike through the back of his head.

What if I don't want to?

CHAPTER FIFTEEN

Berggren woke to a bloodcurdling scream. Niesha and Eshtak still slept next to him, but Calen was missing. At first, he thought he'd dreamt it. By the time he wiped the sleep from his eyes and slid his clothes back on, the stronghold raged with chatter.

Couldn't go a single day without something going wrong after barricading tunnel three.

"Breech!" Hardin yelled.

That single word gave rise to panic. People began fighting over tools and weapons.

Berggren shouted, "Listen up! We continue to act this way, we'll all be dead by nightfall. Yes, the zhebəllin have found a way inside the stronghold, but there's no need for alarm. I'm certain only a few of them can get through the breech at a time, so we still have the advantage. We must engage them and kill them all."

Mortis emerged from the crowd, his nose still bandaged. "Hold up a minute." Hatred burned in his eyes as he glared daggers at Berggren. "There's a far better way to handle this situation."

Berggren scowled and crossed his arms. "Bet this'll be good."

"And what's that?" Hardin said.

Mortis pointed a finger at Berggren. "We give them exactly what they want."

Berggren frowned. "Why me?"

"Not just you, but also the two rats you call children. Oh, and that grotesque little man-child, too." Mortis smirked, obviously proud of himself.

"Not a chance, you conniving little weasel," Berggren said.

Mortis crossed his arms over his chest. "Save your breath. I've already negotiated the terms with their leader."

Berggren grabbed Mortis by the front of his shirt and jerked him forward. "How dare you think—"

The pickaxe handle came out of nowhere and cracked Berggren right in the side of the head. The entire room shook in his vision before turning on end. The ground rose to meet him and drove the air from his lungs.

"Iceberg!" Niesha screamed.

It was the last thing he heard before everything faded to black.

† † †

Calen had arrived in the main room just in time to witness the single blow that took Berggren down. It stunned him. Never in a million years would he have ever thought it possible. From the looks of it, everyone else thought the same thing.

Niesha lunged for Berggren, snapping Calen out of his daze. He grabbed her by the arm and pulled her back. Fierce as a feral cat, she fought back, and it took all his strength to pull her away from Berggren. He wrapped his arms around her and pulled her deep into the chaos. Eshtak followed.

Niesha squirmed. "Let me go!"

"Stop struggling, or you'll get us all killed," Calen said.

"I won't let them hurt him," she growled.

"I care about him, too, but we won't be able to save him if we're caught."

"Eshtak saves big friend, too."

Niesha settled. "We'll save him?"

"Yes. I've fought zheballin before. They're not very smart." Calen released Niesha. "Come on." He led her and Eshtak into one of the storage rooms and shut the door.

She looked around. "What are we doing in here?"

Calen knelt and pulled a piece of parchment out of his pocket. Unfolded, the parchment covered a two-foot-square section of the floor. He pointed at a small rectangle drawn on the parchment. "This is where we are right now."

Niesha stared at the parchment, eyes wide. "Whoa, is that what I think it is?"

"Yes." He grinned. "I started the map just for fun but then thought it might come in handy if I could map out the entire stronghold, so I did."

Eshtak clapped, and Calen grabbed his hands. "We must keep quiet."

"Eshtak sorry."

Niesha's cheeks turned red, and she looked away.

"What's wrong?" Calen said.

"I just… well…" She finally met his gaze and shrugged. "I feel bad that I didn't think you were that smart."

A few months ago, a remark like that would've devastated Calen and sent him spiraling down into the depths of despair. Now, it brought a smile to his lips, especially coming from Niesha. She was the most intelligent girl he'd ever met, and it astounded him every time he remembered she'd seen just six name days.

Calen tousled her hair. "I'm pretty good at playing dumb."

Niesha giggled. "I don't think it's an act."

"Maybe, maybe not," Calen said.

"Eshtak not dumb."

All three of them giggled for a few moments, but then a somberness settled over them.

Calen pointed at several lines on the map that connected most of the rooms with each other and the main room. "These air shafts will allow us to stay hidden while we figure out a plan to rescue Berggren."

Niesha looked from the map to the grating over the shaft on the opposite wall. Her brow wrinkled. "Not to sound rude, but are you sure this plan of yours is doable?"

Calen frowned. "What do you mean?" She poked him in the stomach with her finger and giggled. He scowled. "Funny. For your information, I've already verified I can fit in them."

"Eshtak fits too."

The door burst open. Hardin, covered in blood, stepped into the room and slammed the door shut behind himself. Then, he barricaded the door shut with several boxes before slumping down in front of it.

Bang! Bang! Bang!

The door jolted, but Hardin's barricade held.

Calen quickly folded up the parchment and shoved it into his pocket. He stood and faced Hardin. "What's happening out there?"

Hardin nearly bolted from his skin he stood so fast. "Gods, Calen." He placed his hand on his chest. "You nearly stopped my heart from beating."

Niesha stood. "Berggren?"

"Alive." Hardin shook his head. "For now, anyway."

Black smoke began seeping into the room through the cracks around the door.

"Open the door, Hardin, or this won't end well for you," Mortis yelled through the door.

"We've got a way out," Calen said. He pointed at an air shaft high on the wall.

"Hurry then," Hardin said. "They don't know the three of you are in here."

"Come with us," Niesha said.

Hardin shook his head. "If I do, they'll figure it out." The smoke grew thicker. "Hurry!"

After stacking a few crates beneath the shaft, Niesha entered it first. Eshtak and Calen quickly followed her. Once inside, Hardin placed the grate back over the air shaft opening and then moved the stack of crates off to the side so that the zhebəllin wouldn't be drawn to the shaft.

"Good luck," Hardin said.

Calen managed to turn himself around inside the shaft just as the door burst into flames. Hardin made quick work to unbarricade the door and then yanked it open. He retreated several paces. Mortis stepped through the flaming door, a metal bar in his hand. Three zhebəllin entered behind him.

Mortis surveyed the room. "You alone in here?" Hardin nodded. "We'll see about that."

The zhebəllin scoured the room, breaking open all the crates. Each sniffed the air, but none took notice of the air shaft. Calen had no doubt they would've been caught if it hadn't been for the smoke.

Thank you, Ʒäțūr.

Mortis snarled at Hardin. "On your knees, traitor."

Hardin stood in defiance. "The only traitor in this room is *you*."

Two of the zhebəllin kicked the backs of Hardin's legs, and Hardin dropped to his knees with a grunt.

"You claim I never have anything positive to add to a conversation. Well, here's a positive for you," Mortis said. "You're dead."

Metal glinted in the torchlight.

Thwack!

Calen cringed.

Hardin collapsed in a heap and lay still.

Mortis spat on Hardin. "One down, three to go." He and the three zhebəllin exited the storage room.

Calen lay in the air shaft for several seconds, watching Hardin and hoping and praying he would stir.

But the only things that moved in the room were the clouds of smoke, the flaming door, and the expanding pool of blood beneath Hardin's head.

Calen wept as he turned around in the shaft and faced Niesha and Eshtak. He shook his head in response to their questioning eyes.

The three of them crawled farther into the shaft until they reached a point where the smoke began filtering up through another section of shaft that likely led to the surface. As the smoke drew up the shaft, Calen closed his eyes and wept harder.

Ɔätūr, help us.

CHAPTER SIXTEEN

Aria stood alone in the throne room, staring up at a monstrosity of twisted black and silver iron that kings of the past had called their throne. From its ruby seat situated within the gaping maw of a black dragon to the silver iron wings arcing high overhead, the throne demanded attention as soon as one entered the massive room.

Matching black tapestries featuring a red serpentine eye flanked the throne, each fifteen feet wide and forty feet high. Twenty columns of black granite swirled with gold rose to meet the sixty-foot-high ceiling of red birch wood inlaid with golden vines. There were no windows to give light to the room, yet none were needed. Sixteen golden sconces adorned every column, and ten golden chandeliers, parallel to the columns, ran straight down the middle of the room. Unlike the torches used in the multitude of other rooms spread throughout Galondu Castle, the throne room used none. Instead, oil lamps fed by pipes hidden in the columns and chandeliers gave the room light and life.

Aria traversed the six gold-clad steps and approached the throne. Despite its formidable appearance, she found the throne to be quite comfortable once she settled into it. It pleased her, especially given the day she faced.

A single clap brought forth Brema from beyond the throne room doors. The homely girl carried with her a purple velvet pillow. Atop the pillow sat a sparkling silver crown encrusted with rubies, emeralds, and diamonds. The crown once belonged to Queen Veshna Carac, the wife of King Magus Carac. Aria found it more beautiful than she'd remembered when Pravus had shown it to her right before they went to war. Now, it was hers to wear.

She'd never pictured herself wearing such a thing, but Cinolth and Credan both insisted that it would give her the proper demeanor and an air of superiority while dealing with her people in court. That was another insistence on the part of them both. She questioned the need to hold court at all. As far as she was concerned, there were far more important things that needed to be done.

Earlier that day, Credan had led her through the formalities of court and what was expected of her as Queen, but none of it mattered. She'd do it her way, the people be damned. If they didn't already fear her, they would by the time they left her court.

Aria sighed as she watched Brema approach. A humble chambermaid, Brema wasn't a sight fit for the people. Credan had made that abundantly clear earlier in the morning. Despite their differences as of late, Aria agreed with the man. However, she trusted no one else to make her look the part she intended to play. Therefore, she would have Brema adjust her hair before placing the silver crown atop her head. Once finished, the girl would return to the shadows and her daily chores.

Brema stopped at the foot of the stairs and curtsied. "Mistress—" She froze for a moment. Color flushed her pale cheeks, and the pillow she held trembled. "—I mean Queen Rosai."

She's learning.

"Come forward."

Brema approached the throne and tripped on the fourth step. Somehow, she managed to catch herself while simultaneously preventing the crown from tumbling off the pillow. Brema blushed again. "Please forgive my clumsiness."

Aria glowered. "Do your job, and I'll forget everything."

A few minutes later, Brema stepped back and stared at Aria. She beamed with pride. "I must say, you're a picture of radiance, my queen."

A light unto the world.

Aria dismissed Brema and smiled to herself, but the joyous feeling faded. Had all gone as planned, Pravus and Alderan would be at her side right now, and her father would be dead. Instead, she sat alone on a throne, about to hold court for the first time.

The crown, light as it were, still felt strange and weighty atop her head. At some point, she'd get used to wearing it, and that day couldn't come quickly enough. If the day favored her, perhaps she'd never need to hold court again.

A true farce.

Aria took a deep breath and stared straight ahead. "Enter."

Credan joined her at the throne and stood just to her left. He looked far more nervous than she felt. It certainly didn't bode well. A dozen guards dressed in royal mail marched into the room and flanked the throne, fanning out down the steps. As far as she was concerned, they were unnecessary. She had no qualms defending herself.

She scowled at Credan. "Send in the first victim."

"The first citizen," Credan corrected. "As you wish." He signaled to the guards who stood just outside the throne room doors.

A man and his wife entered the throne room. Both wore a red band on their left arm. The man bowed low, and the woman curtsied once they reached the foot of the steps up to the throne.

Aria watched them for several moments, relishing the power she wielded. "Rise."

The man spoke, his gaze never reaching hers. "Queen Rosai, we bring news of the utmost importance from Atrum Moenia."

Aria sat straighter. "Proceed."

"Work has begun on the marble statues that will bear the likeness of your holiness," the man said.

"Yes, I know. This is happening in every city and town across the realm." Aria glared steel right through the man. "Once the statues are completed, I expect daily worship and weekly sacrifices to them."

The woman took the man's hand. "What my husband is trying to say is that we fear what some might do once those statues are in place. There are some who speak against you and vow to defy your creed."

Aria scoffed at the woman. "All who resist worshiping me will be used as examples. Their blood will paint the roads red. Anyone caught without a red band on their arm will be beaten on their first offense and face death on their second offense. I cannot be clearer on this matter." She slid forward on her seat. "Please tell me you've come with something of value. Perhaps you've spotted the traitors featured on the posters that hang throughout the realm? I assure you, that would be news of the utmost importance."

The woman looked to the floor and rubbed the back of her neck. "No, my queen, but—"

"Enough." Aria seethed. "Leave my court before I decide to have you both killed for wasting my time."

The couple quickly bowed and made haste toward the throne room exit. A dozen more citizens came through the doors with fruitless news before Aria could take no more. She turned to Credan and glared at him.

Beads of sweat dripped from Credan's brow. "Yes, my queen?"

"Assure me that the others have not come to waste my time as well."

He swallowed hard and pulled at his shirt collar. "I would be uncomfortable making such a declaration."

"Uncomfortable?" She rose from the throne and faced Credan. "Have none of these people been screened before entering my court?"

Fear flashed in his eyes. "That... isn't tradition."

Aria quaked. She snatched the crown off her head and shook it at Credan. "Damn tradition and damn this wretched court!" She tossed the crown on the throne seat and stormed away.

Something or someone will burn for this.

† † †

Traveling with a bunch of orcs provided no advantages for a man of Wrik's intellect, especially as a prisoner. He had no delusions it would, and yet the lack of conversation baffled him. He'd never known a race to be so self-absorbed. Granted many humans thought of nothing but themselves, but most would still engage in some level of conversation even if it only centered around themselves.

It came as no surprise that the higher races looked down on lower races such as the orcs. Orcs lived and acted like savage beasts, and the lot of them stunk worse than a room full of defiled chamber pots. Without Murtag to keep them in line, they'd likely have killed each other or him already. Given his current state of uncleanliness, he would almost prefer death to facing Aria. Regardless of the animosity between them, he still valued her opinion of him.

Although a prisoner to them, the orcs still provided Wrik with a few necessities: brackish drinking water that smelled worse than ox urine, a full day without sustenance of any measure (the palm-sized ball of mold with an immeasurable hint of bread essence didn't count), and swift punishment for his various escape attempts, one of which would leave his left thigh scarred for life.

Ahead stretched the mile-long wall Aria used to create the gateway between the northern part of The Plains and Galondu Castle. It offered Wrik his only saving grace. Had the gateway not been working, death would've found him long before they ever reached the castle. As it were, setting foot inside the castle and facing Aria would likely end his life. Then again, death at her hand would prove a far more suitable fate than being left at the mercy of Murtag and the other orcs.

Murtag and the other orcs stopped in front of the massive gateway and stared at it. After a few minutes, Wrik spoke up. "Send me through, and you'll see that it's safe."

"You're a wizard," Murtag snarled. "As I said before, I'm far smarter than you."

"Are you? What you're suggesting is that every single person who went through the gateway a few weeks ago must've been a wizard of some sort. Tens of thousands of soldiers. I'll admit, that would truly be remarkable."

Murtag backhanded him. "Another word, and I'll cut out your tongue and feed it to you."

Wrik raised his shackled hands and stepped back several steps.

Murtag summoned over an orc named Thurg. The beastly fiend defined grotesque. Layers of fat surrounded his midsection, yet bulging muscles carved his arms and legs. A fattened bull. Tendrils of yellowish-green snot hung from his porcine nose.

With a grunt, Murtag shoved Thurg through the gateway. On the castle side of the gateway, Thurg patted himself down and then turned back, raising his thumb.

An arrow ripped through the front of Thurg's skull. Thurg fell face-first, his head coming back through the gateway.

Hundreds of soldiers clad in black armor—many carrying crossbows—approached the gateway from the castle side. One of the soldiers, a captain according to the braids he wore over his left shoulder, stepped forward. "Go back to wherever you came from, or you will meet the same fate."

Murtag glared at the captain. "I have business with the queen."

"Impossible." The captain drew his sword. "Our queen would never deal with the likes of your kind. You've been warned. Leave now."

Wrik stepped up next to Murtag. "I think you misunderstand the gravity of the situation at hand." He held up his hands. "As you can see, I am a prisoner of this beast. As such, I demand an audience with Queen Rosai."

The captain grinned. "You're as thick as your friend."

"Am I?" Wrik studied the man for several moments. "How about you make haste and inform Queen Rosai that Wizard Wrik Isler awaits her at the gateway."

The captain turned and addressed his men. "If any of them make an attempt to cross through the gateway, execute them all."

"Yes, captain," the soldiers said in unison. The soldiers parted as the captain walked through their ranks and toward Galondu Castle.

"Now we wait," Wrik muttered.

An hour later, a different soldier, also a captain, approached the gateway. With a scowl on his face, he turned and addressed the soldiers. "By order of the queen herself, we are to permit these beasts passage to the castle. I will personally escort them to her. Now, all of you fall back and continue to defend the castle at all costs."

As the soldiers faded back into the background, the new captain turned and faced Murtag. With a sigh, he signaled for them to cross through the gateway and follow him.

Wrik's heart began beating quicker as they approached the castle. How quickly would she dispatch him? Given that she'd sent a shade after him, it surprised him a bit that she hadn't gone to the gateway herself and executed him there.

As they rounded the corner of the castle, Wrik spotted Aria standing at the castle gates in all her splendor and beauty. Form-fitting black trousers and a red top with flowing sleeves. He could not take his gaze from her.

Aria wore a smile, but the closer Wrik got, the better he could see that she'd changed somehow. Physically. He couldn't quite grasp the difference.

Perhaps her eyes?

He stared into them. Deep down into her tortured soul. War and grief had left her little more than a hollowed-out shell of the young woman he thought he knew.

Until she tried to kill me.

Aria's gaze met his for an instant. Her smile faded to a frown. Then a scowl.

Like the wind, she approached in silence but with fury. Arms at her sides. Palms forward. Fingers spread.

Sweat moistened Wrik's palms as purple bolts of energy crackled between Aria's fingers. In a few moments, he'd be dead. With everything he'd seen, read, and planned, he'd never expected or contemplated an end like this. He willed his life to flash before him so that he could revel in all the things he'd accomplished, but only one thought came to him in that instant.

Her focus isn't on me.

Aria stalked toward Murtag. Without context, Wrik couldn't understand the situation unfolding before him. As far as he knew, Murtag had followed her orders, so why the wrath?

"What's the meaning of this?" She seethed.

Murtag fell on one knee. "My queen, I've done just as you asked of me."

She pointed at Wrik. "No, what you've done is shackle and collar one of my closest friends. Explain yourself before I end your life."

Closest friend? What game is she playing at?

Murtag looked up at Aria with a hint of defiance. "You said to bring anyone who returned to that spot to you. I've done just that."

Aria turned to Wrik, the energy still crackling between her fingers. "Is this true?"

"Yes, my queen," Wrik said, "but I swear it's not what you think."

"I'll be the judge of that." She turned and walked back toward the castle entrance. "Wizard Wrik, follow me. The rest of you will return to that spot and continue your watch until further notice."

Murtag rose and glared at Wrik. "As you wish, my queen." He shoved Wrik with his shoulder as he turned around to leave. "If I ever see you again, you're dead." He and the other orcs headed back toward the gateway.

Wrik couldn't care less about Murtag and his empty threats, but Aria drove fear into his heart. He would've preferred for her to have just killed him. Now, he didn't know what she would do to him. What he needed was an escape plan. He set his mind to it as he followed Aria into the castle.

Gods… what will I tell her?

† † †

Aria waited for Wizard Wrik in the war room. Something about the room always made her feel closer to Pravus. It was almost as if a small part of him remained there. As absurd as it were, the feeling of his presence never faded. She'd heard rumors about spirits who lingered between worlds, but she couldn't bring herself to believe such nonsense. Pravus believed in nothing. He likely spent his days now in the clutches of Diꝫäfär.

And where am I headed?

Wrik entered the room, disrupting her thoughts. "Thank you for allowing me time to bathe before we spoke."

"I wouldn't have stomached sitting with you in a closed room while you smelled like sweat and sewage. As you know, I'm with child, and many odors leave me nauseous."

"Well, I'm glad to be clean once again."

"Good. Now, let's discuss the issue at hand. Why did Murtag find you in the exact same spot as the little dragon who killed my brother?"

"It's simple, really." Wrik began to pace. "Once the news arrived about Lord Pravus's death and the death of Alderan, I was beside myself with grief, especially given the way Alderan died. Then, I noticed you had reactivated the gateway. I knew in that moment that I must go and investigate the little dragon incident myself. While doing so, Murtag mistook me for an enemy and shackled and collared me. I don't blame him, though. He was just following orders. However, I assure you that I had nothing to do with Alderan's death. As with you, I considered him a friend."

Aria mulled over Wrik's explanation. "And did you discover anything during this investigation?"

"Nothing I'm sure you don't already know."

He's hiding something from me, but what?

"Humor me," she said.

Wrik removed his spectacles and began cleaning them as he paced. "Well, based on the prints left at the scene, the dragon appears to be no dragon at all."

Something certainly felt off with Wrik. She'd never experienced so much tension while in his presence before. He'd always appeared comfortable around her in the past. What had changed between them other than the fact that she was now the queen?

Could that be it?

She couldn't be certain. Until she was, she must keep him close. For now, she'd accept his explanation. After all, she had another avenue of getting to the truth.

"I will remove your shackles and fetters, but the collar must stay on until this matter has been settled."

"Do you really think that necessary, Lady Aria?"

"I am the queen, Wizard Wrik. You will address me as such."

"Yes, of course. Forgive me. I've come to know you so well as the former that I hadn't given your status change a thought. I will do my best to address you as Queen Rosai henceforth."

"See that you do."

Wrik stopped pacing and bowed. "As you wish, my queen."

"Good. Now, there is one other matter I'd like your assistance with."

"Name it, and I will do my best to please you."

"Cinolth tells me that there are wizards capable of retrieving memories straight from someone's head. Are you aware of such wizards?"

Wrik placed his spectacles back on his face and gazed at the candle flame that flickered between them for a good long time. "Yes, of course."

He hesitates to answer again. Why?

Wrik cleared his throat. "They are called fizärd mämärä. Memory wizards in our tongue. Speaking of which, were you aware that your brother possessed this gift?"

"Alderan?" Aria's throat tightened. Just the mentioning of his name conjured a torrent of emotions in her gut and mist to her eyes. She turned away and bit her lower lip until she regained control of herself. "No... the two of us never spoke of such things."

"I'm sorry, truly." He cleared his throat again and then continued, "Although not entirely rare, Lord Rosai rid the world of several wizards with such a gift. However, I believe I might still know of one."

Aria faced Wrik. "Summon them at once."

"Yes, of course. Keep in mind that it will take a day or two as she doesn't reside here. May I ask as to your intentions?"

"You may, but the matter is of no concern to you."

"Yes, but she may want a reason for the summons."

"I am the queen!" Rage stirred within her. "Is that not good enough reason for her to come at once?"

Wrik tipped his head slightly. "Yes, my queen. Always. I will send for her at once."

"Good." Aria focused her gaze on the map of the Ancient Realm spread across the table. "You can see yourself out."

"As you wish."

Aria looked up just as Wrik reached the door. "And Wizard Wrik?"

He glanced back. "Yes?"

"Make sure you stay within the castle walls."

"And where would I go?"

She smiled. "Nowhere... if you value your life."

CHAPTER SEVENTEEN

Zelanora and Master Savric stood at the bow of the ship, watching the waves crash against the southern coast of the southernmost island of the Shattered Realm as they sailed past. The island's beige, sandy beaches stretched far into the distance, forming what looked like a massive desert.

Zelanora pulled her windswept hair from her face. A few strands of hair clung to her lips, wet with ocean spray and flavored with sea salt. She spat and blew them away. "How many islands make up the Shattered Realm?"

Master Savric leaned on his staff as he surveyed the vast array of islands. "It is impossible to say for certain because the makeup of this realm is ever changing. Last I checked, there were dozens of islands. Perhaps there are more now."

"You mean new islands are still being formed here?" Zelanora said.

Master Savric nodded. "It is a possibility, given that Ɂätūr has never stopped creating, but what I speak of is the continual breaking apart of the islands."

"I don't understand." Zelanora leaned on her elbows and rested her head in her hands. "What would cause the islands to break up?"

"If you knew your ancient history, you would." Morcinda joined her and Master Savric at the bow.

Zelanora turned and faced Morcinda. Given their encounter with the seahounds the previous day, the woman looked radiant, her pale skin aglow and her dark hair shining in the early afternoon sun.

How does she stay beautiful out here in the middle of the ocean?

A tinge of jealousy crawled into Zelanora's voice, "For your information, I studied ancient history quite extensively, just not the history of this realm."

Morcinda feigned a smile. "And for your information, this region wasn't always known as the Shattered Realm. Long ago, it was called the Kingdom

Realm. History tells us that the Kingdom Realm was one of the most beautiful places on our planet." She swept her arm toward the islands and scowled at them. "As you can see, the Cartographers' War changed everything."

"I've heard of that war before but didn't know that this was the area where it took place." After a time, Zelanora frowned. "Why do we keep sailing past islands? Shouldn't we search them all for this Korin woman?"

Master Savric chuckled. "Not if we prefer to keep breathing, which I will admit is an activity I am quite fond of." He chuckled again then cleared his throat. "As you will come to understand, dangers lie at every turn in this region of the world, especially for humans and more so for those of us who wield mezhik." He patted Zelanora on the back. "Fear not, young one. We will seek information about Korin in Calamentum."

"And what's in Calamentum?" Zelanora said.

Master Savric grinned and then winked at her. "An old friend and keeper of unattainable knowledge."

Unattainable knowledge?

† † †

Calamentum stood before Savric and Zelanora, a shell of what once had been a glorious city of trade. Stone walls surrounded its small footprint, scorched and in various stages of disrepair. Not understanding its history, one might think the entire city had been built out of pure obsidian, down to the last stone of its narrow roads, but they would be wrong. Prior to the Cartographers' War, the city featured buildings made of brick, granite, marble, and stone, none of which were dark in color. A vast forest once surrounded the city, too. Now, only gray carcasses remained of the trees to the north. A petrified forest. To the south, east, and west, few trees survived. It was a wonder that the people who remained in Calamentum found ways to grow food and survive.

Zelanora held her hand over her nose. "What is that horrific smell?"

Savric sniffed the air and wrinkled his nose. "Remnants of wizard's fire. As bad as it smells, it will not kill you. However, holding your hand over your nose might."

Zelanora lowered her hand and looked about, her eyes wide. "Maybe I should have stayed on the ship with Morcinda."

"Do as I do and say nothing unless directly spoken to and you'll be fine. Understood?" She nodded. "Good." Savric drew his hood over his head and Zelanora did the same with hers. "Follow me."

They traversed several cobblestone streets until they came upon a single-story building without windows, doors, or roof. It looked exactly as it had so long ago. He led them up to the stone doorway and stopped.

Zelanora looked around. "Why are we here?"

Savric held a finger to his lips and then scanned the roads and buildings. As far as he could tell, no one lurked about. However, this was saurian territory. Therefore, his eyes were of little use for the task. Well, at least without a touch of mezhik. Had they been almost anywhere else in the world, he would've lit the place up and exposed anything or anyone hiding in the shadows. Today, he would make do with instinct, and it told him that they were not alone.

He pulled Zelanora close and whispered in her ear, "See the crude crescent moons etched into either side of the doorway?"

"Yes."

"When I say 'now,' you will touch the two marks simultaneously with your palms and step through the doorway. Whatever you do, do not hesitate."

"Got it."

Savric nudged Zelanora into the doorway and then turned and faced the road. Calling upon his mezhik, his palms began glowing with light.

"Kill them," hissed one of the invisible saurians.

† † †

Zelanora gasped as silver blades materialized out of thin air from multiple directions, each gleaming in the sunlight. She swallowed hard and braced herself for the worst.

Master Savric knows what he's doing.

She had to believe it.

A moment later, at least a dozen blades twirled toward her. Many more likely flew at Master Savric from the opposite direction.

Master Savric grunted and stumbled into the back of her. Her heart leapt in her chest. "No!"

The blades fell to the ground, each connecting with a sphere of light that hadn't been there a moment before.

A light shield!

"Now!" Master Savric said.

Zelanora pressed her palms against the crescent moon marks in the cold stone and stepped forward through the doorway. The piles of rubble and open air disappeared, replaced by a large room constructed of stone. Master Savric entered the room right behind her and dropped to his knees. His staff clattered as it hit the floor.

The low ambient light made it difficult to see much of anything, but there was no mistaking the dagger hilt that protruded from Master Savric's left shoulder. She knelt next to him.

"Should I pull it out?" Zelanora said.

"That not be the wisest choice."

Zelanora whirled around. A stout woman carrying a torch approached. She grabbed Master Savric's staff and stood with the staff pointed at the woman. "Don't come any closer."

The woman cackled. "Ye be a pathetic excuse for an adversary, I ever seen one."

"It is okay, Zelanora," Master Savric wheezed. "She is the one we have come to see."

Zelanora lowered the staff. "Sorry, I didn't know."

"Name's Gerda." The orange haired woman handed Zelanora her torch before pushing past. "A saurian blade must be shrunk lest it burrow itself deeper."

"I'm Pr—" Zelanora realized the fewer people who knew her the better. "—Zel. You can call me Zel."

Gerda grunted acknowledgment then reached into her apron and pulled out a small sack bound with twine. The sack held a mixture of substances: white powder, yellow clay, and some green leaves with yellow veins that Zelanora didn't recognize. The woman took a pinch of the white powder and yellow clay and shoved them inside her cheek along with two of the leaves.

After a minute of chewing and sucking, Gerda pulled a brown wad from her mouth with her finger and placed it around the blade, next to Master

Savric's skin. The blade physically shrunk in width. Zelanora blinked several times, certain her eyes had tricked her.

Gerda placed a finger on either side of the blade and grabbed its hilt with her other hand. "This gonna—" She yanked the blade out. "—hurt."

Master Savric howled and held his shoulder. "Bugger bees, woman!"

Gerda eyed Zelanora and grinned. Brown bits from the salve were still stuck to her teeth in several places. She worked to get one of the larger chunks off with her tongue and then spat it out after finally dislodging it.

Ew!

Gerda lifted Savric's chin and proceeded to examine his face before grunting. "No word from ye fer years, then ye show on me doorstep, malnourished and whatnot." With a final grunt, she said, "Sure this ain't no social visit."

Savric held his shoulder and sighed. "I truly wish it were, my dear friend."

"Sure ye do." Gerda snatched the torch back from Zelanora and pushed past her again. "Follow me."

Zelanora knelt next to Master Savric. Blood oozed between his fingers and soiled his light brown robes further. "Would you like me to try and heal that for you?"

Master Savric eyed the wound, then shook his head. "Save your strength, dear. It will heal well enough on its own." He proffered his hand. "However, you may assist me in attaining my feet once more."

She helped Master Savric up and handed him his staff. Then, the two of them followed Gerda into another part of the building.

† † †

Savric sat across the stone table from Gerda. Zelanora sat next to him. He pushed an empty porridge bowl toward the center of the table and patted his belly. It would do wonders to strengthen him and heal his shoulder. Plus, it would keep his stomach silent for another hour or so.

He leaned over the table and winced as the pain in his shoulder bloomed anew. He groaned and sat up straight. "Now that we have all the formalities and necessities out of the way, how about you tell us everything you know about a woman named Korin."

Gerda's eyes narrowed, and she looked to the shadows in the corners of the room. "Where ye hear that name?"

Savric glanced over at Zelanora. "From the lips of a dying man."

Gerda slammed the saurian blade onto the table. "And what ye want with her?"

"Truthfully, I am uncertain," Savric said.

"She be nothing more than legend," Gerda said. "A white-clad spectre who haunts the darkness. An avenger."

Zelanora leaned forward. "What else do you know of her?"

"Ye know all I know." Gerda rose from the table and snatched up Savric's bowl.

Savric pulled on his beard. "Tell us where we can find her, Gerda. It is of grave importance."

"Ye said ye uncertain." Gerda picked up the saurian blade and twirled it between stubby fingers. "Were ye not a friend, I'd slit yer throat fer lying."

"I would never lie to you, Gerda. Ẑäṭūr be my witness. We are uncertain as to why me must find her, but find her we must. As a friend, I implore you to further assist us."

Savric and Zelanora waited a good minute while Gerda stared into the distance. Finally, she said, "Sail east, beyond the Extimus Wilderness. Ye find her where kings and queens reign no more."

Savric rose from the table. "Thank you, Gerda. We owe you a great debt."

"Be gone, and never return lest I kill ye with me own hand." She winked at Savric, then turned to walk away. Over her shoulder, she said, "Use me back door. It be less compromised." With that, she left the room, fading into the darkness.

Savric grimaced. "I believe it is time that we explore the Cadivus Ruins."

† † †

The Cadivus Ruins, once a prominent castle of the kings and queens of old, rose from the barren grassland not far from shore. Its black and gray structure mimicked that of an upturned hand, pieces of its walls and spires protruding upward like fingers. It was one of the few places in the Shattered Realm that Savric had never visited before, nor had he ever wanted to. Cadivus had been the epicenter for everything vile and evil that came out of the Cartographers' War. Many volumes of books documented its history of brutal violence and bloodshed.

A stain on this world, Ɂäțūr.

Morcinda pulled the ship into the harbor. Two other vessels sat moored to the peer, each ready for sailing. The three of them exited the ship and walked up the pier. By the time they reached land, a group of hooded archers clad in white had them surrounded.

A handful of the archers were short-statured but stocky, so Savric surmised them to be dwarves or one of the other many half-races and not children. The rest of the group exhibited human features, and most of those a female form.

A strange welcoming party.

One of the human females held no weapon. She stepped forward and lowered her hood. Her lavender eyes matched her short-cropped hair. A silver ring pierced her lower lip, a contrast to her dark skin.

The female clasped her hands behind her back and stood with her feet spread slightly. "Your presence here is unwelcome. Turn around and leave, and we will not pursue you."

Savric stepped forward, staff in hand. "We seek counsel with the one called Korin."

"You are misinformed, wizard. I assure you that no one here goes by that name." The woman raised her hood back over her head. "Leave at once." She turned away.

Time to drop another name.

Savric stood tall. "You do well to protect your leader, but I assure you that we come under the direct authority of King Pius Zaridus."

The woman froze for a split second, and Savric noticed. "That name means nothing here," she said.

Zelanora came and stood next to Savric. "And yet your heart races at the mere mention of it, doesn't it?"

The woman turned back and eyed Zelanora. "Lower your hood, sorceress."

Zelanora peered up at Savric. He patted her arm. "Go ahead, young one. Do as she asks."

Zelanora lowered her hood and stared defiantly at the woman. "Satisfied?"

"Two born of mezhik..." Her gaze moved to Morcinda. "And what are you?"

Morcinda's left hand rested on the hilt of her dagger. She lowered her hood with her right hand. "Keep lying to us, and I'll relieve you of your life."

The woman smiled beneath her hood. "It's been far too long since I've seen an *äallf äkfeţik* in the flesh."

Savric cleared his throat. "As I said before, we seek counsel with the one called Korin."

The woman studied the three of them for a long time. Finally, she said, "I am her." Korin turned and motioned for the others to lower their weapons. "Come inside where we can speak... freely."

† † †

To Zelanora's surprise, the entire first floor of the ruined castle remained intact. As they traveled deeper within its walls, she couldn't help but feel a sense of home. Sure, its stones were black and gray and not a pristine white, but it still reminded her of the King's Palace in Vallah. She wondered what it might've looked like back when the entire structure stood.

Perhaps one was modeled after the other.

A single floor beneath ground brought them into a cavernous room. Based on its majestic architecture and the paintings that adorned its walls, she was certain it once served as a temple to one of the many heathen gods. Now, a simple stone seat stood at the front. Dark blue curtains stretched the width of the room behind the seat, concealing anything that might lie beyond.

Korin walked up to the seat and sat down facing them. She lowered her hood and crossed one leg over the other. Without a doubt the woman commanded a presence. Zelanora admired her, not because of anything the woman had done but because of what she represented. A young woman both in control of a kingdom and an army. Given the chance, Zelanora would lead her kingdom the same way.

Many of the others from the pier gathered behind Zelanora, Morcinda, and Master Savric. None bowed to Korin, so neither did she.

Korin eyed Master Savric. "Speak freely, wizard. What business does King

Zaridus have with me?"

Master Savric stroked his beard. "As I said before—"

"King Zaridus is dead," Zelanora blurted. Master Savric turned and glared at her, but no one else in the room reacted to her news. It wasn't what she'd expected.

Korin uncrossed her legs and leaned forward in her seat. "Then why come at all?"

I've been asking myself the same question this entire journey!

Never once did she come up with an answer other than fleeing for her life. It hadn't been her choice to leave, yet she still felt like a coward and knew she'd be viewed as such in the eyes of her people once she returned.

If I ever do.

Zelanora peered over at Master Savric, expecting him to reply. He leaned heavier on his staff than he had after facing the seahounds. Weary. Far frailer than she knew him to be.

What happened to him?

"The great dragon has awakened, and the Ancient Realm has fallen," Morcinda said.

Korin sat up. "The great dragon?"

"Cinolth The Dark breathes again," Master Savric said.

A loud murmur fell over the room. "Can it be?" someone said.

"You have the power to help them understand," Master Savric said to Zelanora through mindspeak. *"All you need do is use it."*

Zelanora nodded and eyed the leather pouch strung over Morcinda's shoulder. "Give it to me, and I'll show them."

Morcinda reached into her pouch and retrieved the black dragon scale. She handed it to Zelanora.

Gooseflesh rippled up Zelanora's arms as she approached Korin.

"Halt!" a woman yelled. Zelanora turned and faced a dozen crossbows aimed at her.

"Lower your weapons," Korin said. All lowered their weapons; a few with a hint of reluctance. "Come to me, child."

I am no child!

Zelanora wanted to scream it from the top of the toppled ramparts, but she held fast to her tongue. Instead, she turned and approached the seat. "This is one of Cinolth's scales." She held it out, and Korin took it.

Korin examined the scale for several minutes while Zelanora stood there. Once satisfied, she said, "It is indeed a dragon scale, but how am I to believe it came from Cinolth The Dark?"

Show her, Zel.

"Hold out your hand with the dragon scale." Korin did, and Zelanora took the woman's hand, pressing the dragon scale between their palms. Her hand trembled and felt like ice against Korin's warm flesh. She closed her eyes, concentrated on the smooth feel of the dragon scale, and touched it with her mezhik.

As it did the first time she touched it, the dragon scale spoke to Zelanora. Showed her such evil deeds it made her toes curl and her heart race. She pushed the horrific images from her mind and pictured them flowing down her arm, through her hand, and into Korin's open palm. The passage of time ceased to exist as the images continued to flow between them.

"Auh!" Korin jerked her hand away from Zelanora, her eyes wide. The dragon scale fell to the floor. "How can this be?"

"Mezhik," Savric said.

Zelanora opened her eyes, winded as though she'd been running. Weakness crept into her muscles and drew her to her knees. Korin swooped down from her perch and knelt next to her. Placed an arm around her shoulders.

In that moment, Zelanora noticed something that her mind could not comprehend. Korin wore a necklace beneath her white armor. In and of itself, a necklace would mean nothing, but this necklace was like no other in the world. Ice blue stones, like her eyes, alternated with black, green, and red stones. Not just stones but jewels. Zelanora had designed it herself many years ago. Only one person in the world ever wore it.

She peered into Korin's eyes, and her heart skipped a beat. "You can't be..."

The fabric of reality, woven tightly around everything, stiffened. Then, without sound, shattered.

Although her eyes never blinked, never looked away, never changed from their beautiful lavender, Korin no longer appeared the same. Her dark skin paled, cheekbones rose, chin narrowed, and her once lavender hair grew down past her shoulders in chestnut brown locks.

The woman kissed Zelanora's forehead, then smiled. "Welcome home, my love."

The entire room darkened around Zelanora and Korin. "Mother…"

CHAPTER EIGHTEEN

Cyrus sat in silence, staring at the book Gnaud had found about the spires. Having read every word, it left no room for interpretation outside of what Gnaud had told him. Still, it must be done. However, he would have to find a way to do it all himself. The others would be both a hindrance and a liability.

He rose from the table. The others looked to him in silence. "It will take more time, but those spires must come down." He held up his hand and kept the others quiet. "All of you will stay here in the Great Library with Gnaud while I destroy them."

Theyn roared. "It's a suicide mission, and I will not allow it!"

Cyrus glared at her. "This isn't your choice to make."

"Oh my! You cannot do it," Gnaud said. "Everything will be lost."

"The world will be lost if I do nothing." Cyrus slammed his fist against the table.

Zerenity spoke up, "No, Cyrus. I don't think you understand what Gnaud is saying."

Cyrus clenched his fist. "Enlighten me."

"If you destroy the spires, all of Nasduron will be lost." Zerenity swept her arms outward. "*All* of it."

Cyrus scoffed. "The Great Library has protections of its own. You will all be safe here."

"No," said Gnaud. He plopped down on the table in front of Cyrus. "This library is tied to the final spire in ways you don't understand. Sure, it will surface, but not without... consequences."

"Yes, I know," Cyrus said. "All of its knowledge will be destroyed, but I'm willing to make that sacrifice for the better of the world."

Tears flowed from Gnaud's eyes. "I will not stop you from doing what you think is right or best."

Cyrus rubbed his bicep. "It is our best and only option right now."

Theyn grabbed Cyrus's arm. "For a man with vast knowledge, you can be so dense at times."

Cyrus scowled. "How so?"

"The knowledge that will be lost sits right in front of you." Theyn released his arm and sighed. "Is that a sacrifice you're willing to make? Is that a choice made by you alone?"

Gnaud…

Cyrus drooped in his chair, stunned. How had he missed something so vital? He and Wrik had risked their lives to save Gnaud, and now he opted to sentence Gnaud to certain death?

No, it was Nardus who saved Gnaud, not me.

Cyrus leaned back and grabbed his head. "Ƨätŭr. My God. I am a fool."

Gnaud leapt off the table and into Cyrus's arms. "If my life stands in the way of saving the world, who am I to say no?"

Cyrus wrapped his arms around Gnaud and held Gnaud's head to his chest. "We will find another way, Gnaud. Ƨätŭr never fails us."

Zerenity raised an eyebrow. "Well then, let's think about other options."

"What about the mezhik mirrors?" Rakzar offered.

"You'd die if you tried to go through one of them," Theyn said.

Zerenity nodded. "Correct. Plus, no such mirrors exist in Nasduron." She looked over at Cyrus. "Right?"

"Yes, you are right." Cyrus released Gnaud, and Gnaud crawled back upon the table and sat down. "Placing a mirror here would've defeated the purpose of hiding Nasduron beneath the ocean."

Theyn eyed Cyrus. "You're a mage. You can control all the elements. Wouldn't it be possible for you to create a pocket of air, like a bubble, and lift us all to the surface?"

"Even if it were possible for me to do so, there's no way for us to breech the barrier that protects Nasduron aside from disabling the spires," Cyrus said. "It would also require more mezhik than I possess to keep a spell like that active long enough to reach the surface. We are miles deep."

Ridan slumped on Bakkan's back. "Then what's left? Where does that leave us?"

Cyrus rubbed his left bicep. "I'm not sure."

Zerenity stood and walked over to the table where Urza lay. "Why would they have sunk Nasduron without a way to return it to the surface?"

"I never said that they did." Cyrus watched Gnaud clean his spectacles. As with most things, mezhik almost always provided a way to undo what had been done, the sinking of Nasduron no exception. "However, it can't be achieved from here."

"But there's a way," Theyn said. "Whatever it is, can't we get Wizard Wrik to do it?"

"It's not that simple." Cyrus stood and began pacing as his mind traced memories far in his past. "The wizards who constructed and conjured the spires also created a horn they called *Felzmiere's Hūrn*, a name honoring one of the first mages to have existed. If the horn is blown at just the right spot and at just the right time, Nasduron will rise from the depths. Otherwise, Nasduron and the person who blows the horn will be ripped apart." He grabbed a chair and slammed it down. "But none of that matters. After Nasduron sank, they banished the horn from our world for fear of Magus getting hold of it."

Ridan gasped. "Other worlds exist?"

"At least one," Cyrus said. "We call it the Shadow World."

"Honestly, I never understood the name," Gnaud said, placing his spectacles back on his face.

"There is a simple explanation. It was named that because everything there is just a shadow compared with our world." Cyrus sat back down. "Mezhik is almost non-existent, and what does exist is warped and damaged."

"So, there's no way to get this *Felzmiere's Hūrn* back?" Zerenity said.

Cyrus eyed Zerenity. "The issue doesn't just lie in retrieving the horn but also in our ability to use it. It must be done from the surface and only in a specific spot, neither of which we can do."

"Ugh!" Ridan fell back against Bakkan's back. The mastiff familiar shifted his weight. "Then we're back to the beginning. Stuck here without a future."

"Ɀätūr will show us the way," Zerenity said.

Rakzar shook his head slowly. "I wish I could believe that."

"As do I sometimes," Cyrus said.

Zerenity grabbed Cyrus's shoulder and shook him gently. "Where has your faith gone? Are you not one of the seven? *Ūrdär Dhef 2äfn Dhä*? Sworn to uphold the laws of 2äţūr?"

"I was once… but Nardus has had more of an influence on me than I ever imagined possible. The loss of his family…" He rubbed his left bicep. "My family. Where was 2äţūr in that? How could he just ignore what was about to happen? Sit back and do nothing?"

"We all make choices, Cyrus," Zerenity said. "You know as well as I do that he allows us our freedom, and that same freedom sometimes comes with a cost."

"But everything?" He shook his head. "How is that fair to anyone?"

Theyn came to his side and put her arm around him. "You've not lost everything."

"Yet." He forced air from his nostrils. "Shanara—Aria—is all I have left."

"From your former life, but you still have me," Theyn said.

Cyrus pulled Theyn close and buried his face in her thick, beautiful hair. "I know, and if I were to lose you too, I'd reach into the heavens and rip 2äţūr from his throne."

"I know you would." Theyn leaned her head back and kissed him.

Every moment near her brought Nardus closer to the surface.

I've become so weak.

Rakzar proffered his hand. "Killing Aria will be our last option. I swear it." Cyrus clasped Rakzar's hand and gave him a curt nod.

"Agreed." Zerenity looked around at the others. "We will do everything in our power to find another way to stop Cinolth. We give you our word."

Everyone else agreed.

Cyrus spat on the ground. "And if it comes down to it, she will die by my hand." He rose from his chair. "Now, if you all will excuse me, I must find a way to reconcile the two sides of my mind. I cannot fight a war while one rages within."

Theyn grabbed his arm as he started to walk away. He stared at her. "What?"

"You are of one mind, my love. We all see the truth in your actions and words."

"Then why am I at such odds with myself?"

"Seek forgiveness and offer it, too," she said.

"I've forgiven you, Theyn. Long ago." He kissed her on the forehead.

Theyn clung to his arm. "I know, but that's not what I'm talking about. You need to forgive yourself and your god. Do this, and I'm certain your mind will heal."

"I'm not so sure." He peeled Theyn's fingers off his arm, walked out of the Great Library, and headed straight for Ʒäṭūr's temple.

It's time you and I have words.

† † †

Cyrus knelt on the white stone floor and lifted his eyes toward the golden altar that stood before him. So much time had passed since he last spoke with Ʒäṭūr, and now words failed to pierce his lips. What does one say to a God who has forsaken his son? A God who turned his back during Cyrus's greatest time of need. His darkest day.

"Where were you?" he cried. His voice, dripping with anguish and rage, echoed throughout the great hall. "I begged you not to take my family, yet you hid your face from me that day. You allowed me to wallow in my own anguish and drown myself with ale. Had you been there, Vitara and Savannah would still be alive. Had you been there, I wouldn't have missed Shardan and Shanara grow up. Now, you've taken my eldest son and turned my daughter against me. What did I ever do to deserve this? I served only you!"

A great wind stirred, extinguishing all the candles in the hall. Then, a familiar presence filled Cyrus's mind. *"Through the darkness of your life, I've always been with you. Held you. Comforted you. Cried with you. Even when you shut me out, I never left you. You are my son. My loved one. I've never forsaken you, nor will I ever."*

Cyrus stared into the darkness. "If you were there, why didn't you lift a single finger to help me when my family was attacked and killed? You could've prevented it all."

"You cannot see the end from the beginning, nor can you see how a single

event ripples through time, creating so much change, but I can, and I do. In your time of despair, you forgot the love you shared with your family for several years. A love which many never experience. You also failed to see the truth before your eyes and buried children who weren't your own.

"Through all that, I was still there. You damned me. Forsook me. Turned your back on me, yet I waited patiently for you to return to me. Do you think your reunion with your two children came by accident? A mere coincidence? Never! I plucked you from your pit of despair and placed you directly in their paths. Yet you still refuse to see my hand in it. Open your eyes, my son. See the truth that lies before you. Reconcile your past, present, and future. Forgive yourself."

Cyrus fell on his face and wept. "My God, I am broken."

"Never, my son."

"I war with myself during every waking moment. I know not who I am or what purpose I serve."

"You're who you've always been. Who you will always be. You are my son."

"But am I Cyrus or Nardus?"

"Yes."

That final word echoed through Cyrus's mind as the candles relit, bringing life back into the hall. He rose back to his knees and wiped tears from his eyes and snot from his nose. The golden altar reflected his own image, but the way the light hit its surface from multiple directions left his face split right down the middle. As he stared at the reflection, he began to see not just the two sides of his face but one side of his face and the other of Nardus's.

Two sides of a coin.

The longer he stared at the reflection, the clearer it became that a single face stared back at him. Neither Cyrus nor Nardus but a combination of the two. He touched his own face as though for the first time.

Stubble protruded from his cheeks, jaw, chin, and around his mouth. "A trait of Nardus."

Intense yet kind eyes stared back at him. Brown with yellow flecks. "An amalgamation of the two of us."

The tips of his fingers tingled as he drew upon his mezhik.

Cyrus.

Tears wet his cheeks again as he gazed upon himself. "I… forgive you." He raised his arms and tilted his head back. "Ƨäṯūr. My God. Forgive me and bless me, for I am your son!"

"You are forgiven!"

† † †

The only thing Rayah was certain of was that the archway kept her attention most of the day because it was nearly dark when she exited the building. In all that time, she hadn't had a single thought of Alderan or the others. Why it'd drawn her with such rapt attention, she didn't know, but now she needed to get back to the Great Library and find out if the others had been successful in taking down any of the spires.

When Rayah arrived back at the library, Urza lay on top of one of the tables. She looked horrible. Blood covered most of her armor and soiled the top of the table as well. Her chest rose and fell, and her eyelids twitched.

"What happened to you?" Rayah said.

The others weren't around, but she heard voices coming from the direction of the kitchens. She touched Urza's arm for a few moments, said a prayer, and then headed toward the others.

Inside the kitchens, everyone except Cyrus stood around one central table, eating chunks of bread dipped in a stew that smelled of potatoes and carrots. Her stomach rumbled. She couldn't remember the last time she'd eaten something. She took a bowl and scooped some broth into it. Grabbing a piece of bread, she settled next to Rakzar and Ridan.

"So, how did it go with the spires?" Rayah said. "How's Urza?"

"She'll survive," Rakzar said.

"We're still trapped here," Ridan said.

Rayah dipped a chunk of bread into the broth and let it soak. "Until the spires can be destroyed, right?"

"That's not possible," Zerenity said. "We cannot take them down. Gnaud discovered a book behind one of the bookshelves that talked about how the spires were formed and the fact that if a spire is destroyed it will flood that section of the city. Doing so would kill us all."

Rayah stopped chewing. "Then what are we supposed to do?"

"Sit here and rot," Rakzar said.

"We're back at the start," Ridan said. "This situation is entirely Cyrus's fault."

Theyn growled. "You know that's not fair."

Rayah hated the bickering. It reminded her of the time she spent with Alderan and Rakzar while trapped in the cell beneath Castle Portador Tempestade. She was about to change the subject when Cyrus walked into the room with Urza, her arm draped over his shoulders for support. Rakzar walked over to them and placed Urza's other arm over his own shoulders. They led her over to a chair.

"You're looking a lot better," Rakzar said.

"I've got Cyrus to thank for that." Urza grimaced when she sat down. "Another day, and I'll be as good as new."

Rayah stared at Cyrus and cocked her head. "You look different somehow."

"Yes," Theyn said. She stroked Cyrus's cheek. "He's finally at peace."

Cyrus kissed Theyn. "I am, thanks to you." He turned to the others. "I know I've led many of you to confusion as to who I am, including myself, so allow me to make a final declaration. Although we should always look to the past for insight and knowledge to lead us into the future, we should never dwell on it. Long ago, I lived a life as Cyrus Nithik, but that time has passed. Help me move forward and embrace the future. Henceforth, my name shall forever be Nardus Remison."

"As it should be," Theyn said. Rayah and the others agreed.

After several minutes of silence, Rayah finally piped up. "I discovered something today."

Gnaud walked across the table and sat down in front of her bowl of broth. "And what was it you discovered?"

"As I was walking through Nasduron, I stumbled upon a symbol carved into one of the cobblestones. Then, I noticed another. A trail of them became visible, so I followed it across the city to a large building."

Gnaud's eyes lit up. "Yes, yes, of course! The stones. As the spires were being built, the stones were embedded into the streets all across Nasduron as a way to lead the people through the darkness once the city sank to the bottom of the ocean. After all, they knew the sun could not penetrate the depths of the ocean."

"But why lead them to a building?" Nardus said. "What's the significance?"

Rayah closed her eyes and pictured it. "It was a magnificent building. It made me think of Alderan and how great it would've been to have held our wedding there. Naturally, the thought made me cry. I'm not sure if what happened after that was due to my tears or just a coincidence, but the floor opened and revealed a stairwell. At the bottom of the stairwell stood a grand archway. A blue, watery surface filled the archway."

Nardus eyed Gnaud who sat on the table. "Gnaud, my oldest and wisest friend, do you know anything about this archway?"

"Or has the memory of them escaped you like the spires did?" Urza said.

Gnaud crossed his arms. "Dear ʕäṭūr! I am older than all of you, Nardus included. As such, I'm entitled to forget a passage or two from time to time."

"I completely understand." Zerenity tapped her chin. "This archway sounds like a portal."

"Yes," Nardus said, "but to where?"

Gnaud twisted his whiskers between his fingers. "I think I can explain. Erecting the seven spires took the strength of many, and not just wizards and sorceresses. Not a single person left Nasduron beforehand, each playing a role that would guarantee the plan's success. After the seven spires were erected, the wizards cast Nasduron to the bottom of the ocean.

"As you now know, no one could leave once that happened. However, it was never the plan to trap everyone here. The architects knew that Nasduron's limited resources would never sustain all the people. They also knew that it would take just a single individual to keep the place functional. This is the reason that they built the archway and embedded stones in the streets to point people in its direction."

"But why would they need directions?" Nardus said.

"As I said before, they believed Nasduron would be cast into darkness once it sank to the bottom of the ocean," Gnaud said. "Therefore, the people needed a path to light their way toward the exit. As they erected the spires, they came to realize that the mezhik they poured into them created what they called a prism effect. When light above, so Nasduron would be below."

"An exit!" He looked to Rayah. "You must take me there. Now."

† † †

Nardus stood before the archway buried beneath the performance hall. Rayah had described its every detail with perfection, right down to its alluring pull. Her strength to resist it surprised him. Luckily, the others agreed to wait up in the performance hall while he investigated.

Kneeling, he read the words written in the ancient language that were etched into the stone floor. They prickled his skin. "Gnaud, I think you need to see this."

Thirty seconds later, Gnaud bounded down the passage toward him. His eyes immediately grew wide as he took in the archway. "Dear Ζäţūr."

"Listen to this." Nardus read the inscription aloud, "Beyond lies the point of no return."

Gnaud nodded, his gaze focused on the archway. "Yes."

Nardus rubbed his left bicep. "I can read the symbols around the archway, but I don't understand their significance or the meaning of the inscription." He sat on the floor and met Gnaud's gaze directly. "Do you know the meaning of the inscription? Was something written about it in the book about the spires?"

"Oh, my! No." Gnaud peered up at him. "But I do understand it." He breathed on his spectacles and rubbed them with a kerchief from his pocket. "Because of the importance of the knowledge within Nasduron and the Great Library, precautions had to be taken to ensure it didn't fall into the wrong hands. This archway provided a means of escape for the people of Nasduron but also came with a price. It is a one-way portal, as you might've guessed by its inscription."

Nardus nodded, and Gnaud continued, "However, I fear it is more than that. From what I remember, when a person passes through the archway, an ancient mezhik marks their blood. This mark prevents them from remembering the location of Nasduron while it remains hidden beneath the ocean."

"And therefore the only way this mezhik can be broken is with *Felzmiere's Hūrn*," Nardus said.

Gnaud nodded. "I believe you are correct."

"Mezhik be damned." Nardus spat, then scowled at the archway. "And where does this portal lead?"

Gnaud shrugged. "I was never privy to that information."

"I understand." Nardus sighed and pulled on his hair. "Ugh. We now have a means of escape, but it also means that I may never see you again."

A grin spread across Gnaud's face. "I doubt that. You've always had a way of bending or breaking the rules."

Nardus chuckled. "Easy to do when the rules are your own, but this... I'm not so sure."

"Have faith," Gnaud said.

Nardus nodded, then called for the others. He explained everything to them about the archway once they arrived, and answered all their questions to the best of his ability.

Ridan sat on Bakkan's back and stared at the archway. "What are we waiting for?"

Although he couldn't speak for the others, Nardus knew exactly why he hesitated. "As I said, we know nothing about what lies on the other side of this portal, nor can we see anything. It might be safe, but it could also kill us."

"Well, there's one simple way to find out." Rayah flew into the blue water and disappeared. Ridan and Bakkan followed right behind her.

"I hate water," Rakzar growled.

"You're not alone." Urza took Rakzar's hand, and they went into it together.

Zerenity looked at Nardus and smiled. "Ⅾätūr willing, we'll all be waiting on the other side." She turned and walked through the archway.

Nardus hugged Gnaud one last time. "Until we meet again, my friend." Gnaud wiped tears from his eyes as Nardus turned and walked into the water with Theyn.

CHAPTER NINETEEN

Aria screamed and sat upright. Heart pounding. Sheets soaked with sweat. The bed coverings lay unused next to her. A woeful mourn arose as her bedchamber doors cracked open wide. Then, a ghoulish beast cloaked in shadows stepped through them and approached.

She cowered on the bed and retreated to its far corner. "Stay away from me!"

The beast gave pause. Leaned forward, head cocked to one side. "Queen Rosai, are you unwell?"

She recognized the beast's voice. No, not a beast but a man. "Master Credan?"

"Yes."

Why would he call me Queen Rosai?

Credan stepped into the light of the lone candle burning on the bedside table. "Are you unwell?"

"Now that you're here, I'm feeling better." Her pulse slowed as she moved back to her side of the bed and sat on its edge. Her feet dangled close to the floor. "It was nothing more than a nightmare."

"I understand." Concern oozed from his eyes and dripped from his words. "Would you like me to have a glass of warm milk fetched for you?"

"That would be nice." She stacked several pillows up and then leaned back against them. Master Credan was already back to her bedchamber doors. "Master Credan?"

The man turned, his features cloaked in shadows once again. "Yes, my queen?"

Queen? Am I still asleep?

Aria grabbed the skin on her thigh and twisted it hard. Pain registered immediately.

No, I'm definitely awake.

She decided Master Credan must've misspoken. He still stood at the door, awaiting a response. "Please do not mention this to Lord Rosai. I'd loathe for him to think me an adolescent and unworthy of marriage."

Credan stiffened. She thought it odd, but he was an odd man. "As you wish… Lady Aria. Close your eyes and rest. Your glass of milk will arrive shortly."

"Thank you."

Master Credan closed the doors behind himself, leaving her alone with her single candle.

"I'm not afraid of you," she whispered, and blew out the candle. Sleep quickly met her in the darkness and pulled her into its arms.

† † †

Aria stood at the precipice. Bodies lay strewn across the field of charred grass below. Broken. Bloodied. Dismembered. Dead. Both beast and fowl ravaged the dead. A feast she would not partake of.

Human, orc, gnoll, zheballin. Race made no difference. They all bled, and all met similar fates.

She turned away. Stepped back from the cliff edge. That's when she heard the cry. Raspy. Guttural. Unmistakable.

"Help me."

Chills engulfed her.

"Help me."

Aria turned back and scanned the field. Fires still burned. Smoke skewed her vision.

"Help me."

A sense of urgency swept through her as she descended the cliff and began searching through the bodies. The first few gagged her. Brought bile into the back of her throat. She choked it down and continued picking through the carnage.

"Help me."

With each cry, the voice became more familiar. She stood at the cusp of recognition, yet her mind could not make the leap.

"Help me."

Frantically, she searched. Body after body. So many dead.

"Help me."

She saw him then. Lying on his back. Ash gray. Head to toe.

Her eyes burst with tears. Gushed rivers as she knelt next to him.

"Help me."

This one she knew. This one she loved. More than life itself.

A tear—her tear—struck his face. Left a hole right through him. Right to the ground.

"Help me."

She reached out and touched his face, and he turned to ash.

"Alderan!"

CHAPTER TWENTY

The young man woke with a loud gasp.

A hand quickly covered his mouth. "Be quiet, flamewalker. We're almost there."

Jagger.

He nodded, and she removed her hand. "How long have I been asleep?"

"Maybe an hour. As I said, we're almost there."

Snowy cliffs rose on the left. To the right, a snowy drop off. The bottom beyond his vision. He tightened his arms around Jagger's waist and squeezed Eis a little tighter with his legs.

After a time, he finally said, "I think I know my name."

"How?"

"I dreamt of a young woman with red and blonde hair, but it felt like more than just a dream. Like either she was there with me or that I was there with her. She knelt over me and wept as I lay on the ground. Over and over, I asked her for help. I could tell by the look in her eyes that she knew me. She called me Alderan."

"Alderan?" Jagger chuckled. "What kind of name is that?"

"I don't know. Why does it matter?"

"Well, it certainly doesn't sound like a name one would give to a flamewalker."

"For the last time, I'm not a flamewalker."

"Yes, you are. You came from within the flames. How else would you explain it?"

"Fine, whatever. But I'm certain my name is Alderan."

Silence hung between them for a time before Jagger finally broke it. "What else do you remember?"

Alderan closed his eyes and focused his mind on the single thing he thought he knew: his name. At first, he found nothing but a deep pit of darkness, but then the edges of his memory began to brighten. Morphed into pictures.

He started describing it to Jagger. "A battlefield stretches as far as the eye can see. It reminds me of the one in my dream with the young woman." He thought about it for a moment. "I think it might be the same one."

"A battlefield?"

"Yes. There's a massive black dragon, too. Evil exudes from him like a disease."

"What's a dragon?"

"Generally speaking, a dragon is a terrifying beast with wings, claws, sharp teeth, and a long tail."

"Sounds like the beasts from our prophecies. Drezhn."

"Drezhn is the name for them in the ancient language. They are one and the same," Alderan said.

"Gods… they exist." Jagger groaned. "What else do you remember?"

"Blood and bodies lie strewn across the field. And there's a man. He stands with defiance against the dragon. He… he…"

Jagger prodded him. "He what?"

"He holds back… time."

Jagger scoffed. "That's an impossible feat."

"And yet… he did it." Alderan squeezed his eyes tight and focused on the man. "I know him. His name is Nardus. My father."

Memories flooded his mind. All the events that led up to that moment on the battlefield came back to him. Then, he remembered what came next.

"A small dragon attacked. Not me, but the young woman from my dream. She's my sister, Aria. I knew I had to save her no matter the cost. Then, I was there. Standing between her and a stream of dragon flames."

"You don't remember running over to her?"

"I didn't." Alderan opened his eyes. "I teleported. I've done it once before, too, but I'm not sure how."

"Mezhik," Jagger said.

"Yes, but it's more than that." The answer struck him. "Rakzar, a gnoll friend of mine, calls me an emotional wizard. Not as in a certain type of wizard but as in a wizard who can use mezhik when emotions run high."

Jagger smiled. "A second nature, so to speak."

"Right." The rest of the memory came to him. Fire exploded from his mind and burned him alive. Consumed him. He buried his face in Jagger's back and screamed.

Somehow, Jagger managed to tackle Alderan. She held her arm over his mouth. "You're going to get us killed," she whispered.

Alderan fought against the burning sensation. Knew it was only in his mind. Finally, it subsided. He tapped Jagger's arm, and she released him.

"I'm sorry." He wiped his eyes and stared up at Jagger. "The dragon flames hit me, and I felt them burning me alive again. I'm sorry."

Jagger glanced around. "It's okay."

"After the flames hit me, I remember lying on the ground and staring up at Aria, just like I am with you now. I also remember saying goodbye to the love of my life, Rayah." Alderan smiled as he thought of her. "She's a beautiful woman, and her wings are breathtaking."

Jagger frowned. "A human with wings?"

"She's a dryte." Alderan's smile faded. "My heart aches for both of them."

"Because they think you're dead?"

"Yes, but it's more than that. There's so much strife between them." Tears wet his cheeks again. "Between Aria and me, too. We've been at odds for some time."

"But you saved her life."

"I know, but we fought that war on opposite sides."

"I can't imagine how difficult it would be to fight against your own blood. I'm not sure I could ever oppose my father."

"Aria's more than just my sister. She's my twin. Until recently, we shared an unbreakable bond."

"What happened after you said goodbye?"

"I woke up in a dark cave. You know the rest better than I do."

Questions filled his mind. Bombarded him.

"There are so many things about what happened to me that I just don't understand. I wore an amulet that protects against dragon's fire, so how did I still get burned?"

"You're certain it ever worked?"

"Yes. Cinolth, the massive black dragon, spewed fire at me not long before that, and his flames didn't touch me."

The more Alderan thought about it, the more certain he became that he'd died on the battlefield.

Then how am I still alive?

He sat up and scratched his head. "How did I end up rising out of a firepit here in Reothadh?"

"Somehow, you're connected to Gwendor."

For several moments, Alderan couldn't make sense of any of it, but then the answer struck him. He reached up and pulled the front of his shirt down. The red mark from the necklace he'd taken from Wrik was no longer there. Instead, he had a scar.

"What is it?" Jagger said.

"I used to wear a necklace. Or rather I had one that embedded itself into my skin somehow. Wrik, a wizard friend of mine, said that the necklace came from a special friend of his."

What kind of friend had it been?

He released his shirt and peered over at Jagger. "You mentioned something about a man named Gwendor."

"Not a man but a bird."

"Oh, that's right. Gwendor was a bird."

Alderan's pulse began to race. Wrik's necklace held a long feather from a bird. A feather he'd never seen before.

"The feather… it brought me back to life."

"A feather?" Jagger scoffed. "That makes no sense."

"I remember hearing a legend as a boy about a bird known as the phoenix. It would live for a long time, and when it died it would rise again from the ashes."

Jagger gasped. "What you describe sounds just like Gwendor."

Could the legend be true? Is that what happened to him? Gwendor's feather brought him back to life?

"I think—"

Jagger moved. She put a finger to her lips and motioned for him to follow her. Eis kept watch as they crawled over to the ridge.

Far below sat a village. Alderan could tell because of a thick ring of torchlight, but the distance far exceeded his vision, especially given that it was the middle of the night.

"What do you see?" he said.

"My father. He's bound with rope and stands before the council and the entire village."

"You can see all that?"

"Yes." Jagger leapt to her feet. "Father!"

† † †

For a moment, the entire world halted as Jagger's gaze met Grimbold's. There were so many things she wanted to tell him. So much left unspoken between them.

I've returned for you, Father.

Grimbold's lips moved. It took a second for the sound to reach her ears. "Run!"

Elder Markum kicked Grimbold square in the chest. Grimbold staggered backward and disappeared into the depths of the pit.

"No!" Jagger lunged forward, but something held her back.

Images of hunters flashed in her mind.

Eis.

She brushed away tears of anger and turned to the flamewalker. "We're being hunted. One woman, one man. I can smell their ferzh. Or rather Eis can."

The two of them quickly mounted Eis.

Suddenly, one of the ferzh emerged from the shadows to the west. The woman riding the beast grinned. "Hello, Jagger. Thought ya'd get away, did ya?"

Jagger glared at Sasha. "Where's your lover?"

Another voice came from behind them to the east. "Right here."

Riptan.

Sasha and Riptan blocked them from going anywhere but down.

"There's no point running," Sasha said. She and her ferzh, Wortlos, inched forward. "We'll track you down no matter where you go in

Reothadh."

Jagger's fingers twisted into Eis's mane as she anticipated what would come next.

Thewt!

"Go," Jagger said to Eis through mindspeak. Eis plunged down the side of the mountain.

"You shot me, you fool!" Sasha said.

Riptan roared.

Jagger didn't look back.

† † †

The descent down the mountainside took far less time than the climb had, but Alderan and Jagger had failed to gain any distance from the ferocious beast that chased them. The forest provided them with just enough cover to avoid the barrage of darts but not enough to evade the beastly male.

"Who is he?" Alderan said.

Jagger growled. "His name is Riptan, and the ferzh he rides is Brecher. Riptan will never stop hunting us."

Alderan glanced back. Through the trees and brush he glimpsed Brecher again. The ferzh dwarfed Eis and put fear in his heart.

Ahead, moonlight shone on rocky terrain. Beyond that, a sea of ice. They would likely make it to the coast, but where would they go from there?

We'll be out in the open and trapped.

Alderan clutched Jagger's waist a bit tighter. "What's the plan once we reach the water?"

Jagger huffed. "How would I know?"

"I take it this wasn't part of the plan."

"Yes, flamewalker—" Jagger refused to call him by his name. "—my plan included being chased by a skilled hunter shooting poisonous darts at us with his zabatana until we ran out of land." She growled. "Admittedly, it's working perfectly."

Poisonous darts!

Alderan swallowed hard. "What was your plan before everything went wrong?"

Jagger glanced over her shoulder. "I didn't have one. Is that what you want to hear?"

It was exactly what he didn't want to hear. "How were we ever supposed to leave Reothadh?"

The forest thinned, then faded as they broke into the open. The large rocks forced Eis to slow. Riptan would have to slow down, too, but it would give him the advantage.

Thewt!

Eis staggered but kept moving forward over the rocks.

"Eis has been hit," Jagger confirmed. Alderan looked back and saw the yellow dart sticking out of Eis's hindquarter. He reached back and pulled it out.

Thewt!

Eis staggered again. Alderan latched on to Jagger just as Eis's hind legs collapsed beneath her.

Behind them, Riptan roared with laughter. "Give up, Jagger!"

"Never!"

Somehow, Eis found the strength to stand again. The coast lay just twenty yards ahead. They might make it that far, but what purpose would it serve?

"Even if we manage to disarm and subdue Riptan, won't others of your clan eventually come after us?"

Jagger nodded. "We must find a path that leads us beyond Reothadh."

"Across the sea?" No docks, piers, boats, ships, or any other unnatural elements could be seen anywhere along the coast.

We're doomed.

Eis carried them to the coast and collapsed by the water's edge. Alderan and Jagger turned and faced Riptan. The male dismounted Brecher just five yards away, zabatana in hand.

Riptan snarled, "I gave you the chance to come willingly. Now, you will face the clan, bound and shaved."

To the south, Alderan could just make out what looked like another island. It must've been at least fifteen miles away. No chance of swimming such a distance, even if there hadn't been ice floating in the water.

Eis managed to stand again. Alderan and Jagger stood to either side of her. Both reached out and clutched part of her mane. Eis growled at Riptan. Brecher growled right back and stalked forward.

"What now?" Jagger said.

The wind kicked up. Swirled around Alderan, Jagger, and Eis.

Jagger looked at Alderan with terror in her eyes. "What's happening?"

Riptan raised the zabatana to his lips and blew.

Thewt!

Alderan closed his eyes and pictured the distant island.

Riptan roared, but the sound faded into nothing.

His entire body tingled for just an instant, then faded. When he opened his eyes, Riptan no longer stood before him. Instead, a great stretch of water lay ahead.

Jagger grabbed him and crushed him in a hug. "I knew you'd save us."

It was then that he realized his rebirth had changed him. He no longer struggled to touch the source of his mezhik. It flowed within him. A river of life. He pulled away from Jagger and stared at his hands as he flexed them.

Perhaps I am no longer the emotional wizard.

CHAPTER TWENTY-ONE

Credan stood on the southern rampart and stared down at Atrum Moenia while he awaited Cinolth's arrival. He hated heights, and they hated him, too. The longer he stood there, the more nauseous he became. Before long, he'd be facing the regurgitated contents of his stomach. Given the circumstances of his unscheduled meeting with the overgrown reptile, perhaps a purge would serve him best.

With hands gripping the parapet, he leaned over its edge. The small town tossed about as though it were a boat anchored to a violent sea. He opened his mouth but then heard it.

Thump-thump. Whoosh! Thump-thump. Whoosh! Thump-thump. Whoosh!

He turned and watched Cinolth approach from the north. The big dragon closed the distance quickly and kicked up a flurry of dust and wind as he landed. Credan stumbled backward a step and almost toppled over the parapet before catching himself. The misstep left a gash across his right palm and blood on the black stone. Oddly enough, the pain crushed his nausea and stopped the world from spinning around him.

"Tell me you have good news." The words rumbled and smoked from Cinolth's lips.

"I've located Reubane, as requested."

"Don't misconstrue your role, Credan. You are nothing more than a servant. I command you to do my bidding. Failure will result in death."

Credan nearly choked on his own spit. "Yes... master."

"Explain why Reubane isn't here instead of you."

"I've run into a slight problem. As I said, he's been located. However, I am currently without a means to release him from his containment."

"And why is this my problem?"

"Understanding the nature of this task, I surmised enlisting Queen

Rosai's help in the matter would prove problematic."

"Make yourself clear before I grow bored of you and relieve you of your pathetic existence."

"I am in need of a wizard so that I can release Reubane."

Cinolth lowered his head to Credan's level. "You knew this when we first spoke."

"I... Well... Um..."

"Lie to me, and it will be the last thing you utter."

"Yes, I did, but I didn't realize it was a problem at the time. I thought I would enlist Wizard Wrik to assist me, but he's nowhere to be found."

"Breathe a word of this to Wizard Wrik, and I will snack on your limbs while you watch."

Credan's legs gave out, sending him to his knees. Pain raced through his legs. He winced and forced it from his thoughts. "Yes, master."

Cinolth closed his eyes for several moments before speaking again. "You will have your wizard within two days."

"I don't understand."

"Tens of thousands follow my command."

Yes, of course. His mind-controlled army.

"And how will I find this wizard?" Credan said.

"His name is Qotan, and you will not." Cinolth snorted smoke in Credan's face. "He will find you."

Credan dipped his head. "Very good, master."

Cinolth rose and spread his wings. "Do not fail me again."

Credan covered his face as Cinolth whipped the air with his wings and took to the sky. Once the dragon flew out of sight, Credan took a deep breath and sighed. As fierce as Lord Rosai could be at times, he never feared for his life the way he did in Cinolth's presence. In fact, the fear Cinolth conjured within him matched only that of the time he spent serving Fekᴇzhn dhä Räd a lifetime ago.

I owe you everything, Pravus. May the gods show you mercy.

He wrapped a kerchief around his injured hand and rose. The thought of Reubane running loose again struck almost as much fear within him as the thought of dying by Cinolth's hand.

Gods... what have I gotten myself into?

CHAPTER TWENTY-TWO

Twice during the night, Calen, Niesha, and Eshtak narrowly escaped discovery as they explored the air shafts of the stronghold further. The zhebəllin posted two or three guards at the entrance of every room and worked through the night building, filling, and suspending cages from the ceilings with anchors and rope. The cages were exactly like the one he escaped from in the tunnels beneath the Daltura Hills. The only difference was the zhebəllin didn't dig pits beneath these ones and fill them with spikes.

As of the last count, cages filled seven rooms. Calen recognized many of those who were caged as people sympathetic to Berggren or simply opposed to Mortis, but so far none of the cages held Berggren. After witnessing what Mortis had done to Hardin, his hope of finding Berggren still alive all but dried up. He knew Niesha and Eshtak felt the same way even though neither of them made mention of it. The fire that once lit Niesha's eyes had become little more than a spark.

The three of them lay on their stomachs in one of the shafts, facing each other. Calen reached forward and lay his hand over Niesha's. He said nothing and didn't need to. Her eyes swelled with tears. She nodded and then turned around in the shaft. She moved ahead, and he and Eshtak followed. With dozens of other rooms left to explore, a thread of hope remained.

Ɂätūr, keep the big man alive.

Light filtered into the shaft through the grating ahead. As far as Calen could remember, this room wasn't on his map. Niesha halted, and Calen crawled up next to her. It took a moment for Calen's eyes to adjust to the bright light. Berggren lay on a slab of rock with his arms and legs spread wide. Thick leather straps anchored his ankles, wrists, neck, and forehead to the slab. Crusted blood covered the side of his head and face where he was struck with the pickaxe handle the previous night. Although his eyes remained closed, his chest continually rose and fell.

Thank you for keeping him alive, Ɂäʈūr.

Three zhebəllin stood next to an open iron door that led into a dark corridor. Mortis paced with a bloody dagger in his hand, his face twisted with rage. "How long does it take to fetch a bucket of water?" None of the zhebəllin responded. Mortis turned to the zhebəllin, cleared his throat, and then said something in a language Calen didn't understand. Two of the zhebəllin nodded and exited the room.

"He speaks zhebəllin," Niesha whispered.

Calen nodded but kept his gaze focused on Mortis. "Yeah, I got that."

Given the rarity of dealings with zhebəllin in any capacity, why would a man like Mortis know their language? Calen couldn't make sense of it.

A few minutes later, a different zhebəllin entered the room carrying a large wooden bucket. Water sloshed over its edges and splattered on the floor. He set the bucket down next to the slab and then exited the room. Mortis barked something at the remaining zhebəllin. The zhebəllin nodded and exited the room as well, pulling the door shut behind him.

Mortis walked over to the slab and smacked Berggren's face, but Berggren didn't stir. "Not so tough now, are you?" He inserted the point of his dagger underneath Berggren's shirt and drew it down from Berggren's neck to his belly, slicing the shirt open. Then, he pulled the shirt open, exposing Berggren's torso.

"By the gods!" Mortis stepped back, eyes wide. His dagger fell to the ground.

Niesha gasped and quickly covered her mouth, but the damage had been dealt. Mortis's gaze shot straight to the air shaft as he bent down and fumbled for his dagger. "Reveal yourself—" His fingers grasped the dagger. He stood back up and held it to Berggren's throat. "—or he dies."

Niesha reached for the grate and Calen grabbed her hand. She glared at him, and he shook his head at her. After pointing at himself and motioning toward the grate, he checked his pocket to make sure he still had the dagger they'd found last night. His fingers found its hilt, and he quietly sighed. Moving past Niesha, he pushed the grate open. It clattered to the floor.

Mortis sneered and kept the blade at Berggren's throat. "Knew I'd find you little rats if I waited long enough."

Calen slid out of the shaft and dropped to the floor. His hands wouldn't stop shaking, so he stuffed them in his pockets. "Harm Berggren, and it'll be the last thing you do." His voice squeaked.

That was pathetic, Calen.

"I call your bluff." Mortis's blade slid across Berggren's throat an inch, leaving a small red line in its wake. A few drops of blood trickled from the wound. "Tell the girl and that thing to come out of the shaft, or I'll finish the job."

All the horrific events from the last few months swirled inside Calen's mind, stirring up a torrent of emotions. He missed his aunt and Master Savric more than words could express, and he'd grown quite fond of Berggren and Niesha over the last few days. The last thing he wanted was for any harm to come to them or Eshtak.

Now that he knew the identity of the man he'd met in Daltura weeks ago, it changed nothing. The day he stood up to the zhebəllin and freed the children of Daltura, something had changed within him. Sure, he still looked like the fat kid he'd always been, but he no longer repulsed himself. Instead, he'd come to realize a hero isn't defined by what they look like but by how they act in the face of danger. He strained to keep his bladder in check, but fear wasn't something to be ashamed of, either. It would keep him alert.

Niesha and Eshtak dropped to the floor next to him.

"Bad man zhebəllin."

Calen didn't understand what Eshtak meant, but then the stank of urine burned his nostrils. He didn't need to look to know it'd been Niesha who peed her trousers, but it made him smile. Not because he found it funny but because he'd once been her. Her fear filled him with bravery and courage. After all, he must be brave for his new little sister. He smiled bigger as he reached over and squeezed her hand. Eshtak grabbed his other hand.

Mortis stepped around the slab. His gaze pierced Calen's forehead. "Find something funny?"

Berggren groaned. Mortis ignored him and stalked closer to Calen, Niesha, and Eshtak.

Ɂäṭūr, give me strength.

"You make me feel ten times smarter," Calen said.

Mortis's scowl deepened. "I have no idea what that's supposed to mean, but I look forward to spilling your blood."

Calen swallowed hard, then released Niesha's and Eshtak's hands. He peered down at Niesha. "I've got this. You and Eshtak free the big man." She nodded, then glared at Mortis.

Every part of Calen wanted to cry out as he drew his dagger, but the last thing he wanted to do was attract the attention of any zheballin posted outside the door. Instead, he growled and charged toward Mortis.

Mortis snarled and slashed at Calen as the two of them collided. Mortis's blade sliced right through Calen's shirt and nicked his forearm. The cut stung and drew blood, but Calen held fast to his dagger.

As they circled, Calen noticed his blade dripped with black blood. Mortis's shirt blossomed black, but he didn't seem to notice. Instead, Mortis jabbed at Calen several times. Calen blocked the attacks as best he could, but the last jab found real estate just below his bellybutton and plunged deep.

Calen exhaled and bit his tongue as Mortis's blade retracted. He ignored the pain and swiped down with his dagger. The blade found flesh of its own. Ripped through it like butter.

Mortis howled, and his dagger fell to the ground. Black blood spurted from his wounded hand.

Calen doubled over and clutched his stomach. A sticky wetness covered his fingers. He refused to look at himself. Feared it would drain his strength and send him into darkness.

Instead, he focused on Mortis's bloody hand. Three missing fingers. The tip of his thumb lobbed off.

Mortis groaned. His skin bubbled. Limbs contorted. Face distorted. Skin pulled away from his lips.

Calen couldn't look away as the man he knew to be Mortis morphed into a gangly beast.

A zheballin.

Calen gasped. Staggered backward. Right into the slab where Berggren lay.

Dazed, he could do nothing as a large hand reached out and snatched his dagger away.

He slid to the floor, the pain overwhelming. Nothing had ever burned so bad.

The thing that had once been Mortis snarled. Retreated, but not fast enough.

Calen's dagger found the beast's shoulder. Drove the beast back into the wall. But none of it was Calen's doing.

Berggren towered over the beast. Arm cocked back. Ready to administer the final blow.

"Wait," Mortis or the beast gurgled.

Berggren's arm lowered a few inches. "For what?"

"Keep me alive. You survive." The beast looked to be in agony, its face twisted.

"You're worth nothing," Berggren growled.

"King has value."

Berggren twisted the blade in the beast's shoulder. "Expect me to believe you?"

The beast groaned and pointed to itself. "Kaja, king of zhebəllin."

"Liar." Berggren raised his fist again, poised to strike.

"Wait." Calen pulled himself to his feet with the assistance of Niesha and Eshtak and hobbled over to Berggren. "Think about what he's saying."

"Nothing to think about," Berggren barked.

"Don't be foolish, big man," Niesha said. "You always act before thinking."

Berggren gruffed. "Explain it then."

Calen took a deep breath and regretted it as pain shot through his abdomen like lightning. He doubled over and took several shallow breaths before he could speak again. Finally, he said, "It explains why he can speak their language and how he supposedly negotiated with them. It also explains how they were able to breech the stronghold so quickly after we fortified it."

Niesha nodded. "He's right, big man. Explains everything."

Berggren sighed. "Suppose it does, but it don't explain how he changed from a human to a zhebəllin."

"Hold on." Niesha bent down and picked up one of Mortis's fingers. She held it up so Calen and Berggren could see it. "Maybe this does."

It took a moment for Calen to identify the ring still pushed onto the severed human finger because of it being covered in black blood. A quick glance at the other severed fingers brought further understanding. The two without a ring and the thumb tip had all transformed into zhebəllin fingers.

And she's only six?

Calen took the human finger from Niesha and stared at it. "A mezhik ring…" He pulled the ring off, and the finger morphed in his hand. He jerked his hand back and let the zhebəllin finger fall to the ground.

Berggren turned and eyed Kaja. "Get us to the surface, and you'll live to see the next sunrise."

Kaja grinned, displaying a mouthful of wickedly sharp teeth. "Deal."

Calen didn't trust the zhebəllin king to keep his word, but what choice did they have? They were trapped in the room, and Berggren would never fit into the air shaft. Plus, he'd never be able to crawl around with a hole in his gut, either. He closed his eyes and did the one thing he knew would help: he prayed.

Niesha took his hand. "Pray for me, too."

"Eshtak too."

Calen swallowed back tears and nodded.

Ɂäṭūr, guide us, heal us, and keep us safe.

CHAPTER TWENTY-THREE

Morcinda sat on the temple seat, her mind still unable to rectify the events surrounding Queen Lanara and her death ten years earlier. She'd been there when it'd happened. Saw Lanara plunge over the castle wall. Witnessed her broken body lying on the stone pathway in a pool of blood. It took the better part of a year for her to move beyond the tragedy. She knew the woman for decades and considered her a friend. Few ever attained such an honor in her life, and no one had since her death.

But she's not dead.

She unsheathed her ivory-handled dagger and stared at it. Lanara had given it to her just a week before Lanara died. Said it would keep her safe on the high seas.

She knew then.

Lanara walked into the temple. "Thought I'd find you in here."

"Collecting my thoughts."

"I know you far better than that, Morcinda. You're angry with me."

Morcinda stared at the woman as she approached the seat. "Would you blame me if I was?"

"Never. You have every right to be."

"I mourned for you for months."

"And I mourned for you, too."

"No! You don't get to say that. *You* left *me*, Lanara, not the other way around."

"I had no choice."

"Save your lies. We all have a choice in everything we do."

Lanara knelt in front of the seat. "You know that's not fair. Yes, you lost a friend that day, but I lost *everything*. Do you know what it's like to hide from yourself for so long that you forget who you once were? I buried Lanara that day, same as you."

"For what?"

"To save the kingdom. My family."

"Save them? Your death nearly tore them apart."

"Rictar and Zelanora knew nothing of our plan, and it had to be that way."

"What happened? What drove you to such a decision?"

"You know the decree Pius made about those who possessed mezhik."

"Yes, and I never understood why he would make such an asinine decision given his knowledge of who you were."

"Therein lies the first issue." Lanara looked at her own hands. "Pius knew nothing of my gift when he made the decision, and even if he had, he would've had no choice but to make it anyway. The magistrates, lords, and peasants of the Three Kingdoms feared those like me and implored Pius to protect them. I assure you that he would've made the decree no matter the circumstance, but his advisers, council, and lords also made it clear that they would seek to remove him from power if he refused."

"But all of that happened long before you faked your own death."

"Yes, and I never would've needed to do so if Pius hadn't caught me using mezhik one night."

"Are you saying that he forced you into this?" The thought enraged Morcinda.

"Yes." Tears wet Lanara's cheeks. "Once he found out my secret, he could hardly look me in the eye anymore. I had betrayed his trust by keeping the truth about my family history from him. I lay no blame on his shoulders for what he felt necessary to do once he found out."

"I knew your secret."

"Yes, but you're far more perceptive than most people. Plus, you were my truest of friends."

"Then why didn't you continue living the way you had all the years before? And why did you keep all this from me?"

"Pius said it was impossible to continue as though nothing had changed. I knew he was right, but I begged him to reconsider anyway for the sake of our children. Mentioning them drove him to rage. He threatened to expose me if I didn't figure out a way to disappear for good. Once I'd come up with a plan to fake my own death, he insisted that no one could ever know the truth but him. As hard as it was to accept, I finally agreed. To be certain I would never go back on my word, he forced me to seal my promise with blood. That seal prevented me from returning or telling anyone the truth. His death must've broken it."

Zelanora stepped out of the shadows, her face twisted with agony. "You never loved me, did you?"

"With every breath and every beat of my heart." Lanara stood and tried to embrace Zelanora, but Zelanora pushed her away.

"Stay away from me, you liar!"

"Every word is true, my love. I did what was necessary to protect you and Rictar."

"Protect us?" Zelanora thrust her arms in the air. "You abandoned us!"

"Never! If I hadn't faked my own death, the people would've learned the truth. Once they knew, they would've killed you both for fear of either of you possessing mezhik."

Zelanora crumbled to the ground and wept. Lanara knelt next to Zelanora and embraced her. Morcinda felt sick for Lanara and the girl. Pius had ruined both their lives and escaped without punishment. Rictar died never knowing the truth.

Savric entered the temple with a bowl in hand. He stopped short of the seat and cocked his head. After swallowing a bite of food, he said, "What have you done, Morcinda?"

✝ ✝ ✝

Savric stormed out of the temple and returned to the small room Lanara had provided for him to sleep in. Rage consumed him, an emotion he rarely experienced or expressed, but the situation warranted it. His firsthand experience dealing with King Zaridus proved the man held a great deal of disdain for those who possessed mezhik. However, he had never contemplated that King Zaridus would have forced his own wife to abandon her life and deceive the kingdom using the very thing he loathed. Were the wretched man still alive, he would give him far more than a piece of his mind.

Traitorous snake.

He sat down at the table in the corner of the room and retrieved the book from within his robes. The fountain pen stabbed the first page, leaving a small pool of ink in its wake. As the ink faded, he took a deep breath and focused on what he intended to share with Nardus.

With his rage subsided, he began writing: *"Queen Lanara lives, her death an illusion. Lanara will be a great asset in defeating Cinolth and his army if she can be persuaded to join our cause. I have yet to discuss the matter with her, however I am certain she will be willing to do the right thing no matter the cost. If I am correct in this assumption, I believe the people of the Ancient Realm will rally around her and Princess Zelanora. No matter the answer, Morcinda and I will set sail for the Ancient Realm in a few days. Our goal will be to recapture and reclaim the King's Palace in Vallah. With Lanara's help, we can veil our progress and remain undetected. Pray for our success and the help of Lanara. -Savric"*

Satisfied with the message, Savric tapped the page with the fountain pen and watched the words fade away. Not a few days before, Zelanora demanded they return to the Ancient Realm, but would she still want to do so now that she knew the truth of her mother and the heart of her people?

Savric raised his head.

Ƨäţūr, make it so.

CHAPTER TWENTY-FOUR

Even though he wore an invisibility cloak and the ring that transformed him into a saurian, Rakzar kept to the shadows as he traversed the dank, narrow roads of Dyserth. Few people were out at such a late hour, but it would only take one person to recognize any of them and alert the authorities or one of Cinolth's mind-controlled minions.

A notice hung from almost every door to be on the lookout for persons of interest. Likenesses of Nardus, Theyn, Rayah, Zerenity, and Rldan accompanied them. For whatever reason, he and Urza had been excluded. Along with the ring and the cloak, they could use the oversight to their advantage. Doing so would leave just two of them vulnerable. Still a risk, but it was their only option.

Rakzar tore down one of the notices and stuffed it into his pocket. Then, he entered a dark alley and removed the cloak. Once he pulled the ring off his finger, he shed his lizard skin and growled. It would be the last time he'd ever wear the damned thing.

Ahead, a scrawny but tall man rounded the corner and entered the alley. He stumbled forward, either drunk, blind, or both. A moment later, Rakzar had the answer. The man reeked of ale.

The man leaned against one of the walls and unfastened his trousers. Urine splashed against the wall, and its odor drifted down the alley.

Rakzar shifted his weight.

The man froze once he realized he wasn't alone. He turned and peered into the darkness while he fumbled with his trousers. "Someone there?"

"Your worst nightmare."

Rakzar was on top of the man before the man had a chance to move. He covered the man's mouth with his hand. "Alert anyone, and it'll be the last thing you ever do, understood?"

The man, wide eyed, nodded wildly. Rakzar removed his hand, and the man whimpered.

"The name's Dru, and I'm not a drinking man."

Rakzar scoffed. "And I'm no beast."

Dru shook his head. "No, really. Downed my first drinks in years tonight."

"Don't care." He stood and pulled Dru to his feet. "Move on, and forget you ever saw me."

"But you're one of them, right?" Dru said.

"One of who?"

"You serve the…" He whispered, "The drezhn."

"Why would—" Rakzar caught himself. "Yes, I do."

"I saw something earlier." Dru looked around cautiously. "I know where you can find the ones listed on the notice."

Rakzar's pulse quickened. "Who have you told this to?"

"N-n-no one. Took to the drink to work up my courage." Dru sighed. "I need the coin after this past winter. Lost almost everything, including my wife of forty years."

Rakzar grabbed the man's arm. "Show me, and I'll make sure you get what's coming to you."

The man trembled. "Look, I uh, I…" He raked his head with his fingers. "You're right. I should just move on."

"No longer an option." He pushed the man out of the alley and into the road. "Lead the way."

† † †

Urza stood in the shadows and watched Rakzar approach the barn, but he didn't come alone. For some reason, a drunkard led the way. She smelled him clear across the field.

Click! Click!

Cold steel slid into her open palms. She twirled the blades with anticipation.

"Stand down, Urza." Nardus stood next to her.

She hadn't heard him approach, and it disturbed her. But what disturbed her more was the fact that she hadn't smelled him, either. She took inventory of herself.

I must be slipping.

"You're not slipping," Nardus said. "I'm downwind from you, and I teleported here."

"Fine, but why are you in my head, wizard?"

"No need to read your thoughts when your actions speak volumes."

She sheathed her blades. "I see."

"Relax. You'd know if I were in your head."

She turned and faced Nardus. "Would I?"

Nardus smiled. "I'll show you sometime, but right now we need to find out who the man with Rakzar is."

"Agreed." She growled. "Whoever he is, it doesn't bode well for him."

Zerenity appeared in a whirlwind. "You called for me?"

Nardus pointed toward Rakzar and the man. "We need to know if they're alone."

"I'll scout the area," Urza said.

Nardus shook his head. "That won't be necessary."

† † †

Zerenity and Nardus waited outside the barn while Rakzar and Urza escorted the skinny man named Dru into the barn cellar. Afterward, she knelt, placed her palms against the dry soil, and closed her eyes. She said a brief prayer and then called upon her mezhik and poured it into the ground.

A few minutes later, nature responded. Zerenity's eyes shot open, and she peered up at Nardus. "Three lifeforms approach from the same direction. About a half mile out."

Nardus grimaced. "Either Dru is a liar, or those who approach overheard his conversation with Rakzar."

Zerenity stood and peered into the darkness. "What would you like me to do?"

"Depends on them. No bloodshed, if possible."

"Agreed." Zerenity smiled. "I have an idea."

Nardus chuckled. "I'm sure you do."

She reached out with her mind. *"Rayah."*

"I'm here," Rayah said.

"We need your assistance."

"Be there in a minute."

Once Rayah arrived outside the barn, Zerenity filled her and Nardus in on the plan.

Rayah wasted no time and dove straight into the ground.

Nardus smiled. "You're a wise woman, Zerenity."

Her cheeks warmed. "Long ago, that might've been true. Now, I simply look for ways to ease the pain of others. She's a strong girl, and taking her mind off Alderan for a spell will do her good."

† † †

Rayah flew beneath the ground, the feel of the soil something she hadn't realized she missed until that moment. The last time she'd done so, it'd cost Alderan his life. Had it been for any other reason than saving the others, she wouldn't be doing it now.

I couldn't save you, but I won't fail your father.

It didn't take long for her to locate the three people. One woman and two men. All humans. Each wielded a weapon. None would have a chance against her.

Rayah started with the man at the back of the group. She followed him for several steps before reaching up and pulling him down into the ground. The plan was to bury them up to their necks, and she had every intention to do so, but rage got the best of her. The man wound up at least seven feet below ground. Once she secured the other two, she'd pull him back up.

The other two hadn't noticed their companion missing yet, but she'd only have the element of surprise one more time. She went for the other man and pulled him down to his waist before the woman with him reacted.

† † †

Lightning flashed in the distance, lighting up the cloudless, moonless night. Nardus swore. In an instant, he moved from the barn to the field and conjured a light shield around himself just before the sorceress attacked with another bolt of lightning. His shield held, but the woman's mezhik was strong enough to push him back a good foot.

Lightning crackled at the woman's fingertips. "Identify yourself, wizard."

"Me?" Nardus glared at the woman. "You first."

Vines shot up from the ground and ensnared the woman's legs. The lightning in her hands morphed into fire. She reached down and grabbed the vines, turning them to ash in an instant. Her face twisted with rage, highlighted by the massive ball of lightning that grew between her palms.

"Enough!" Zerenity shouted, arriving behind the woman in a massive whirlwind.

The woman turned and thrust her hands toward Zerenity, but the massive ball of lightning didn't shoot from her hands. Instead, it fizzled. She reached for the ꙅäbräꙅär now around her neck, but more vines shot up from the ground and constrained her. The woman roared.

Nardus reached out to Rayah with his mind. *"Are you okay?"* She didn't answer, but he felt her presence. He knelt and placed his hands on the ground. The soil began vibrating as he poured his mezhik into it. Two fissures formed in the ground, opened wide like giant golem mouths, then spat up three bodies. Rayah and two men.

The two men coughed up dirt before sitting up. Thanks to Zerenity, vines made quick work binding their hands and feet.

Rayah, her clothes and hair scorched black, lay still. Nardus crawled over to her and pulled her into his lap. He smoothed back her blackened hair, and his fingers met a sticky gash on the back of her skull. Using mezhik, he stitched the wound back together and healed it. The effort left him spent of energy.

Rayah's eyelids fluttered then opened. She groaned as she reached up and probed the back of her head. "Why does my head feel like it's been split open?" Her nose wrinkled. "And what's burning?"

"You were struck by lightning." Nardus peered up at the woman bound with vines. "Turns out we've captured a sorceress."

"I could've killed her, but I didn't," the woman said.

Nardus pushed Rayah off his lap and stood. "Had I not been here, she and your two friends would've died."

The woman snarled. *"She* attacked *us."*

Zerenity stood next to Nardus. "Do you deny approaching us with drawn weapons?"

"Would you have done it a different way?" one of the men asked.

"Depends on the intent." Nardus rubbed his left bicep. "You here to collect a reward?"

"Quite the opposite," the woman said. "We came to stop the gnoll."

"Rakzar." Rayah stood and stretched her wings. "His name is Rakzar, and he's with us."

The woman frowned. "You employ a gnoll? Are you unaware of their evil nature? It will turn on you the moment it has a chance."

"He, not it," Nardus said. "And we do not employ him. He is a friend and has proven his loyalty on numerous occasions. Now, tell us who you are."

The woman straightened. "I am Lilith Lightborn, daughter and heir to King Rikard of the Lost Realm."

Zerenity gasped. "The Lost Realm?" She glanced up at Nardus. "Is it possible?"

Nardus recalled reading about the so-called Lost Realm when he was just a boy. Lore had it that the realm once flourished, but then the king at the time fell violently ill and died the next day. The queen, a powerful mage, became so overwhelmed with grief that her mezhik spilled over the entire realm, causing it to vanish.

He shrugged. "I've lived long enough to know anything is possible."

Lilith held up her arms. "Unbind me, and I will prove it to you."

"If what you say is true, why have you traveled all this way?" Zerenity said.

"Until recently, our realm stood alone in the world. Sailing away from it would bring you right back to the other side. Then, a few months ago, everything changed. Vessels would leave port and no longer appear on the other side of the realm. Eventually, we sent expedition teams out. My vessel was one of them. Suffice it to say I've traveled here to fulfill prophecy."

Nardus touched Lilith's bindings and they turned to ash and fell away. "What is your proof?"

Lilith reached into her shirt and pulled out a silver necklace with a triangular-shaped, vibrant yellow pendant. Inside the pendant hung a six-sided white star with a sapphire center. "Do you recognize it?"

Nardus's pulse quickened. "The triad."

Rayah's eyes widened as she stepped closer. "What does it do?"

Lilith smiled. "It amplifies mezhik." She released the necklace and then removed the ƨäbräƨär from her neck. The collar turned to dust. "Now, who are you?"

"My name is Nardus Remison, but I was once known as Cyrus Nithik. I am a mage and the last of *Ūrdär Dhef 2äfn Dhä*."

Lilith's eyes widened. "The Order of the Seven? If that's true, how are you still alive?"

Zerenity's eyes narrowed. "If you're truly from the Lost Realm, how would you know anything about the order?"

"A crystal shard." She said it as though it warranted no additional explanation.

"And this shard does what exactly?" Rayah said.

"It allows us to view the other realms." She frowned. "Or rather it allows Clawthorne, the last of our realm's drezhn, to view and record significant events in the other realms. She has lived millennia and is the only one who can interpret the shard. It is the way we know your history... and your future."

Zerenity cocked her head, her eyebrows raised. "You know the future?"

"Yes, and no. It's more prophecy than anything else."

"I believe you," Nardus said, "so why have you come here?"

"To help you survive and win a war."

Nardus rubbed his left bicep. "It sounds like you already knew me, so why did you attack us?"

"Clawthorne provided me with a location and a vague description of you, so I had to be certain."

Zerenity scoffed. "Are you saying you came all this way to help us fight a dragon?"

"No." Lilith's eyes met Nardus's as she removed her necklace. "I came to give you this." She took Nardus's hand and placed the necklace in it.

A surge of energy filled Nardus. Replenished him. Brought clarity to his mind.

Nardus stared at the triad. "I don't understand."

"When the time comes, you will."

After a time, he looked into her eyes. "Without this, you'll be... ordinary."

"If a sorceress is ordinary, then I guess that is true. However, you will be extraordinary." Lilith smiled. "Clawthorne told me that the fates of our realms are intertwined. Both will either be saved or destroyed." Her smile faded. "Besides, what good will the triad do me if I am dead?"

Nardus put the necklace on and tucked it inside his shirt. "One day, I will return this to you."

"Of that, I have no doubt." She turned to Zerenity. "Please unbind my men, and we will be off." Zerenity obliged.

Nardus scowled at Lilith. "I thought you said you came here to help, so why are you leaving?"

"I did, and I have. The triad is the only help I can offer you. My path and fate lies elsewhere."

"Fine, but I still have one question," Nardus said.

Lilith peered at him with anticipation. "Yes?"

"How long have you been here in Dyserth?"

"A few weeks." She frowned. "Why?"

"We just lost a war. Had you found me sooner, we might've won."

"Had I found you any earlier, things would not have been as they must be." Lilith crossed her arms. "And never forget that you lost a battle, not a war. There is a difference." She nodded with satisfaction, then turned to her men. "We must return to our vessel. The journey ahead is long, and I am quite tired."

Nardus eyed Zerenity. "We have a long journey ahead as well."

"Indeed."

Nardus, Zerenity, and Rayah parted ways with Lilith and her men and headed for the barn cellar.

Inside, Urza knelt over Dru in the far corner with a blade to his throat. "Savor your next breath. It will be your last."

"Back off, Urza." Nardus walked over to them.

Urza growled. "He deserves to die."

Nardus touched Urza's shoulder. "Our mission is to help innocent people, not kill them."

"Innocent?" She eased up. "He would turn us in for a few coins."

"Then why did he seek encouragement from a glass of ale to do so?"

"How would I know?" Urza stood.

"Because he didn't want to do it." Nardus retrieved three silver coins from his coin purse and tossed them at Dru. "Consider that payment for your discretion."

Dru scooped up the coins and scrambled to his feet. "Thank you, sir. You are far too generous."

Nardus stared hard at the man. "Leave us two of your horses, and tell no one we were here."

Dru swallowed hard. "Two is all I've got. I won't be able to work the farm without at least one of them."

Nardus sighed and handed Dru another silver coin. "This will get you a new horse. Now, leave us."

Dru bowed. "Never saw a thing. Swear it on my life." He bolted out of the cellar.

"Gather around," Nardus said. "We've nearly reached the point where we must split up."

The eight of them, Bakkan included, gathered in a haphazard circle. Nardus eyed each of the others, all warriors he now considered friends. As tough as the last few months had been on them all, he knew it would be far tougher going forward.

Lilith had been right, though. They'd lost a battle, not the war. With Ӡätūr's help and the power of the triad, they might still have a chance. However, he needed to know which of them were willing to risk their lives and fight on.

Only one way to find out.

He stared at Ridan. Fierce warrior and attitude without end in a small package. "I know you've been away from home far longer than you planned, and you lost someone close to you, so I'd understand if you—"

"We're right where we want to be—" Ridan stroked Bakkan's head. "—so don't even think about trying to send us packing. I won't allow Normak to have died for nothing."

Nardus nodded at the dwarf then turned to the two gnolls. "Rakzar? Urza?"

"You're the father of the White Knight," Rakzar said. "Because of that, I'll go wherever you need me to go."

Click! Click!

Urza twirled her blades in her hands. "Someone has to keep Rakzar alive."

"Good." Nardus turned to Zerenity. "And you?"

Zerenity wiped a tear from her eye. "I'll do everything in my power to find a way to save Aria from Cinolth and herself."

Rayah flew over to Nardus and wrapped her arms around his neck. "Don't you dare ask me if I'm still willing to fight."

Nardus squeezed Rayah and then set her down. "Not a chance."

"Are you not going to ask me?" Theyn grinned when he looked at her.

Nardus chuckled. "I'll be the first to admit you're better off at sea."

"Once, that was true." She stood on her tippytoes and kissed Nardus's cheek. "Unto death, I go where you go."

"Then it's settled." Nardus looked to Rayah then Ridan. "Once we make it through Oriens Pass, the two of you will travel north and retrieve *Hemär Dhef Əllít* from deep within the Oblivio Mountains. With it in our possession, we will be prepared to destroy Cinolth's heart once we find a way to defeat him. The rest of us will head back to the battlefield south of Elatos."

"And where will we find you once we've retrieved the hammer?" Rayah said.

"Hopefully in the last place anyone will look for us," Nardus said. "The King's Palace in Vallah. It lies in ruin."

Ridan slammed the butt-end of her spear into the ground. "We will not fail."

Ɛätūr, I pray her words hold true.

Outside, Nardus set his sights on the Sol Deus Mountains to the west. On horseback it would take a few days to reach the other side. Thankfully, they had enough supplies from Nasduron to last a few weeks, so there was no need to return to Dyserth. He and Zerenity mounted the two horses and Theyn shifted into her cat form. Then, the eight of them headed out.

Ɛätūr, keep us safe.

CHAPTER TWENTY-FIVE

Aria stood outside the castle gates with Credan and Wizard Wrik, awaiting the arrival of the sorceress named Cydna. Wrik had told her very little about the woman other than she could retrieve memories.

Although Aria held Wizard Wrik in high esteem, she couldn't help but feel a rift had formed between the two of them. In the past, he'd always been happy to see her, but the last time they spoke he hardly looked her in the eye. Today, he hadn't said a single word to her. Perhaps her keeping him collared left him bitter, but she must exercise caution. If for some reason Wrik was behind the attack that killed Alderan, she needed him close. However, she'd remove the collar if Cydna cleared him of wrongdoing.

The sound of pounding hooves reached the castle long before the gray carriage came into view. Once it pulled up to the gates, a young woman emerged. Chocolate skin, piercing yellow eyes, ruby lips, and silver hair that waterfalled over slender shoulders. She wore white robes beneath a royal purple cloak.

Wizard Wrik stepped forward and greeted her with a kiss on the top of her outstretched hand. "Mistress Cydna, it has been far too long."

Mistress is about right.

"My beloved Wrik. It's been seven years, six months, fourteen days, and—" Cydna looked toward the sky. "—eleven hours, but who's counting?"

Wizard Wrik chuckled as he led Cydna over to Aria. "My queen, I present to you Mistress Cydna."

Cydna curtsied. "The honor is mine, Queen Rosai."

"I'm certain it is." Aria turned and headed through the gates. "Follow me, I've little time to waste."

Once inside, Aria turned back. "Credan and Wizard Wrik, you will wait for us in the throne room." She swore some of the muscles in Wizard Wrik's face twitched but couldn't be certain. Perhaps she'd struck a nerve.

Good.

Aria swept her arm toward an offshoot corridor. "This way, Cydna."

She and the young woman traveled deep into the interior of the castle, far below ground. Once they reached a room with a black iron door, she led Cydna inside.

The stench hit her. Drove bile up into her throat. She choked it back down but knew it would surface again if they spent much time in the room. Cydna said nothing, nor did the rank odor seem to faze her.

She's not with child.

Aria refocused on the ten-foot-square cage that sat in the center of the room. More specifically, the gnoll who lay atop a bed of straw within it. His back to them, he feigned sleep, but Aria knew better. She'd been informed of his hesitance to interact with anyone.

"On your feet, Durqel." She barely choked the words out.

The gangly beast rolled over. His mismatched eyes met hers, and he sat up. "My queen." He stood, stumbled forward, and fell on his knees. If possible, the gash in his neck looked far worse than it had four days earlier.

You won't suffer much longer.

Aria turned and addressed Cydna. "This beast holds the key to my brother's death within his pathetic mind. Retrieve it for me, and you'll be rewarded."

"As you wish." Cydna eyed the cage. "In order to fulfill your request, I'll need full access to the subject."

"Who's the subject?" Durqel said.

"You are." Aria called in one of the guards and had him unlock the cage. Cydna stepped inside, and Aria closed the door behind her. "Make it quick."

Cydna knelt and touched Durqel's neck. The beast howled but didn't shrink away from her.

Aria grabbed hold of the cage bars. "You're not here to heal the beast, Cydna. Do what I've asked of you, or I'll find another to replace you."

Cydna glanced up at Aria, her face twisted into a scowl. "If I simply do as you ask, he will die before I have the chance to retrieve any information, let alone specific memories. Healing him is necessary."

"Fine, but only go as far as necessary." Aria retreated to a stone bench against the far wall and sat down. Her head quaked.

Once Cydna finished partially healing Durqel's wound, she had him lie back down on the straw bed. She placed her hands over his temples and closed her eyes. "What are we looking for?"

Aria leaned back against the wall. "Durqel witnessed a dragon turn into a person but can't seem to remember what the person looked like other than that they were tall. Tell me who they are or at least what they look like."

An hour later, Cydna opened her eyes. "I've found your woman."

Aria's heart stuttered. "A woman?"

"Yes, but I'm uncertain as to her actual features."

Aria stood and walked over to the cage. "Explain what that means."

"I'm certain it was an older woman, but she had the sickness."

The sickness?

Understanding rocked Aria. She grabbed onto the bars for support, her legs unsteady. "Are you sure of this?"

"Grey skin, black veins, and black eyes." She looked up at Aria. "What else could it be?"

Cinolth betrayed me.

† † †

Wrik sat on the first step leading up to the throne. Credan paced. Had there been carpet, Credan would've worn a hole through it. The two of them hadn't spoken since arriving in the throne room, and it had suited Wrik just fine, but now Credan had worked up enough energy to give him cause for concern.

Finally, Wrik said, "Why do you pace as though your life depends on what Cydna finds?"

Credan threw his arms up and continued to pace. "How does it not? If the sorceress fails to retrieve any information, I fear Queen Rosai will br—" Credan stopped and shook his head. "Never mind."

"Finish your thought, Credan." Wrik stood. Towered over the little man. "Queen Rosai will what?"

Credan waved his hand. "It's nothing. My concerns lie elsewhere, not with the queen."

"You're lying." Wrik grabbed the front of Credan's shirt. "What are you not telling me?"

Aria and Cydna entered the room. Wrik let go of Credan's shirt.

"What's the meaning of this?" Aria stalked forward with rage in her eyes.

She knows.

He looked at Cydna, his betrayer. She smiled as though all was well.

Aria halted in front of him and Credan. "Explain why my two most trusted advisers are at each other's throats when I need them more than ever."

Me a trusted adviser? Interesting.

Wrik and Credan looked at each other. Clearly Credan had no idea as to what to say, but Wrik did. "I was simply demonstrating how those ghastly orcs handled me. During my moment of recollection, I fear I might've gone a bit further than necessary. I sincerely apologize, Master Credan."

Credan straightened his spectacles and nodded. "Apology accepted, my friend. I am thoroughly horrified at your mistreatment."

"Good." The edge in Aria's voice remained. She reached out, and the ƨäbräƨär pulled away from Wrik's neck and flew into her hand. "Forgive me for insisting you wear this, Wizard Wrik. I hope you understand why I found it necessary, given the circumstances."

Wrik bowed. "Yes, my queen." He eyed Cydna. "I'm overjoyed that Cydna was able to help in the matter of the *little dragon*. Might I inquire as to what she discovered?"

Aria seethed. "Cinolth."

Well done, Cydna. Well done.

Wrik feigned anger. "A betrayal then? That wretched beast will be the end of us all."

"Not if I have any say in it." Aria turned and stormed out of the throne room.

Wrik turned to Credan. "What's become of Queen Rosai?"

Credan scowled. "What are you talking about?"

"Her…" Wrik searched for the right word, the matter delicate. "…beauty has faded."

Credan's face paled. He looked around the throne room. "Make no mention of it if you want to keep your life."

"I would never say anything to her face."

Credan sighed. "As you know, Lord Rosai created many grand illusions with his mezhik. From what I understand, Queen Rosai was one of them."

Realization came to Wrik. "His mezhik is fading because of his death."

Credan nodded.

Gods, that man had no end to his deceit.

† † †

Aria burned with so much rage and hatred that her footsteps scorched the rocks as she marched toward the center of the atrium. Cinolth, the vile betrayer, awaited her. Had she the power, she would've struck him dead where he stood.

Cinolth's presence entered her mind. *"Your rage is impressive. It prevents me from knowing your thoughts."*

"I know," Aria growled.

"You've discovered the truth of the little dragon."

"And your betrayal."

Cinolth's head slithered down to her level. "My betrayal?"

"I gave you life, and you returned the favor by trying to kill me!"

Smoke billowed from Cinolth's nostrils. "Explain yourself before I swallow you whole."

Aria balled her fists. "Pale skin, black veins, and black eyes. Sound familiar?"

"Impossible."

"You killed my husband. Nothing is beyond you."

"You're so determined to cling to a man you think is your friend that you can't see the truth. Think about what you're saying. Why would I try to kill you? What purpose would it serve? My life is tethered to yours."

"I'm no fool. You knew my brother would try and save me, and you knew his sacrifice would sever the bond I shared with Pravus. Risking killing me was worth it for you. You eliminated two of the only influences in my life within a few moments."

"I understand why such an explanation makes sense to you, but you're forgetting one important detail."

"And what is that?"

"I'll admit that I took advantage of the situation once I realized your bond with Pravus had broken, but the prophecy of your brother made no more sense to me than it did to anyone else. However, no one understands prophecy better than Wizard Wrik."

"He is my friend!"

"No, he is a liar."

"Why would he do any of this? And why would Cydna lie to me about what Durqel witnessed on the plains?"

"Did Durqel confirm what Cydna told you?"

"No, but that's because he still couldn't remember."

"You are still a foolish girl. How can you trust a woman you know nothing about over me? That woman is a friend of Wizard Wrik. Can you not see the truth? They've deceived you and turned you against me."

"You've done a fair job of that all on your own. And, for the record, I trust no one."

"Good. I suggest you redirect your rage into a more meaningful task. Persuade Cydna to tell you the truth."

Aria reached out with her mezhik. The ground quaked, and the massive chains that hung from the dragon poles began to clang against their poles.

Cinolth looked around. "What are you doing?"

Five of the chains rose like snakes, whipped their heads, and shot toward Cinolth. Cinolth spread his wings but wasn't quick enough to combat the chains. One chain ensnared his neck, and the other four his wrists and ankles.

Cinolth raged and lashed out at the chains. "You think these will hold me?"

"They were made for this very purpose."

Cinolth roared. "You are so naive!"

"If Cydna's story changes, I will release you."

The scales on Cinolth's chest and belly glowed with a reddish-purple hue, and then he spewed orange, red, and purple flames at the chains that bound him.

Aria collapsed to her knees, a portion of her energy depleted. The massive chains melted from Cinolth's wrists and ankles and dripped from his neck.

Cinolth's serpentine eyes narrowed. Tortured her soul. "Try something like that again, and I will show you just how powerful I truly am." He roared as he beat his wings and rose into the air. One last glance, and then he flew up and out of the atrium and disappeared beyond the castle walls.

Rage coursed through Aria's veins. She stood and reached out to Credan with her mind as she stormed out of the atrium. *"I'll be in the persuasion room. Bring Cydna to me at once."*

† † †

As soon as Credan escorted Cydna out of the throne room, Wrik knew his time at Galondu Castle had come to an end. Cydna was an old friend and would likely buy him a little bit of time, but she wasn't the type who could endure pain for long. His heart ached knowing he'd never see her again, but her death might prove to be the catalyst that would save the world.

Or at least my life.

Wrik returned to his secret room to retrieve the single item that he believed could either persuade King Forlin to join their cause or get himself killed for possessing it: the signet ring of Ellesmere. The äəllfin ring was worth more than any other item he'd ever possessed, and the thought of parting with it left him feeling a bit bitter.

A necessary sacrifice to see this to the end.

Once he fetched the ring, he exited the room, locking the door behind himself and resetting the trespass ward. In a single step, he teleported up to the northern ramparts. Blackwind, the fastest and fiercest of the nítfinzh, greeted him with a trill.

"Hello, girl." She nuzzled his chest, and he rubbed the top of her smooth head. "We don't have time for pleasantries today, but I promise I'll make it up to you."

Her bright yellow eyes peered up at him, and she bobbed her head when he smiled. He quickly grabbed her saddle and strapped it on to her. It was then that he detected a charge in the air. The hairs on his arms and the back of his neck rose.

"Aria." Wrik turned and faced her. The blood drained from his face.

Gods, what has she done?

Blood covered Aria's clothes, smeared her face, and dripped from her hands and hair. "Cydna and I had a hand to heart talk."

Wrik cleared his throat. "And you've come to see me off?"

Dark clouds gathered in the sky as Aria stalked forward. "I thought you were my friend."

"I was. Thought I might've loved you at one point, too."

Fire and lightning swirled in her palms. "What happened? Why did you turn against me and try to kill me?"

Anger rose into Wrik's throat. "You of all people have the nerve to ask me that?"

"What did I ever do to you?" Aria growled.

"Pravus sent an assassin after me, but that wasn't good enough for you when they failed to kill me, was it?"

Aria's eyes narrowed. "I know nothing about an assassin."

"No, of course not. And I suppose you'll deny sending the shade after me, too."

"I don't even know what that's supposed to mean."

"Deny it if you want, but I verified it was your aura around it. No one could've summoned that beast but you."

"I don't understand."

"Neither did I, Aria. You broke my heart."

"And you killed Alderan."

"That was never my intention."

"You didn't know he'd sacrifice himself to save me?"

"Rage blinded me. The only thing I thought about was killing you after what you did."

"I did nothing!" Two balls of fire and lightning flew from Aria's hands and fizzled inches from Wrik's chest.

"An aura never lies." Wrik mounted Blackwind.

"You will die this day, Wrik!" A multitude of lightning bolts shot down from the sky, setting fire to the red tarps that covered the open-air stables.

"You possess power far greater than mine, but my intellect surpasses yours by leaps and bounds. I knew a day like this might come, so I drew runes around this place to protect myself from an attack. Your mezhik is worthless here."

Aria screamed and fell to her knees.

A thought struck Wrik. He'd never contemplated Cinolth having the power to control Aria's mezhik, especially without her knowledge of it, but the possibility of it struck a nerve within him. Twisted his insides.

Perhaps she isn't lying.

The more he contemplated it, the more certain he became of it. It made him also recognize the fact that he'd prevented Nardus and Alderan from killing Cinolth.

Gods… Alderan and Cydna died for nothing.

"I'm sorry, Aria."

She looked up at him, her eyes bloodshot and seething with hatred. "It's too late for that."

"That beast controls more than just your mind. Ask him about the shade."

Wrik connected with Blackwind's mind and urged her to take flight. The graceful beast stretched her wings and lifted them off the rampart with just a few wing beats.

"Alcedonia," Wrik said to her through their link. Blackwind carried them south, beyond the castle, and then banked to the west. Once the castle faded from view, Wrik took a deep breath and settled into the saddle.

Gods, I've made a mess of things.

CHAPTER TWENTY-SIX

Alderan, Jagger, and Eis continued south for the second day after escaping the clutches of Riptan and his beast. Neither of them knew where it would lead, but they had no choice but to keep moving. Eis and Jagger were impervious to the cold winds and blowing snow, but they nipped at Alderan relentlessly. Jagger lent him her cloak, but it didn't help protect his feet. He couldn't remember the last time he'd felt them without an accompanying barrage of needles.

He would've used mezhik to keep himself warm, but teleporting the three of them twice had left him depleted of energy. On top of that, he'd come to another realization. Despite all the things he'd learned from Zerenity, she never once mentioned the fact that cold weather zapped energy even faster than using mezhik. It would've been useful knowledge. But then again, it still wouldn't have made a difference to their situation. In addition to the teleporting and cold, a lack of food also played a role in his depleted state.

In the two days on the run, they'd come across virtually no civilization or creatures of any kind. In turn, that meant no food source. He began to wonder if anything existed beyond Jagger's village.

"Up ahead," Jagger said.

Alderan saw nothing but snow. "What is it?"

"Some kind of stone structure."

Twenty minutes later, Alderan caught sight of what looked like ruins of an ancient castle through the flurry. "I see the structure, but it looks to be long abandoned."

Eis stopped abruptly, and Jagger dismounted. She peered ahead. "Definitely not abandoned." She knelt and placed her hands on the ground. "We've got company."

"What kind of company?"

Jagger shrugged. "Not sure, but from their size I'd guess humans like you."

"Thought I was a flamewalker."

"You are *the* flamewalker, but you're still a human."

Alderan peered ahead. "How many are there?"

"It's hard to tell exactly, but I'd say several dozen." Jagger rose. "Looks like there's some sort of seaport to the east of the ruins. I see a large vessel with some sort of fish woman on the bowsprit."

"Fish woman?" Alderan dismounted and nearly collapsed, his legs far weaker than he'd imagined. Eis laid down. "Maybe I can get us closer."

Jagger glanced back at him and scoffed. "Look at yourself. You hardly have the strength to stand right now. Trying to teleport us would likely kill us."

She was right, but Alderan didn't like it. "Then what do you suggest we do?"

"I'd say run, but Eis is just as spent as you."

"Then I say we fight."

Jagger shook her head. "You are foolish, flamewalker. As I said, there are dozens of them."

"Maybe so, but I'm sure you're stronger than all of them combined."

"Even at full strength, it would be futile. Besides, they'd have you killed or captured before I could fight them all."

She had a good point. The only viable solution was to keep moving and hope their welcoming party was a friendly one. "I guess we take our chances and meet them in the middle."

"Agreed." Jagger stared at Eis for several seconds, and then Eis stood. "Eis says she can carry you as far as the ruins but no farther."

Alderan nodded and mounted Eis with Jagger's help. Jagger stayed on foot and led them toward the ruins. Before long, a small army of white-clad archers met them in the middle of the frozen tundra and surrounded them.

"We come in peace." Alderan almost laughed at how stupid it sounded after he said it.

Guess I'm still an oaf.

Three hooded figures approached, their faces obscured by shadows. Each carried a bow on their back. One of them said, "Visitors twice in one week." A male voice. The man glanced at the other two with him. "What are the odds?"

"Until today, I would've said zero," a female said.

Jagger stepped forward. "We seek food, water, shelter, and safe passage."

"Nothing else?" The man lowered his hood.

Silver hair, twisted in braids, covered his head and rested on his broad shoulders. Blue eyes contrasted his dark skin. A silver line ran straight down the center of his forehead and branched into three lines at the bridge of his nose. The lines gave his face the illusion of being cracked. Two silver rings pierced the right side of his lower lip. He stood a hand length shorter than Jagger.

"I am Thieren." Thieren peered up at Jagger. "I've not seen one like you before. Where did you come from?"

"The name's Jagger." She crossed her arms. "I hail from Reothadh."

"Nothing escapes Reothadh," the other person with Thieren said. *Another female.*

"Perhaps not, but we did." Alderan pulled back Jagger's cloak and extended his left arm, palm up. "Trust me, it was far from easy." His teeth chattered.

Thieren's expression darkened. "A third wizard."

"My name is Alderan Somneri, and I am from the Ancient Realm."

He studied Alderan's face. "And you seek Korin, too?"

Alderan glanced over at Jagger. "I'm sorry, but I'm unfamiliar with that name."

Jagger shook her head. "I've never heard of a Korin, either. As I said before, we need supplies and shelter. We wish no ill will toward you."

"And your beast?" Thieren said, eying Eis. Eis growled low.

"Her name is Eis." Jagger stroked Eis's mane. "I assure you that she will not attack unless provoked."

Thieren looked to each of the two females with him, then nodded. "We will provide you with some food and water, but then you must leave this land. You are unwelcome here." He raised his hood. "Come with me."

The three of them followed Thieren and his brigade of white-clad archers toward the castle ruins. As they rounded the eastern side of the ruins, Alderan spotted the ship Jagger had mentioned. His pulse raced with recognition.

The River Maiden!

"Thieren, wait," Alderan said.

Thieren stopped and turned around. "My patience runs low, wizard. Speak your mind with haste."

"Yes, of course. Take us to the elf named Morcinda."

Thieren glowered at him. "Morcinda is our guest. You are not."

"Tell her that I am here," Alderan said. "I promise that she'll want to see me."

"You're in no position to make demands."

Alderan pushed his hair behind his ears. "It is a request, nothing more."

"I know men like you," Jagger said. "You seek power that isn't yours and fail to understand your place. Let Korin decide our fate. She is clearly your leader."

Thieren growled, turned, and stormed toward the entrance to the ruins. Alderan prayed that Jagger hadn't squandered his only chance to return home.

Once inside the ruins, Thieren and several others escorted Alderan, Jagger, and Eis down several stairways and through many hallways before reaching a thick iron door. Thieren unlocked the door and led them into a dimly lit corridor.

Jagger halted just beyond the door. "What's the meaning of this?"

"A precaution, nothing more," Thieren said. "I give you my word."

Jagger fumed. "There's no—"

Alderan grabbed Jagger's arm. "Trust me, everything will be okay. Morcinda's my friend." She scowled at him but nodded.

Dozens of old dungeon cells line the long corridor. Most of the cells either had no door at all or were missing portions of their containment walls. Only the cell at the end of the corridor remained intact. Thieren led them to it and ushered them inside.

"You will remain here while I speak to Korin on your behalf. In the meantime, I will have water and food brought down to you." Thieren stepped into the corridor and locked the cell door. He peered through the small, rectangular iron slot built into the wooden door. "I will return within the hour with an answer from Korin."

Thieren and the others exited the dungeon. Then, the iron door slammed shut and the lock clunked into place. Alderan sank to the floor, his legs too weary to hold him any longer. Jagger plopped down on the stone bench at the back of the cell. Eis lay at Jagger's feet and closed her eyes.

Jagger sighed. "I suppose this is all part of your grand plan, flamewalker?"

"In a way, yes." Alderan smiled. "Did you notice anything when Thieren brought us down here?"

"Yeah, we're the only ones locked up in this wretched place."

"Exactly!" He swept his hair out of his face and leaned against the wall. "There were also no guards posted outside the main door, and all the corridors coming down here were vacant. I'm willing to bet there are less than sixty people in this entire castle."

Jagger leaned forward and propped her head up on her hands. "How does any of that help us?"

"It likely won't. At least not until they bring us some food."

"And then?"

"And then you'll break us out of here."

"You value my strength more than you should."

"And you doubt yourself more than you should. The hinges on our door are rusted nearly through. A good kick or shoulder slam, and we'll be free."

"From this cell, yes, but not from the dungeon. The outer iron door is quite thick, and its hinges showed no sign of rusting."

"And that's where I come in. I can teleport us to the other side of the door."

"You told them you're a wizard and showed them your mark, and you think they didn't plan for that?"

Alderan frowned. "Well…" He drew a blank. They hadn't collared him, but that didn't mean they had no other means to hinder a person who could wield mezhik.

Jagger turned sideways and lay back on the bench. "We're at their mercy. Pray the gods save us."

Ɂäṭūr, help us find a way out of here.

† † †

Savric lay on the bed and stared at the strange patterns in the rock ceiling. Given enough attention, the patterns danced about. His eyes began to cross, and his eyelids became desperately heavy.

A knock at the door drove him to a sitting position. At some point, he'd dozed off. "Come in."

Morcinda entered the room. "We set sail within the hour. I suggest you make preparations."

Savric scowled at her. "Such as?"

"That stomach of yours. The way you eat, we'll run out of food in the middle of the ocean."

Savric chuckled and rubbed his belly. "I assure you that my—" His stomach quaked and groaned with hunger. "I will follow my nose to the kitchens at once and fill my belly and the coffers of my robes to the point of bursting."

Morcinda nodded curtly. "See that you do."

It didn't take long for Savric to pinpoint a food source. The succulent scent of bone broth with peas and carrots wafted through the hallways and led him straight to the kitchens. An older woman—about his age—tended to a small pot of steaming goodness. Her brow wrinkled as he strode her way.

She shooed at him. "Out with yeh, yeh vermin."

Savric applied his best smile. "Madame, I believe we have yet to become acquainted. I am Savric Naphor of the Ancient—"

"Don't care who yeh be. This here broth got two stomachs teh feed, and neither be yers." She took the pot and filled two bowls.

"Are they not?" Savric feigned disappointment. "Then to whom does this marvelous food belong?"

"Wizard an a halfbreed."

A halfbreed? Interesting, indeed.

"I understand." He proffered his hand. "Please allow me to assist you in delivering them."

The woman looked him up and down and squinted. "Seem fit enough."

She handed him one of the bowls, grabbed a large paper package, and then scooped up the second bowl. "Name's Trina. Behave yerself, an yeh might get somethin' special. This way, an don' drag yer feet, neither."

The two of them exited through a door at the back of the kitchens and descended far beneath the ruins. Savric envisioned himself a spry young man, but the dozens of stairs they descended jarred his bones and shot pain into his knees and hips. Not only did his bones ache, but by the time they reached a large iron door, he sucked wind harder than a bellows before stoking a fire.

Trina handed him the paper package and then fished a large key out of her pocket. She fumbled with the key for a good thirty seconds but couldn't manage to insert it into the lock. Instead, she kicked the door. "Curses to yeh!"

Savric smiled. "Allow me, Trina." She glared up at him and hesitated before exchanging the key with the paper package.

"Tis me shaky bones."

Savric slid the key into the lock and turned it three times before the mechanism fully disengaged. The door groaned as it swung inward. Just a few torches lit the expansive corridor. Even with poor lighting it was obvious the cells were in disrepair.

He stepped around a pile of rubble. "Do you keep prisoners down here often?"

Trina shook her head as she headed farther down the corridor. "These be the first. Came with the mornin'."

"And their charge?" Savric said.

She stopped, cocked her head when she looked at him, and shrugged. "Not being us, suppose."

Savric didn't like the sound of it one bit. He didn't know Queen Lanara, but Morcinda did. She trusted the woman and expressed the care with which Lanara handled herself and delicate situations. Keeping prisoners directly opposed her friendly disposition.

What else are you hiding, Lanara?

† † †

Alderan lay on the stone bench deep in concentration. No matter how hard he tried, he couldn't feel Aria's presence. In the past year, he'd learned a lot about their bond and how certain things prevented it from being detected. The *zäbräzär* had blocked everything, but even when neither of them wore the wretched collar, the link they once shared faltered. The blood and mezhik bonds Aria formed with Pravus and Cinolth dulled his bond with her, and great distances certainly played a part as well. A myriad of other reasons likely existed, but the night almost always brought them together.

Tonight, we'll see each other again.

Jagger called to him, "Flamewalker, someone's coming."

He rose and joined her at the door. Indeed, someone approached. Their feet dragged across the rock floor.

"Two of them," she said. "Huh…"

"What?"

"Both of them are older, and they're alone. Plus, they've left the outer iron door wide open."

Alderan smelled food, and his stomach rumbled. "Guess Thieren didn't lie about sending food down."

Jagger scowled. "Forget the food. Now's our chance to escape."

"Perhaps we should eat and then escape."

"No time," she whispered.

"Step back from the door," a woman with a deep, shaky voice said.

Jagger pushed Alderan against the wall, took three steps back, and then charged the door.

Crack!

The door didn't break from its hinges but exploded outward.

Bang!

The door twisted on its hinges and slammed against the outer wall.

Dust and debris filled the corridor.

A woman cried out as Jagger and Eis charged forward and cleared a path.

Alderan protected his eyes with his arm as he exited the cell and headed down the corridor.

"Feathers! Are you alright, Trina?" a man said.

Recognition stopped Alderan in his tracks. When he turned around, a ball of light rose out of the dust.

Jagger grabbed his shoulder and turned him around. "Come on, flamewalker. We've no time to waste."

"I know that voice." He shrugged her hand away and turned back toward the light.

His heart thrummed in his chest as the dust began to settle. Alderan peered through the dust. "Master Savric? Is that you?"

"I dare say, Trina's foot has become ensnared."

Alderan rushed back toward the cell and the light. A man with his back turned to Alderan wrestled to lift the cell door trapping the old woman's leg. Without thinking, Alderan willed the cell door to move, and it did. The door lifted off the woman's leg and flew straight into the cell and crashed against the stone bench.

Crippling pain drove Alderan to the ground as it pulsed through his head. "My dear boy" was the last thing he heard before succumbing to it.

† † †

After healing Trina's leg as best he could, Savric led the halfbreed named Jagger and her ferzh Eis back up to the kitchens. Jagger managed to carry both Alderan and Trina at the same time. He marveled at the young woman's brute strength but still couldn't wrap his head around what had transpired. Sure, he understood everything about the breakout Jagger performed, but that's not what confounded him. His mind returned over and again to the message Nardus had left in the Ūrdär Dhef Ƨäfn Dhä book: *"Shardan is dead. -Nardus"*

Nardus never would've lied about the death of his son, so the two most confounding questions of Savric's lifetime swirled in his mind: how is Alderan alive, and how did he wind up in a dungeon cell beneath the Cadivus Ruins thousands of miles from the Ancient Realm?

Morcinda entered the kitchens. "Master Savric, we're about to set—" She gasped when she noticed Alderan lying on top of one of the tables. She staggered back several steps. "It cannot be!"

"Indeed, yet here he lies."

Morcinda shook her head with disbelief. "How?"

"I am uncertain." Savric stroked his beard as he stared at Alderan. "However, we must inform Queen Lanara of the situation."

"Situation?"

"Bring her here at once, and I'll have Jagger—" He gestured toward Jagger with his hand. "—explain."

Morcinda nodded and exited the kitchens. Trina, her leg healed enough to stand on, labored over another pot of broth, albeit a much larger one. Alderan would require a generous portion to begin his recovery from exerting himself much too far.

Thank you Ƹäƭūr for keeping him alive. Er, twice.

Morcinda returned with Queen Lanara, Princess Zelanora, and several others.

Queen Lanara looked between Jagger, Eis, and Alderan, her brow furrowed. "What's the meaning of all this? Who are these people?"

Jagger came forward. "We are refugees of Reothadh."

"Reothadh?" Queen Lanara scoffed. "Nothing escapes from there."

"That's what I said," one of the females that came in with Queen Lanara said.

Queen Lanara turned to the woman, her face flushed. "Vera! You knew of this and said nothing?"

Vera nodded with reluctance. "Thieren forbade us from doing so."

"He hasn't the authority to make such demands," Queen Lanara said.

"Don't I?" Thieren stepped into the room, flanked by half a dozen others. The others held bows with arrows nocked. "You're on your way out, Korin, and I'm the single candidate for succession to the seat."

"You're wrong, Thieren." Queen Lanara stood without fear before Thieren. "That seat's been filled."

Thieren laughed. "You think anyone will stand in my way once you're gone?"

"It is our way," Queen Lanara growled. "My decision is final."

"So is mine." Metal flashed in Thieren's hand just before he drove a dagger into Queen Lanara's side.

"Mother!" Zelanora cried. Savric grabbed her and pulled her back.

The air crackled. Not with energy but with the sound of melting ice. Then, the fabric of reality cracked and shattered, changing what everyone had perceived as real.

Queen Lanara stood several feet from Thieren, her side unpierced and his blade without blood. She glared at him. "If you think anyone would serve a man such as yourself, you're more delusional than I had imagined."

Thieren spat on the floor. "Mezhik won't save you, Korin."

"You're right, Thieren, mezhik has nothing to do with this." She nodded, and the six who flanked Thieren turned their bows on him. "On your knees."

"You'll regret this moment for the rest of your life." Thieren growled and threw his dagger straight at Zelanora.

Savric had no time to react as the blade twirled right past his head. He cringed, expecting a cry of agony, but none came. Instead, the blade dropped to the floor behind him with a clatter.

Thieren dropped to his knees and fell face-first onto the floor. Two arrows protruded from the back of his skull.

"You saved my life," Zelanora said.

Savric turned around to see Jagger standing in front of Zelanora.

The halfbreed shrugged. "Takes more than a metal blade to pierce my skin."

"Broth's ready." Trina turned, took in all that had happened behind her back, and shook her head. "Don' expect me teh scrub the floor."

After a hearty meal of broth and bread, Savric and the others made their way out to the port and Morcinda's ship. Queen Lanara said her final goodbyes, and then she and Zelanora boarded. Savric and Morcinda followed after Alderan insisted he could manage on his own. Savric watched Alderan and Jagger embrace from the ship's railing. Then, Alderan hugged Eis's neck and made his way on board.

Savric placed his arm around Alderan as the ship pulled away from the port. "I dare say, you have an adventure worth telling, and I am keen on hearing every last word of it."

Alderan chuckled softly as he gave one final wave to Jagger and Eis. He wiped a tear from his eye. "Do you think it is wrong of me to leave her like this?"

"She made her choice, my boy, and she understands your destiny far better than most." He squeezed Alderan's shoulder. "Ɂätūr willing, she will rescue her father with the help of Vera and the others."

Alderan nodded. "If it's alright with you, I'd like to turn in for now. I'm still feeling quite weak."

"As you wish. I will look forward to hearing your tale another day." Savric smiled. "Perhaps tomorrow."

"Tomorrow."

Zelanora took Alderan's hand and led him toward the cabins below deck.

As the islands began to shrink in the distance, Savric turned and headed to his own quarters. Another battle brewed on the horizon, and he prayed they'd be ready when it came.

Let it be your will, Ɂäțūr.

CHAPTER TWENTY-SEVEN

Calen lay in the dark beneath the boughs of a massive pine tree. He knew this not because he could see it but because of its soothing aroma and the bed of soft needles beneath him. His stomach still burned around the wound, and pain nearly paralyzed him every time he tried to move on his own.

Guilt chewed on his conscience. The others would be better off without him. He only slowed them down and put them at risk of being captured or worse. And no matter how much he begged, the three of them refused to leave him behind.

The others spoke in hushed voices, thinking him asleep.

"We need to find a healer," Berggren said. "That wound of his has turned black as night."

"I've seen wounds like that before," Niesha said.

"Eshtak sees wounds too. Eshtak not lose friend."

Tears slipped down Calen's cheeks.

Ɂäţūr, I'm not ready to die.

A soft breeze rattled the tree branches and carried with it the voice of an angel. Calen had never heard Niesha sing before. Never knew she could. But the lullaby she sang brought back memories of his aunt. He lay there and listened to her sing:

> *When the wind howls late at night*
> *Twists your toes with oh such fright*
> *Remember that I'm right by your side*
> *And know you'll never need run or hide*
>
> *I'll keep you warm and keep your soul safe*

Within my arms and loving embrace
Fear not my child, unto your last breath
For I hold the key, even to death

† † †

Berggren placed his hand over Niesha's mouth and pulled her close. "Quiet, young one. We're not alone."

Dozens of pairs of red eyes shone in the darkness. The unblinking mass circled the small camp.

Eshtak snatched the dagger out of Berggren's scabbard and stood tall. "Big man takes friends." He drew the dagger across his own palm, cutting it deep. "Run!"

Berggren gasped. "Gods, Eshtak! What are you doing?"

Eshtak tossed the dagger on the ground, spread the fresh blood across his chest and down his arms, and then ran right through the sea of red eyes and into the darkness. Most of the red eyes turned and chased after him. The remaining ones seemed focused on the bloody dagger lying on the ground. Berggren just stood there, stunned.

What just happened?

Niesha retrieved the dagger and held it in front of her. One of the eyes flew toward the blade. She cocked her head. "Is that a beetle?"

Berggren knelt. Although he had never seen a creature quite like the one that landed on the outstretched blade, he believed the girl was right. The large beetle began feasting on the blood. Two of its kin joined in and had the blade spotless within seconds.

Niesha dropped the dagger and pulled on Berggren's sleeve. "These things are attracted to blood."

"Got that," Berggren said, his gaze fixated on the beetles as they flew toward a large pine.

Niesha yanked his sleeve harder. "Calen's wound!"

Understanding rocked Berggren. Eshtak had drawn them away to save Calen. He snatched up the dagger and sheathed it. By the time he and Niesha reached Calen, the beetles had already chewed through Calen's bandages.

Calen screamed. Tore at his wound as the beetles burrowed into his stomach.

Berggren hated what must be done. Swallowed down bile even as his knuckles connected with Calen's jaw.

Calen's scream ended abruptly, and his body lay still.

Niesha grabbed Berggren's arm. "What have you done?"

"Stop talking and do as I say. No questions." Niesha nodded, her face white as snow. Berggren retrieved his dagger again and handed it to her. "I'll fish the beetles out, and you kill them. Understood?" She nodded again.

Berggren took a deep breath and shoved his fingers into Calen's wound. Between the grotesque and sticky feel and the stench of decaying flesh, he could hardly breathe or think. What made matters worse was the size of his hands and fingers. He had no chance of fishing out the beetles without killing Calen first.

Niesha stared at Calen's stomach. "What's wrong?"

Berggren pulled his fingers out. "You're gonna have to fish them out, and I'll kill them."

Tears poured down Niesha's cheeks. "Me?" She swallowed. Choked. Drew a deep breath. "What if I accidentally kill him?"

"You don't do it, and he dies." He took the knife from her and looked at Calen's gaunt face. "I think we're running out of time."

Niesha moved closer to Calen, closed her eyes, and shoved her fingers into the gaping wound. A few seconds later, she pulled out one of the beetles. It writhed and snapped at her. Berggren grabbed it and tried to squish it in his palm, but the little bastard was hard as a rock and somehow managed to bite him, too.

"Bugger!" By the time Berggren figured out how to de-wing and skewer the creature, Niesha had another one for him.

The third beetle burrowed far deeper than the first two. Niesha buried her hand up to her wrist in Calen's gut before she finally retrieved it. Berggren dispatched of it and then tore off his shirt and wrapped it around Calen's midsection.

Niesha wiped her hand on her trousers. "Now what?"

Berggren had no answer. Calen needed a healer, but they were somewhere in the middle of the Orbis Mountains. The entire area was unfamiliar to him. They could be just outside a village or a hundred miles from one. His choice could either save or kill Calen, but indecision only had one path.

"Northeast. We head toward the Hotah River and Vallah." Although she didn't argue, Berggren could tell Niesha had something on her mind. "Spit it out."

Niesha shrugged. "I was just wondering if we might run into the enemy if we head to Vallah."

"We could." Berggren lifted Calen into his arms. "As I'm sure you know, the enemy is all around us. So, I'm not sure that it matters. What I do know is that we might possibly find something or someone in Vallah that could help Calen."

"Good enough for me." She stood and walked out from beneath the tree boughs. "So, which way is northeast?"

Berggren emerged from beneath the tree with Calen in his arms. He motioned to his left with his head. "That way."

She turned in the direction Berggren had indicated. "And what about Eshtak?"

"He's far smarter and more resourceful than I'd imagined. I'm certain he'll catch up with us at some point."

"I like him."

Berggren chuckled. "Me, too. Now, let's get moving before something else decides to attack us."

"Good idea." She surged forward. "I'll lead the way."

I'm sure you will.

CHAPTER TWENTY-EIGHT

After releasing Cinolth from the dragon poles, Aria headed straight for her bedchamber. When she arrived, Brema had a tub filled with hot water waiting. She stripped off her bloody clothes and slipped down into the water.

It took the better part of an hour for Brema to scrub the blood from her skin and wash it from her hair. Once Brema finished, Aria had her fill the tub with fresh water, lavender, and herbs. Then, she dismissed the girl for the night.

She lay back in the tub and allowed the herbs to work their way into her muscles, relieving some of the tension. However, nothing would settle her aching heart or mind.

Even with all the time she'd spent locked up in Dragnus's dungeon, she'd still never felt as alone as she did in that moment. Not one person she loved remained alive, and all those who still lived had betrayed her or eventually would. Never again would she let someone get close to her or allow herself to feel love. She reached into the water and stroked her belly.

You will be the last, my love.

Once the water cooled, she rose from the tub and retreated to the balcony. The crisp night air prickled her wet, bare skin, leaving her chilled. The view of Atrum Moenia reminded her of the first night she spent at Galondu Castle. She'd shed her clothes and curled up next to the hearth. Perhaps she'd do the same tonight.

A knock at her bedchamber door pulled her from the past. She slipped into a robe and stood before her bed. "Enter."

Credan popped his head through the cracked door. "Is there anything I can do for you, my queen? Anything you require?"

"Loyalty," Aria snapped.

"Always, my queen."

"Make sure I'm undisturbed tonight."

Credan bowed. "As you wish." He ducked back out and closed the door.

Aria stood before the hearth and let her robe slip from her shoulders. It fell into a pile, and she spread it on the floor and lay on top of it. The flames jumped about, and the fire crackled. The longer she stared at it, the more her mind drifted. Viscus D'Silva rose from its depths and pulled her into the past.

As it once had before, Alderan's presence consumed her. She knew it to be nothing more than a deception of her mind, yet she clung to it as though it were a lifeline. Yearned to be with him again. As she slipped into the hands of sleep, she met him aboard a sailing vessel in the middle of the sea.

† † †

Credan led Reubane through the castle and up to the southern ramparts. When they arrived, Cinolth was already waiting.

"Qotan found you," Cinolth said.

Credan shook his head. "He never came, so I found another way."

"You are wrong. He remains here. I can feel his presence."

Credan and Reubane both looked around. "You're… certain?" Credan said.

"He stands at your side." Cinolth moved his head closer. Stared at the empty space next to Credan. "For some reason I cannot see him, either."

Reubane scowled. "You control the spirits then?"

"An impossibility." Cinolth snorted. "Nevertheless, I've severed my connection with this phantom."

"And what is it you want from me?" Reubane said.

Cinolth eyed Credan. "Leave us."

What is it you're up to?

Credan bowed. "Yes… master."

Once he reached the far stairwell, Credan slipped into the shadows and watched Cinolth and Reubane. The distance made it impossible to overhear their conversation, and the dark night distorted his vision, but one gesture Cinolth made was quite clear. The dragon had extracted something from within his chest and handed it to Reubane.

Fear crept into Credan's bones. "What kind of damnation have I unleashed?"

He turned and dashed down the stairwell with reckless abandon.

I must warn Queen Rosai.

† † †

Qotan stood in the shadows, stunned. A moment earlier, he had lain on Zerenity's guest bed. Now, he found himself atop the ramparts of what he believed to be Galondu Castle, a distance of almost six hundred miles. Well versed in mezhik, the physical leap astounded him. Further confounding were the beastly man and the massive dragon who stood less than a dozen paces away. As far as he could tell, neither had spotted him. He hugged the wall and willed himself into the dark shadows.

Although he'd never seen a dragon in person before, he never doubted their existence, nor had he believed them to be extinct. Standing within such close proximity to one thrilled him more than he'd ever admit to anyone, especially Savric, but the encounter frightened him, too.

Was I summoned here somehow?

He dismissed the notion as quickly as it entered his mind, yet he knew there must be a good explanation as to his miraculous travel. However, one didn't come right out and present itself. The more he pondered his situation, the more concerned he became.

Have I lost my mind?

A quick check of his faculties confirmed them to be in order.

Then I must be dreaming.

He raised his sleeve, grabbed a wad of skin between his thumb and forefinger, and twisted it hard. The immediate pain response crushed his theory, but it also left no clues behind as to how he came to be in the presence of a dragon.

What is this then?

The beast spread its massive wings and beat the air with them, kicking up dust and debris. Qotan shielded his eyes as the dragon took to the sky. The thunderous sound of drums and cracking whips rang in his ears as the beast circled the castle before flying north and disappearing into the night.

The strange man no longer stood on the ramparts, either. Qotan stepped out of the shadows and surveyed the area. As far as he could tell, only one exit existed. Yet the man hadn't walked past him to get to it.

So, where did he go?

Qotan walked over to the parapet and peered over the side of the castle. Given the lack of moonlight and his ocular disadvantage, he couldn't see anything.

How strange this night is.

He rubbed his chin then reached out for his staff, but it didn't fly into his hand as it usually did. As his mezhik conduit, weapon, and walking stick, he never traveled anywhere without it. The fact that he hadn't brought it with him gave him further concern. It would require investigation, but more pressing matters loomed ahead.

It had been far longer than he could remember since he'd stepped foot inside Galondu Castle. From what he recollected, the castle was a maze of corridors, halls, and stairwells. He also remembered the mirror located at the end of one of those corridors. Unfortunately, his keen sense of direction wasn't what it used to be. Had Savric been there, he would've chided Qotan for it.

I pray you are safe, brother.

Qotan sighed as he headed toward the stairwell. Given the sheer size of the castle, it would likely take him days to locate the mirror, especially while evading detection. On the bright side, while he remained there, he might be able to ascertain the reason for his visit and his loss of memory. A thought struck him as he scratched his chin.

Perhaps it has something to do with that nasty vine.

† † †

Reubane clawed his way down the south side of the castle and landed on the royal balcony without a sound. He slipped through the curtains and entered the bedchamber. Smoldering coals provided the only light in the room, but it was unnecessary for a man such as himself. Long ago, Reubane had found himself capable of attaining the abilities of those he killed. Night vision was only one such gift.

The curtains were drawn around the massive bed. There, he would find her and fulfill his mission. Afterward, she would satiate his darkest needs.

All the days spent locked in the dungeon blurred together. A hundred or several thousand made little difference to a man who could never die. One thing was certain, though. He would never allow himself to be locked up again.

Behind the curtains sat an empty bed, the covers unruffled. He drew them back and buried his face in the sheets. Her scent permeated them. Drove him to the edge of madness.

She will be mine.

On the floor before the hearth, she lay. A wanton seductress. Ready for the taking.

Reubane removed his shirt and stood over the woman. Every breath wheezed from her luscious lips. Unspoken words of desire. Soon, she would reveal her darkest secrets and beg him for death.

He retrieved the strange gray shard from his pocket and stared at it. Studied it. It held some sort of ancient power. Distinct. Foreign. Its identity eluded him.

He knelt over her. Straddled her. She slept on as though under a deep spell.

Are you dreaming of me?

He chuckled softly. "You will be soon."

Bending down, he drank in her scent. Lavender. Sage.

The artery on the side of her neck pulsed with life. Her blood the nectar of gods. How sweet she'd taste. The first bite of a juicy apple.

I will savor you.

Reubane sat up and palmed the shard. His pulse quickened with anticipation.

"Plunge it into her heart," the dragon had told him.

He raised his arm.

Crack!

The bedchamber doors burst open.

The woman stirred. Then, her eyes opened. Beautiful, green eyes fringed with red stared up at him.

Credan and several guards rushed toward Reubane, weapons drawn.

Reubane thrust the shard into the woman's chest and stood.

She gasped. Wheezed. Clutched her chest.

But the shard left no wound. Drew no blood.

Odd…

† † †

The pain lasted just an instant. A pinprick. Nothing more.

But it ripped Aria away from Alderan and his new world beyond the veil.

A man stood over her, his brow furrowed. She'd never seen him before. Bald head, bushy black beard, and a bare chest littered with scars. Grey eyes searched hers. He must've had as many questions as she did.

"Step away from the queen!"

The loud voice startled Aria. She glanced back and saw three soldiers standing at a distance, their weapons drawn. Credan stood behind the three soldiers.

Aria sat up, and the strange man backed away.

Credan stepped around the soldiers. "On your knees, Reubane."

Reubane… where have I heard that name before?

Reubane's lips spread wide, revealing a set of yellow, sharpened teeth. He eyed Aria once more. "You and I will finish our business later."

Aria scowled. "What business?"

"The dragon and I made a deal." He turned and sprinted toward the balcony.

Aria rolled up onto her knees, conjured a fireball, and thrust it at Reubane. The curtains burst into flames right behind Reubane, and then the fireball struck him in the back. Reubane plunged over the edge of the balcony. Aria and the others rushed out to the balcony and peered over the banister.

She expected to see Reubane still falling or splayed out on the ground far below, his flesh eaten with wizard's fire, but neither were true. Impossible as it were, the man had simply vanished.

Aria grasped the banister and arched her back as fire erupted in her chest. The sensation spread throughout her body before fading. Once it did, she found the sorrow within her heart extinguished. A desire to burn the world and everyone in it was all that remained.

CHAPTER TWENTY-NINE

After separating from the others several days ago, Rayah, Ridan, and Bakkan trudged through the fresh spring snow that covered the ground just south of the Quietus Forest. It wasn't a lot of snow, but it certainly slowed them down. The frigid air forced Rayah to walk instead of fly. She still remembered the time her wings froze and never wanted to go through such a painful ordeal ever again.

For the last half hour, the only audible sounds were those of the crunching snow beneath their feet and an occasional cough from either her or Ridan. Scarves helped keep the cold from their lungs, but it also prevented them from breathing easily. Soon, they'd reach the forest and gain reprieve from the biting wind. She couldn't wait.

Ridan spoke few words during their journey, and Rayah didn't blame her. They'd both lost someone very close. However, she wondered if the dwarf spoke much before losing Normak or if not talking much was just her thing. Either way, Rayah decided she would give Ridan space and keep her mouth closed as much as possible. Given her nature, though, it was an impossible task.

"We were going to get married, you know."

Ridan grunted and pushed Bakkan a bit harder.

Rayah did her best to keep up as she continued to talk, "He was everything to me, and I loved him more than life itself. But I... I kept a secret from him."

Ridan sighed. "Feel free to keep it from me, too."

Ouch!

Rayah fought herself to keep quiet but failed again just as they reached the edge of the forest. "You don't like me much, do you?"

Bakkan stopped, and Ridan dismounted. She glared at the densely packed trees. "My feelings toward ya are irrelevant."

Rayah rubbed her arms. "That's not true. Once we enter this forest, I need to know you'll have my back no matter what happens or what we face."

"Did I leave ya behind when we went after Käíeꙅ after ya expended all yar energy and couldn't walk or fly?"

Rayah had somehow forgotten about the reconnaissance in the canyon. "You didn't, but how can I be sure it wasn't just a show for Normak and the others?"

"I've given ya my word." Ridan grabbed her spear off Bakkan's back and then led him into the forest.

Rayah huffed and followed them into the thicket beneath the canopy of golden firs and silver pines. Ridan's quick and rough pace dislodged much of the snow from the overhead boughs, all of which seemed to find real estate atop Rayah's head.

She's doing it on purpose.

Rayah slowed down a little to keep herself from being buried in snow. As she weaved her way through the trees and deeper into the forest, she noticed that the trees grew ever thicker and began to choke out most of the daylight streaming down from above. Ridan would likely have the same issue and slow down, so she stopped for a moment to catch her breath.

After a few seconds, Rayah realized that the only sound she heard was that of her own breathing. No wind, no birds, no Ridan. Fear drove her forward, and she paid the cost for it as branches whipped her from every direction. By the time she pulled herself together and stopped again, she'd lost track of where she was and which direction Ridan went.

Rayah was about to call out to Ridan when she heard a soft whisper in her ear. Turning in a circle, she found herself alone. When she stopped, the whisper returned. Closing her eyes, she concentrated on it. The words strayed beyond recognition, but their melody drew her in. As the whispering lullaby drifted farther, she followed. Soon, she found herself running to keep up with it. Nothing else mattered but chasing after it. She must know its source.

Thoughts of Ridan and Bakkan, of herself, dissipated until nothing remained within her mind but the soft whispers and the desire they instilled upon her. Rayah began to wonder who she even was, but those thoughts soon faded into nothing as well.

I'll be anything you want.

† † †

An hour into the forest, Ridan realized she hadn't heard Rayah say anything for at least half that time. She slowed to a halt and listened to the forest. Nothing stirred, not even the wind through the trees.

"Rayah!" The sound of her voice fell flat, likely traveling little more than a twenty-foot diameter in such dense vegetation.

Ridan chided herself for being so short with Rayah. She'd never been one for lengthy conversation and certainly never expressed her feelings, especially when it hurt so much to think about. Normak was far from perfect, but it was one of the reasons she cared about him. He would've renounced his own birthright if it meant gaining favor with her.

Apart from physical attributes and a never-ending desire to talk, she likened herself to Rayah. They were both headstrong and feisty and would stop at nothing to avenge those they loved. Perhaps she could learn to be friends with Rayah.

Gotta find her first.

Ridan scratched Bakkan between his ears. "Looks like we're gonna have to backtrack a bit to find Rayah."

Bakkan snorted and glanced back the way they'd come.

"Yeah, I know, but we can't just leave her to die."

Bakkan growled and shook the snow from his back, and then he turned around and headed back the way they'd come. Ridan followed close. Twenty minutes later, Bakkan stopped and growled low. Something was wrong.

Ridan closed her eyes and listened to the forest once again. At first, she heard nothing, but then a soft lullaby tickled her ears. She gasped, and her eyes shot open.

"Fiɜbärz!"

Pulse racing, she hopped into the saddle strapped to Bakkan's back and tucked herself against his withers. She held on tight and said, "Seek!"

Bakkan tore through the forest without restraint. With such thick fur, very little ever hurt him, especially a few whipping, scratching branches, but

Ridan didn't possess such a thick layer of protection. Her armor dulled most of the shots, but a few caught her right in the face. One smacked her right between the eyes and drew blood. She knew it had not just because she felt the blood but also because it had found its way down the side of her nose and to the corner of her mouth.

Fifteen minutes later, Bakkan burst into a small clearing and slid to a stop. At first, Ridan didn't understand why he'd done so, but then she saw what he did. Just ahead, Rayah lay on the ground in front of an entrance to an underground den. Thousands upon thousands of purple flies swarmed around her.

Ridan dismounted and edged closer to where Rayah lay. Vibrations from their wings reached her before the sound hit her ears.

Purple flies don't sing!

The fiʒbärz swarmed around her head. Tickled the hairs in her ears with their lullabies. Ridan stormed forward, immune to their evil whispers. She grabbed Rayah by the arms and shook her, but Rayah didn't wake.

Ridan changed tactics and began swatting at the fiʒbärz, but it only seemed to enrage them. They attacked in swarms, but their teeth proved too small to penetrate her skin. She grabbed Rayah, hauled her over her shoulder, and carried her over to Bakkan. By the time she finished strapping Rayah to Bakkan's saddle, she realized more than just the fiʒbärz stalked her.

She grabbed her spear off Bakkan's back and commanded him to run. Bakkan snorted his disapproval before turning and dashing into the trees. Turning back, Ridan faced not just a massive swarm of fiʒbärz but also three black foxes with brown stripes on their sides and a silver streak that stretched from the back of their snouts all the way to the tips of their three tails.

The foxes snarled and bore their vicious teeth as they circled Ridan. Drool dripped from their maws, and their amber eyes revealed an intelligence far greater than basic animal instinct. Each of the foxes eyed her spear with disdain.

Ridan took her spear and drove its tip into the frozen ground. The foxes stopped circling and gazed up at her with what she could only describe as curiosity. She knelt, her hand still wrapped around the spear shaft. "I've not come to harm ya."

"Liar," the fiɜbärz whispered. "You attacked us."

"Yes, but only after ya lured my friend here."

"A dinner guest," they said with a hint of malice.

Ridan stood, disgusted by the foul little creatures. "There will be no feast."

"No feast, no escape," they said. The foxes tightened the circle.

"Withdraw, and I'll return with a young buck. Refuse, and I'll make certain ya all die of starvation." She ripped the spear out of the ground and struck a fighting pose. "Decide now, for my patience has faltered."

The three foxes backed away and then returned to their den. The fiɜbärz undulated as they swarmed and circled her head. "You have one day." As one, they dispersed and faded into the trees.

† † †

Rayah woke to the sound of crackling wood and the smell of smoke. She bolted upright, expecting to find herself in the middle of a raging forest fire, but instead met Ridan's eyes through the flames of the small campfire. Her head ached, and she couldn't recall how they'd arrived at the base of a rocky mountain. The last thing she remembered was entering the Quietus Forest.

Ridan stood. "Was starting to wonder if ya was ever gonna wake."

Rayah rose on her knees and rubbed the stiffness from the back of her neck. "What happened?"

"Fiɜbärz. They lured ya away with their wretched lullabies."

"How did we escape?"

Ridan shook her head. "*We* didn't escape. I saved ya from them." She plucked a makeshift torch off the ground and lit it in the fire. "Come on, I think I might've found what we're looking for."

Rayah pulled herself to her feet. "You've located *Hemär Dhef Əllíṭ*?"

"Not quite, but I'm fairly certain I've found the entrance that leads to its location." Ridan mounted Bakkan and motioned Rayah over. "Hop on behind me. Bakkan knows the way, and it's quite treacherous."

"The campfire…" Rayah looked around. Snow covered every surface a foot beyond the campfire's perimeter. The fire would have no chance of spreading. Still, she didn't like the thought of leaving it, so she gathered several handfuls of snow and doused the fire.

No need to save me again, Rakzar.

It took a good forty minutes and a great deal of strength for Bakkan to reach the small outcropping hidden behind a wall of large boulders. The climb had been nearly vertical at times and the surface sheer ice. Rayah knew she never would've made it all the way up on her own. The blustery winds and freezing temperatures would've prevented her from using her wings, and the drastic change in elevation left her lightheaded. Had she attempted it, she would've fallen to her death.

Rayah dismounted and peered over the boulders. The Quietus Forest, blanketed with snow, lay several thousand feet below. She pulled her coat tight as shivers raced down her spine.

Ridan stood next to her. "Beautiful spot, right?"

"Yes, but how did you find this place?"

"Normak taught me many things, including how to map areas. He showed me how to spot paths and trails unrecognizable to most. It didn't take me long to recognize this trail."

Rayah peered down at the spot where they'd ascended. Trail was not one of the words she would've used to describe it. She sighed. "I'd be lost without you, Ridan."

"No, ya'd be food for the fizbärz and their beasts."

Rayah placed her hand over Ridan's. "You know that's not what I meant."

Ridan nodded and turned away but didn't move her hand. "Same, and sorry about earlier. Normak left a crater in my heart that will never be filled."

"It's okay, and I understand." She bent down and kissed the top of Ridan's hand. Then, she turned and faced the solid rock face. "Now what?"

Ridan retrieved the burning torch she'd wedged into Bakkan's saddle and handed it to Rayah.

She frowned at the torch. "What am I supposed to do with this?"

"Look closely at the rock face. Severe weather has eroded portions of its surface over the centuries, but ya can still make out the symbol."

Rayah moved closer and squinted at the rock face. Sure enough, a symbol had been etched into the rock. Three flames. The symbol for fire. She touched the surface with the torch flame. Sparks skittered across the rock, and then the rock began to bubble and fizz. She jumped back as the rock sloughed into a puddle on the ground, revealing a tunnel entrance where it once stood.

She and Ridan glanced at each other, and then Rayah entered the tunnel. Its smooth rock walls were hewn, not with mezhik but with chisel, evidenced by small marks every few inches. Whoever created the tunnel did so with painstaking effort.

Several strides in, the tunnel widened into a small, circular room with a white sand floor. Three iron sconces hung from the walls, one to either side of the entrance and another opposite the entrance. Two of the three torches remained, both extinguished. Nothing else existed in the room. No furniture, doorways, or symbols on the walls, floor, or ceiling.

Ridan groaned. "Now what?"

Rayah knelt and examined the sand floor. Given that the mountain consisted of grayish-black rock, it seemed odd that the floor would be covered with white sand. It certainly wasn't natural, so someone must've hauled it all the way up there.

She glanced up at Ridan. "Why would anyone go to the trouble of hauling sand up the side of a mountain?"

Ridan smiled. "To conceal something."

"Exactly." Rayah placed the torch in the empty sconce. "Guess it's time to get our hands dirty."

The two of them, along with Bakkan, dug around in the sand for almost an hour but found nothing beneath its surface. It didn't make sense. The sand had to serve some purpose.

Ridan sat back on her heels. "This is pointless."

"Yeah, and it looks like we're starting to lose some light." Rayah stood and retrieved the burning torch from the sconce. She used it to light the other two torches and then returned it back to the empty sconce.

The floor began to tremble, and then the sand at the center of the room started filtering down into two parallel cracks in the floor that weren't there beforehand. Rayah, Ridan, and Bakkan shrunk back and hugged the walls, their eyes fixated on the floor. Two more cracks appeared, parallel to each other and perpendicular to the first two. The cracks grew until each intersected the others, forming a rectangle. Dust fell from the ceiling as the sound of rock scraping against rock filled the room. The rectangular object shuddered as it began rising from the floor. As it did, Rayah noticed not only its whitish-golden hue but also that its edges were beveled at a forty-five-degree angle, the sand sliding off them. The rectangular box rose four feet out of the floor before halting. Then, the trembling and noise ceased.

Ridan took a step toward the rectangular box. "Is that what I think it is?"

Rayah's heart hammered as she approached it. She gathered a deep breath and expelled it atop the box, blowing away the thin layer of sand that remained upon it. Her efforts revealed a silver coat of arms. The sun in the top left corner and a crescent moon in the lower right, separated with a long-handled hammer. Below the coat of arms was an inscription inlaid with silver. It read: "Bräţäkţär Ef Əllíţ."

Protector Of Light.

Rayah straightened. "A sarcophagus."

Ridan came to her side. "Yeah, and I bet the hammer lies inside."

Nerves shook Rayah's hands. "What do we do now?"

"We open it."

"How do we know it's not a trap?"

"Nardus said no such thing."

"He didn't mention a sarcophagus, either. Especially one with a warning."

"Warning?" Ridan studied the sarcophagus. "Guess it depends on the interpretation. I think it's the person's title."

"Exactly," Rayah said. "And how do you know we won't have to face this person once we open it?"

"Hmm…" Ridan continued to stare at the sarcophagus. "Hadn't thought about that."

Rayah shuddered. "That's all I can think about."

"We've faced far worse than the spirit of a fallen warrior, right?"

Rayah didn't disagree, but it still didn't calm her nerves. Either way, they'd come for the hammer. Leaving without it wouldn't be acceptable.

She took a deep breath, removed her coat, and then donned her special gloves. The blades trembled on her belt, ready to do her bidding. "Let's do this."

Ridan retrieved her spear and wedged the spear tip into the crack between the sarcophagus and its lid. She glanced at Rayah, and Rayah nodded. Ridan yanked down on the spear shaft with a grunt. At first, the spear just bent under Ridan's weight, but then the sarcophagus lid slid over an inch.

A strong wind rushed forth from the cracked sarcophagus, blowing out the torches and casting the small room in darkness. Ridan and Rayah stepped back. Bakkan growled, his eyes glowing in the darkness.

A yellow, ethereal glow emanated from the sarcophagus, and then the lid flew into the air and crashed into the ceiling.

Crack!

Rayah and Ridan crouched low and protected their faces as the lid exploded into a million pieces and rained down from the ceiling like starlight. As frightening as it was, Rayah couldn't help but feel a sense of awe. She'd never seen anything like it before.

The room burst with light as a man clad in shining armor as bright as the sun sat up in the sarcophagus. "Who dares awaken me?" The man rose until he stood inside the sarcophagus.

Neither Rayah nor Ridan said a word or made a move. Bakkan stood motionless, too.

The man turned and faced Rayah and Ridan. His glowing eyes peered into their souls. "I am Verin, *Brätäktär Ef Əllít*. Why have you disturbed my slumber?"

After a few moments, Rayah finally found her voice. "We've come for *Hemär Dhef Əllít*."

The glowing man stepped down from the sarcophagus. He towered over her and Ridan. Rayah cringed, fearing what might come next.

Verin said, "Your journey has been for naught. The hammer has been gone for centuries."

Rayah and Ridan glanced at each other. Ridan said, "I don't understand. How can it be gone?"

Verin cocked his head. "Was it not used to destroy the dark heart?"

"No, and that's why we've come for it," Rayah said.

Verin sighed, and the light from his armor dimmed. He leaned against the sarcophagus, defeat upon his face. "Then I've been deceived."

"Deceived?" Ridan edged closer to Verin. "By whom?"

"A man I once considered a friend." He glared at some space over their heads and rubbed his eyes. "Gazsi."

Rayah had never heard the name before. She peered over at Ridan, and Ridan shrugged. "How can we find this Gazsi?" she said.

"No one finds Gazsi." Verin gazed at them both for several moments. "Gazsi finds you." He turned and crawled back into the sarcophagus.

"Wait," Rayah said. Verin just stared at her. "There's something I don't understand."

"Speak quickly, for I am old and in need of rest."

Rayah drew closer to the sarcophagus. "The ancient texts say that you served Magus and hid the hammer for him. If that's true, then why do you call yourself *Brätäkṭär Ef Əllíṭ*?"

"The texts do not lie. I served Magus for years, and I did take the hammer at his request, but by that time I'd come to realize I fought for the wrong side. For the wrong God. As punishment, I bound my soul to this place in servitude to Ʒäṭür. I will never truly rest until *Hemär Dhef Əllíṭ* returns to me." Verin lay down and closed his eyes.

From that moment, everything happened in reverse. Starlight rose to the ceiling and reformed the sarcophagus lid, then the lid crashed back down on the sarcophagus, expelling the ethereal light. Ridan's torch flickered back to life in its sconce, and the sarcophagus sank back into the sand until no signs of it remained. Then, the sand smoothed itself out.

Rayah removed her gloves and pulled her coat back on before facing Ridan. "Now what?"

"We kill a buck and then head for Vallah."

Rayah frowned. "Kill a buck?"

Ridan winked at her. "Had to make a deal to free ya." She mounted Bakkan and patted the space behind her. "Come on, we've got a long journey ahead of us."

Rayah dreaded returning to the King's Palace empty-handed, but what choice did they have?

Ʒäṭür, please help Nardus understand who Gazsi is and where to find Hemär Dhef Əllíṭ.

CHAPTER THIRTY

At first light, Rakzar and Urza set out toward the battlefield where everything had changed. Most his life, he had believed death was the end of existence. Nothing more than a thin veil separated life from eternal darkness, and death pushed you beyond that veil. Then, he stepped into the ocean and drown. He swore in that moment he'd felt a presence and witnessed a bright light before returning to the beach and to his body. Still, he knew his life would end in darkness. What he didn't know was whether the White Knight's had. He prayed it didn't.

As they neared the area south of Elatos, one thing became clear: he and Urza could walk right through enemy camps without fear of capture. Not a single person or beast bothered to turn their head as they passed by. He'd have to report the news to Nardus once they met back up at the King's Palace in Vallah. It was something they could certainly use to their advantage.

After traveling a bit farther, Urza stopped. Rakzar recognized the spot where the White Knight—Alderan—had turned to ash. Although the ash had long since blown away, the ground remained charred.

Miss you, friend.

Rakzar was about to turn away when he caught a glint of something out of the corner of his eye. He walked over and knelt next to Alderan's outline. The dirt wasn't just charred but had melted into glass. Rakzar dug around it and found it to be several inches thick. As hot as dragon's fire was, he didn't believe it could turn dirt and sand to glass with a single burst. Only wizard's fire burned that hot and continued to burn.

What had caught his eye lay within the glass. He used one of his axes to shatter the glass and then dug a pendant out of it with his claws. He recognized the pendant as the one Nardus gave to Alderan to protect him from dragon's fire. The same pendant that failed to do its job. Rakzar almost tossed it away but then thought better of it. Nardus might want it back. Might want to examine it to see why it had failed to protect Alderan. Then again, Rakzar had already discovered the answer. It wasn't dragon's fire at all that killed the White Knight.

Urza returned to Rakzar's side with three pieces of a recurve bow. "Not sure how the dwarves are going to fix this."

Rakzar examined each piece. He wasn't a weapons expert by any means, but the breaks looked clean and provided a good surface to adhere to. "Not just any dwarf. Torbrek Stonebreaker. If it can be fixed, he'll do it."

Two soldiers clad in black walked over to Rakzar and Urza. Both had their swords drawn but not at the ready. Rakzar's first instinct was to kill them both, but then he remembered where he stood and that no one thought of them as the enemy. He handed the bow pieces back to Urza.

The tallest soldier peered up at Rakzar and scowled at him. "Wrong place for scavenging, dog."

Rakzar ignored the man's racist slur but glared at him. "You dare waltz over here and interrupt the queen's business?"

"Queen's business?" the smaller soldier said. The two men exchanged frowns.

"Yeah, that's right," Urza said. "This bow belonged to the queen's brother. She wants it repaired and returned to her at once."

"Does she?" The taller soldier glanced at the bow pieces and wrinkled his nose. "Used to work the armory. No one could fix that bow."

"No human," Rakzar said.

The taller soldier raised his sword toward Rakzar. "You, a dog, insulting me?"

Click! Click!

Urza lunged forward and drove one of her blades underneath the man's chin and right up into his skull before the bow pieces hit the ground. The man's eyes grew wide. She ripped the blade out, and the soldier gurgled and fell to the ground, dead.

The shorter soldier dropped his sword and backed away with his hands raised. "Not here to cause trouble."

"Neither are we," Rakzar growled.

Urza licked the blade clean before returning it and its twin to their sheathes on her forearms. The soldier turned and walked away, leaving a pool of urine behind. She bent down and relieved the dead soldier of his coin purse.

Rakzar picked up the bow pieces and placed them inside a large leather sack. After strapping the sack to his back, he dropped on all fours. "Come on, Urza. We've got a long journey ahead."

† † †

A few hours later, Urza and Rakzar arrived at the shoreline of Trivers Lake where they'd fought Käíeƹ and buried Normak. Urza had promised Ridan that they'd return Normak's body to Tectus. Little did she know how well Rayah had buried it. An hour later, they finally unburied Normak enough to pull him from the sand. His body had preserved in the cold, damp sand far better than Käíeƹ's did out in the elements, but it smelled a thousand times worse.

Urza turned and looked at Käíeƹ's corpse. Something had clearly made a snack of her. Mostly bone remained. "I'd ask if you wanted to carry him or her, but there's no way in the nine realms I'm touching her."

Rakzar shuddered. "Torbrek wants her, he can come get her."

He bent down and pulled the crystal dagger from the sand by its black hilt. As delicate as it had seemed, the blade remained in a single piece. He slid it into the sheathe Verdik Shardshaper had made for it, then rose. "You take Normak today, and I'll carry him the rest of the way tomorrow. Deal?"

"Fine, but if anyone asks why I have a dead dwarf strapped to my back, I'll take my anger out on you. Understood?"

Rakzar growled with laughter. "I'd pay good money for an artist to paint a picture of that!"

Urza contemplated burying one of her blades in his side. Not a fatal wound, of course. Just one deep enough and wide enough for him to think twice before making her the punchline for any sort of joke.

"Bet you would," she said.

After Rakzar secured the dwarf to Urza's back, the two of them headed north toward the Gala River. With luck, they'd make it as far as Scindo Flumen before resting for the night.

As they ran, Urza couldn't keep from thinking about her dwarven friend.

How will Torbrek react to Normak's death?

† † †

A few hours after sunrise, Rakzar and Urza reached the foothills of the Procerus Mountains. From there, they traversed the hidden trails that led to the cave entrance to Tectus. Hours later, they reached the cave entrance and met the same two dwarves guarding the entrance as they had the first time they came looking for Torbrek Stonebreaker. Normak had mentioned the two of them were twins.

Gorfek, the dwarf with the red beard, glowered at Rakzar. "Yeh back, are yeh?" He glanced around Rakzar and Urza. "Where be the others?"

"Ridan and Rayah are on another quest," Urza said.

"An' Normak?" said Worfek, the dwarf with the orange beard.

"That's one of the reasons we're here." Rakzar turned around.

The two dwarves gasped and swore, "By the gods!" They raised their weapons.

Gorfek said, "Yeh shouldn'a come 'ere."

Urza knelt. "We didn't do this to him, but the one who did lies dead by Normak's hand on the western shoreline of Trivers Lake. His bravery helped save the rest of us."

Worfek nodded. "Normak be brave as a silver bear an fierce as a black lion."

"Aye," Gorfek said.

Rakzar turned and faced the two dwarves. "Let us pass. Torbrek needs to know what happened to his brother."

Gorfek and Worfek lowered their weapons and stepped aside. "Gods be wit' 'im on 'is journey to the other side," Gorfek said.

Rakzar and Urza made their way down to the fifth level of Tectus with little more than a few gasps and curses from some of the dwarves they crossed paths with along the way. By the time they reached the armory, word had already made its way to Torbrek. He stormed through the doors brandishing a pair of three-balled flails.

"How in the nine realms did you let my brother die?" He swung one of the flails. Its spiked balls bit into the rock wall a few inches from Rakzar's left shoulder with a *crunch* and tore away a small section of the wall when he yanked it back.

Urza and Rakzar stepped back. Urza said, "Calm down, Torbrek. We'll tell you everything."

Torbrek buried the three ends of the second flail in the floor just inches from Urza's feet. Rage filled his eyes. "My brother's strapped to that beast's back like some sort of trophy kill, and you want me to calm down?"

"We had no other way to transport him," Rakzar said. "Let's move inside the armory, and we'll lay him on one of the worktables."

Torbrek slammed the first flail into the floor then tossed both flail handles aside. "This way."

Rakzar and Urza followed Torbrek into the armory and all the way to the back. Torbrek had clearly raged his way through the entire armory. Rakzar didn't blame him. Had Normak been his brother, he likely would've reacted in the same manner.

Torbrek cleared the contents of the table by tossing everything onto the floor. "Lay him down here and be gentle."

Rakzar dropped on all fours, and Urza untied Normak from his back. Then, the two of them placed Normak on the table and stepped back. At first, Torbrek just stood there and stared at his brother as though he expected him to rise from the dead and speak, but then he leaned over the table, took Normak's decayed hand in his, and wept.

Once Torbrek gained control of his emotions, Rakzar and Urza walked him through all the events that led to Normak's death and then the ones that followed it. They left nothing out, including leaving Käíeʒ's body on the shoreline.

Torbrek paced and pulled on his beard braids. "A living and breathing dragon..."

"Yes, and that's the other reason we're here." Rakzar took the sack from his back, pulled out the three pieces of Alderan's bow, and lay them on the table. "This bow was the only thing strong enough to wedge an arrow between Cinolth's scales."

Torbrek returned to the table and gave the bow a quick glance. "Dwarves do not make bows."

"Yes, we know," Urza said.

"Then why would you bring it to me?"

"Take a closer look at it," Rakzar said.

Torbrek huffed. "Very well." He picked up one of the ends and began to examine it. "Definitely not human made." His brow furrowed as he held it up to the light. "Nor is it elvish." He torqued the piece in his hands. "This is—"

"Not from our world," Urza finished. "We know. And that's why we brought it to you."

"Yeah, I understand that now." Torbrek frowned and scratched his chin with the bow end. "I will need some time to understand the materials used."

"Understood," Urza said. "However, there's one more issue."

"Which is what?"

Urza sighed. "The arrows that went with the bow were lost in the chaos of the battle."

Torbrek set the bow end back on the table and returned to Normak's side. "Arrows can be forged."

"Yes, but can they be forged with the power to pierce Cinolth's scales?" she said.

"I'm not sure I follow what you're asking."

"His scales are impervious to most types of mezhik," Rakzar said, "and his scales are virtually impenetrable because of their thickness and the way they're layered. His only weak spots lie at the pits of his arms."

Torbrek walked over to a chest of drawers and began rummaging through them. "Few weeks ago, a traveler came with some strange tales of sentient vines and a sickness that turned the skin white and the veins and eyes black." Torbrek pulled two black objects from the drawer and handed Rakzar and Urza one each. "Claimed those were left by the sentient vines after they withered and died."

"Dragon scales," Urza said.

"According to Nardus, these are scales from Cinolth," Rakzar said. "Something about a curse when he was killed during the Great War."

"Yes, I've heard the tales. I'll be right back." Torbrek headed back into the main part of the armory and returned a minute later with a spear. He handed it to Urza. "I believe we're on the cusp of discovering how to pierce these scales."

Rakzar scoffed. "Are you talking hours, days, weeks, or years?"

"Days at most. Look at the divots on the underside of those scales."

"Yes, I see," Urza said, examining her scale. "So, what created them?"

Torbrek crossed his arms over his chest. "I used the tip of a dragon's claw that Normak found long ago while hiking through the Procerus Mountains. Attached it to the end of an arrow."

Rakzar wasn't nearly as impressed. "This is still a far cry from piercing it."

"Of course it is." He turned and began stoking the fires of a large furnace. "Now, give me an hour to finish a task. I will meet you on the third level."

"For what purpose?" Urza said.

"A grand party must be thrown in honor of my brother."

"I thought the third level was all agriculture and mining."

"True, but it's also where we go for the largest gatherings." He grinned wide. "Gatherings with the king and queen!"

† † †

Urza stood just beyond the massive gates that led down to the fourth level of Tectus and awaited Torbrek's arrival. Rakzar, ever impatient, paced next to a massive field of amber wheat. Utilizing a vast network of reflective crystals, the dwarves had designed a way to bring sunlight to their crops. And, given the consistent temperatures below ground, the crops produced food year-round. It was an impressive and ingenious system.

After a short wait, Torbrek strode up from the lower level, fully clothed in shining gold dwarven armor. Had she not known the dwarf, Urza might've mistaken him for royalty. Three dwarves clad in matching black armor fell in behind Torbrek. Each of them carried a battle axe draped over their right shoulders. Behind those three marched an entire brigade of dwarves clad in dark red armor. Gold-and-red banners draped from the poles of their long pikes.

Another brigade followed the first, each dwarf clad in gold and red armor that matched the banners carried by the first brigade. Unlike the others, they carried no weapons. However, they donned black leather belts with several pouches.

The alchemists.

Growing up, Urza had heard legends of the dwarven alchemists. They used elements of nature to wage war, much like the wizards and sorceresses of the human race, and their skills rivaled that of the elven druids.

Next came King Morlek and Queen Dommoure. Although she'd glimpsed the queen once before, Urza had never laid eyes on the dwarven king. He rode in on a pure white mastiff and wore white gold armor and a matching helmet that commanded attention. His gray eyes were striking.

The queen rode next to him on a mastiff of her own, but hers was solid black. She also wore armor, black as midnight, yet the light created a rainbow of colors everywhere it hit the armor. The beauty of her armor surpassed that of King Morlek's. She too had gray eyes.

The king and queen had no children of their own. Even if they had, royalty in dwarven society was not a station one was born into. Instead, the dwarves had a system of election. Once someone was elected, they would reign either until death or until they reached an age of 400 years. Unlike many societies, a queen could run to rule the clan. If elected, her husband would serve as king in name only. Also, unlike some societies, the crown never passed from king to queen or vice-versa.

Urza eyed the king once again. Given his youthful features and grayless red hair, he likely had centuries before reaching the age of retirement.

The royal entourage followed close behind the king and queen. Magistrates and counselors, advisers, and even a jester. All dressed in armor in shades of green, blue, and purple. Urza deemed her own leather armor inadequate for such an occasion.

"Thought this was supposed to be a party," Rakzar said.

Urza had been so absorbed in the procession that she hadn't noticed Rakzar return from the wheat fields. "The party isn't here."

She and Rakzar fell in behind the royal entourage, along with droves of dwarves. Given their vast numbers, Urza imagined the entirety of Tectus must've come to pay respects to Normak. The sentiment nearly overwhelmed her.

As they passed through the center of the third level of Tectus, she became more and more aware of how she and Rakzar stuck out. The two of them were giants among the short-statured dwarves. She quickly became more self-conscious than she thought possible, especially when she felt their stares locked on the back of her head.

This isn't me.

The procession headed through a wide tunnel filled with a rainbow of sparkling light. It wasn't far before the short tunnel transitioned into a massive cavern. Crystals and gemstones covered the massive cavern, including the floor. Unnatural light bounced off every surface and caused the entire cavern to feel as though it were spinning.

At the far end of the cavern sat two thrones encrusted with jewels. The king and queen retreated to them. Tables lined the outer rim of the cavern, each filled with mounds of breads, meats, and cheeses. Alongside each table were massive wooden drums filled with ale. Before long, the entire room danced, sang, and cheered in the name of Normak.

Urza nursed a mug of ale. The bitter taste didn't sit well on her tongue. Rakzar leaned against one of the outer walls with his arms crossed and a scowl on his face. Had she anywhere else to be besides standing next to him, she would've been there.

After what felt like hours of drinking, King Morlek toasted the memory of Normak. Afterward, the crowd slowly dissipated. Torbrek was among the last to leave. Urza and Rakzar followed him back to the armory.

Inside, they returned to the back room. Normak's body was gone.

"What happened to Normak?" Urza said.

"He's been laid to rest with my parents and sister." Torbrek scowled at the empty table where Normak had lain. "I noticed his winged boots were not on his feet."

"Ridan took them," Rakzar said.

Torbrek nodded. "Figured as much." He turned to the large furnace. "See yourselves out, and come back in two days. I'll have what you need then."

Urza and Rakzar showed themselves out and returned to the upper level of Tectus. There, they made their way to the best of the three inns in Tectus: Oakengut's Inn and Pub. It was the same establishment where they'd watched Normak dance and sing atop the tables. Urza stopped and closed her eyes for a moment as they passed the pub part of the establishment. Normak danced in her mind one last time.

Farewell, friend.

CHAPTER THIRTY-ONE

Everything happens for a reason. That's what Nardus used to tell himself long ago. Long before he was ever known as Nardus. Yet somewhere along the way he stopped believing it. Found the sentiment hard to swallow. Rebuked those who dared quote it to him.

Now, everything had changed, but not because he had resolved the issues within himself. Nor was it because he entrusted his life to Ɂät̪ūr once again. No, the explanation for his change in perspective was far simpler. It boiled down to two words scrawled on a page. Yes, there were far more than two words written, but none of the others carried the weight of the first two. It would be impossible.

Every few minutes, he checked the book again. Verified those two life-altering words still remained and that his mind hadn't played a wicked trick on him. To be certain, he had Theyn confirm them. Three times.

Still, he found those two words difficult to swallow. Difficult to believe. No matter how true they might be, he could never be certain until he witnessed it with his own eyes. Touched his son's face once again. Wrapped his arms around him and held him tight. Even then, it would be difficult. After all, how does one rise from the dead? No mezhik held such power.

The final act played over in his mind. Victory was at hand, Cinolth in his clutches. But an instant later, his world fell to ruin as dragon's fire consumed Shardan. Turned him to ash. Ripped him away from the world.

Nardus held his head. Pulled on his hair.

How can he live?

The question churned in his mind relentlessly. Distracted him from everything. Everyone. He'd fallen to his knees and praised Ɂät̪ūr for the news, yet he still questioned it. Questioned everything.

How is it possible?

"Nardus!" Theyn grabbed his arm.

"I'm here," he said, though it wasn't quite true.

Once he finally focused on the moment, he realized that the two of them were alone for the first time in more than a week. Theyn sat on the floor in front of a massive stone hearth, facing him. A fire blazed, crackled, sparked. Kept the night's chill at bay.

"It's time we talk about the future," Theyn said.

At first, he thought she meant the next battle, but her eyes said more. She moved closer. Took his hands in hers.

"What is it you expect of me?" The words sounded harsh even to his own ears. He sighed. Squeezed her hands. "I'm sorry. That came out wrong."

"It's okay, my love."

"No, it's not. What I meant to say is that I don't understand what you mean. All our futures hang in the balance as long as Cinolth lives."

"Yes, and that's why we must discuss it." She stared into his eyes for an eternity. The silence between them ate at his very soul, but he refused to break it. Theyn finally did. "What I mean is that I need to see our future."

"What's the point in peering into a future that might change or that could be misinterpreted?"

"As dark as it seems, knowing what might lie ahead of us gives me a sense of peace and hope."

"Even when you're skewered by a dragon's claw?"

"Especially then." Her infectious smile curled his own lips. "Did it not save our lives in the spire?"

Nardus conceded. "Yes, but how long did we live in fear of that moment?"

"I will not force you to do it, but it would mean everything to me if you did."

Nardus turned and stared at the flames for a few moments. "I'll allow it, but then I'll fight every moment to prevent whatever we see."

"And what if it's one of us dying of old age?"

"Then I'll fight even harder to never let you grow old."

"That's not something you can control."

"Perhaps not, but I serve a God who can and does."

"How are you so certain about your god? Is my god somehow inferior to yours?"

"Zhedäꙅ Ɔʊn is a false god, Theyn, and I can prove it."

"How so?"

"Has this god of yours ever spoken to you or performed a miracle?"

"No, but that's not how it works."

"No? And why do you think that is?"

"Like any god, Zhedäꙅ Ɔʊn is far too busy to respond to someone like me. I am nothing but her servant, so why would she have reason to speak to me?"

"When my God speaks, the foundations of the world quake with fear and wonder. And, when I pray to him, he responds in many ways, but he always responds. As you know, I begged him to bring my family back to me, and he did. Perhaps not in the way I expected, but he did, nevertheless. Shardan has died twice now, yet Savric tells me he lives again. A miracle!" He reached up and cupped the side of her face. "Has your god brought the dead back to life?"

She scowled. "No, but that's not fair."

"Why not? Is it because your god is inferior to mine? Or is it that your god is false?"

Theyn pulled away. "As I said, she's busy."

"Have you offered her food sacrifices?"

"Yes, daily at times."

"And she's consumed them?"

"No, but—"

"There can be no but. Long ago, I witnessed Ɔät̪ūr reign fire from the heavens and consume a sacrifice given in his name. In that moment, I knew no other god existed but him. Shed yourself of your false god. Renounce your affiliation to Zhedäꙅ Ɔʊn and serve the one who existed before the foundations of the world. Join me, Theyn. Serve Ɔät̪ūr with all your heart."

Tears glistened in Theyn's eyes. "You're asking me to throw away everything I've ever known to be true."

"Yes, because the things you understand to be true are nothing more than the lies of Diꙅäfär."

"I don't know. I must think about it."

"Very well." He kissed her hand then released it. "Come over here and do what you must."

Theyn pushed Nardus onto his back and crawled onto his chest. After piercing her thumbs with her fangs, she placed them on his temples. As it had twice before, mezhik tingled against his skin as Theyn's mind joined his.

"Ready?"

Nardus groaned. *"I am."*

He quickly slipped down into what felt like a dream. Moments later, Theyn withdrew her thumbs. They both gasped and held their chests. Theyn lay against him as the pain subsided.

"Nothing has changed," she said, sorrow in her voice.

"I still die in battle."

She nodded, and tears wet his neck. "I still didn't see who threw the spear into your back."

"Obviously, I didn't either."

"How do we fix this?"

Nardus sighed. "I'm not sure if we can, but I'll do my damnedest to try." He stroked her head. "At least we win the battle."

"Yes, but does it end the war?"

He wasn't sure he wanted to know the answer. "Pray that it does."

Nardus closed his eyes for a minute. Nearly drifted off to sleep when the sound of shattering glass rose from deep within the ruins of the King's Palace.

† † †

Zerenity conjured a ball of light as she dashed down the corridor toward the room where Nardus and Theyn had settled. The two of them emerged from the room just as she arrived. She looked beyond them and farther down the dark corridor. "You heard it, too?"

"We did." Theyn shifted into her cat form.

"Sounded like it might've come from the kitchens. The two of you follow me and stay close." Nardus took off down the corridor.

Zerenity did all she could to keep up with Nardus and Theyn. By the time she reached the doors that led into the kitchens, her chest heaved, and her lungs burned with fire. It took several seconds for her to catch her breath. Neither Nardus nor Theyn breathed hard.

Wait until you're my age.

Another glass broke just on the other side of the doors, and she extinguished her light.

A voice bellowed from within. "Zhedäʑ ʕʊn… help me find something to stop the bleeding."

"That's—"

"Berggren!" Theyn burst through the doors.

Zerenity conjured another ball of light and followed Nardus through the kitchen doors. Her eyes first took in the mountainous man, his hands and clothes covered in blood. Then, she saw the young man sprawled out on one of the counters.

Calen.

She rushed over to him. Niesha knelt on the counter next to Calen and held a bloody rag against his stomach. The poor girl hardly blinked when Zerenity pulled her hand away from Calen. The rag resisted a little as she peeled it away. Greenish-black flesh surrounded a gaping wound full of cheesy, yellowish pus. The pungent odor curdled what remained in Zerenity's stomach from supper earlier that night.

Dear ʕäʈūr.

She stepped back. "Nardus, come take a look at this. I'm not sure I can do anything for him."

Nardus inspected the wound. "You're an herbalist, are you not?"

"Yes, but—"

He glowered at her. "Gather supplies to make a salve for the wound. Theyn, go help her." He turned to Berggren. "What happened?"

"First, we were attacked by zhebəllin in the stronghold. They captured me, but Calen, Eshtak, and Niesha rescued me. During the rescue, Calen took a jab to the gut."

Nardus looked back at Calen's wound then to Berggren again. "That can't be all that happened."

"We were attacked by blood beetles a few nights ago." Niesha cringed but continued, "A few of them got into the wound, so I had to fish them out with my hand." She held up her hand. It was crusted with dried blood past her wrist.

Zerenity just stood there, her mind stuck trying to process what'd happened to Calen.

Nardus snapped at her, "The longer you hesitate, the more likely it is that Calen dies."

Zerenity swallowed hard. "Yes, of course." She and Theyn left the kitchens in search of something that would combat the corrosive saliva of blood beetles.

† † †

Nardus had never seen a wound as infected as Calen's. He didn't understand how it hadn't taken the boy's life already, so he thanked Ɛätūr for the opportunity to save him. As the night drew into morning, he continued to alternate between cutting away the rotted and dead flesh around and within the wound and using his mezhik to stitch the tissue back together. During that time, his thoughts kept returning to the theme he'd explored earlier in the night.

Everything happens for a reason.

Only a true God could have orchestrated the events over the last few days to bring each of them where they needed to be. Right then, every doubt faded from his mind about his son. Shardan lived. The news of his resurrection or whatever one might call it led Nardus back to Vallah and the King's Palace. Had he not been there, Calen would be dead. However, it took far more orchestration than that. It all started with their escape from Nasduron and the encounter with Lilith beneath the barn outside Dyserth. Had she not given him the triad, he wouldn't have had the strength or stamina to work on Calen through the night.

Everything happens for a reason.

It was also no coincidence that Zerenity had come with him. Her knowledge of herbs and the salve she created would enable Calen's wound to fully heal. Without it, the infection would have eventually spread beyond the containment of Nardus's mezhik.

Everything happens for a reason.

Had Theyn not been there, Zerenity never would've located the herbs.

Theyn's keen sense of smell enabled them to locate what was needed beneath the rubble. As he saw it, the list of orchestrated events was endless.

Nardus wiped sweat from his brow and sighed.

"He'll live, right?" Niesha said.

Nardus turned and faced her. She'd been so quiet all night that he'd forgotten she was still there. "He will, thanks to you."

Niesha scrunched up her face. "I didn't do anything but remove a few bugs."

"If you hadn't, they would've eaten him alive. You're a hero."

She hung her head. "No, I'm not. I didn't want to do it, but the big man said I had to."

"Just because we do something we're asked to do doesn't make the act less heroic. Many people would've refused to do what you did or might've even run away."

"But I was afraid." She looked back up, then stared at her hand. "What if I'd pulled something out that should've stayed in? I could've killed him."

Nardus moved over next to her and leaned against the table. "Impossible."

She looked up at him. "What do you mean?"

"As I said, had you done nothing, he would've died. Therefore, the only possible change to his outcome by you acting would be to save his life. Do you understand?"

Niesha cocked her head then nodded. She chewed on her lower lip and stared at Calen. Finally, she said, "You're different than the big man."

Nardus chuckled. "Is that a good thing or a bad thing?"

She shrugged. "Not sure it's either." After chewing her lip some more, she said, "He treats me like a parent would, but you treat me like a person." She frowned and shook her head. "That didn't come out the way I intended it to. I mean you don't treat me like I'm six."

"Well, you're far more mature than any other six-year-old I've ever met." He studied her face for a few moments. "Should I?"

Niesha looked up at him again, her eyes wide. "No!"

He put his arm around her and squeezed. "It's settled then." Her greasy, brown hair tickled his nostrils. He inhaled and regretted it. "Ugh."

Niesha wiggled away from him. "Yeah, I know. I'm quite ripe." She wrinkled her nose. "You're past expiration, too."

He laughed. "I'm sure we all are."

Theyn walked in and eyed the two of them. "What's so funny?"

"How about you take Niesha and find somewhere to bathe."

Niesha looked at herself. "What's the point if I have to put these soiled rags back on when I'm done?"

"I saw a bunch of clothes when Zerenity and I were looking for herbs. There might be a few that'll fit you." Theyn held out her hand in front of Niesha. "Come on."

Niesha took Theyn's hand and hopped off the table. Then, the two of them headed out of the kitchens, hand in hand. Nardus smiled.

Theyn would make a perfect mother.

The thought struck a nerve. After everything he'd been through with Shardan, Shanara, and Savannah, could he handle having another child? He didn't have an answer. For now, one wasn't needed.

And if we survive the war?

CHAPTER THIRTY-TWO

Everything Wrik knew about mezhik and dragons had been turned upside-down a few days back. He'd never read a single book about dragons using mezhik, but Cinolth was no ordinary dragon. Cinolth had proven it by cursing the world upon his death and then returning from the dead.

But how had he used Aria's mezhik without her knowledge?

The question haunted him. Yet he held no doubts as to Aria's innocence after seeing the look on her face when he left Galondu Castle. The farther he traveled down the prophetic path, the more blood he found on his hands. He never planned on killing anyone or causing anyone to die that wasn't predestined to, yet he had.

Far too many to count.

In truth, he couldn't pinpoint the place in his life where he veered from observer of prophecy to fulfiller of prophecy. The steep slope he stood upon had nearly cost him his life more than once. Now, he needed to figure out how to right the wrongs he'd caused. He also needed to figure out how he could get back on Aria's good side now that he knew she didn't want him dead. Or at least that she hadn't before he screwed everything up and killed her brother.

Alcedonia lay at the foot of the Aether Mountains. He would soon risk his life again facing the ire of the äəllf äkfeţik. Winning the war would be impossible without a mage like Cyrus, and the aquatic elves held the key to freeing him from Nasduron.

Wrik was about to make his entrance in Alcedonia when Blackwind began chirping and bobbing her head. It wasn't unlike her to get excited when she was hungry, but she'd just fed less than an hour ago. Without warning, Blackwind rose, wrapped her leathery wings around him, and pulled him to the ground. His spectacles flew from his face.

"*Blackwind!*" he said through their link. "*Let me go!*"

She groaned, wrapped her wings tighter, then rolled the two of them beneath the shadows of the trees and into the thick brush. Wrik struggled to free himself without hurting her, but then he heard the sound.

Thump-thump. Whoosh!

The sound nearly stopped his heart.

Cinolth!

The two of them lay still as Aria and the massive beast made several passes over the area. Blackwind's heart thundered in his ear as Cinolth drew near again. He'd never known before how much she feared Cinolth, but he didn't blame her. She'd make for a decent-sized meal if Cinolth caught her.

Thump-thump. Whoosh!

The sound pounded his ears without relent.

Thump.

Wrik couldn't breathe. Couldn't see much without his spectacles but blurry shapes. Something in the small clearing moved, then stopped. He cursed himself for losing his spectacles.

"Fire's been out for several hours," Aria said. The clearing was far too small for Cinolth to land, so she must've dismounted from the air.

Gods, don't let her find my spectacles.

"Strange," Aria said. "There's a pile of rocks just sitting here by the fire pit, and they don't match those nearby."

A pile of rocks?

Wrik was certain there were no rocks piled up by the fire pit, so where had they come from?

Snap!

The broken twig sounded far closer than Wrik would've liked. He held his breath as the shadows began to move. Blackwind trembled.

Stay calm, girl.

"If you're out here Wrik, know that I'm coming for you." Aria stood just feet away.

After what felt like hours, Aria turned and walked away, the leaves crunching beneath her feet. Had she conjured a light ball, Wrik and

Blackwind would be dead.

Why didn't she?

Sometime later, Aria and Cinolth finally moved on, the sound of Cinolth's wings fading in the distance until the silence of the forest returned. With a bit of encouragement, Wrik managed to get Blackwind to let him go. He stood and returned to the clearing. His blurry eyes searched the sky, his pulse still elevated. Droves of dark clouds provided plenty of cover for a large dragon, but they could never hide the deafening sound of his beating wings.

As he stood there, Wrik wondered if Aria and Cinolth just happened to be searching the Aether Mountains for him or if someone or something had tipped them off. Either way, he realized that he must be more careful. Cinolth had eyes everywhere.

He rubbed Blackwind's belly. "You did good, girl." She bobbed her head and trilled. The beautiful sound settled his mind and brought his pulse back down to a normal level.

Wrik knelt and searched the ground for his spectacles but didn't find them.

Did Aria find them?

It was a stupid thought. If she had, she would've burned the forest down to find him. So, the question of where they landed remained. He wished Blackwind was a sentient creature. Her intelligence was unquestionable. She understood a plethora of commands, but no command he knew of would get her to help him find his spectacles.

He rose and sighed loudly. "Should've had a spare pair made."

"Looking for these?" came a screechy, high-pitched voice.

Wrik whirled to his left and conjured a fireball. The additional light distorted his vision further. "Who's there?"

"Name's Vorath, but everyone calls me Screech." Something small moved to Wrik's right. "Extinguish that fireball of yours, and I'll be happy to give you your contraption back."

Wrik let the fireball fizzle out then held out his hand. "They're called spectacles. Hand them over." A gelatinous blob drenched his hand and oozed between his fingers. "Ugh!" He closed his hand and found the spectacles buried within the putrid slime. Thankfully, he had a strong stomach. "What the gods did you do to them?"

"Thought they might be some sort of strange food." Screech snickered. "Turns out I was *way* wrong."

It took a good minute for Wrik to get the spectacles clean enough before he felt comfortable placing them back on his face. When he finally did, he regretted it immediately. The reprehensible stench burned his nostrils and made him tear up.

Wrik rubbed his eyes with his fingers. "What did you eat before you tried consuming my spectacles?"

Screech snorted. "Coulda been just about anything. I'm really not picky, and I'll try anything once."

With his vision restored, Wrik glared at the strange little dragon that stood before him.

Brown, rock-like plates covered Screech's entire body except for his chest and belly. They were tan. A small patch of brownish-black spots covered the top of his head and his chest, both a diamond-shaped pattern. Two small black horns protruded from the top of his skull, just above pointed black ears. Deep-set serpentine eyes jittered in their sockets. Bright yellow with brown centers. He had a smooth snout lined with sharp teeth, and three bony nubs protruded from beneath his narrow chin. He stood just three feet tall on his hind legs, and each of his two leathery wings looked to be no more than two-and-a-half feet wide. A round-tipped tail whipped the air behind him, and small, bony nubs trailed down the length of his back.

"How long have you been following us?" Wrik said.

"Following?" Screech chuckled, sneezed, then coughed up a wad of phlegm. He spat it on the ground. "Sorry about that. Turns out I'm highly allergic to fear."

Wrik scowled. "Answer the question."

"Never followed. Just found. I've been searching for you for quite some time." Screech cocked his head. "You are Wizard Wrik, right?"

Hearing his own name caught Wrik off guard. "How do you know who I am?"

Screech stretched out his wings, then sneezed violently. The force sent him reeling backward and into a reverse somersault. He lay on his stomach for a few moments and sneezed twice more before picking himself back up. "Sheesh." Snot drooled from his nostrils. He licked it off with a long, gray tongue. "Sorry about that."

Gross.

"As I was about to say, Peorvem The Ancient sent me to find you."

"I see." A single explanation arose in Wrik's mind, and he didn't like the implications of it. "Have you come to deliver a message?"

Screech scoffed as he looked down at himself. "Do I look like a messenger dragon? No. No, I do not. I'll have you know I'm a fierce fighter." He spread his wings wide, puffed out his chest, brandished his curved claws, and growled. The sound he produced reminded Wrik of an angry kitten.

Wrik laughed. "Yes, I'm sure you are."

Screech scowled and crossed his arms over his chest. "I once took on a killer moth. *All* by myself."

"And did you win?" Wrik said.

"That's really not funny." Screech pouted, and his gaze fell to the ground. "Admittedly, I did not, but it wasn't for lack of trying."

"I'm sure you gave it your best effort." Wrik shook his head. "Anyway, you've come without a message and you're obviously not here for my protection, so—"

"Hey!" Screech flicked the ground with his tail. "I'll have you know I saved your life today."

Wrik scoffed. "By cowering in the shadows?"

"Funny. Real funny. Before I cowered in the shadows, as you say, I scooped up your specta-thingies. Luckily for the both of us, that scary woman didn't see them or me. I'm great at hiding."

"Right. You were the pile of rocks Aria saw."

"Figured that out all on your own? Good job." Screech pointed at his own chest. "My quick thinking saved your life."

Wrik knelt and raised his arms. "No, no, you're absolutely right. You did save my life, and I am indebted to you."

Screech nodded. "Yes, you are." He whipped his tail back and forth, thumping the ground. "And now you'd like to know what it is you can do to repay me, right?"

"Not quite, I'm afraid. Despite these telling and informative revelations and your show of bravery in the face of imminent peril, I am not at liberty nor in a position to repay any incurred debts at this juncture. Also, I must admit that I'm still at a loss as to the purpose of your visit." Wrik leaned forward. "Why have you come?"

"You use big words," Screech said. "I could use big words, too, but I choose not to do so. Now, as to the purpose of my visit?" He beat his wings and lifted himself off the ground several feet. Wrik stood to meet the little dragon's gaze. "I prefer the term quest rather than visit. I'm certain you agree that it better suits the situation we find ourselves in. So, let's just say I'm on a quest for Peorvem. As such, you are the treasure I've long sought. Now that I've found you, I must gather you up and return you to Peorvem."

Wrik nodded. "So, this is a summons."

"Peorvem said he would call upon you when the need arose."

"Indeed. But why did he send you when he could've just summoned me with the toe ring?"

"He did and waited several days, but you never arrived."

"That's preposterous." Wrik reached into one of his pockets and retrieved the toe ring. The brass pulsed. "Gods… I've been quite preoccupied and haven't looked at this ring for a week."

Screech smirked. "And that's why I'm here."

Wrik thought of Noella and sighed. Enlisting the help of the aquatic elves to help minimize the tidal waves once Nasduron rose from the depths would have to wait.

I must inform Cyrus.

"I know the way to the Valley of Dragons and to Peorvem's chamber," Wrik said, "but there's something I must do first."

Screech shook his head. "Not an option. Much time has been wasted already. We must return at once."

"A few minutes can be spared."

"And what could you possibly do in a few minutes right now that you couldn't do on the way to the valley?"

"What I must do would make little sense to you." He pushed the little dragon aside. "As I said, I know the way. I will see you there soon."

Screech flew back in front of Wrik and pointed a claw at him. "You know of the backdoor?"

Wrik started. "Are you telling me that there's a backdoor into the Valley of Dragons?"

Screech nodded. "It's the only way you'll be able to reach Peorvem."

Wrik held up the toe ring. "Not when I have this."

"Yes, and that might get you into the valley, but you'll never make it down to Peorvem's chamber. Our queen, Quldrai, refuses to grant anyone access to the ancient one right now. If you tried, she'd kill you and eat you."

Wrik sighed. "I don't doubt it."

Screech settled back down on the ground and paced in front of Wrik. "Yes, but there's more. Your níţfinzh cannot reach the heights of the valley. However, without her help your efforts will be futile."

"I'm uncertain as to what you mean, but I'm sure it'll become clear later." Wrik turned to Blackwind and stroked the underside of her chin. "Don't go anywhere. I'll be right back."

"Right back?" Screech folded his wings behind himself. "No time!"

Wrik ignored the little dragon and set his mind on Nasduron. He stepped out of the Aether Mountains and into the Great Library. "Cyrus! We have a situation that cannot wait."

"Oh, my!" Gnaud somersaulted off a table deep within the library and sprinted toward Wrik.

"Whoa! What is this place?"

Wrik peered down and cringed. Screech held onto his robes, the little dragon's serpentine eyes as wide as they would go. "Gods, you're not supposed to be here."

Gnaud slid to a stop several yards away. "Dear Ȝäţūr!" His spectacles magnified the fear in his eyes. "Did you... Is that... What in..."

Wrik groaned. "Yes, Gnaud. It's a dragon."

Screech released Wrik's robe and trotted toward Gnaud, his teeth bared and a low growl emanating from his throat.

"Oh, my!" Gnaud backed right into a table leg.

Screech laughed and pointed a claw at Gnaud. "The look on your face!" He laughed harder.

Gnaud's brow furrowed as he smoothed his shirt and then straightened his spectacles. "Laugh it up, dragon boy."

Wrik glanced around the library. "Where are Cyrus and the others?"

"It's Nardus now," Gnaud said.

But the realm needs Cyrus.

"Fine, but where is he?"

"I'm afraid that you've missed them by several days."

Wrik didn't quite understand. "Are you saying that they're still working to take down the spires?"

Gnaud shook his head. "No, I mean I'm the only one here. The others have all left."

"You're not the only one here, now." Screech turned to Wrik and pointed at Gnaud. "Does this guy seem a little off to you?"

Wrik ignored Screech. "How did they manage to leave?"

Gnaud stepped around Screech and hopped up on the table next to Wrik. "Rayah found an archway. I thought Nardus would've told you."

"I've been preoccupied for many days, and we have no way of reaching each other. That's why I came here."

"Well, as I'm sure you've already guessed, the assistance of the äəllf äkfeṭik is no longer needed."

"Yeah, I gathered that. It'll save me from a potential and unnecessary death."

Gnaud gasped. "Oh, my! You must consider it a blessing then."

Screech walked toward one of the shelves and began rummaging through the contents it held. Wrik shook his head. "When you see Nardus again, tell him I've gone to the Valley of Dragons."

Gnaud plopped down on the table and sighed. "I'm afraid relaying messages to Nardus won't be possible."

Wrik frowned. "Why not?"

Tears wet Gnaud's furry cheeks. He removed his spectacles and wiped his eyes. "Nardus and the others will never be able to come here again."

"Did he—wait, what?" Wrik pulled a chair out from beneath the table and sat down facing Gnaud. "What do you mean by that?"

"It was a condition of using the single-direction archway."

Interesting. He smiled to himself. *Nasduron's knowledge will be mine alone.*

"Did he say where he was heading?"

"Yes, to retrieve Alderan's bow. From there, they will head to Vallah and the King's Palace."

"Isn't Vallah in ruins?"

Gnaud put his spectacles back on and pushed them up his nose. "Oh, my, yes, and likely the last place Cinolth's army would think to look."

Wrik had to admit the logic of it made sense. "Very well. I must leave, but I'll return soon."

Gnaud smiled. "I look forward to seeing you again."

"Likewise." Wrik looked over at the shelf where Screech had been, but the little dragon wasn't there anymore.

The last thing I need right now is to have to take care of a young dragon.

Wrik stood and pushed the chair back underneath the table. "Screech, it's time to go."

The little dragon popped his head over one of the shelves. "Another minute."

"Now," Wrik growled.

Screech huffed. "Fine, but you're bringing me back." He climbed onto the top of the bookshelf, spread his wings, and glided over to Wrik. Some sort of yellow trinket hung from his neck on a black leather cord.

Wrik glared at the little thief. "Nothing here is yours to take."

Screech peered down at his newfound treasure. "But it matches my eyes."

Wrik started to say something else, but Gnaud held up his hand and smiled at Screech. "Please consider it a gift."

"Yes!" Screech lifted the trinket up and held it in his hands. "The others will be so jealous."

Wrik bent down and eyed Screech. "The others must never know of this place. Understood?"

The little dragon looked around and nodded. "Not sure what this place even is or how we got here."

"And you never will." Wrik rose and proffered his hand to Screech. "Time to go."

Screech took Wrik's hand, then the two of them stepped back out of the Great Library and into the small clearing where Blackwind awaited. He mounted Blackwind and then motioned for Screech to join him.

Screech backed away from Blackwind. "Uh, yeah. Um… you do realize I've got wings of my own, right?"

"Yes, but you'll never be able to keep up with us."

Screech clutched his trinket and pouted. "No one ever believes in me."

Wrik sighed. "We don't have time for this. Either you get on, or we leave you behind. Your choice."

"I'm the only one who knows where the backdoor is." He moved closer and poked at one of Blackwind's legs. She snorted and bobbed her head. "You sure this thing is safe to ride?"

"Her name is Blackwind, and she's the fastest and most nimble of the níţfinzh." Wrik leaned over and proffered his hand. "Come on."

"Does she fly really high?"

"As high as possible."

Screech swallowed hard. "I'm uh… well… you know."

"Are you trying to say you're afraid of heights?"

Screech lowered his head and nodded.

Wrik laughed. "You do realize that you're a flying dragon, right?"

"Yeah, but I keep as close to the ground as I can when I fly."

"Come on."

Screech took a deep breath and grabbed Wrik's hand. Wrik hauled Screech up onto Blackwind's back, right behind himself. The little dragon trembled.

Of all the dragons Peorvem could've sent, why this one?

Wrik glanced over his shoulder. "You start sneezing that gelatinous slime of yours onto me, and I'll toss you right off. Understood?"

"Got it." A puff of dirt wafted behind Screech. He snickered. "Oops!"

"Ugh!" Wrik waved his hand in front of his nose. "Did you just expel musty dirt from your rear?"

"Guilty, but I promise that it only happens when I'm anxious. Or when I'm hungry. Sometimes when I'm eating, too."

I don't even want to know what comes out of him when he's angry or sad or excited.

Wrik scowled. "Just hold on to my robes and keep your bodily functions in check."

Screech shrugged and grinned. "No promises." He grabbed Wrik's sides and closed his eyes.

Wrik faced forward, leaned into the saddle, and stroked Blackwind's neck. "It's time to fly, girl."

Blackwind bobbed her head several times, then beat her wings and leapt into the air. Screech's claws sank into Wrik's sides, and Screech moaned like a wounded cat.

This is going to be a long flight.

After coaxing Screech into easing up on his painfully sharp grip, Wrik directed Blackwind to head toward the Procerus Mountains. As they flew through the valleys between some of the peaks of the Aether Mountains, dark clouds began gathering overhead. The wind picked up and howled through the canyons. Lightning lit the sky, and the heavens rumbled. Then, the sky broke open and drenched them.

Blackwind fought hard against the storm, but the violent winds and pouring rain proved a worthy foe, tossing her all about. After an hour of hard-fought progress, Wrik finally gave in and commanded her to find a place to land. Had he not done so, she would've fought the storm until it brought her down.

Peorvem will have to wait a bit longer.

CHAPTER THIRTY-THREE

Rage still burned within Aria as West Hotah came into view on the horizon. Even though several of Cinolth's army had reported sighting Wrik flying toward the Aether Mountains earlier that morning, their search had turned up nothing. Now, they approached the first city to have completed the marble statue dedicated to her.

West Hotah featured few structures beyond a few stories tall, and none that rose above the western hills. Given the specifications of the statue, it would be visible throughout the entire city. She caught sight of the back of the twenty-foot-tall statue as they made their final approach.

Gooseflesh enveloped her, driving away the last of her rage as Cinolth landed amidst a large crowd gathered before the statue. The statue would serve as a god to the people and a reminder as to whom they served. Not long ago, she would've loathed seeing such a vulgar display of power, but now nothing could've felt more right. As queen, she deserved to be worshiped and would demand it of everyone, regardless of their faith.

"Have your moment," Cinolth said through mindspeak, *"for soon I will have mine."*

At first, she hadn't understood why Cinolth refused to have statues made in his image too, but now she shared all his thoughts. To him, humans were revolting, and she shared most of his sentiment. However, he desired the dragon throne. Quldrai ruled but without authority. Cinolth deserved the throne. He was the true heir to it, and soon he would challenge her for it.

Aria dismounted. Silence fell over the entire crowd as they bowed to the ground before her. She drank in the power and relished it.

Pravus would've loved this moment.

Although she still loved the man, she no longer felt sorrow toward him. Nor did she feel sorrow for her brother. The night in her bedchamber with the man named Reubane had changed everything. Had she been given the choice as to whether she wanted a piece of Cinolth's heart inside her, she wasn't sure what she would've chosen. Now, she wanted nothing else, their bond sealed.

As she walked through the crowd, she noticed none of them were under Cinolth's influence. It didn't surprise her given his nature. Why would he allow his servants to worship her?

Her gaze slowly traveled up the length of the statue. Every detail spoke to who she was from the bottom of her boots all the way up to her face, but that's where the likeness ended. Mezhik crackled at her fingertips as rage boiled to the surface.

She turned and faced the bowing crowd. "Bring me the stone masons responsible for this at once!"

Six men and two women peered up from where they bowed. None of them spoke or moved further.

Aria seethed. "On your feet." The eight stood. All kept their gaze toward the ground. She stalked them. Circled them. Smelled their fear. Had she not been so furious, she would've enjoyed the moment. "Which of you were responsible for sculpting my face?"

One of the two women raised her hand. None of the men did. Aria stormed over to the woman. Lifted the woman's chin until the woman's brown-eyed gaze met hers. "Tell me your name."

"Ella, my queen." The woman's voice quavered.

"Study my face and that of the statue. Tell me what you see."

Ella's eyes moved back and forth across Aria's face before she took several steps back and craned her head toward the statue. After a minute of studying it, she said, "The statue resembles you perfectly, my queen."

Aria roared. She swept her arm up and forward. Ella flew backward ten feet and landed on top of a burly man. Although conscious, neither Ella nor the man tried to move. Mezhik crackled at her fingertips once again.

She glared at the other seven. "Which of you believe Ella captured my likeness?"

The seven glanced amongst each other. None of them raised their hand or spoke up. All of them were liars. With only a thought, she conjured a fireball and thrust it at the closest of the seven. The dark-skinned man had no time to react before the fireball hit him square in the chest. It consumed him before he had a chance to scream. The crowd, their faces plastered to the ground, didn't move, but many of them began to sob softly.

One of the six who still stood, a young man with brown hair, trembled. Urine soaked his trousers and tears wet his cheeks. Aria stalked toward him.

"Has your answer changed?" she said. The young man nodded but kept his eyes focused on the ground. "This statue shares my likeness?" The young man nodded again.

Aria stood there and stewed.

How many more share his delusion?

She looked across the crowd. A few others had gathered around the fringe. None of them bowed. One gestured toward her with his second and third fingers extended when her gaze met his.

The lewd bastard!

Aria raised her arms with a growl and then thrust them down. A hole opened in the ground and swallowed the man. Panic rippled through the crowd, creating chaos. People trampled each other as they ran for cover.

"It's time we make an example," Cinolth said through mindspeak.

Aria wrapped her arms around herself and hunched over. Then, she reached deep within herself and drew upon her mezhik. With a deafening roar, she swept her arms outward and thrust her chest forward. A semi-circle of fire and lightning arced outward, consuming dozens of people still struggling for cover.

Screams and wails filled the air, along with the stench of burning flesh.

Using mezhik, Aria flew onto Cinolth's back. She grabbed hold of his lower neck spike. "Burn the city to the ground."

"With pleasure."

Cinolth took to the sky, circled around, and began bathing the city with fire. Aria poured her mezhik into Cinolth's dragon fire, causing it to burn hotter and spread farther. Within half an hour, the entire city burned and smoldered. Black smoke filled the air for miles. They didn't bother searching for survivors. Those who lived would spread word of her wrath. No one would smite her again.

Drained of energy, Aria directed Cinolth to head back to the castle. When they reached Galondu Castle, Cinolth landed at the center of the atrium. She slid off Cinolth's back and landed hard in the sand. She lay back, spent.

Cinolth snaked his head down to her. "You did well, my queen." The smell of sulfur still burned upon his lips.

She reached up and stroked his maw. "As did you."

He snorted smoke, and she withdrew her hand.

"Regain your strength." He looked up toward the heavens. "In three days, we will take back my throne."

Aria nodded. "Nothing will stop us."

Cinolth roared, then took to the sky, kicking up a storm of sand in his wake. Aria lay there and watched him fly high above the castle and then disappear as the sand settled. Even with him gone, the smell of sulfur and smoke filled her nostrils with each breath.

I'm in need of a bath.

She was about to reach out with her mind when she noticed Credan approaching from the east. He slowed and bowed before reaching her position.

"You're just the man I need," she said.

Credan smiled down at her. "Am I?"

"Send word to Brema. Have her draw me a bath at once."

"As you wish." He looked around. "Would you like me to summon someone to help you back to your bedchamber?"

"I'll manage."

"Very well." Credan turned and started walking away.

"There's one other thing."

Credan stopped and faced her. "Yes, my queen?"

Suddenly, her pulse began racing. Did she really want to know the truth? Could she handle it?

Spit it out, Aria.

Aria sat up. "Have you noticed a recent change in my appearance from when I first arrived?"

Beads of sweat formed and ran down the sides of Credan's face. He stammered, "Um, I, well, yes, I would say so. The red streak in your hair would be a hard thing to miss."

"Anything else?"

"I believe the red fringe around your irises is new, too."

The man held back the truth. Anger surged within her. "And what of my face?"

Credan drew closer. Knelt before her. Wrinkles creased his brow. "May I ask what this is about?"

Fear gripped her. Drew her back to the mirror in her bedchamber. Back to the young woman with the broken face.

It's true, then. I killed all those people for showing me the truth.

"It's nothing." She waved him off. "Forget I ever asked."

"As you wish, my queen." He rose and walked away.

Pulse still racing, she pulled herself to her feet. Soon, she would need answers as to why her beauty had faded, but for now she needed a bath, food, and sleep. Perhaps not in that order. She staggered out of the atrium and hugged the walls as she traversed the corridors and stairwells up to her bedchamber.

How can I call myself a god if my mezhik drains so quickly?

Brema met her at the door and helped her into the bedchamber. Aria sank to the floor, but Brema still made quick work of removing her clothes and carrying her over to the copper tub. For such a scrawny girl, she had the strength of an ox.

Aria slid into the tub. The heat from the water worked its way into her bones and weighed down her eyelids. In just seconds, she felt herself slip down into the darkness of sleep.

There, the entire world burned.

CHAPTER THIRTY-FOUR

Nardus lay in the darkness, Theyn at his side. He stroked her bare back and ran his fingers through her hair. As usual, she smelled marvelous. The bath they shared earlier had done wonders for him, too. Blue light chased away the darkness, then disappeared. A few seconds later, it happened again.

Ɂäəll Dhef Ɂäfn Dhä.

He slid his arm from beneath Theyn and retrieved the leather-bound book that lay on top of his discarded cloak. The seal pulsed with blue light once again. After reciting the holy words, its golden clasp clicked open. He flipped the book open to its first page. Using the fountain pen located within its front pouch, he touched the page. Ink bled onto the page, forming words: *"The night cloaks our arrival into Vallah and the King's Palace. We will dock at the royal port beneath the palace and will need your assistance to gain entrance into the palace itself. Below, you will find an expertly drawn map that will lead you to the hidden passage. See you soon, father. -Alderan"*

Nardus sprang to his feet and dressed.

"It's the middle of the evening," Theyn groaned. "Where are you off to?"

Excitement strangled his vocal cords. "Shard—no, Alderan will soon arrive."

Theyn bolted upright. "Even under cover of darkness it'll be a huge risk. Won't they be seen?"

He stuffed the book into a leather satchel and slung the satchel over his shoulder. "No."

After strapping his scabbard on, Nardus slid Brinzhär Dädh from within it. The sound of steel rang through the room, and the golden blade shone in the darkness. Its power seeped into the flesh of his palm. How good it felt. Satisfied its release would be clear, he slid the sword back into its scabbard.

"I'm coming with you." Theyn pulled on a fresh pair of tan trousers and a black blouse, then stepped into her boots. "Where are we headed?"

"Alderan sent me a map with the location of a hidden passage. It leads down to the royal port beneath the palace."

"You've called your son Alderan twice now."

"Yeah, I figured it's the right thing to do." He rubbed his left bicep and allowed his fingers to linger on the two scars flanking it. "We all must move forward."

Theyn reached up and pulled him into a kiss. Her tongue caressed his. Sent chills through him. He pulled away, wrapped his arms around her, and held her close.

My second true love.

Her warm, moist breath penetrated his shirt with each breath as she pressed her ear against his chest. "I've never heard your heart beat so fast."

"I've never had a son return from the dead twice."

Theyn slipped out of his arms and took hold of his hand. "Well, let's go find him."

† † †

After studying the map Alderan had sent, Theyn led Nardus out of the bedchamber and into the first of many rubble-filled corridors within the King's Palace. Although Nardus and Zerenity had placed warning wards around the handful of bedchambers their group occupied, they'd not done so with the rest of the palace for fear of another wizard detecting them and alerting Cinolth and Aria.

So far, they'd come across no enemies hiding in the palace, but a single detection by one of Cinolth's minions could cost them their lives. None of them knew exactly how the bond between Cinolth and his infected worked, but based on past experiences, it seemed as though the communication pathway had no bounds. If true, Cinolth would know their location within moments if one were to discover them. No matter what the truth might be, killing one of the infected would be a last resort. However, any other enemy outside of Cinolth's control would be dealt with without mercy.

Theyn paused at the corner of intersecting corridors. Based on the map, they needed to go right, but a massive mound of rubble, broken furniture, and other debris blocked their path. She turned to Nardus and whispered, "Now what?"

"As far as I see it, we've got three choices. Either we find an alternate path, I teleport us to the other side of the rubble pile, or I use mezhik to clear us a path."

Theyn eyed the corridor again. "Since we don't know how far the rubble field extends or what lies beyond it, the second option is definitely out."

"Fair enough." He rubbed his chin. "Given the potential for a thunderous collapse, I believe the third is equally unsafe."

"Agreed." She peered into the shadows ahead. "Looks like we find a way around it."

"I don't remember passing any corridors or doorways that led in the direction we need to go," Nardus said.

"Me neither, but it looks like there might be a room just ahead on the right."

"Guess we'll find out."

Sure enough, a short alcove about thirty paces down the corridor led to a pair of wooden doors. The door on the right stood slightly ajar. Perfect darkness lay within.

Theyn put her nose to the opening and drew a deep breath. Decay filled her nostrils. She jerked back and covered her mouth but couldn't suppress a rogue cough.

The doors flew open. Ripped off their hinges. Disappeared into the darkness and crashed somewhere within. Nardus and Theyn retreated to either side of the alcove as an ogre stepped through the doorway and into the corridor. The disgusting beast slurped up strings of snot as it sniffed the air.

"Gorch smells human flesh."

Theyn shifted and crouched low, ready to pounce. The beast wiped its nose and slammed its fist into the wall right above her. A glob of snot dripped from Gorch's hand and landed right on top of her head.

I just bathed!

Nardus unsheathed Brinzhär Dädh. The metal *sha-shing* drew Gorch's attention. The beast staggered toward Nardus, swinging wildly with its fists.

Ogres notoriously had bad vision, but their thick skin and brute strength often made up for it. Gorch would likely be no exception.

Theyn crept closer, shouted "now" to Nardus through mindspeak, and lunged onto the beast's back. The ogre groaned and circled. As sharp as her claws were, they couldn't match the toughness of Gorch's skin and found no purchase as she slid down his back.

Gorch kicked at her and caught her right in the ribs. Bones cracked, and the air expelled from her lungs as she slid across the corridor and slammed into the wall. She fought through the pain but couldn't catch her breath, each gasp excruciating.

Nardus roared, and the corridor flashed with reddish-orange light.

Gorch's head tumbled from his wide shoulders and hit the floor with a wet thud. Then, Gorch's body crashed down right in front of her like a felled tree, quaking the floor.

Theyn closed her eyes, held her side, and wheezed.

"Let me help," Nardus said. He moved her hand and pressed against her side.

At first, the pain threatened to incapacitate her, but then Nardus began pouring his mezhik into her. As he did, the pain eased, and she began to relax. When she opened her eyes, she saw a flash of movement right behind Nardus but knew it was too late.

† † †

Theyn's eyes reflected movement. Nardus spun around, conjuring a fireball simultaneously. Behind him stood Niesha, her eyes bulging from her eye sockets. He quickly extinguished the fireball and scowled at the young girl.

"You almost got yourself killed," he said, peering into the stretch of darkness behind her. "Are you alone?"

"Yeah," Niesha said.

"This is no place for a little girl to be roaming around in the dark."

She huffed. "I'm not a little girl."

"You are, but that's beside the point. What are you doing out here?"

"I heard you leave earlier, so I followed you."

Nardus pointed at the decapitated ogre. "As you can see, it's not safe."

"I'm not stupid. That's why I brought this knife." She held it up. Fresh blood dripped from its blade.

Theyn sat up and leaned against the wall. "What happened?"

"You got kicked—"

She glared at Nardus. "I know what happened to me." She looked at Niesha. "Why is there blood on your knife?"

"Because I'm more careful than the two of you." She pointed back down the corridor with the knife. "You were being stalked by a ginormous rat. Now, you're not."

Nardus shared a glance with Theyn. Neither of them had noticed the rat or Niesha for that matter. He shook his head. "You're just full of surprises, aren't you?"

"Sure am." She looked around. "Where we headed now?"

There was no point in sending her back to Berggren on her own. He pointed toward the dark alcove. "We see where that leads."

Niesha growled and brandished her knife. "I'm ready for anything."

Theyn grunted as she pulled herself to her feet. She favored her ribs and held her hand on her side. For now, she'd be okay. He'd work on her more later.

"Let's hope we find no more trouble," Theyn said.

"Agreed." He stared into the darkness beyond the alcove. Given the amount of noise they'd already made, he decided it might be wise to proceed with a little more light, so he conjured a small ball of white light. "Follow me."

The massive room lay in ruin and reeked of death. Half a dozen corpses lay on the floor, all but one cleaned to the bone. Based on their small size and the shape of their unique skulls, they had to be zheballin. From the looks of it, the ogre had been there at least a few days.

Guess he did us a favor.

Double doors stood open toward the back of the room on the right side. As luck would have it, the doors led right into the corridor that was blocked. To the left, the corridor terminated at a large, semi-circle fountain made of white marble with gray veining. It featured a knight clad in teal armor wielding a sword and shield. The shield bore the coat of arms of House

Zaridus.

Black iron sconces hung on either side of the fountain. Neither bore a torch.

Nardus eyed Theyn. "You take the right sconce, and I'll take the left."

She frowned. "And do what?"

"Turn it to your right as far as it will go when I say so." Theyn nodded and grabbed the sconce. He grabbed the one on his side. "Now."

Both sconces turned all the way upside-down before stopping. His clicked into place, and he assumed hers did too. They both stepped back and stared at the fountain.

After a few seconds, Niesha crossed her arms. "Is something supposed—"

Clank! Clank! Clank! Clank!

The fountain and the wall behind it began turning and didn't stop until the entire thing had circled ninety degrees, leaving a five-foot gap behind the wall.

"Whoa," Niesha said. "It's a secret passage."

All three of them stepped back as a figure cloaked in purple emerged from the darkness. The woman lowered her hood as she stepped into the light. Princess Zelanora followed right behind the woman. Age aside, the two of them were nearly identical.

Niesha eyed the first woman. "You're…"

The woman knelt in front of Niesha. "I am Queen Lanara. And to whom do I speak?"

"Just plain Niesha. No royal title or anything."

Queen Lanara smiled. "It is a pleasure to make your acquaintance."

Niesha scowled. "Doubt it. No one's ever happy to meet an orphan."

Nardus couldn't help but laugh. He understood how Berggren had grown so fond of her. How could anyone not?

Queen Lanara rose. Her lavender eyes met Nardus's. Took stock of him. "Are you really him?"

Nardus bowed slightly. "I am."

Her gaze turned toward Theyn. "And you must be the shifter."

"Yes." Theyn lowered her gaze but made no attempt to bow or curtsy.

Princess Zelanora moved past her mother and hugged each of them. "It's so good to see you're all alive."

Shardan!

How had he managed to forget about his son? Anticipation grew in his gut as Savric and Morcinda walked out of the passage. He edged closer to the fountain, his pulse thundering as he squinted to see through the darkness. The shadows swirled. Pulsed. Teased him. Then, Alderan stepped into the light.

† † †

Strong arms wrapped around Alderan and lifted him from his feet before his eyes had a chance to adjust to the light.

"Praise Ƨätūr!" Nardus set him down and grasped his shoulders. "It really is you."

Alderan smirked. "Who else would I be?"

Nardus stepped back and studied Alderan, tears in his eyes. "You died on the battlefield. I saw it with my own eyes." He glanced back at Theyn. "We all did."

Theyn hugged Alderan. "Welcome back."

"Thanks, I guess."

The whole situation felt awkward, but not because Theyn and his father were so happy to see him alive. In their eyes, he'd died just over a week ago, but for him he'd simply been away. He couldn't imagine what they and the others must be going through.

Rayah!

No one else had come to greet them but the little girl named Niesha. Alderan's pulse quickened, and he began feeling queasy and lightheaded. "Where are the others?"

Nardus embraced him again. "Take a breath, son. We all survived the battle, Rayah included."

Relief flooded Alderan as he held onto his father and drew several deep breaths. His thundering heart slowed, and he pulled away. He searched within himself for his connection with Aria but came up empty.

His lips trembled. "And Aria?"

"Alive." Nardus smiled. "What you did saved her life."

Alderan pushed his hair behind his ears and stared at the floor. "And

Cinolth's."

"Yes, but your selfless act broke the bond she shared with Pravus."

His mind raced with ideas of what that might mean. "Then she's joined us?"

"No," Theyn said. "The beast still controls her."

"Yes, but we have one less foe to contend with," Nardus said. "After you broke their bond, Cinolth killed Pravus."

Pravus is dead…

It was a fact that the man hated him and had treated him poorly, yet hearing of Pravus's demise left him hollow. At first, he didn't grasp the reason for his unorthodox response to the news, but then it hit him. Even with all Pravus's faults, Aria still loved him. The man clearly loved her, too.

She must be beside herself with grief.

Thinking of Aria triggered another thought. He looked to his father. "Does Rayah know I'm alive?"

Nardus shook his head. "Not yet. No one else does except Zerenity."

Anger swelled in his chest. "Why would you keep that from Rayah? From the others?"

"We lost the battle, son, but the war isn't over."

Alderan fumed. "That's no excuse."

"In truth, it is. Having said that, Rayah and Ridan were sent on a mission before I received news of your resurrection."

"Fine, but what about Rakzar and the others?"

"As I said, the war isn't over. Rakzar and Urza were about to head into the enemy's camp when I found out, so I made the decision to keep them in the dark to keep them from being distracted."

Alderan groaned. "That makes no sense."

"It does," Theyn said. "Urza would've been fine knowing the truth, but Rakzar cares for you far more than he lets on. Your death hit him hard. If he'd been told the truth, it would've put his and Urza's lives in danger. They will find out when they return."

Rakzar took my death hard?

In a millennium, he never would've thought Rakzar gave two figs about him. Knowing the truth left Alderan elated.

Crack!

Alderan and the others turned toward the corridor. Nardus closed his hand, and the ball of light floating above them winked out, casting darkness over the corridor.

Thud! Thud! Thud! Thud!

A loud, deep groan filled the corridor and reverberated in Alderan's chest. "Gorch not wake."

Alderan's palms dampened. "What was that?"

"Wait here," Nardus said. He drew Brinzhär Dädh and charged down the corridor and through a set of open doors before the glow of his sword faded.

† † †

A while later, Zerenity and the others sat around a table. She tapped her chin with her finger as she studied Alderan who sat across from her. "There's something different about you, darling."

Alderan looked down at himself and shrugged. "I'm just me."

"You are… yet you're not." She leaned across the table for a closer inspection. His face looked just as she remembered, and his green eyes shone with life. "Could you stand up and turn around for me?"

"Sure." Alderan stood and circled twice before sitting back down.

"Feathers, woman," Savric grumbled. "The boy is no impostor."

"Never said he was, Savvy." She frowned. Something about the boy had changed. She was certain of it. "I know it sounds absurd, but would you mind pulling up your sleeves and showing me your arms?"

"Nothing's changed. I still have a few wizard marks." Alderan pushed back his sleeves, and everyone at the table gasped, including him.

"Ʒät̪ūr's mercy," Zerenity said.

Crimson feathers ran up the outsides of Alderan's arms, from wrist to shoulder. Alderan stood and backed away from the table, his eyes fixated on the feathers. He lifted his shirt, but there were no matching feathers on his torso. However, the same didn't hold true when he pulled up the legs on his trousers. Feathers identical to those on his arms covered his legs.

Zerenity stood and walked around the table to get a closer look. The feathers looked just as real up close as they had from afar, yet when she touched one of them on his forearm, she felt nothing but skin. How could her eyes see feathers but her fingertips feel skin?

Ẑäṭūr, what is the meaning of this?

She turned to Savric and the others. "Have any of you ever seen anything like this before?"

None of them had.

Nardus stared at Alderan's arms with a grim expression on his face. Finally, he stood. "Come with me, Alderan. We need to talk." He eyed the others, then said, "Alone. The rest of you should start figuring out how we're going to prepare for a war while being hunted."

Zerenity's eyes narrowed.

Nardus knows more than he's letting on. Why is he holding back on us?

"I will see that it's done," Queen Lanara said.

"Good." Nardus turned and escorted Alderan out of the room. Zerenity and the others gathered around the table and began discussing defenses.

† † †

Nardus sat down next to Alderan on a stone bench and stretched out his legs before settling against the block wall. Admittedly, he didn't know his son as well as he would've liked, but they'd only known each other for a few weeks, and one of those was after Alderan died. Still, he was certain the boy held back information. It both puzzled and concerned him.

What does he have to hide?

Alderan stared at his right arm and traced the feathers with his finger. "What does this mean?"

"That's a good question, and I think you have an answer for it."

"Why would I?" He yanked his sleeve back down and stared forward.

"I'm not sure, but you're a terrible liar."

"How would you know?"

"Every time you lie to someone, you cannot look them in the eye."

Alderan turned and glared at him. "And now?"

"What do you know of it?"

"Noth—" Alderan's gaze shifted away. He punched his own leg. "Ugh."

Nardus placed his hand on Alderan's shoulder. "How can I help you if you refuse to let me in?"

"I've seen how you are." He leaned forward and buried his face in his hands.

"How am I?"

"You're irrational when it comes to Aria and me."

"Because I care for you and want to protect you both?"

"Yes."

"How am I any different than any other father?"

Alderan sat up straight. "You act before you think."

Nardus chuckled. "Well then, you are your father's son."

"Promise you won't go on a rampage, and I'll tell you everything I know."

"Tell me everything you know, and I'll try and stay calm no matter what it is."

Alderan sighed. "Fine." He swept his hair out of his face and leaned against the wall. "It all started when I first met Wizard Wrik."

Nardus listened while Alderan told him about Wrik's secret room and how Wrik had captured him. How Wrik had brought Aria to see him and how he came to possess the necklace with the feather. By the time Alderan finished telling him everything that'd happened, Nardus knew what must be done.

You lied to my face, Wrik.

CHAPTER THIRTY-FIVE

Despite three and a half days and concerted effort, Qotan still hadn't come across an explanation as to how he wound up at Galondu Castle, nor had he located the mirror. To his credit, though, he had managed to avoid detection. Savric would've been proud of him for that at least.

Ahead on the left, light poured forth from a partially opened door. Two voices carried out into the corridor. One female and one male. However, their conversation didn't have enough volume for his aged ears to decipher it.

Without sound, Qotan moved closer. Craned his head to hear better. Yet it still wasn't ideal. His pulse increased as he peered through the crack in the open door. A young woman dressed in black hunched over a long table. On the other side of the table stood a bald man who wore spectacles. The man's eyes followed whatever the woman was pointing out.

"This is where the Valley of Dragons lies." Qotan didn't recognize the woman's voice. "In two days, Cinolth and I will go there and challenge their queen."

Cinolth? Impossible.

The man nodded. "And you will return victorious, my queen."

Qotan froze. As far as he knew, King Zaridus still ruled the Ancient Realm, and his son, Prince Rictar, was next in line. The likelihood of Princess Zelanora ever ruling sat at zero. Plus, Princess Zelanora didn't have blonde hair with red streaks. Nor did any of them reside at Galondu Castle.

Then who is she?

The young woman reached over for something, turning her head just enough for him to get a glimpse of her face. Despite her damaged face, he recognized her immediately.

Aria.

Savric had mentioned seeing Aria in Daltura a few weeks back, but he had never alluded to her gaining such stature. Her presence perplexed him.

How can this be? And why does this man call her queen?

Paralyzed in thought, Qotan failed to conceal himself or teleport away before Aria pulled the door open wide. Her attention remained on the bald man behind her, but the man's stare met Qotan's. At least that's where the man's eyes focused, yet the man made no mention of Qotan's presence to Aria. Nor did his expression allude to the fact that someone stood in the corridor behind her.

How peculiar.

Aria turned, stared at Qotan, then walked right through him. Qotan gasped. Not because she'd stolen his breath but because of the impossibility of what'd just happened. Moments later, the man did the same thing.

Qotan's heart thrummed. Pummeled his ribcage. Caused his skin to hemorrhage with beads of sweat. He looked down at himself. Inspected his palms. Reached out and touched the open door. Felt the grain of the wood on his fingertips.

I am not dead.

A thought struck him. Morphed into a plan. He went and stood in the middle of the corridor and yelled at the top of his lungs, "Aria!"

Aria, not ten paces away, stopped and turned back toward Qotan and the room.

The man stopped, too. "Is something wrong, my queen?" A frown furrowed his brow.

"Everything is fine, Credan." She swept her fingers through the end of her long braid. "I just thought I'd forgotten something back in the war room."

The two of them turned, walked down the corridor, and disappeared around the corner of an adjoining corridor. Qotan looked down at his hands again.

Ɂäţūr, what is happening to me?

Qotan spent the next hour storming through the castle and making contact with everyone he encountered. None acknowledged his presence, and each passed through him as though he were an apparition. He tried disarming a soldier but couldn't grasp the man's dagger. Toppling a chair gave rise to another soldier, but the man wrote it off as some freak accident.

He settled on a bench in the atrium and rested his elbows on his knees.

I do not understand, Ʒäʈūr. My brother sees me… but is he the only one who does?

Within his mind, he relived recent events. In King Zaridus's court, no one took notice of him. Nor had they in Vallah or on the docks before boarding *The River Maiden*. No matter how many memories he retrieved or how far back he went into the past, a pattern began to emerge. The only human contact he'd had since mirror hopping decades earlier had come from his brother.

It is true, then? Am I dead?

Sorrow filled his heart, and he wept.

Sometime later, he pulled himself back together and wiped the tears from his eyes. Given what he'd learned of himself, he recognized a unique opportunity.

With Savric's help, I can gather information from anywhere, and he can report it back to King Zaridus.

Reinvigorated, Qotan sought the mirror once more. And, as luck would have it, he stumbled upon the corridor where it hung on the wall less than twenty minutes later. After verifying he was alone, Qotan set his mind on Tyrosha and touched the mirror. His reflection and that of the dark corridor faded from the mirror's surface. Darkness lay beyond. He conjured an orb of light and stepped through the mirror and into Zerenity's closet. Black armor lay at his feet. It matched that of the soldiers who patrolled Galondu Castle. Dozens of other garments were strewn about the closet.

Has something happened to Zerenity?

Gooseflesh tingled on his nape as he pushed his way through several rows of clothes and exited the closet. A short-statured man with big, bright green eyes sat on the edge of Zerenity's bed. Tears streaked his face.

Qotan cocked his head. "And who might this be?"

The little man looked up at him, smiled big, and pointed a thumb at himself. "Eshtak."

Qotan stumbled backward and caught his robes on the closet door handle. Fabric ripped as he fought to catch himself. The little man moved with alacrity, grabbing Qotan's hand and pulling him back to his feet before he crashed to the floor.

The event left Qotan breathless. He leaned over with a hand on his chest and stared at the little man. "You see me?"

Eshtak nodded wildly. "Eshtak sees old man. Old man not sick." He wrapped his arms around Qotan's legs and buried the side of his face against Qotan's hip. "Eshtak happy to see."

For the life of him, Qotan couldn't remember ever meeting Eshtak. "How do you know me?"

Eshtak pulled away and spun in a circle. "Eshtak friends with brother."

"You know Savric?"

He nodded. "Eshtak knows Master Savric. Eshtak good friend."

Qotan explored the house and searched the yard. Eshtak followed him everywhere. The place looked as though it'd been deserted for some time.

"Where is my brother? Zerenity?"

Eshtak shrugged. "Master Savric sails. Pretty lady gone."

"When will they return?"

"Eshtak not know."

Qotan sighed. The sun had already disappeared behind the mountains. Soon, it would be dark. "I will search for my brother tomorrow."

"Eshtak too?"

He chuckled. "Very well."

Eshtak twirled around the yard so much, Qotan began to feel dizzy.

Back inside, Qotan lit a fire in the fireplace. Then, the two of them settled into a pair of rocking chairs and watched the flames dance for a while. The heat drove the ache from his bones and pulled the tension from his shoulders. The only thing that might've felt better would've been an evening in one of the Tyrosha bathhouses.

This will have to do for now.

Qotan spent the next hour on the edge of his chair as Eshtak told him of the sickness, the war, and the fall of the Three Kingdoms. Gut wrenched, he leaned back in the chair and closed his eyes. Tears streaked his cheeks and hung on his jaw. He made no attempt to keep them from falling.

Queen Aria...

CHAPTER THIRTY-SIX

Nardus crouched beneath the trees not far from the stronghold entrance. Theyn knelt at his side in cat form, and Savric, Zelanora, and Zerenity knelt next to her. The night hid the five of them well enough, but Cinolth's mind-controlled army had beaten them there. From the looks of it, the army had yet to gain entrance. And, given the unruly nature of the zhebəllin, it wasn't likely that they would. The discord between the two groups would play in their favor.

He used mindspeak to communicate with Zelanora. *"You're certain there are no mezhik wards or rune spells surrounding the stronghold?"*

"Yes," Zelanora said through mindspeak. *"My father forbade mezhik of any kind, as did his predecessors. They never would've allowed a wizard or sorceress to help, nor would they have wanted them knowing the location of the stronghold."*

It made sense, if only in the context of a mindset firmly against mezhik. Either way, her word would have to be good enough. Zhebəllin weren't known to exhibit patience, especially when it came to a food source like human flesh. As such, the citizens enslaved by them would likely suffer a tragic end soon.

Nardus mindspoke to Theyn and the others all at once. *"We have no idea of what we're about to go up against, so be prepared to fight as soon as we teleport into the stronghold. Understood?"* Agreement was unanimous. *"Good. Let's go."*

He grabbed onto Theyn's mane and teleported them just beyond the entrance gate. Theyn immediately lunged at the lone zhebəllin and ripped its throat out before it had a chance to raise an alarm. Savric, Zelanora, and Zerenity appeared moments later.

The stench of zhebəllin permeated the air as they crept down the long, dark tunnel that led into the main area of the stronghold. Groans, wails, and shrieks sounded from every direction, echoing off the walls. Several zhebəllin lay asleep against the walls.

Zerenity stepped into the open. Her open hands glowed with a green hue as she drew upon her mezhik. Vines began growing out of the ground and wrapped themselves around the necks of the sleeping zhebəllin. She clinched her fists and thrust her arms down at her sides. The vines tightened like nooses and choked the zhebəllin. One of them managed to cry out before its head became free of its body.

Not the entrance we were going for.

Nardus unsheathed Brinzhär Dädh and let its mezhik fill him as its ring echoed through the cavernous space. Golden light surrounded him and lit the darkness. Zhebəllin flooded the area, snarling and weapons brandished. Then, chaos ensued.

In an instant, the others were swept into the fray.

Nardus surged forward, the blade an extension of himself. Every slash met flesh. Drew black blood. Ripped through bone. Sprayed ichor.

As the fight wore on, the zhebəllin became smarter, using humans as shields. However, the disgusting tactic made little difference. Somehow, the blade understood the difference between friend and foe as he spun, charged, parried, and slashed his way across the room, never once drawing blood that wasn't black.

With a violent, thunderous crash that echoed throughout the room, Nardus's deadly dance concluded. His eyes focused on a single goblin who stood atop the stage section of the main stronghold area. In and of itself, the event would've been insignificant. However, the zhebəllin held a long blade to the throat of a large, yellow cat.

"Theyn!" Nardus roared.

Her voice entered his mind. *"Trust me, I have him right where I want him."*

For an instant, he didn't understand, but then he realized her plan. The zhebəllin who held her stood at least a head taller than the others and fit the description Berggren had given them. Somehow, she'd located their king.

"Kaja," Nardus said through mindspeak.

"Chop off the head, and the others will scatter like night bugs."

Kaja spoke. "You cannot win."

From the corner of his eye, Nardus witnessed Savric slam the butt end of his staff into the floor. A blinding light ushered from the crystal atop the staff and swept across the stronghold. All the zhebəllin seethed and hissed, each covering their eyes. Except Kaja.

Kaja ripped the blade across his body, but Theyn was no longer in his grasp. She'd shifted and slid beneath the deadly blade. With dagger in hand, she drove her fist up underneath Kaja's chin. A silver blade soaked in black blood erupted from the top of Kaja's skull. His eyes rolled back, and he collapsed when Theyn let go of the dagger.

Zelanora knelt. Closed her eyes.

The air shimmered. Tingled.

Mezhik.

Memories surfaced from the depths of Nardus's mind. Zhebəllin gasping, choking, vomiting. Skin bubbling. Sloughing off. Every one of them that touched, bled, or ate a human suffered a miserable death.

The zhebəllin in the stronghold began shrieking with terror. Many dropped to the floor and convulsed. Others fought among themselves to escape through one of the tunnels. None stood their ground.

Nardus smiled and sheathed Brinzhär Dädh.

"Nice work, everyone," Nardus said to the others through mindspeak.

Within the hour, every zhebəllin remaining in the stronghold lay dead in a pool of its own black blood. Nardus, Theyn, and Zelanora worked to free the citizens of the Three Kingdoms from their cages while Zerenity and Savric used wizard's fire to burn the zhebəllin bodies. Given the size of the stronghold and all its rooms, both tasks took several hours.

In all, they found thirteen bone pits spread through the stronghold. Thankfully, only six contained remains. Based on the size of the empty pits, Nardus estimated the zhebəllin had devoured a few hundred people. It sickened him. Had they arrived sooner, perhaps they would've saved half of them.

The thought of blaming Ɛäṭūr crept through the shadows of his mind, but then he remembered an important fact. Had Berggren, Calen, Niesha, and Eshtak not escaped, they never would've known about the attack. All the citizens of the Three Kingdoms would've perished at the hands of the zheballin. Nardus closed his eyes and said a quick prayer thanking Ɛätūr instead.

† † †

Once Zelanora and the others gathered the remaining citizens into the main area of the stronghold, she climbed onto the stage and faced the people for the first time since her father's death. Although she'd sat in court many times with her father and brother, she'd never addressed the people. Doing so would've raised her father's ire and constrained her to her bedchambers for a solid month. Rictar, her brother, had done just that on several occasions and spent a good portion of one summer alone. Although he had loved their father as much as she did, their relationship was oft strained. Rictar changed after their mother died. She likely had, too. Now that she knew her mother's death to be a lie, part of her resented her mother and hated her father.

Would Rictar have felt the same? Would he have forgiven them?

She swallowed hard.

Will I?

Tossing the question from her mind, she focused her gaze on the people who stared up at her. Many of them had been beaten, injured, and abused. Others were no longer present and would never be again. She couldn't imagine how many people the Three Kingdoms lost in the devastating battles.

Too many.

Anger rose into her throat as she came to terms with where she stood and what it would take to rebuild her father's kingdom. First, they must win the war, and it would take the entire realm to do so. With her mother's help and that of Nardus and the others, it could be accomplished.

We will do this.

Pride swelled in her chest as she folded her arms behind her back and addressed her people. "My fellow citizens, I stand here tonight not as your princess but as one of you. Like many of you, I've also lost family and friends. Loved ones."

"Here, here!" a young man shouted. Blood still caked his hair and the left side of his face.

Zelanora nodded at the man. It would take men and women like him to bring Aria's reign of terror to an end. "Our enemies have stormed our gates, torched our cities, and left us for dead. However, we are still alive. We are still strong. And we will fight back." Several people cheered and others clapped. Once the noise died down again, she continued, "The night we face is dark, and it might remain so for weeks to come, but rest assured that the light cannot be vanquished. We fight for justice. For freedom. We fight for the right to live. Mark my words when I say we will not fail."

"We've lost everything," someone said. "So, what is there left to fight for?"

Another said, "How many more of us will die?"

The room buzzed with heated conversation. It would take more than a few words to unite the people. What they needed was reassurance, but she didn't know how to provide it when she needed some herself.

How can I convince them?

Zerenity joined Zelanora and placed her hand on Zelanora's side. The simple gesture reinvigorated her.

Zelanora held up her hand and waited for the talking to cease before continuing again. "The only way one can lose everything is to lose their life. We are all still here." She looked to the man with bloody hair, then to several others. "Are your lives not worth fighting for?"

"We're farmers and carpenters," an older man said. "Stone workers and blacksmiths. Fishermen. Fathers and mothers. Children." He raised his arms. "Explain to me how we're supposed to stand up to an evil sorceress and her dragon? To their vast armies?"

Zelanora knew what she had to do. Knew the one thing that might finally convince her people to fight. Yet she also knew it would place her in imminent danger.

One way or another, they will come to know the truth about me. Therefore, it must come from me.

She held her hands out and stared at them as she drew upon her mezhik. Green flames rose from her palms. Twisted and danced as they formed a fireball. Her gaze rose. Met those of her people. "We fight fire with fire."

Gasps filled the stronghold.

"She's a sorceress, like her mother!" an old woman said.

One woman screamed and then fainted into the arms of the man standing behind her.

Another man shook his fist at her. "You're the one who brought this upon us!"

Nardus joined Zelanora and Zerenity and scowled at the people until they quieted. He pointed a finger at Zelanora. "This young woman—your princess—had *nothing* to do with the attacks on your cities. Nor did her mother. King Zaridus—your *dead* king—" Many of the people began to weep or wail. "—knew of the coming threat and did nothing." His eyes flashed with lightning. "If you want someone to blame, then look to his ineptness."

A man toward the back of the room cried out, "He blasphemes our king!"

"No!" Savric materialized on the stage and shook his staff at the crowd. "I personally delivered the message of war to King Zaridus, and he thanked me by throwing me out of his courts."

Theyn—still in her cat form—leapt onto the stage. Those nearest the stage backed away. She paced back and forth several times, then shifted into her human form. The crowd grew silent with fear.

Zelanora watched her fireball fizzle out before addressing the people again. "You've been lied to for far too long," she said. "Mezhik was never your enemy. It can be your enemy no more than the air you breathe or the water you drink. Yes, it can be used for evil, but it can also be used for good just as easily. It is the same as your water or food. Add poison to them, and they'll kill you. Inhale too much smoke from a fire, and it will kill you, too. Fear not what you don't understand but seek to attain knowledge." Muscles tense and fists clenched, Zelanora stood tall. "Like it or not, we stand against your enemies and will defend you unto victory or unto death." She shook her fist in the air. "Who among you will stand with us?"

At first, no one moved. Scarcely breathed. Sniffles rose from every corner of the room. Then, the young man with the bloody hair raised his hand as he looked around the room. "My name is Kris, and I'll stand with you, Princess Zelanora."

A few seconds later, another hand joined Kris's. "As will I," the woman said.

Many of the people looked to one another, unsure of what they should do.

"This is our fight," Kris said. He circled where he stood. "If you cannot fight for yourselves and your families, what is the point in living?"

Another hand rose. Then another. Several more. Soon, more than half the people had a hand raised.

Love and courage filled Zelanora's heart. "Together, we will be victorious!"

CHAPTER THIRTY-SEVEN

Rakzar and Urza stood on either side of Torbrek Stonebreaker and watched him draw the string back on Alderan's recurve bow. The little man managed to pull it all the way back to his face, nearly a foot. The ends of the bow bent back but didn't break. Muscles in his arms, shoulder, and back bulged as he kept the string drawn, and the bow showed no signs of weakness. Nor did Torbrek.

As impressive as it was, Rakzar couldn't be certain the repair would hold up against someone with brute strength, so he insisted on testing the bow himself. In truth, he'd never used a bow before. In fact, he'd never even held one. It felt strange in his large hands. Delicate and foreign.

The thought of it snapping in two when he drew the string shot fear into his mind. It would be a horrible way to lose an eye. Then again, losing an eye would be horrible no matter the circumstance.

Rakzar exhaled and drew. The bow bent slightly, but the string only moved half a dozen inches. He eased up, repositioned his hands and arms, and tried again. The string slipped from his sweaty fingers after just a few inches of drawback, and the arrow barely made it past the end of the bow before falling to the floor. Torbrek and Urza busted up laughing.

He glared at them both, then shoved the bow at Urza. "Let's see if you're still laughing once you've tried it."

Urza took the bow and nocked an arrow. "You think everything is about strength, but you're wrong."

She inhaled as she drew the string back and rested her hand against her cheek. The string touched the tip of her nose. With a wink, she released the string and loosed the arrow.

Whoosh!

The arrow flew seventy feet across the armory and buried itself right in the center of the straw target with a soft *shick*.

"Nice shot," Torbrek said.

Rakzar scoffed. "Beginner's luck."

"Really?" Urza nocked another arrow and drew back the string.

Whoosh!

Whoosh! Whoosh!

Two more arrows quickly followed the first.

Shick!

Shick! Shick!

Rakzar couldn't believe his eyes. Four arrows protruded from the target, each within an inch of the others. Luck had nothing to do with it.

He eyed Urza, and she just shrugged. "Like you said, beginner's luck."

What else don't I know about her?

Torbrek clapped slowly. "Good show, but fixing the bow was only part of it." He withdrew seven black-and-silver arrows from a quiver slung over his shoulder. Rakzar hadn't even noticed him carrying it. "Now these will complete the set." He lay them on the table in front of them.

Rakzar had never seen anything like the arrows before. It was impossible to tell if they were made of metal, obsidian, a combination of the two, or something altogether different. He suspected something different.

Torbrek confirmed it, his eyes glistening with mischief. "It's something I like to call clawmetal."

"Clawmetal?" Rakzar shook his head. "That was the best you could come up with?"

Torbrek scowled. "And I suppose you have a better name?"

"Blacksteel, perhaps?" He offered.

Torbrek's scowl deepened. "Already exists and is far inferior to my creation. As the name implies, these are a mixture of steel and dragon claws."

Rakzar wondered where Torbrek might've gotten his hands on some dragon claws but figured it made little difference as long as they worked. "Makes more sense, I guess." Rakzar picked up one of the clawmetal arrows and examined it. "There are no feathers on it."

"Fletching," Torbrek corrected. He took one and ran his fingers along its shaft. "These arrows need none and will fly true."

"And the point?" Urza said.

"The barbed end will slice through almost anything and secure it."

Rakzar and Urza shared a glance. "Like a dragon's heart," Rakzar said.

"Ah, now, see? You're catching on." He held up a finger. "Wait right here."

Torbrek laid the arrow down and trotted across the armory. He dismantled the straw target and replaced it with a metal stand. Two steel plates hung from the stand, parallel to each other, and each about a foot wide and high. Both plates had a large dragon scale strapped to its center. Once satisfied with their positioning, he returned with an elvish bow.

"Now, allow me to demonstrate." Torbrek strung the elvish bow and nocked one of the clawmetal arrows. "As I'm sure you're aware, elvish bows are known to be the strongest made."

Rakzar knew nothing of bows, but he nodded all the same. "Agreed."

Torbrek drew the string as he inhaled. "As I told you a few days ago, I had been working on something that would penetrate those dragon scales but hadn't perfected it yet."

"Right," Urza said.

Whoosh!

The arrow flew true.

Clank!

As expected, the arrow failed to penetrate the dragon scale. It clattered to the floor.

Torbrek led the three of them over to the first target and pointed at a smudge on the dragon scale. "As you can see, the arrow hardly scratched it."

"It did nothing," Rakzar said.

Torbrek reached down and picked up the felled arrow. "Correct."

Back at the firing end, Torbrek took Alderan's bow and nocked a clawmetal arrow. "Until this morning, it hadn't occurred to me that it wasn't my creation at fault but the delivery method of it."

Understanding came to Rakzar. "It requires Alderan's bow."

Torbrek grinned. In that moment, he reminded Rakzar of Normak. But the resemblance faded with Torbrek's smile.

"Precisely." He drew back the string and loosed the arrow.

Whoosh!

Again, the arrow sailed through the air, but with far more speed.

Crack!

The arrow smashed into the second target. A sound akin to shattering glass followed the crack.

Rakzar squinted to see what'd happened. The first target still hung from the metal stand, and the dragon scale at its center refracted light. The second target had an arrow protruding from it, but there seemed to no longer be a dragon scale strapped to it. The three of them headed back across the room.

Rakzar knelt in front of the second target. The clawmetal arrow had penetrated the steel plate at least seven inches and cracked the plate from top to bottom, but that wasn't what captured his attention. His eyes scanned the floor. Black shards littered it, none bigger than a thorn. The dragon scale had been obliterated.

Gods…

He didn't understand how an arrow could cause so much destruction, but it didn't matter. What did matter was that Torbrek had fixed the bow and produced exactly what they needed.

That scaly bastard is going down.

Torbrek worked the arrow out of the steel plate and examined it. "There's one more thing I want to show you."

Again, they returned to the firing end of the armory. Torbrek returned all but one of the clawmetal arrows to the quiver he carried. Then, he retrieved a gauntlet from another table and slid it onto his firing hand. The gauntlet looked just like the clawmetal arrows, formed of a black-and-silver substance.

Torbrek held up his gauntleted hand. "As you can see, this is made of the same material as the arrows. You'll understand why in a minute." He took the last clawmetal arrow and nocked it on Alderan's bow. After a quick draw and aim, he sent the arrow on its way.

Whoosh!

As before, the arrow met the target with a crack, followed by the sound of shattering glass. If Rakzar had been skeptical of the arrow's ability before—which he hadn't been—its second demonstration would've squashed all doubt.

Torbrek lay the bow on the table. "Now, you might be asking yourself what good the arrow will do if you've got no way to retrieve it once it's embedded in a target. I asked myself that same question last night. Thank the gods I was granted an answer."

The dwarf stretched out his gauntleted hand toward the first target. At first, Rakzar detected nothing, but then he noticed the arrow begin to vibrate. The arrow worked its way out of the steel plate and flew back across the armory and into Torbrek's hand.

Gods...

Torbrek beamed. "Impressive, right?"

The arrows and gauntlet worked just like Rayah's gloves and blades. Rakzar didn't know how Torbrek managed to replicate the same behavior, especially given that he couldn't use mezhik. His puzzlement must've been obvious.

Torbrek looked around the armory with caution. Then, he leaned toward Rakzar and said, "Sometimes, we employ a wizard to help us perfect our armor and weapons. Divulge this secret, and I'll have your heads. Understood?"

Rakzar and Urza agreed. Who would they tell, anyway?

Torbrek removed the gauntlet and placed the final arrow in the quiver. "One last thing to remember. This gauntlet will retrieve all clawmetal arrows not in the quiver. It's important you keep this in mind. Otherwise, someone might end up getting hurt that wasn't supposed to." He handed the bow and gauntlet to Urza and pulled the quiver off his shoulder. Rakzar took the quiver when Torbrek offered it to him.

Urza stared at the bow. "We cannot pay you for this."

"Pay me?" Torbrek scoffed. "Soon, we will owe you a far greater debt than can ever be paid in weapons."

"How so?" Rakzar growled.

"Freedom is priceless." Torbrek sighed. "Had I the king's ear, my brethren and I would be free to join you. What I wouldn't give to avenge Normak."

"Come with us," Urza said.

"Unlike my brother, I am bound in duty. If I were to leave, I could never come back." He shook his head. "This is my home. I've never known anything else."

Rakzar strapped the quiver onto his back. "And Ridan?"

"Ridan… Gods, I love her." He looked up, his cheeks red. "Like a sister, of course. We had our fun once, but her heart belongs to Normak."

Urza said, "Does she have a free pass, too?"

Torbrek snorted and shrugged. "You mean like Normak did? Well, she's the king's niece. As such, she can do no wrong."

Urza gasped. "She never said anything about it."

"And never will," Torbrek said. "If I were you, I'd never mention it to her, either."

"We need to go." Rakzar proffered his hand to Torbrek. The dwarf eyed it for a few seconds before taking it. "Until we meet again, Stonebreaker."

"May the gods look favorably upon you." He released Rakzar's hand.

At least one God.

Urza knelt and hugged Torbrek. "And you, my friend."

Rakzar and Urza made their way up through Tectus and made camp for the night a few hours beyond the city's cave entrance. The next few days would be a hard journey, but Rakzar knew it would pale in comparison to the battles ahead. He took the first watch while Urza slept. It gave him time to process all that'd happened over the last week and a half. No matter how much he would've liked to go back and change events, he knew it wasn't possible. Still, it didn't prevent his mind from imagining it.

Rest well, White Knight. You will be avenged.

CHAPTER THIRTY-EIGHT

Rayah held onto Ridan as though her life depended on it, and in some ways it did. A brief skirmish with a flock of carnivorous hawks left one of her wings damaged. After that, she could only manage flying short distances before tiring. Ridan insisted she ride Bakkan with her.

Although it didn't seem to slow Bakkan down with the two of them on his back, Rayah thought it would've been a better idea to use Normak's winged shoes. The mere suggestion of doing so created a rift between them. At first, she thought Ridan was being petty about the whole incident, but the more she thought about it, the more she realized how wrong she'd been to make such a suggestion. Had Ridan asked her to use something of Alderan's, she likely would've reacted in the same manner.

"I'm sorry," Rayah said.

Ridan glanced back. "What?"

Rayah added more volume to her voice the second time. "I said I'm sorry."

Ridan grunted. It was likely the only response Rayah would receive. For now, she'd live with it.

As they rode on, the evening landscape changed from forests and grass to rocks and hills. The hills morphed into the gargantuan Orbis Mountains to the west and south, and the Tamda River they followed gave birth to Trivers Lake. Vallah lay ahead, its many levels scaling the side of the mountain.

The cloudless night offered clarity, even with just a sliver of moon. Nothing stood between them and the mangled gates that led into the ruined city but foot-high grass. Mountains and forest rose to the north and the lake shimmered to the south. Somehow, the war had missed its northern shoreline.

A bone-chilling howl disrupted the serene night and sent Bakkan skidding through the grass. Ridan launched off Bakkan's back as soon as he came to a halt, spear in hand. Rayah already had her gloves on, so she yanked two blades free of her belt. The three of them crouched low in the grass and peered into the shadows of the forest.

The wind picked up. Sang as it whipped through the grass. Distorted Rayah's vision. She raised her head a little more to get a better view.

Three beasts emerged from the forest. One to the east, one to the west, and one directly north of them. They had nowhere to run. Memories of the day she met Alderan flooded her mind as the gnolls drew closer. A quick test of the ground confirmed her fear: the soil contained more rock than dirt. It wouldn't be an option for escape or for fighting. Neither would flight.

She and Ridan stood, shoulder to shoulder. Bakkan growled low. It would likely be the only thing they could count on from him. As a familiar, he rarely engaged an enemy. Ridan once told her that it was impossible for him to do so, but she remembered him pinning Ridan down when they fought Käíeᴢ. Either way, she wouldn't count on his help.

"Just when I thought the day couldn't get worse," Ridan said.

"Same."

"Lookie what we got here, boys," one of the gnolls said as he quickly closed the distance to just ten feet.

The gnoll to the west stopped about ten feet away as well and sniffed the air. "Smell like dinner."

To the east, the gnoll crept even closer. His yellow eyes were nearly gray, and he looked sickly. A portion of his scalp was missing, and blood covered his left side, which he favored. "Ever had dwarf meat, Crash?"

"Nah, Biff," the first gnoll said. "Bet it tastes like fowl."

The second gnoll howled with laughter. "Everything taste fowl."

Rayah glowered at the one named Biff and brandished her blades. "Do I look like a dwarf to you?"

Biff stood on his hind legs. He would've made Rakzar look short, standing a good eight feet tall. He shrugged. "What doesn't?"

Crash rose on his hind legs, too. "Toad doesn't."

The second gnoll half growled, half croaked. "Not funny."

"Don't know," Biff said. "I think it is. Tell the girls here why we call you

Toad."

"Hops like a toad, croaks like a toad, must be a toad," Crash said.

Ridan took a step toward the one named Crash. "You gonna talk us to death, or are we gonna fight?"

Crash laughed. "Don't damage 'em, boys."

The three gnolls converged.

† † †

Alderan stood atop the King's Palace, his dark blue robes pinned against the fronts of his legs and his black cloak billowing at his back. Once, he'd fought Zerenity on wearing such attire, but now they felt more natural against his skin than trousers and a shirt. Plus, they proved far more resilient against the elements.

He stared down at the massive lake, but its wavy surface failed to capture his attention. Instead, he warred with his mind over the memories of Aria slaying the king in cold blood. It hadn't been her. Knew it in his heart. Yet his mind insisted otherwise.

As he continued to contemplate how both could be true, his thoughts began to shift toward Rayah. Although he didn't share a bond with her like he did Aria, he often imagined reaching into the depths of his soul and connecting with her on a level far more intimate than any he'd ever known. According to his father, Rayah didn't know he lived. He wondered how she would react when she saw him again for the first time. Would she be relieved or scared? Angry, perhaps? If it were the other way around, how would he feel?

It would be the best day of my life, times a thousand.

A chill swept beneath his robes, crawled up the back of his legs, and clawed its way up his spine and onto his shoulders. He drew his hood and gathered his cloak around himself, but it didn't drive away the feeling. Instead, it had the opposite effect. The chill burrowed beneath his skin and slithered down into his heart. Pulse racing, he peered into the night.

A pebble rolled across the rooftop. Alderan spun around, a fireball blazing between his hands. Calen, his eyes wide and hands raised over his face, stood just three paces away.

"For the love of Ɂäţūr, Calen!" Alderan said, extinguishing the fireball. "I could've killed you."

Calen joined him at the railing that surrounded the palace rooftop. "Sneaking up on you was never my intent."

Alderan glowered at him, his heart still pumping furiously. "You're supposed to be resting."

"And you're supposed to be dead." Calen chuckled.

He didn't know Calen very well. In fact, he didn't really know him at all. The portly boy never struck Alderan as someone who would face fear with bravery, yet he had according to Berggren. Anyone willing to take a dagger in the gut to save someone they cared about was alright in Alderan's book.

He laughed. "Guess you have a point."

Calen placed his hands on the railing and leaned over it. "We sure are a long ways up."

"Yeah, and I wouldn't trust that railing if I were you." He pointed out several cracks and two missing supports.

"Right." Calen backed away from the railing. "Never thought I'd find myself living in the King's Palace."

"Neither did I. To be honest—"

Vicious howls filled the night. Alderan knew the sound all too well.

Gnolls!

He and Calen rushed over to the southeastern corner of the rooftop and scanned the city below. The only things that moved were carried by the wind.

Calen pointed toward the east. "Over there!"

Alderan squinted. Three gnolls. Two of them stood over what looked like their kills. The third circled someone very short who wielded a spear. In his heart, he knew it must be Ridan. If so, one of the others must be—

"Rayah!" Like a flash of lightning, Alderan moved from the rooftop to the grass field in a single step.

† † †

After Rayah and Bakkan went down, Ridan thought of nothing but revenge. Twice, she'd struck the beast she fought, jabbing the point of her spear into his thick hide, but the blows only emboldened him.

Crash swiped at her, and she ducked, but not quickly enough. One of his claws dug into her scalp and scraped across the back of her skull. She cried out as the force toppled her. Splayed out on her back, she tried to raise her spear, but Crash had it pinned under his foot.

He stepped on her midsection with his other foot and drove the breath from her lungs. His weight alone could've crushed her. Saliva dripped from his jowls and onto her face as he leaned over her.

"Time to meet your maker," he growled.

His yellow eyes brightened. As did the night. Crash looked up just as a fireball hit him square in the chest. He howled and staggered backward. Swiped at the flames eating away his flesh. Fell backward. Writhed. Gurgled. Stilled.

Ridan pulled herself to her feet and kicked her spear up to her hand. She wheeled around to face Toad and Biff, but they both lay still, consumed with fire. Bakkan lay still, surrounded by a dark pool.

A figure cloaked in black and dark blue robes knelt over Rayah, their hands stretched over her body. Shadows hid their face beneath their hood as tendrils of white light seeped from their palms and into Rayah.

Ridan dropped her spear and moved closer to the cloaked figure. "Who are you?" Her pulse raced as their eyes met.

Gods…

† † †

Rayah lay in the grassy meadow with her eyes closed as sunrays bathed her in warmth and drove the frost from her bones. The side of her head pulsed with pain, and she couldn't remember why she lay there or how she'd suffered the blow, but the sunrays comforted her.

Ƨäţūr's glorious sun.

A familiar voice called her name from a great distance. Haunting as it echoed in her mind. At first, she couldn't put a name to the voice, but as they continued to call her name clarity came to her.

Ridan.

A waterfall of memories flooded her mind. They were almost to Vallah. Saw the city gates. Then… hateful yellow eyes. Vicious beasts. Gnolls. The attack.

Rayah's eyelids fluttered. Heavy as they were, she forced them open.

Hands hovered over her head. Too big for Ridan's. Not just too big, but also teeming with mezhik.

My sunrays.

"She's awake," Ridan said.

"Rayah?"

Another familiar voice, but male. It must be Nardus, yet it didn't sound like him. No, she knew what she heard. Knew the impossibility of it. How hard had she been hit in the head?

The hands moved away, giving her a perfect view of her savior. But the shadows prevented her from seeing his face. Her heart hammered as he drew back his hood. Blonde locks shone in the pale moonlight. Beautiful green eyes.

Rayah knew then what had happened to her, but it still didn't make sense. Didn't feel right. There should be no pain or suffering in Kinzhdm ef Häfn, yet she felt both.

"How can I be dead?" she said.

Alderan lifted her into his arms. Held her close. His warm breath upon her neck. "You're not dead," he whispered.

She breathed deep. Smelled his musk. Felt beads of sweat upon her lips when she pressed them against his neck. "Then I must be dreaming."

Fear grabbed her. Tore at her heart. Twisted her gut. Soon, she would wake, and she'd be alone again. Tears swelled in her eyes. Ran down her cheeks.

Alderan pulled her back. Gazed into her eyes. Smiled the way he always did. "You're not dreaming, Rayah. I am here." He wiped tears from her cheeks with his thumbs, then kissed her.

Rayah wrapped her arms around him and kissed him deep. Tasted spices on his tongue. She wept as they held each other.

Still, she didn't believe. Couldn't allow herself to. Dead do not rise. Not until the final judgment.

If I'm not dead and not dreaming, then what is this, ǯäţūr?

She pulled away from Alderan and stood. "This must be some kind of illusion, or you're a demon."

Ridan rose. Took Rayah's hand and shook it. Shook her. "The man ya love found a way to cheat death to be with ya!"

Rayah jerked her hand away. "It's not possible."

"Were he Normak, I'd be praising the heavens."

Alderan stood and ran his fingers through his hair. "We live in a world of mezhik. How could you possibly think anything is impossible?"

"Because you died!" Rayah shook with both rage and sorrow. "Everyone saw you reduced to ashes." She grabbed her head and groaned. "I've relived that moment in my mind for weeks."

"I understand." Alderan reached toward her.

Rayah retreated. "How could you understand? You're not even real!"

"Think about what you're saying, Rayah. If I wasn't real, then how did I heal you? Why does Ridan see me? Why has everyone seen me?" He sighed. "Look, I know this is complicated, but I never died. I stole a necklace from Wrik by accident, and it saved my life."

Rayah couldn't believe what she was hearing. "First off, how do you steal something by accident? Either you stole it, or you didn't. Second, how can a necklace save your life? Do you not understand how absurd that is? You burned to ash, for the love of Ɂäṭūr!"

He scratched the back of his neck. "Yes, I know, it sounds crazy."

"Crazy isn't the word for it. It's impossible!" Rayah fluttered her wings and took to the sky.

Alderan held up his arms. "And yet here I am."

Rayah's mind swam with thoughts as she hovered over the grass field. None of it made sense, yet she couldn't deny what her eyes saw. What she felt in her heart.

What am I supposed to do, Ɂäṭūr?

An answer came to her. She dropped back to the ground and faced Alderan or the demon pretending to be him. "If you really are who you say, then my bond with you should be intact, correct?"

Alderan shrugged. "Guess so."

"Sit down." Alderan complied, and she sat facing him. "Do you remember what happened when I told you about my assignment and what'd happened to your village?"

Alderan nodded. "Yeah."

"You had knowledge beyond what I told you."

"I felt everything. Experienced it as though I had been there."

"Exactly." Rayah glanced over at Ridan. She lay on the ground next to Bakkan and held him. It made her wonder how much loss one could suffer before breaking.

Has she reached that point?

Alderan squeezed her hands. "Ask me to do anything, and I will."

"While in Nasduron, I spent a lot of time alone thinking about what'd happened and what I might do." She began describing the place and told him about the archway and how they'd escaped through it. He listened intently and remained silent until she finished.

His eyes brimmed with tears, and his hands quavered. "You wanted to kill Aria." He jerked his hands away, stood, and walked toward the lake.

Despite his anger, joy filled her heart.

It really is him!

CHAPTER THIRTY-NINE

Aria stood at the center of her bedchambers. Bloody, broken glass littered the floor. Bit into the bottoms of her bare feet like venomous fangs, spilling her blood. Tears streaked her cheeks, but not from the physical pain. It paled in comparison to the pain within her heart and mind.

Pravus never loved me.

After the incident with the statue in West Hotah a few days ago, she'd demanded every mirror inside the castle be covered, removed, or destroyed. All of them had been, and she had no desire to view her reflection ever again, but the rain—*The damned rain!*—refused to bend to her will. It conspired with the traitorous moon. First, the rain pooled on her balcony. Then, the moonlight peeked through the clouds and seduced her. Bathed her with its beams and transformed the rain pool into a vile, hideous reflective beacon. At first, she ignored it and stared into the distance, but eventually her eyes failed to resist its temptation. Failed to comprehend the lengths she'd gone to avoid such an event. She cursed the moon, the rain, and the small pool they'd created, yet the small pool proved insufficient. Marred her reflection. Provided little more than a shadow of who she really was and what she looked like. It should've been enough. Should've satiated her perverse desire to torture herself, yet it didn't. In fact, it had the opposite effect. She obsessed over the statue and her reflection and warred with herself. Eventually, she could no longer resist. The truth must be revealed. So, she returned to her bedchambers and removed the sheet draped over her full-length mirror. The events following that moment blurred in her mind. Left her standing on a bed of broken glass.

Seething, Aria reached out with her mind and located Cinolth. *"Meet me on the rooftop."*

"I am feeding," came his response.

She hated him. Hated herself. Hated the world.

She teleported to the rooftop and stood atop the southern rampart parapet. The wind whipped around her. Pushed against her legs and kept her unstable. If she were to fall, there would be no one to save her. She moved toward the outer edge of the parapet. All the way until her toes hung off its side.

Aria spread her arms wide and closed her eyes. Released her fear. The wind blew back her clothes and hair. Her stomach lurched as the sensation of falling gripped her. Yet her feet still touched the stone parapet. Opening her eyes, she stared into the black abyss far below. As dark as it was, it might as well have been the edge of the world.

Thump-thump. Whoosh! Thump-thump. Whoosh!

Cinolth approached fast and landed hard, knocking Aria off the parapet. She landed hard on her back and cracked her head against the dense stone. Pain burst forth from the back of her skull and enveloped her head. A single, serpentine eye glared at her just inches above her head. Cinolth's hot breath burned her neck, and the sulfuric fumes choked her.

"Foolish girl," he roared.

Aria sat up as Cinolth withdrew his head. A sizable lump had already sprouted on the back of her head, and her fingers came away with blood on them. "I told you to come."

"So that you can vent your pathetic frustrations and self-doubt?"

"You know nothing of how I feel."

"You're wrong. I feel everything you do, and it sickens me."

"What sickens me is my face."

"Vanity will be your death."

"Pravus lied to me. Don't you get that?"

"Yes, he used his mezhik to create the illusion that he'd healed your face. So what?"

"Why would he do that and not just heal me like he claimed?"

"Your injuries far exceeded his limited healing power. It was the only option he had."

"And why is the mezhik failing?"

Cinolth snorted. "Pravus is dead, and the illusion could only last so long without him constantly adding mezhik to it."

Aria had never contemplated mezhik working in such a manner, but it made sense. She pointed at her face. "And how am I supposed to fix this?"

"We have far greater issues than your broken face."

"I don't care what you think. Tell me how I can fix it."

"Create your own illusion."

"I may be a mage, but my powers aren't limitless. You know I cannot perform illusions."

"Then find someone who can, or find another solution."

Aria huffed. "You're no help."

"Nor shall I be in this matter." He turned and looked toward the north. "Tomorrow, we fly to the Valley of Dragons and face Quldrai."

"Yes, I know."

"Once we've secured my throne, we will return to Vallah."

"Why?"

"One of my followers spotted the winged girl. She was with a wizard."

Aria jumped to her feet. "We need to go now!"

"No," Cinolth roared. "You've had your day and earned your throne. My patience wanes, and I will wait no longer."

Aria crossed her arms. "Then I'll go without you."

"You will do no such thing. Return to your bedchambers and rest. You will need your full strength if we're to dethrone Quldrai."

Rage coursed through her veins. "No!"

"It's not a request."

Cinolth's presence overwhelmed her mind. She fought to sever the connection, but the more she resisted, the greater his hold became. Her vision jittered. Shook her world. Feet slid forward of their own accord, then the dragon, the ramparts, and the night sky vanished.

Aria gasped. Clutched her chest. Dropped to her knees at the foot of her bed and fell onto her side. Rigid as stone. Hot tears slid down her cheek. Itched on her skin. She willed her arm to move. Her hand to wipe the tears. But nothing responded.

Cinolth's voice filled her head. *"Remember to whom you belong."*

"I am yours," she said, but the words were not hers.

Cinolth's mind retracted from her, and she pulled her knees to her chest. Tears flowed from her eyes without restraint. Slowly, she slipped into the comforts of sleep with a single thought on her mind.

I am not my own.

† † †

Reubane sat in a chair in front of Aria and watched her sleep. He'd come to her bedchambers every night since their first encounter and had lain next to her while she slept on more than one occasion. It had been enough at first, but tonight he needed more. He planned to finally take what belonged to him—what had been promised to him—but refrained after witnessing unexplainable events. Those events played again within his mind.

Aria stood on the balcony, her hair tousling in the wind. Every curve exposed beneath a sheer gown. Reubane liked what he saw. Needed it. She looked so peaceful as she gazed into the distance, but then her demeanor changed after her gaze shifted to a small puddle of rain. At first, Reubane thought she'd spotted him, but then she stormed back inside. He followed her. Kept to the shadows as she uncovered a full-length mirror. Her gown slid off her slender shoulders. Piled on the floor. Normally, he would've ogled such a beautiful creature, but he couldn't keep his eyes from focusing on the two fingertips she used to trace her broken face. They lingered on her blistered lips and jagged teeth. The bulge of her left cheekbone. He watched her, enraptured by the tenderness with which she caressed herself. So enthralled, he witnessed only the aftermath of her fist smashing the mirror. Her wail sent gooseflesh racing across his body.

Reubane exhaled a deep breath as he returned from his thoughts, then knelt next to Aria. Her hair, still damp in a few spots, smelled of rain and lavender. He breathed it in as he leaned over her and buried his face in her neck. Her soft, warm skin caressed his nose and cheek, and the veins in her neck pulsed with life. Restraint wasn't one of his many traits, and he knew he'd barreled past the point of no return as his teeth slid across her skin.

You will taste like a fresh strawberry.

Pulse raced. Breath shallow.

Her skin gave little resistance before producing a trickle of warm, coppery liquid. Aria moaned but otherwise did not stir. Reubane lapped up the blood with his tongue, savoring the sweet yet acrid nectar.

A knock at the door drew his attention. The handle turned.

Reubane sat up and sighed. "We will finish this another time." He returned to the shadows as the door opened into the room. After one last glance at Aria, he retreated to the balcony and disappeared into the night.

CHAPTER FORTY

A knock at the door drew Nardus from his sleep. Faint light filtered in through the window, deepening the shadows where it failed to reach. From the looks of it, the sun had yet to crest the western ridge of the Orbis Mountains. He sat up. Theyn wasn't there, but it wasn't unusual for her to slip away. She required far less sleep than he did.

Nardus slipped his trousers on and pulled his shirt down over his head as he opened the bedchamber door.

Calen stood in the corridor, his eyes to the floor as he pushed a small piece of rubble around with his foot.

Nardus yawned. "What is it, Calen?"

He looked up and rubbed the back of his head. "Something happened last night while I was on the rooftop."

"Something like what?"

"It could've been nothing."

"If it were nothing, you wouldn't be standing at my door before sunrise, now would you?"

"No, sir. I guess not."

He ushered Calen into the bedchamber and sat him down on a chair in front of the fireplace. "Speak your mind, son. What happened?"

"After Alderan went to save Rayah and Ridan, I just stood there and watched him fight those gnolls."

"Considering the fact that you should've been in bed resting, you can't be blamed for not helping him. And, even if you wanted to help, the fight would've been over well before you made it down there."

Calen nodded. "I know, but I should've gone and told Queen Lanara."

"And why didn't you?"

"I was about to when I noticed what looked like someone watching. It was difficult to see from the rooftop, but I'm almost positive the person had pale skin."

"You think one of Cinolth's mind slaves saw you?"

He shook his head. "Not me, but Rayah and Alderan."

Nardus cursed and smacked his fist into his palm. "Then we don't have much time before they come for us."

Calen chewed on his lower lip. "That's what I'm afraid of."

Nardus stood and raked his fingers through his hair. "I wish you had told me this last night."

"I would have, but it was late, and you still hadn't returned from the stronghold." Calen groaned. "I tried to stay awake, but the salve Miss Zerenity gave me for my stomach made me really tired. After waiting awhile, I couldn't keep my eyes open anymore. I'll do better next time."

Nardus sighed. "No, you're right. I shouldn't expect the impossible of you, especially given your current circumstance." He feigned a smile. "You did well telling me this, Calen."

"Thank you," Calen said.

Nardus turned and stared at the pile of ash in the fireplace. It reminded him of the battlefield south of Elatos. Of Alderan. They lost that battle not because they were overpowered or outmaneuvered but because of a simple distraction. One small dragon.

Perhaps we need a distraction of our own.

He turned back to Calen. "Gather the others and have them meet me in the hall upstairs. I have a plan."

"Yes, sir." Calen rose and exited the bedchamber.

† † †

Alderan watched as everyone gathered around the same table they had used the night before the first attack on the Three Kingdoms. Every seat at the table had been filled that night, but now just a few seats were occupied. So many people gave their lives fighting for King Zaridus and the Ancient Realm, but what did they have to show for it? What had they achieved?

Nothing.

Rayah sat across the table from him, her gaze locked on him. After uncovering the disturbing revelation about Aria, he could hardly look at

Rayah. Those few moments he did boiled his blood. In no world had he ever thought it possible that the two women he cared about would be at each other's throat.

Nardus entered the hall and stopped at the head of the table. He leaned on its edge with his palms and eyed each of them. "Is this all of us?"

Everyone glanced around the table, including Alderan. To his knowledge, the only two missing were Rakzar and Urza. With any luck, they'd be back in a few days. Everything hinged on their success with the dwarves.

Alderan had grown quite fond of Rakzar and looked forward to seeing him again. Now and again, he thought about all the months he and Rayah spent running for their lives, but it felt so distant now. More like a dream than reality.

"We are few, but we're strong," Queen Lanara said.

Few was an understatement. Cinolth controlled tens of thousands who would fall on their own swords if commanded to do so, and Aria led an army of not just soldiers but ghastly beasts and ferocious foes. In a straight-up war against them, there would be no chance of victory. However, personal ties made each battle far more intimate. Aria and Cinolth both had something to prove by defeating Nardus. That would be their downfall.

Alderan reached out with his mind but felt nothing of his bond with Aria. She could be anywhere in the world or nowhere at all, and he'd never know. The thought scared him.

Keep her safe for me, Ʒäʈūr.

"That we are." Nardus took his seat. "From this point forward, we must operate as though the enemy knows our location and could launch an attack at any point."

Theyn leaned forward in her seat. "Berggren and I have cleared the entire palace, but there are still a few zhebəllin and ogres roaming around the city."

Nardus nodded. "Yes, but they aren't the enemies who will report back to Cinolth."

"We've been discovered, then?" Zerenity said.

Alderan's heart sank. "This is my fault, isn't it?"

"Feathers," Savric said. "One can never be at fault for saving the lives of friends."

"Agreed," Ridan said. She sat next to Rayah and nodded when Alderan looked at her. "Rayah and I would be dead if it wasn't for ya, Alderan."

Rayah touched Alderan's leg with her foot. He glared at her, but it didn't stop her from smiling. "She's right. You saved us even though I'm the one who's supposed to be protecting you."

Stabbing me in the back is more like it.

"Nardus isn't talking about any of that." Everyone turned their attention to Calen. "I'm certain I witnessed a mind-controlled person last night."

The entire room gasped.

Niesha's face paled. "Here in the palace?"

Calen shook his head. "No, they stood at the tree line and watched Alderan fight those gnolls."

Alderan leaned back in his chair and closed his eyes.

This is *my fault.*

† † †

Nardus banged his fist on the table until the conversation died off. It amazed him how twelve people—himself not included—could make so much noise. "Look, I know this isn't the kind of news you wanted to hear, but I do have a plan that might buy us some time."

"We all jump in Morcinda's ship and flee the realm?" Berggren said.

"That is a plan, but not a good one." Nardus stood and walked around the table until he faced Lanara. "From what I understand, you're capable of grand illusions."

She smiled and blushed a little. "What did you have in mind?"

"I'd like you to create an illusion that will mask Vallah and the King's Palace from our enemies."

Lanara's smile faded. "I'm not sure I follow."

"We need time to fortify the palace if we intend to use it as our last stand. Doing so will draw unwanted attention even if what Calen saw turns out to be nothing."

"Let me make sure I'm getting this straight. You're asking me to alter the perception of anyone who views Vallah and the King's Palace?"

"I am, but it's more than just that. Obviously, those of us here will need to see things as they truly are. Otherwise, it will be impossible to make progress."

"What you're asking isn't just impractical or improbable. It's impossible."

"You deceived an entire realm once before."

"Yes, but that was far different. Only a few people witnessed my demise and fewer the bloody aftermath."

"When you say impossible, do you mean to say such a feat cannot be done technically no matter the scale of the illusion?"

Lanara frowned and stared straight ahead for several seconds before answering. "As you know, there is almost always a way to do something with mezhik. However, one must not only have the skill to do it but also the power. Therefore, it is technically possible to do what you're asking."

"And you agree that you possess the skill?"

"Yes, but an illusion of such grandeur would require far more power than what I possess just to conjure it. Once conjured, it would require constant upkeep at a level that would likely kill me."

Lilith's words rang true in Nardus's mind. He smiled, then chuckled.

"Was something I said funny?"

"No, but Ɂäţūr has a way of providing all we need just when we need it most." As he walked back around the opposite side of the table, he took off the necklace Lilith had given him. He stopped next to Lanara's chair. "Hold out your hand." She did, and he placed the necklace on her palm.

Lanara stared at the necklace. "So much power. This is—" She peered up at him. "—the triad?" He nodded.

"Dear Ɂäţūr!" Savric rose from his chair and circled the table to get a look at it. Zerenity followed suit.

Nardus returned to the head of the table and sat down. He stared at Lanara as she took the necklace and put it on. "I'll ask you once more. Can you create an illusion that will mask Vallah and the King's Palace from our enemies?"

Lanara beamed. "Consider it done."

"Good." He turned to Savric and Zerenity. "The two of you will place wards around the King's Palace and the uppermost level of Vallah. It's imperative that we be alerted when anyone comes and goes, but we also don't want to tip our hand to the enemy."

Zerenity patted Savric's hand, then kissed his cheek. "We've got this, Savvy."

Savric's cheeks turned several shades of red. "Feathers, woman! Carry on as you have, and the lot of them will deduce the details of our relations."

Niesha snickered. "Even the big man knows what's going on between you two."

Berggren scowled at her. "Act your age."

"You first." She stuck her tongue out at Berggren.

Nardus chuckled. "Now that we have that settled, it's time we move on to other matters." He looked over at Ridan and Rayah. "The two of you are back, so where's *Hemär Dhef Əllíṭ*?"

Rayah and Ridan looked at each other. Rayah nudged Ridan, and Ridan scowled and shook her head.

Nardus leaned forward and placed his hands on the table. "Rayah, what happened?"

Rayah exhaled. "You want to know everything or just the highlights?"

Nardus looked to the others. "Tell me everything."

"Very well." Rayah began recounting their tale from the moment she and Ridan split from the group at Oriens Pass. "...and that's when we cracked open the sarcophagus and awakened Verin, *Bräṭäkṭär Ef Əllíṭ*."

Nardus stood, and his chair crashed to the floor behind him. "Verin still lives?"

"In some capacity, yes."

"That wretched bastard." Nardus spat on the floor. "Did you rip his throat out?"

"We didn't do anything to him," Ridan said. "We didn't need to."

"He just handed you the hammer and that was it? No fight to the death?"

"Believe it or not, he switched sides and swore an oath to Ɛäṭūr that he would always protect the hammer."

"Bah! Impossible."

Ridan shrugged. "Either way, it doesn't matter."

"No? And why not?"

"He no longer possesses the hammer and hasn't for centuries."

"What!" Nardus slammed his fist on the table and roared. He closed his eyes and took a deep breath. "How are we supposed to destroy Cinolth's heart without it?"

"Well, he did tell us who he gave it to," Rayah said.

Nardus's eyes snapped open. "Who?"

"A man he called Gazsi."

Gazsi.

Nardus righted his chair and sank into it. How long had it been since he'd heard that name? If Gazsi really did have the hammer, then they had little hope of ever retrieving it. He placed his head in his hands and sighed.

Gazsi. Why would you take the hammer?

"What about me?" Zelanora said. "What should I do?"

"You, Berggren, and Niesha will return to the stronghold and bring back those who have masonry, iron, and carpentry skills. We'll need their help to repair and fortify the palace."

Zelanora nodded. "Consider it done."

"I need some time to myself." Ridan rose from the table.

Nardus nodded, and Ridan left the hall. Knowing the toll of losing loved ones quite well, he understood. The loss of Normak had already hit her hard, and Bakkan's death pushed her closer to the breaking point.

Ɛät̲ur, comfort her.

Morcinda stood. "If anyone needs me, I'll be making repairs to my ship. The Gelu Ocean was less than kind to *The River Maiden*."

"A good idea, in case we need to get away quickly," Nardus said.

He turned toward Alderan. "Son, there's something I need you to do for me."

As everyone got up from the table and began exiting the hall, Alderan, Rayah, and Theyn hung back. Calen came up to Nardus.

"Sir, what am I supposed to do?" Calen said.

"Get better."

"Thanks to you and Miss Zerenity, I'm practically good as new." He patted his stomach, grimaced, then forced a smile.

Nardus patted Calen on the back. "I appreciate your willingness to contribute, but another day's rest is in order. Tomorrow, we will discuss where your efforts will be needed. Understood?"

He could tell Calen wanted to argue his case, but the boy had better manners than anyone Nardus had ever met, especially for his age. Instead, Calen said, "Yes, sir," and walked out of the hall.

Once they were alone, Nardus led Theyn, Alderan, and Rayah back to his and Theyn's bedchambers. The four of them settled around a small round table with a single candleholder. The candle's flame flickered and danced, and its wax dripped down its side and collected in its holder.

Alderan spoke first. "So, what's this about?"

Nardus rubbed his left bicep. The two scars would always remind him of the life he lost and the lies he endured, but they also served as a reminder to never give up hope. He had once, and now they faced insurmountable odds because of it.

Yet I still have hope through you, Ɂäʈūr.

He eyed Alderan. "Nasduron."

Rayah sighed. "We can't go back—not that I'd want to."

"Perhaps not, but Alderan can," Nardus said.

Alderan smirked. "I can't go back, either, seeing as how I've never been there."

Nardus's brow furrowed. "Funny."

"Why are we discussing this alone?" Theyn sat back and crossed her arms. "It doesn't feel right."

Nardus reached over and placed his hand on her leg. "Trust me when I say that I understand your concern. However, I have another plan, but it might not bear fruit, so I didn't want to discuss it and get the hopes up of the others."

"I see." Theyn took Nardus's hand and held it. "So, what's this plan of yours?"

"First, I'll show Alderan how to get to Nasduron. Once he's there, he'll ask Gnaud about the heart lockets."

Rayah cocked her head. "What are those?"

"They represent our only chance of getting the hammer back from Gazsi."

Alderan leaned forward. "I'm in. Tell me what I need to do."

† † †

It took just two tries before Alderan stepped out of his father's bedchambers and into the Great Library. A furry-faced creature no more than two feet tall stood on the table. His father had said Gnaud was a gordak, but he'd never heard of one before. The little guy reminded Alderan of a large mouse with his pink ears and whiskers, but the spectacles he wore provided him an air of authority.

"I'm Alderan." He proffered his hand. "You must be Gnaud."

Gnaud looked Alderan over several times, cocked his head, then smiled. "Oh, my! I most certainly am." He took Alderan's finger and shook it. "I've heard a great deal about you from your father. I've never seen him prouder than when he talks about you and your sister. Even if you hadn't introduced yourself, it would've been impossible for me to mistake you for anyone else."

Alderan glanced around the massive room. "There must be thousands of books here."

Gnaud stood tall and puffed up his chest. "Tens of thousands, to be exact. And I've read them all."

"Now that's impressive."

Gnaud chuckled, and his chest deflated. "I'm guessing this is not a social visit, correct?"

"No, but I'll most certainly come back when I've got more time."

"I do hope so." He pointed to a chair. "Please, sit down and tell me what it is you've come for."

Alderan sat down and leaned on the table. Gnaud sat on the table in front of him. "Nardus, my father, said you knew everything there was to know, including the locations of the heart lockets. Is that true?"

"Dear Ɂäṭūr! No one possesses that much knowledge. However, I do know a thing or two about the lockets. In fact, I still have one of them."

"Really?"

"Certainly. Hold on a minute, and I'll go fetch it."

A few minutes later, Gnaud returned to the table carrying a gold chain. A golden, heart-shaped locket dangled from the chain. He handed it to Alderan.

"Beautiful, isn't it?"

Alderan stared at the locket and the tiny keyhole at its center. "Does it come with a key?"

"No key is needed."

"Then how does it open? What does it do?"

"Nardus didn't explain anything about it to you?"

"No, but I think it was primarily because he didn't know you still had one of them."

"This locket serves as a gateway between Centauria and the Shadow World."

"I've never heard of the Shadow World. Is it some sort of conjured realm?"

"Oh, my! Definitely not. As the name suggests, it is an entirely separate world from ours."

Alderan's eyes grew wide. "You're telling me that another world exists outside of our own?"

"Yes, and perhaps it's not the only one, but it's the only one we know of. Late at night, when you're lying in the grass and searching the stars, you might see this Shadow World."

Alderan peered down at the locket again. "So, how does this locket work?"

"Well, there are three lockets. Each function much in the same fashion, meaning that they all serve as gateways between the two worlds, but they each have their own parameters. For instance, the locket you hold will return the wearer back to our world exactly one hundred and eighty days after they leave."

"A form of time travel..."

"Yes, and no. As far as time is concerned, our worlds are not linked. Even if you left our world and stayed in the Shadow World for just a few seconds before returning, one hundred and eighty days would still have passed here."

"I see, so how do you use it?"

"You place it around your neck, and it does the rest."

Alderan lifted the necklace above his head.

"Dear Ɂäţūrl" Gnaud jumped to his feet. "Did you not just hear what I said?"

Alderan laughed as he handed the necklace back to Gnaud. "Yeah, I got it. Put it on and be gone one hundred and eighty days." He laughed harder. "The look on your face was amazing. My father said it would be." He winked at Gnaud.

Gnaud scowled. "I suppose I had that coming after all the pranks I've pulled on him."

"Yeah, he told me about the ancient book you made him think he was tearing."

Gnaud grinned wide. "That was certainly one of my best."

"So, to be clear, the locket is set to return one hundred and eighty minutes later, right?"

Gnaud shook a finger at him. "You keep it up, and I'll go put this heart locket right back where it came from."

"That would be a bad idea, given the circumstances."

"And what circumstances might those be?"

"A man named Gazsi stole *Hemär Dhef Əllíṭ*. My father thinks he took it to the Shadow World with him."

Gnaud nodded. "Yes, I know Gazsi. He is a collector of all things mezhik."

"So, you'll give me the locket?"

Gnaud traced its shape with his thumb. "Yes, but you don't know all there is to know of it yet."

"One hundred and eighty days to return. What else is there to know?"

"No matter where it gets used, the return location is always the same."

Alderan folded his arms. "And where might that be?"

"Summitto Valley."

"That's where the Great War took place, right?"

"The exact location," Gnaud confirmed.

"Seems like a strange place for a return point."

"Thousands of years ago, the world looked far different than it does now."

"Right…" Alderan pushed several loose strands of hair behind his ears. "So, where does the heart locket take you in this Shadow World?"

"I'm afraid I have no answer for that." He held up a furry finger. "However, I do know that the timing is different on the other side. Eleven days pass each time someone uses the heart locket to travel to the Shadow World."

"Eleven days versus a hundred and eighty? Seems lopsided to me."

"It certainly does, but I'm sure the creators of the lockets had their reasons."

"Probably." Alderan stuck his hand out. "I should probably get back to my father."

"Oh, my! Yes, of course." Gnaud placed the heart locket in Alderan's hand. "There's one more thing you should know before you leave. Wizard Wrik was here a few days ago and left a message for your father. He's gone to the Valley of Dragons."

"Did he say why or when he'd return or where he was going after that?"

"No, but I told him he could find your father at the King's Palace in Vallah."

"Good. If you see him again, let him know that he must come to Vallah."

"I will."

Alderan looked around and frowned.

"What is it?" Gnaud said.

"My father explained in great detail how to get here but never mentioned anything about how I would get back."

"The principle should be the same as coming here. Just reverse the destination."

"Right." He smiled. "It was a pleasure meeting you, Gnaud."

"Likewise. Be safe."

Alderan nodded, set his mind back on the King's Palace, then stepped out of the library.

† † †

Calen sat on a chair atop the King's Palace, gazing down at the lake. He wondered what it would've been like to have grown up in such a beautiful place. Until a few weeks ago, he'd never ventured more than a hundred yards outside the town gates of Daltura. Now, he imagined he'd seen the better parts of Centauria. Plains, forests, mountains, rivers, and lakes. Buildings and castles larger than all Daltura combined. Creatures large and small. Good and evil.

Sure, the world still scared him at times, but wasn't that true for everyone? Didn't everyone have fears, real or not? Every minute his aunt remained under the control of Cinolth left him fearing for her life, but that fear didn't prevent him from acting when necessary. On the contrary, it drove him. If he did nothing, she would remain under Cinolth's control until she died. No, he loved her far too much and would do everything in his power to save her.

Calen tensed at the sound of footfall. He turned and watched Nardus, Alderan, and Master Savric approach. The intense look on Nardus's face drove his pulse ever faster and pulled him to his feet, but the hint of sorrow emanating from Master Savric's eyes gave him pause.

Ƨäţūr, please don't let it be about Aunt Tahmara.

He swallowed hard as the three of them gathered before him. He focused his gaze on Master Savric. Dark circles surrounded sunken eyes and folds of wrinkled skin draped over far too prominent cheekbones. The last month had taken quite a toll on his godfather.

Calen waited just a few moments before the suspension got the better of him. "What's wrong?"

"My dear boy." Master Savric offered little more than a pathetic attempt at a smile. "I have never been prouder of you, nor could I be. You have far exceeded my expectations in every manner possible."

Calen just nodded, his mind unable to grasp what was about to happen.

Nardus stood next to Master Savric with his legs slightly spread and his arms crossed. The man intimidated Calen even when he smiled. Actually, the smile made it worse somehow.

"Earlier today, you asked me what you could do to contribute," Nardus said.

Calen's pulse rose, and his hands turned clammy. "Yes sir, and you told me to rest."

"I did, but a matter of great urgency has arisen." Nardus glanced at Savric. "And, after a lengthy discussion with your godfather, we have come to an agreement that this task must be placed on your shoulders—" He raised a finger. "—if you're willing."

Excitement and fear battled within Calen's mind. No matter the task, he resolved himself to do it. "I am."

"I appreciate your enthusiasm," Nardus said, "but what I'm about to ask of you cannot be decided without giving it thought."

What could be so important that they'd want me to do it?

Calen nodded. "I'm listening, sir."

"As you know, Cinolth will never truly be defeated unless we destroy his heart."

"Right, but the hammer was taken."

"Yes, but the hope of retrieving it hasn't been lost quite yet." Nardus pulled a golden necklace out of his trouser pocket and held it in his palm. Its heart-shaped, golden pendant flashed in the sunlight.

Calen's heart thumped in his chest as he stared at the beautiful necklace. "And that will help us find it?"

"In a manner of speaking, yes."

Calen frowned. "How?"

Nardus held the necklace up. The chain twisted back and forth, and Calen followed it with his eyes. "This is what's called a heart locket. It's one of only three ever made. With it, one can travel between worlds."

Calen's eyes widened as he stared at the pendant. "You mean… I…" He dropped onto the chair he'd been sitting on before.

Between worlds?

Master Savric knelt on one knee in front of Calen and steadied himself with his staff. "As you may recall, I once reminded you that wielding mezhik is not what makes a person significant. In fact, it can be a hindrance for some."

"I remember," Calen said.

"Very good, my boy. As you can imagine, traveling between worlds—to the Shadow World—is as dangerous as it sounds."

"The Shadow World…" The name alone sent chills down Calen's back. He gazed into Master Savric's eyes. "Have you ever been there?"

Master Savric stroked his beard. "Alas, I have not."

Calen looked to Nardus and Alderan. "Have either of you been there?"

Alderan shook his head, but Nardus nodded. "I have, and I've known others as well."

Why would they want to send me and not someone like Alderan?

It took Calen a few seconds to come up with an answer that made sense. He eyed Master Savric. "I'm guessing this is an instance where being ungifted is an advantage, right?"

Master Savric scowled at him. "You are far from ungifted, Calen. Mezhik is but one of many gifts bestowed upon us by our creator, Ɛäṭūr. We are all unique, as are our gifts." He patted Calen's knee and smiled earnestly for the first time since cornering Calen. "Your bravery exceeds that of most."

Calen lowered his head. "I may act brave, but I'm usually scared."

"We all are," Nardus said. "However, many let fear control them and rule their lives. It takes courage to face fear and move forward. As many have attested, you've proven yourself capable of this on several occasions."

"Have I?" Calen knew the truth of it, yet self-doubt always lingered in the shadows of his mind.

"Indeed," Master Savric said. "And, to answer your question, I believe your lack of mezhik will benefit you." He looked up at Nardus. "I am correct, am I not?"

Nardus nodded. "You are. Mezhik cannot be trusted to work properly in the Shadow World as it can be here. The unexpected results can be deadly."

You made me for this moment, didn't you, Ɛäṭūr?

An hour later and after two trips to the chamber pot, Calen had all the information he needed to make the decision of his life. Alderan, Nardus, and Master Savric had answered every last question, their patience far exceeding what he would've thought possible. Then again, they were asking him to travel to another world. He had every right to know as much as possible before risking his life.

He stared up at the sky for a few moments, then closed his eyes and prayed.

Ɛäṭūr, keep Aunt Tahmara safe while I'm gone, and help the others defeat the evil in this world.

Calen stood and eyed Nardus. "I will do it, sir."

Nardus smiled. "Thank you, Calen." He handed the heart locket to Calen. "You must go now."

Immediately, energy flowed out of the locket and into Calen's palm. He knew the source of its touch well.

Mezhik.

The strange yet exhilarating sensation reminded him of the day when Master Savric had used mezhik on him to spy on Aria and Lord Rosai at the café in Daltura. He'd come a long way since then, and not just geographically. Still, fear lurked in the back of his mind, ready to pounce on him as soon as the necklace wrapped his neck.

Unlike the past, the fear failed to overwhelm his sense of wonder. Once he placed the necklace around his neck, his life would forever be changed. How many others could say they traveled between worlds? He knew of no one other than Nardus.

This is my destiny.

He stared at the locket and the translucent, red jewel at its center. About the size of his smallest fingernail, its shape resembled that of an ancient keyhole—a bulbous top attached to a narrow rectangle. The namesake for the pendant. Although fitting, he wondered why its maker hadn't designed a key for it as well.

Stop dragging your feet, Calen.

In his defense, travel between worlds warranted a bit of hesitancy. After a long, deep breath, he hugged Master Savric one last time, stepped back, then placed the necklace over his head.

I'll never be just the fat boy anymore.

Calen gasped as waves of energy poured into him. The world quaked, the palace foundations shook, and the rooftop started cracking. Mortar disintegrated between bricks. A light brighter than a thousand suns surrounded him, and a chorus of angels sang in his ears. Either his feet lifted off the rooftop, or the rooftop fell away beneath him.

He exhaled, then couldn't draw his next breath. Fire consumed his lungs. Energy pulled at his skin. Much more force, and it would rip him apart.

Fear gripped him. Twisted his heart. Enslaved his mind.

Something's wrong!

Bit by bit, pieces of himself turned to sand and drifted toward the locket's keyhole. The strange process didn't hurt, and he could still feel even as his fingers disintegrated and sifted into the locket. He closed his eyes and thought of his aunt as the last of the light faded.

CHAPTER FORTY-ONE

At the request of Screech, Wrik directed Blackwind to land on a rocky outcropping west of the higher peaks of the Procerus Mountains—the place where the Valley of Dragons lay. After dismounting Blackwind, Wrik looked around. The location must've been at least ten thousand feet below the valley and a solid mile west of it.

Wrik removed his spectacles and wiped them with a small cloth from within his robes. The flight had left them spotted with rain and remnants of insect guts. Once satisfied no spots remained, he returned them to his face and the cloth to his pocket.

Screech sat on a boulder, digging in his ear with a claw.

Wrik looked around again. "Are you sure this is the right spot?"

"Yep. Used it once myself." Screech extracted a brown wad of earwax from his ear, smelled it, then gave it a lick. "Blech!" He spat several times, flicked the wad off his claw as though he thought it might attack him, then raked his tongue with the very same claw. "Ugh. I don't recommend you ever try that."

Wrik shook his head and sighed. "Are you prone to sticking everything in your mouth?"

"Not stuff I've tried before." Screech cocked his head. "Well, unless I liked it before, then I'd do it again."

I'm surprised he's still alive.

Wrik turned back toward Blackwind and pulled her head against his chest. "Don't travel too far from here because we won't be gone long."

Blackwind bobbed her head right out of his grasp. She squawked, flapped her wings, then took to the sky. Wrik prayed one of Cinolth's minions didn't spot her.

He turned and faced a patch of barren trees. Many of their branches had the start of leaf buds. Soon, the trees would flourish with dense, bluish-gray leaves. Farther up the slope, the trees transitioned to pines and conifers. Beyond that, no vegetation grew because of the extreme altitude, bitter cold, and endless snowfall.

"Where to?" Wrik said.

Screech hopped off the rock, stretched his wings, and stared at the mountain. "Uh… follow me."

Twenty minutes later, Screech finally located the hidden tunnel entrance. When Wrik called him out on it, he vowed on the life of his grandmother that it had moved. Wrik nevertheless swore the little dragon had never actually been there despite his insistence to the contrary.

After another hour and several thousand feet of ascension, the cramped tunnel widened. It quickly branched into a network of tunnels of various dimensions. Some twisted back on themselves, and others dove deeper beneath the mountains. Wrik wondered if any led to the dwarven city of Tectus. He'd never been there himself, but he'd heard enough tales and read enough books that he was practically an expert on the subject. Visiting such a city would be exhilarating, except for the fact that they were dwarves and had a sour disposition toward humans, especially those who wielded mezhik.

By the time they reached what Wrik deemed a familiar area, sweat drenched him from head to toe. Heat radiated off his face and kept his spectacles permanently fogged over. If they had much farther to go, he'd likely collapse from heat exhaustion. Although the size of Galondu Castle kept him in decent shape, these tunnels proved excessively warm. A lava basin must've existed somewhere beneath the mountains. Such a natural feature would explain not just how the tunnels stayed so toasty but also how the Procerus Mountains themselves were formed. It would also explain why the Valley of Dragons felt more like spring even in the dead of winter. To be certain, far more fire-breathing dragons existed than other types and likely contributed to the warmer climate, but such a factor wouldn't be explanation enough. Nevertheless, the valley remained a secret the dragons would take to their graves before revealing it to those whom they deemed as lower races, humans included.

Around a sharp bend, the tunnel gave birth to a massive cavern with a crystal blue lake. Wrik recognized it as Peorvem's lair.

"Yes!" Screech zoomed ahead, skimming the water with his feet as he flew across the lake. "I've returned, master!"

Wrik stopped at the shoreline and knelt on the rocky surface, thoroughly exhausted. He scooped up a handful of water and swallowed it down. Despite its warm temperature, it soothed his parched throat.

Screech flew over and settled next to Wrik, a smirk on his face.

Wrik scowled. "What?"

"Of the two of us, you think I'm the gross one?"

"No doubt in my mind."

"You do realize that an ancient dragon lives in these waters, right?"

"What's your point?"

"You're practically drowning yourself in pee water." Screech fell over and held his stomach as he laughed.

Wrik's stomach gurgled.

Gods… he's right.

Peorvem rose out of the depths, displacing water and creating small waves that raced toward Wrik and the rocky shore. "Wizard Wrik. I am pleased to see you've returned."

Wrik stood and retreated a few steps to avoid getting splashed by the waves. "I would've been here sooner if I'd known you had summoned me."

"Fear not, for you've arrived at just the right time." Water dripped from the scraggly strands of white hair that hung from Peorvem's chin. The blue dragon closed his eyes for a moment, sighed heavily, then opened them again. "Many will be lost this day."

"You sense a war?" Wrik said.

Peorvem peered up at the rocky cavern ceiling as though he could see right through it and the many layers of rock, soil, and dirt. "Cinolth approaches as we speak."

Fear tingled Wrik's spine. "Wasn't he banished from this place?"

"Long ago, and his presence isn't welcome here. However, he still maintains the right to challenge Quldrai for the throne."

"And that's his goal? To challenge Quldrai?"

"Precisely." Peorvem groaned, then sighed again. "He will win." The finality of those words shook Wrik to his core.

I've brought this upon us all.

Cinolth controlled a powerful mage and a mindless army already. If he were to gain power over a drove of dragons as well, he'd be unstoppable.

Unless Aria's killed.

As much as he enjoyed the thought of killing Aria just a few days ago, it now sickened him. Had his actions sealed her fate? Would her blood still be on his hands? He cursed himself for acting with blind rage and ignoring the consequences that would arise.

He peered up at Peorvem. "And why have you sent for me?"

"Because I am a threat."

Wrik nearly scoffed at the notion. How could an old water dragon possibly be a threat to the most powerful dragon to ever live? No reason came to mind.

"Your confusion is not without warrant," Peorvem said, "but I assure you that he sees me as a threat. As long as I live, a chance remains that the dragons will revolt against him. However, if I die, all will bow to him."

Wrik nodded. "That makes sense, but how does my presence here help matters? You know he will kill me the moment he sees me."

Peorvem grinned, displaying a mouthful of sharp teeth. "And that is why we must escape before he gets the chance to kill either of us."

Wrik looked around. "Unless I'm mistaken, only two ways exist out of this cavern, and neither are viable. Quldrai would never let you leave, and the tunnels are far too small for you to traverse."

Peorvem held up a clawed hand. "You are mistaken, my friend."

Wrik frowned. "You think Quldrai will let you leave?"

"Never, but I'm certain the toe ring in your pocket will provide the solution."

Wrik started. "I..." He pulled the toe ring out of his robe pocket and examined it. "So, you're telling me that the mezhik of this toe ring works both ways?"

"Precisely. All such rings do."

More than one ring exists?

Peorvem stretched out his hand. "May I?"

Wrik handed him the toe ring. Peorvem back flipped and dove deep into the water.

Screech rubbed his hands together. "This is going to be great!"

As Peorvem emerged from the depths, he no longer took on the form of a dragon but of a human. Or at least something with a humanoid form. When he stepped out of the water and onto the shore, Wrik noticed one glaring issue. The dragon wore no clothes. It obviously made sense, yet he hadn't been prepared for it. Had he known the toe ring's power and the dragon's plan, he would've brought some clothes with him.

Wrik blushed and averted his eyes.

Peorvem and Screech laughed at Wrik's modesty. Peorvem said, "Though your eyes deceive you, I assure you that I am still a dragon."

Wrik nodded. "Even so, we'll need to find you some clothes."

Screech laughed. "Don't you worry. Got it covered. Well, so to speak." He pointed at his back. "Got a few items in the old bag." He twisted and turned but couldn't reach it. Finally, he stopped trying and glared at Wrik. "A little help?"

Two days with the little dragon, and Wrik hadn't noticed the bag. Was he really that self-absorbed? He reached down and untied the top of the bag. Although it looked far too small to contain much of anything, he managed to pull out a pair of trousers, a shirt, a pair of boots, a leather belt, and a dark blue cloak.

Must be some kind of mezhik bag.

Wrik turned around and faced the cavern wall when Peorvem started shaking himself dry. The imagery it provided disturbed him and would likely do so for years to come. Despite having never worn clothes, Peorvem made quick work dressing himself.

"Well, what do you think?" Peorvem said. "Will I pass for human now?"

Wrik turned around and looked him over. The trousers were a bit baggy and ended at his knees, and the shirt failed to cover the lower half of his torso, but the long cloak made up for it. Although no longer serpentine, his icy blue eyes still looked a bit strange. Wrik couldn't quite pinpoint the issue with them. As with his dragon form, white hair grew from his chin. Long, white hairs provided eyebrows as well, but the top of his head remained bald, just like Wrik's.

"You no longer look like a dragon," Wrik said, "but your blue skin makes it obvious that you're not human, either. That, plus the fact that you're almost ten feet tall."

Peorvem cocked his head. "Are there no high races with blue skin?"

Wrik thought about it. He'd never personally run across any, but he did recall reading about a sentient race of seafaring creatures called seahounds once. From what he remembered, they had blue skin. However, their faces were more akin to dogs or wolves rather than humans. Either way, it would make little difference. Aria and Cinolth wouldn't be searching for a blue-skinned humanoid.

"Anyone asks, you're a rare blue giant." Wrik chuckled. "Joking aside, you'll be fine."

The entire mountain quaked. Wrik stumbled and dropped to one knee to keep from falling. The move likely saved his face, but it wrecked his knee. Pain shot up all the way into his hip. The quaking ceased as abruptly as it had begun. He, Screech, and Peorvem shared glances.

"What the gods was that?" Wrik said.

Peorvem said, "I believe Cinolth has made his presence and intentions known."

"By bringing the entire mountain down?"

"In essence, yes."

Wrik bit back pain as he stood and examined his bloody kneecap. It had already become swollen, but it likely wasn't broken. He reached within himself and called upon his mezhik. The pain subsided and the swelling lessened as he released a bit of it into his knee.

The cavern quaked again.

Peorvem groaned. "I believe our window of opportunity is closing."

Screech grabbed his stomach, and a small cloud of dust rose behind him. "Think it just did." Another cloud rose as he pointed at the ceiling.

Wrik looked up and immediately saw the problem. Several cracks appeared in the cavern ceiling that hadn't been there just moments before, and they continued to widen.

Gods...

† † †

Aria sat on Cinolth's back, perplexed by the massive boulder Cinolth had tossed into the center of the valley. She'd asked him about it right after he picked it up, and he'd said she would understand. However, she didn't. Yes, the other dragons scattered, and most appeared to be scared, but Cinolth's presence alone had that effect.

"Explain the rock," she said.

Cinolth's response came via mindspeak. *"For millennia, this valley has served as the home of dragons. During all that time, there have been but a handful of rulers. Unlike human societies, where wars are waged for power, we have but one rule. To ascend the throne of dragons, a challenger must toss a large rock into the valley. Once the challenge has been made, the current ruler must either step down or meet the challenge. If the challenge is met, the duel will be to the death, and any interference by the other dragons is not only prohibited but punishable by death."*

"And how long does the challenger have to respond? What if the challenge goes unmet?"

"Never has that happened." Cinolth blew smoke from his nostrils. *"No matter her response, Quldrai dies this day."*

Aria sat tall, proud to be part of such a momentous day, yet her mind kept tripping over the thought of Rayah escaping while she placated Cinolth. Why had Rayah been headed to Vallah when it lay in ruins? More importantly, who was the wizard that saved her and her little friend from certain death?

Was it you, father, or someone else?

† † †

Even as Wrik, Peorvem, and Screech ran toward the lower tunnel entrance, Wrik sensed they wouldn't make it. Debris rained down from overhead. Everything from dust to pebbles to jagged rocks the size of small houses threatened their lives with each step.

Wrik glanced back for an instant to verify Peorvem and Screech were still with him.

Screech screeched.

Peorvem shouted something unintelligible.

Wrik turned back just in time to witness a massive rock slam into the ground less than three feet in front of him. Forward momentum slammed him into the side of the rock and jarred him. The frame of his spectacles jabbed the side of his face but didn't break.

Peorvem reached out and caught Wrik by the back of his robes before he dropped to the ground, but then the ground dropped out from beneath him.

The massive rock disappeared into a black void, and Wrik dropped at least six feet before dangling in the air.

Gods, I'm next!

Ripping fabric sounded in Wrik's ears as the seams of his robes began to give under the duress of his weight. He reached up to try and find some sort of purchase, but his hands just flailed. The failed attempt caused him to lurch down several more inches.

Screech flew into the fissure and grabbed Wrik's feet.

Peorvem grunted. Despite his size, the old dragon didn't have the strength to continue holding Wrik's entire weight.

This can't be the end.

† † †

Cinolth's rage fueled the fire in his belly and scorched Aria's legs despite her wearing thick leather. Several minutes had passed since Cinolth literally threw down his challenge for the throne, and Quldrai had yet to make an appearance. Dozens of dragons gathered around the valley bowl, but none dared approach.

Cinolth roared, "Come out and face me, you coward!"

Ahead, the side of the hill began smoking above a large tunnel entrance.

"What do you think that is?" Aria said.

A green dragon sat back on its haunches a short distance from where Cinolth stood. "You've awakened the beast," it said. "Prepare to meet your maker."

The ground quaked, and then a volcano of dirt, rock, and flame burst into the air where the hill had been smoking. A large red mass shot up through the center of the explosion, carrying the debris with it for more than fifty feet before disappearing into the massive brown cloud it created. Then, a roar unlike any Aria had ever heard echoed through the valley.

Aria's skin prickled as she searched the sky. Finally, her eyes located the red mass. It came screaming toward them. Pulse racing, she said, "Now what?"

"Protect yourself," Cinolth said through mindspeak. Aria had no idea what that meant or what to expect, but she wouldn't have long before finding out.

Dust and debris continued to fall from the sky as the massive red dragon slammed into the ground just a few feet in front of Cinolth. The valley shook, and the ground cracked, but Cinolth stood his ground. The two dragons stared each other down. As big as Cinolth had become, Quldrai still dwarfed him.

Have we made a mistake?

† † †

Wrik prayed to the gods. To anyone who would listen. But it made little difference. His life was over the moment Peorvem let go of his robes.

Yet somehow, he didn't immediately plummet to his death. The impossible defied, he began to rise instead.

He looked down. Screech still held his feet. Somehow, the little dragon found a way to summon the strength of a dragon ten times his size. With Peorvem's help, the two of them lifted him out of the deep fissure and back to solid ground.

Although out of breath and spent of energy, the three of them headed into the lower tunnel.

Boom!

The ground quaked again, but far stronger than before, and the pale blue light produced by the lake disappeared in an instant. None of them had a chance to look back before rushing waters swept them off their feet and down into the dark tunnels.

† † †

Aria dismounted from Cinolth and took her place alongside the other dragons who had formed a circle around Cinolth and Quldrai. The situation was surreal, and she couldn't help but wonder if she might be the first human to ever witness a challenge to the dragon throne. The notion excited her. She looked around the circle.

Soon, all of them will bow at my feet.

Quldrai stared Cinolth down, and fire spewed from her lips with every word. "I've heard the legends about you and your fall from grace. A shame your own kind rejected you, but now I can see why. You pride yourself on cruelty and indenture those around you into servitude. A true leader needs no such trickery." She spread a wing wide. "The dragons you see in this valley follow me willingly. You will never understand how it feels to wield such power without lifting a claw."

Cinolth took a step toward Quldrai. "Perhaps not, but I enjoy a challenge."

Quldrai grinned, and her eyes narrowed. "As do I."

"Then you accept my challenge and the implied terms?"

"I look forward to crushing your bones and feasting on your flesh." She looked past Cinolth and right at Aria. "Both of you."

A hint of fear crept beneath Aria's skin. She rubbed her arms, but the feeling remained. It grew with the first flash of red.

Cinolth took the brunt of Quldrai's swipe with his left shoulder. It knocked him to the side, but her claws failed to penetrate his scales.

"Yes!" Aria shouted, but her excitement was short-lived.

Quldrai spewed fire at Cinolth, then lunged at him with surprising nimbleness. In contrast, Cinolth seemed a bit sluggish, easily crumbling beneath her weight. Aria had never known him to be so slow, and it concerned her.

The two dragons rolled across the valley floor, ceaselessly biting and clawing at each other as they fought for dominance. So far, neither had done much damage, but the real threat would be to their wings. Without them, maneuverability would be drastically limited as they both relied on them for both stability, strength, and speed.

A sickening crunch of bones swept through the valley, followed by a deafening roar.

The two dragons separated, and the damage became clear. Cinolth's right wing hung unnaturally. Blood glistened in the sun as it ran down his side.

Quldrai grinned, then launched another attack.

† † †

Something firm smacked Wrik in the back, nearly knocking the breath from his lungs. As it was, the water made it impossible for him to breathe. He conjured a ball of light, but it proved useless within the murky water.

Wrik thought plunging into an abyss would've been a horrible death, but now he regretted Peorvem and Screech saving him from it. Drowning would be far more painful and less immediate.

As his life flashed through his mind, he began to realize he had but one regret, and a strange one at that.

I'm sorry I couldn't make things right with you, Aria.

Although drawn to her, he'd come to realize he didn't actually love her. Truthfully, he didn't love Noella, either. If he were honest with himself, the only thing he truly ever loved was prophecy. This realization triggered yet another regret, and one far more painful. If he loved prophecy so much, why had he worked so diligently to achieve a certain outcome?

What did it gain me? Death?

For a moment, Wrik thought a boulder or some other debris had pinned his ankle down, but then something began pulling him through the water. Without a light source and no sense of direction, the motion gave him the feeling of falling.

His lungs burned. He'd expelled the last of his breath ages ago, and now he fought to keep from inhaling two lungs' worth of brackish water. Never had he experienced an urge so strong. Why didn't his brain realize it would kill him if he were to do so? He poured every ounce of willpower into keeping his lips sealed as he clamped his thumb and finger over his nostrils.

Gods, I can't do this!

† † †

Blood splattered the valley floor as the two behemoths continued to battle for dominance. Each had gained the upper hand several times, and both bled from various wounds.

Quldrai lunged on top of Cinolth's back and dragged him to the ground. She pinned him down. Blood dripped from her maw. "Leave this place and never return, and I'll let you live."

Cinolth twisted his head back. "And what makes you think you have the upper hand?"

Quldrai grabbed the base of Cinolth's broken wing in her claws and squeezed.

Cinolth roared.

Aria cringed.

"One good tug, and you'll never fly again," Quldrai said.

Cinolth struggled beneath her weight, yet he remained defiant. "Do it, and it'll be the last thing you ever do."

The ground began trembling. Quldrai's gaze locked onto Aria. "Stay out of this, wizard!"

A yellow dragon with green spots reached over and grabbed Aria by the throat. "Do as she says, or I'll snap your neck."

Aria choked out, "It's not me!"

Quldrai roared, then grabbed Cinolth's neck with her mouth and shook her head violently.

The yellow dragon tossed Aria to the ground. She rose on her hands and knees and called upon her mezhik, but nothing happened. What troubled her further was how weak she'd become. Had the yellow dragon done something to her?

The ground continued to quake and split. It took her several moments to realize the cracks had a pattern

She reached out to Cinolth with her mind. *"What's happening? Are you doing this?"* He failed to respond.

† † †

"He's dead, isn't he?"

Peorvem said, "Quiet, Screech."

Wrik coughed up a lungful of water and spat it across the rocks. When he opened his eyes, he realized he couldn't see. He reached for his spectacles thinking he must have lost them while being swept into the tunnel, but they still sat on the tip of his nose.

Wrik groaned. "I'm blind."

"Doubtful," Peorvem said, "but you might have one vicious headache real soon."

"Already do, but why can't I see?"

"For starters, it's dark in here," Screech said.

Gods…

Wrik felt foolish as he conjured a ball of light. The small space lit up. It hardly contained enough room for the three of them, and seemingly no way out except through a water-filled tunnel.

Wrik sighed. "Ugh. We're trapped in here, aren't we?"

"You could say that," Screech said. "I mean I personally would rather not think about it, but go ahead." A cloud of dust filled the space.

"Screech!" Wrik thumped the little dragon.

Screech scowled. "Sorry, but I'm nervous."

Wrik stared at the water. He swore it was rising. "What happened back there?"

Peorvem stroked the hairs on his chin. "The cavern ceiling collapsed and caused the entire contents of the lake to disperse. Unfortunately, our tunnel exit was blocked by debris."

"Blocked so well that the tunnel filled up with water," Screech said.

Wrik didn't like the sound of any of it, and his headache was getting worse. "And where do you think we are now?"

"Not sure." Screech took a deep breath. "Feels like we might be running out of oxygen, too."

"Damn," Wrik said. "First, I almost plummet to my death, then I nearly drown, and now you're telling me that I'm going to suffocate to death? If I somehow survive *this* death threat, what might come next?"

"Death by fire. That's my guess. Cinolth will dig us out and then roast us."

Wrik leaned back against the rock. "Nice, Screech. Real nice." He extinguished his light and closed his eyes even though he sat in perfect darkness.

"Now what?" Screech said.

That's a good question.

† † †

No matter how hard she tried, Aria couldn't get back to her feet, and it had nothing to do with the quaking ground.

Quldrai released Cinolth's wing and whipped her head around, dragging Cinolth's body along for the ride.

Aria watched with abject horror, unable to do anything to save him.

The ground ceased its quaking, but then a purplish-black fog rose out of its cracks and gathered into an undulating mass.

Quldrai released Cinolth's neck and backed away. "Mezhik derk?" She looked between Cinolth, Aria, and the fog, her eyes wide. "What's the meaning of this?"

He's the one dragon who can use mezhik…

Realization settled in. Somehow, he'd taken her mezhik. Or at least that's what it felt like to her.

Cinolth pushed himself up on one arm and pointed at Quldrai with his other as he stared at the fog. "I command you to take her life."

Heeding his command, the purplish-black fog swept across the valley floor, right toward Quldrai.

Quldrai opened her mouth and spewed fire at the fog, but the flames hissed and fizzled when they contacted the fog. Tendrils of fog entered Quldrai's mouth, nostrils, eyes, and ears and continued to flow into her until none of it remained outside of her. She rose on her hind legs and roared, then slammed her fists into the ground as she came down on all fours. The valley trembled. Then, she collapsed on her side.

All the dragons groaned as blood ran from between Quldrai's scales and pooled around her.

Quldrai exhaled a final breath then lay still as her eyes narrowed and turned to glass.

Cinolth dragged himself over to Quldrai and rolled her onto her back. With a mighty roar, he plunged his fist into the right side of her chest and ripped her heart out. Blood covered his fist and dripped from his claws as he opened his hand and deposited the heart into his mouth, swallowing it whole.

Quldrai's body burst into flames and turned to ash within seconds. Then, a mighty wind carried the ash into the heavens.

† † †

By the time the ground stopped shaking, the rubble surrounding Wrik,

Peorvem, and Screech had shifted, and not for the better. Wrik sat in a puddle of water, and it continued to rise.

Crunch, crunch, crunch.

"Now we're going to drown and suffocate at the same time," Screech said. It sounded like his mouth was full of something. "Then again, I suppose it's basically the same thing, right? Lack of oxygen and whatnot."

Wrik groaned. "Do you not have an off switch?"

"Pretty sure I got no switches at all," Screech said. "What exactly is a switch anyway?"

Crunch, crunch, crunch, crunch.

Wrik conjured a ball of light again. "Forget the switch, what is that incessant crunching noise?"

Screech froze, a rock in his hand. He slowly set it down and lowered his head.

Wrik scowled at the little dragon. "Are you eating rocks?"

"Sometimes I like to eat when I'm nervous."

"But rocks?"

"It's his natural diet," Peorvem said.

Wrik couldn't believe what he just heard. "Are you saying Screech *enjoys* eating rocks?"

Screech shrugged. "I'm a rock dragon. What did you expect?"

Wrik slapped his own forehead and stared at Screech. "Your lack of thought doesn't surprise me." He looked over a Peorvem. "But you? We're sitting here trapped under a mountain of rubble, yet we have a dragon who loves to eat rocks."

Peorvem scowled. "One dragon cannot eat a mountain of rocks."

"Maybe not, but he could potentially eat enough to free us, right?"

Peorvem looked at Screech. "How hungry are you?"

A cloud of dust filled the tight space again. Screech grinned. "There's no limit to my appetite, but there will be a few… consequences." More dust filled the space.

Wrik shook his head. "Gods, just get it over with."

Screech chuckled, then set to work gnawing on the rocks above them.

† † †

Silence settled over the valley as Cinolth rose on all fours. His gaze alone drove the breath from Aria's lungs. Vitriol dripped from every word that came out of his mouth. "Bow to your king!"

For a few moments, none of the dragons moved, but then a dozen of them bowed and swore their allegiance to Cinolth. The others stood, defying their new king. Rage filled Aria's heart.

How dare they insult him!

The entire valley erupted in chaos. Battles ensued across land and air. Fire dragons pitted themselves against ice dragons and other fire dragons. An earth dragon scooped up dirt and soil in its mouth and spat it back out with deadly force, knocking a white dragon out of the air. A female water dragon scrounged to find a power source, only to be met with a barrage of fire from the jowls of an orange dragon with red streaks along its body. The vicious attack left the water dragon smoldering.

Aria gathered her arm beneath her and pushed against the ground, but she still lacked the strength and energy to pick herself up. Although her mezhik had returned, she was beyond depleted. Performing the simplest of spells would likely push her beyond her limit and take her life.

A green dragon with leafy wings and wooden horns stalked toward Aria. Hatred burned in her emerald eyes.

Aria reached out to Cinolth with her mind. *"Save me, or we're both dead."*

"Birch is on our side," came Cinolth's reply.

Birch scooped Aria into her clawed hand, held Aria against her breast, and took to the sky. Fatigued, Aria fought to keep her eyes open. Two other dragons joined Birch, one gray and brown and the other one a solid yellow—not the yellow one with green spots who had attacked her earlier. The two of them fended off three dragons as the valley floor pulled away.

Just before losing the battle with her eyelids, Aria witnessed something unimaginable. Horrific. Out of the rubble left behind when Quldrai first shot out of the ground climbed Wizard Wrik. She'd recognize his large frame and silver robes anywhere.

She closed her eyes and touched Cinolth's mind again. *"He's..."*

CHAPTER FORTY-TWO

Qotan and Eshtak stood outside Zerenity's house, both puzzled by the string of quakes. Although not rare in the Tyrosha area, Qotan had never experienced so many in such a short period of time. To his knowledge, the single volcano located within the Procerus Mountains had been dormant for millennia, yet he still couldn't help but wonder if volcanic activity played a part. As far as he could tell, no smoke or ash darkened the sky, and he detected no sulfuric fumes.

Eshtak bounced from foot to foot and pointed toward the northeast. "Eshtak sees dragon!"

Qotan shielded his eyes with his hand as he looked skyward. It seemed as though his old eyes were becoming more worthless by the day. A small, dark splotch marred his vision and moved southward.

"Eshtak sees more!" The little man began counting them. Eleven in all.

What does this mean?

Not far from the west came thunderous cracking sounds followed by several loud booms.

"Dragon falls!" Eshtak sprinted into the forest.

Qotan's stomach lurched. "Dear ʕät̪ūr."

He found a long, thick stick not long after entering the forest and used it to help him traverse the uneven terrain as he followed Eshtak's trail deep into the woods. Ninety minutes later, he came upon an area with at least a dozen recently felled trees. In the midst of the carnage lay a silver dragon with black splotches. Eshtak knelt next to the beast, his hand on its side.

Eshtak glanced back at Qotan as he approached. Tears streaked his face and ran down his chin and neck. "Dragon dying. Friend helps?"

Qotan knelt next to the massive dragon. The beast groaned, each breath exacerbated by a massive gash in its chest. Blood oozed from the wound.

He leaned close to the beast's ear. "Tell me your name."

When the dragon didn't respond, Eshtak said, "Dragon named Elros. She fights hard."

Qotan tried to touch the dragon, but his hand slipped right through her. He sighed heavily. How would he be able to do anything for her in his current state?

He sat back and hung his head. "I fear there is nothing I can do."

"Eshtak helps." The strange little man reached out and took Qotan's arm by the wrist. "Friend helps Elros now."

Qotan didn't understand. "I am sorry, but—"

Eshtak pressed Qotan's hand against Elros's side. Unlike before, it didn't pass through her. Instead, his fingers touched her clammy skin.

He gasped and eyed Eshtak. "Dear Ɂäʈūr, how is this possible?"

Eshtak shrugged and smiled. "Eshtak helps."

Qotan reached within himself, drew upon his mezhik, and began pouring it into Elros. Slowly, her wounds began to heal. An hour later, Qotan collapsed with exhaustion, his energy spent and his spirit weak.

A foreign presence entered his mind. Even if he'd wanted to, he wouldn't have been able to prevent the intrusion in his weakened state.

"I am indebted to you," Elros said. *"Allow me to serve you as needed."*

Qotan closed his eyes, the weight of his eyelids far too heavy to keep open. *"You owe me nothing,"* he said through mindspeak.

"No, my friend," she said, *"I owe you everything."*

† † †

Qotan woke to the smell of seared venison. His stomach rumbled and churned with hunger. How long had it been since he ate a meal? Moreover, how long had it been since he required one? Over the years, he rarely ate, always finding an excuse to not be present. Savric had scolded and lectured him on numerous occasions about it, but words never stoked his appetite.

To his dismay, they were still in the forest. Based upon the elongated shadows, a few hours had elapsed. Eshtak came over and helped him sit up and then returned to a small fire. Qotan leaned against one of the felled trees and accepted a sizable portion of venison from Eshtak when Eshtak returned to his side.

Succulent juices ran down the sides of Qotan's chin and filled his mouth when he took the first bite. Perhaps it wasn't the greatest piece of meat he'd ever consumed, but his memory failed to recall anything as tasty. Two portions later and his stomach bulged beneath his robes. He belched with great volume and force, and Eshtak howled with laughter.

Elros didn't even look over. She lay on a bed of tree limbs to Qotan's left and picked at her teeth with a sizable rack. An eight-point buck from what he could tell. Based on its size and the fact that Eshtak carried no weapons, she must've caught the deer.

"Thank you," he said. Elros didn't respond, so Qotan touched Eshtak's arm.

"Old friend thanks," Eshtak said.

Elros nodded, then continued to pick her teeth.

How strange it must be for her to misplace me every time I am not in direct contact with her and Eshtak.

Eshtak reconnected Qotan and Elros, and then the three of them spent the next forty-five minutes talking about Cinolth and how he'd challenged Quldrai. The way Cinolth had won the battle disturbed Qotan. From the way Elros described it, Cinolth had used mezhik derk. To his limited knowledge, dragons were unable to use mezhik outside of simple rune spells, and even those practices were rare among them.

If I am right, we are in far greater danger than anyone could have predicted.

"We must leave before nightfall." With a sense of urgency and renewed fear, Qotan tried to pull himself up but still lacked the strength. Given the level of his weakness, it would take many more hours and additional quantities of food before he would fully regain his strength. For now, he'd have to rely on Eshtak's help to get back to Zerenity's house.

Elros rose and stretched her wings, careful to keep in contact with Qotan. Her features were nothing like that of Cinolth's. Where hardened scales covered his body, hers was covered with thick, reptilian skin. Plus, she didn't have any spikes or bony nubs on her body. She stood about eight feet tall when on all fours, and her wings spanned just twenty feet.

"I will carry you." Elros's voice, though deep, wasn't unpleasant to the ear. In fact, Qotan found it to be quite soothing.

Qotan shook his head. "As with me, you have yet to fully recover."

"You misunderstand me, wizard. It was not an offer but a statement of fact. Given your frailty and Eshtak's small stature, I'll easily carry your weight." She kicked the deer rack aside.

Qotan sighed. "Very well." He eyed Eshtak. "I may require some assistance."

Eshtak bent down and picked Qotan up as though he weighed nothing. A few minutes later, the two of them sat on Elros's back. Already, her skin had warmed significantly, the clamminess gone. Muscles bulged beneath Qotan as Elros beat her wings and lifted off the ground. As she rose above the trees and headed east, Qotan couldn't help but smile.

If Savric could see me now.

The flight back to Zerenity's took just ten minutes. Elros landed in Zerenity's back yard with far more grace than Qotan thought possible. She knelt, making it far easier for them to dismount.

Qotan placed his hand on Elros's shoulder. "Thank you for all you have done, Elros. Consider all debts paid."

"Until Cinolth's heart is ripped from his chest, I owe a debt to the realm." She turned her head and stared at him. Her black eyes, outlined in sapphire, pierced his soul. "Where will you go from here?"

"Tomorrow..." Qotan chided himself. Nothing in his body functioned the way it used to, and he must take hold of that truth and compensate for it. "Forgive me. The day after tomorrow, Eshtak and I will journey to the Three Kingdoms area to search for his friends."

Elros nodded once. "Very good. I will take you there."

"I cannot ask you to assist us further," Qotan said. "Given your defection, your life will be in far greater danger if you continue to assist us."

"I forfeited my life the moment I stood against Cinolth and those who knelt before him. No matter where I am or what I'm doing, that fact will not change. Therefore, your concerns for my life are without merit. However, if you deem my presence will put your lives at greater risk, I will concede and go my own way."

Qotan stroked his chin. "I must admit that searching an entire mountain range would be far easier from the sky. I will also admit that these old bones are unfit for such a long journey without some sort of transportation. Given these truths, I accept your offer for assistance. Are you in agreement with me, Eshtak?"

"Eshtak loves Elros!" He bounced back and forth on his toes.

Elros yawned. "Very well. I will find myself a quiet spot to sleep near here and will meet you back here the morning after tomorrow."

After biding Elros goodnight, Eshtak helped Qotan inside and settled him into one of the rocking chairs in front of the fireplace. A few minutes later, Eshtak had a fire blazing.

Bones warmed, Qotan settled back in the chair and rocked himself to sleep, his thoughts not on the future but of dragons.

CHAPTER FORTY-THREE

As soon as Rakzar and Urza rounded the western edge of the Orbis Mountains, the extensive damage to Vallah became apparent. In simple terms, the white city lay in ruins. Walls and buildings lay in heaps of scorched rubble and twisted iron, and the stench of sulfur—of dragon's fire—clung to every surface. He'd been so focused on getting Zerenity to the stronghold after their encounter with Murtag that he hadn't realized how much damage the city had taken.

The two of them made use of the ladders the orcs had used to breech the city and then began their ascent toward the King's Palace. Most of the houses were either burned down or razed to their foundations, and piles of rubble and debris blocked large sections of the main thoroughfare. Several zheballin scurried about, picking through the garbage heaps in hopes of finding food or something of value. Each met the sharpened end of Rakzar's axes or Urza's blades.

By the time they reached the highest level of Vallah, they were worn out from both travel and battle. The King's Palace stood before them, a literal shell of what once represented the might and majesty of the Ancient Realm.

Rakzar traversed the broken steps and peered inside. "Looks like no one's been here for some time."

Urza came up behind him and sniffed the air. "Something's amiss."

He smelled it too, but only for an instant. "You're right. I feel a presence watching us but see nothing. It reminds me of a time when I fought a saurian with an invisibility cloak." Rakzar swiped at the air but came up empty.

Click! Click!

Urza's blades dropped in her hands as she backed away from the entrance. "I don't like this."

"Neither do I, but maybe that's the point. A deterrent." He stepped into the palace. "Nardus!" His voice echoed through the large space.

The air shimmered the way light on a watery surface does. The effect lasted for several seconds before the air cracked and shattered. Rakzar raised his arm to protect his face, but the shards never hit him.

When Rakzar lowered his arm, Nardus stood not two paces in front of him. Theyn, in her cat form, sat on her haunches to Nardus's right. To Nardus's left stood a blonde woman Rakzar had never seen before. Older but not old, she wore a scowl that could've ripped the flesh right off his face.

Nardus proffered his hand and smiled. "Glad to see you made it."

The gesture didn't throw Rakzar off nearly as much as the smile did. When they'd parted days ago, Nardus had been withdrawn. Before that, he'd raged at every turn. The loss of his son had devastated him.

What's changed?

Rakzar shook Nardus's hand as he glanced over at the woman who still scowled at him. "Easy enough when you look like me."

Urza came up beside Rakzar. "What's with all the theatrics?"

"It's the only way we can begin to rebuild without tipping off the enemy," the woman said.

"It also helps keep beasts like you away."

Rakzar whirled around. The White Knight stood before him, dressed in robes. "Not this again," he growled.

The White Knight cocked his head. "What's that supposed to mean? Are you not happy to see me?"

Rakzar grabbed his own head. "First Amicus and now you. I know you're not real, so go away."

Urza touched Rakzar's arm. "I see him, too."

Alderan laughed. "The two of you look like you've just seen a ghost."

Rakzar reached out and poked Alderan's shoulder with a claw, then recoiled. "I don't understand. You're supposed to be dead."

"Yeah, I've heard that quite a few times recently." He spread his arms wide. "Bring it on in, you ugly furball."

Rakzar grabbed Alderan and pulled him into a bear hug, lifting him off the ground. Alderan groaned and beat Rakzar's back with a fist.

"Ease up before I really do die," Alderan choked out.

Rakzar put Alderan down and stepped back. "You died. I saw it with my own eyes. How are you still here?"

The sound of thunderous wings filled the room, then the King's Palace quaked. Everyone looked to the ceiling as dust rained down.

"Cinolth!" Nardus shouted.

† † †

Nardus teleported from the entrance to the King's Palace to the stairway that led onto its rooftop. Lanara and Alderan must've had the same thought, each appearing nearby moments after him.

"Unless he's broken through the illusion, he won't be able to see us," Lanara said.

Nardus nodded, then crept up the stairs, Alderan and Lanara right behind him. Once he cleared the floor of the rooftop, his eyes were drawn toward the dragon.

It's not Cinolth.

The silver dragon, her black eyes rimmed in sapphire, stared right at Nardus. Her lips curled into a smile. "I remember you."

Am I missing something?

Nardus approached with caution. "Have we met?"

"No, but you were in the Valley of Dragons not long ago. I'd never forget the first human I've ever seen." She knelt, and something slipped from her side.

"What was—"

"Friend!" Eshtak bolted right past Nardus and into the arms of Alderan.

Nardus chuckled. "I was about to ask how you knew to come here, but now I understand."

"Perhaps you can enlighten me," Lanara said.

"Eshtak, the little man with the tattoos, is protected from mezhik. Because of it, he cannot be fooled by illusions."

Lanara eyed Eshtak and frowned. "I see..."

"His touch can help others see through illusions, too," Alderan said.

Concern wrinkled Lanara's brow. "If what you say is true, we cannot allow him to fall into enemy hands."

"Agreed." Nardus turned back to the dragon and dipped his head. "My name is Nardus Remison, and this woman is Lanara Zaridus, former queen of the Three Kingdoms."

"And I am Elros The Thunderer."

Lanara moved closer to Elros. "A storm dragon?"

Elros nodded. "One of a kind."

Zerenity stepped out of a whirlwind, and Savric appeared with a flash. The two of them looked around the rooftop for several seconds, but then Savric gasped.

† † †

Savric couldn't believe his eyes. "Brother, is it truly you?"

Qotan slid off the dragon's back and approached. He frowned. "I see you have commandeered my staff. I had begun to wonder if I would ever see it again."

"I broke mine while saving your life, remember?"

Qotan stroked his chin. "A foolish act, indeed."

The two of them embraced, then Savric looked Qotan over. The man no longer had pale skin, black veins, or black eyes. "How are you not still under Cinolth's control?"

"Alas, I am uncertain."

Nardus touched Savric's arm. "Are you unwell?"

"Why would you—" The answer struck Savric. "Yes, of course. Eshtak, would you mind coming over here for a minute?"

Eshtak skipped and twirled as he made his way across the rooftop. "What friend needs?"

Savric pointed at Qotan. "Show him."

Eshtak grinned and grabbed Nardus's hand. "Friend sees friend." He reached out with his other hand and took Qotan's hand.

Nardus gasped. "In the name of Ɛäţūr!"

Qotan cocked his head. "You are the one?"

"The one what?" Nardus said.

"The First Mage of *Ūrdär Dhef Ɛäfn Dhä*. Cyrus Nithik."

"Once upon a time, I was." He held out his free hand. "Call me Nardus."

Qotan took Nardus's hand and dipped his head. "I am Qotan Naphor, *Fizärd Ōírdh* and brother of Savric Naphor."

"An earth wizard," Nardus said. "Skills like yours could come in handy."

Eshtak let go of Qotan's and Nardus's hands and skipped away.

"You're still there," Nardus said to Qotan.

Qotan peered down at their joined hands. "Only for the duration of our physical bond. Once broken, I will become invisible again."

Savric smiled. "To all but Eshtak and me."

Zerenity shouted, "Something's flying toward us!"

Savric and the others looked to the sky, but he saw nothing. It wasn't surprising given the rapid deterioration of his vision as of late. At some point soon, he would need to have more powerful spectacles made.

As he looked around, he realized everyone in the palace now stood on the rooftop. "Clear the roof!"

† † †

Vallah quickly approached. The war-torn city appeared beyond repair. Much of the King's Palace lay in ruins, yet its rooftop looked to be intact.

Wrik reached out with his mind and spoke to Blackwind. *"Land on the rooftop."*

She bobbed her head and tucked her wings. The mountains and trees flew past in a blur as the palace raced toward them. At the very last moment, Blackwind spread her wings and caught the wind. The jolt nearly toppled Wrik from her back. A quick glance over his shoulder confirmed Peorvem and Screech were still with him.

Blackwind drifted down toward the rooftop and touched down with the force of a feather.

Screech slid off her back and hugged the stone roof. "Never thought I'd feel the ground so close again." A cloud of dust rose from his backside.

Wrik shook his head and dismounted after Peorvem. For a moment, the palace looked deserted, but then the air crystallized and shattered. Nardus and several others appeared before him, including a silver dragon.

"I take it you got my message," Nardus said.

"Yes, but it wasn't easy getting here. Dragons patrol the skies."

Nardus looked past Wrik. "And who have you brought with you?"

Peorvem moved to Wrik's side. "Do you not recognize me?"

"Should I?" Nardus said.

"I aided you in the restoration of your memories."

Nardus stepped back and cocked his head. "Peorvem?"

"It is good to see you."

"The name's Screech." He shrugged. "Well, actually it's Vorath. But you can call me Screech if you want."

"I'm Nardus."

"Yeah, figured." Screech pointed up at Wrik. "This man talks about you without end. Nardus this, blah blah, Nardus that, blah blah."

Nardus eyed Wrik. "Does he, now?"

Wrik crossed his arms. "Trust nothing that comes out of that talking boulder's mouth."

"Hey! I resemble that remark." Screech grinned. "See what I did there?"

"We got it, Screech," Peorvem said.

"The rest of you should head downstairs and to the hall." He glared at Wrik. "Wrik and I have a few matters to discuss."

"I figured as mu—"

Nardus grabbed Wrik's arm and teleported them somewhere within the King's Palace.

† † †

Nardus slammed Wrik against the wall. "Give me one good reason why I shouldn't end your life right now."

Wrik, although a much larger man than Nardus, didn't attempt to fight back. "Perhaps we should start with you giving me a reason why you should."

"You think me a fool?"

"The greatest mage to ever live? That's absurd. I worshiped you and the others of the Seven as though you were gods."

"Gods." Nardus spat. "There is only one, and we served him. The way I see it, you serve only yourself and Diz̈äfär."

"Gods!" Wrik shook his head. "You can't possibly think that."

"No? Then why would you betray me, one of your gods?"

"I never betrayed you. It was your daughter who betrayed me."

Nardus shoved Wrik, then turned his back on him. "You're a liar, Wrik."

"How so?"

Nardus turned and faced the big man. "I saw how Shanara—Aria—treated you. She considered you a friend. I also know about the feather."

"Yes, and now you know why Alderan didn't die."

"I do, but he wasn't your target. Aria was."

Wrik crossed his arms. "You're right, Nardus. I intended to kill Aria, one of the few people in the world I care about. Makes perfect sense, right?"

Nardus growled. "None of it makes sense."

"Well, if you'd give me a chance to explain everything instead of accusing me of things you don't understand and threatening my life, maybe you'd understand more."

"Fine." Nardus retreated to one of the two chairs sitting next to a small table. "Help me understand."

Wrik joined Nardus at the table and removed his spectacles. He began talking as he cleaned them. "It all started with the prophecy about Alderan and Aria. Pravus, a man far less competent than you might believe, relied on me to explain it to him. Naturally, I told him exactly what he wanted to hear. As long as neither he nor Aria killed Alderan, his bond with Aria would remain unbreakable. As you know, that wasn't entirely true."

"Yes, I know. Alderan's sacrifice broke their bond."

"Precisely." Wrik placed his spectacles back on his face. "As a prophet and student of history and prophecy, I had no intention of ever interfering with prophecy. However, I realized a rare opportunity had presented itself to me when Alderan placed my necklace around his neck. At that moment, I knew it would later come into play. I just didn't know how at the time."

Nardus leaned forward in his chair. "So you plotted his demise?"

"It was nothing like that. I watched the battle from afar, war a grotesque and unnecessary construct I loathe to engage in. As I did, I realized what you were setting up to do. Right then, I knew the answer to breaking the bond between them. I—"

"You ruined everything and cost us the battle, not to mention all the lives that have been lost since then."

"Yes, I did, and as tragic as it may be, I would do it again."

Mezhik crackled at Nardus's fingertips. "Your loyalties lie with the beast?"

"Never! That scaly bastard sent a shade after me."

"And you live to tell of it?"

"I died for a time, but then Peorvem revived me once the shade returned from whence it came."

"Peorvem saved you? How?"

"The dragon ring. None of the others knew I was human."

"I see." Nardus rubbed the scars on his arm. "Back to the battle. Why did you stop us from killing Cinolth?"

"I had no choice." Wrik leaned over and clasped his hands together. "As I said, I study history and prophecy. If I had allowed you to kill Cinolth, all those under his control would've died with him."

"You can't know that."

"I can, and I do. To spite you, Cinolth's last act would have been to command those he controlled to stop breathing. His control is so absolute, they would have no choice but to comply. That is why I not only had to stop you from killing him in that moment, but also why I had to attack Aria. It accomplished both tasks needed to change the path of prophecy."

"And what if Alderan hadn't sacrificed himself for his sister? Or what if I had moved to save her instead? Or Zerenity? Savric? You would've killed one of us for nothing. Did you think of that before you risked taking her life or someone else's?"

"Given their unique bond, I knew exactly how Alderan would react. His love for her is absolute."

"At best, you're reckless."

"Perhaps, but what I did not only saved countless lives, it also broke Pravus's hold over Aria and allowed him to be eliminated."

Nardus couldn't argue that much of Wrik's logic was sound. He also had to admit that his bias toward Wrik's actions stemmed from his children being involved. Had they not been his, he likely would've handled the situation far differently. Perhaps just like Wrik. However, his mind kept returning to the catalyst.

"You're right, but there's one thing I just can't get past."

"And what's that?"

"If Alderan hadn't intervened, your fireballs would've killed Aria."

"Yes, and it sickens me even now to think about such a scenario, but she's also the key to everything. If I had killed her, it would've killed Pravus and

Cinolth, too. The war would've ended right there."

Although his anger still simmered, Nardus couldn't come up with a reason to continue berating Wrik over what he'd done. If Alderan hadn't come back, the situation would've been far different. The thought triggered another flareup.

"If you knew Alderan would rise from the dead, why didn't you say anything when you saw us all grieving over him in Nasduron?"

Wrik sighed, then nodded. "Honestly, I wasn't entirely sure the feather would work. I also didn't know how it worked. In my mind, he should've risen back up moments after he died. When you arrived in Nasduron without him, I thought it had failed. Whether you believe me or not, I consider Alderan my friend, and living with the knowledge that I'd killed him left me devastated. Seeing what it did to Rayah sickened me."

"You could have given us hope, but you chose not to."

"False hope is far worse than no hope at all. If the feather hadn't brought him back, it would've been like he'd died twice. I couldn't risk that happening. I refused to watch any of you go through that."

"Saint Wrik." Nardus spat on the floor. "For now, I believe you, but if I ever hear anything that contradicts your story, you will answer to me."

"Understood."

"Good." Nardus stood. "We must get back to the others. There is much to discuss."

Wrik stood and smoothed his robes. "For what it's worth, I consider you a friend as well."

Nardus rubbed the scars on his left bicep as images of Vitara and Savannah flashed in his mind. Cold. Dead. Arrow pierced.

Bradwr's face rose from the depths of his mind. His best friend. And betrayer.

Friends aren't worth having.

† † †

Nardus and Wrik walked up the stairs and entered the hall. Theyn pulled Nardus aside as soon as he walked through the doors.

Anger filled her eyes. "Where the gods have you been?"

He smiled, then kissed her. "Wrik and I have come to an understanding."

"You're gone for an hour, and that's all you can say? Given the way you exited the rooftop, I thought you might've killed each other!"

"You've no faith in my ability to defend myself?"

She ground her teeth and sunk her claws into his arm. "I go where you go, remember?"

Nardus pulled his arm away and nodded. "You're absolutely right, and I'm sorry, but right now there are far more important matters to discuss. Besides, the entire room is watching us."

Theyn glanced over her shoulder, and her cheeks blossomed a pale red. She took a breath and nodded, then the two of them joined the others around the table. Each time they met, the group grew. Everyone was there, save Calen. Twenty in all, including himself and the invisible man.

"Zelanora, Berggren, and Niesha. Glad to see you made it back. Were you able to convince some of the skilled people from the stronghold to help rebuild Vallah?"

"A little more than a dozen," Zelanora said. "They will begin work in the morning."

"Not as many as I'd hoped, but better than none." Nardus looked across the table at Peorvem.

He still found it hard to wrap his mind around the old water dragon sitting at the table in some sort of human form. Peorvem smiled at Nardus as though privy as to what he was thinking. Wisps of white hair hung from Peorvem's chin and curled on the table in front of him.

After pounding on the table with his fist, the room fell silent. Elros, the storm dragon, lay at the end of the table, her head resting atop it. He met her gaze. "My understanding is that you witnessed what happened a few days ago in the Valley of Dragons."

Elros raised her head. "Yes. Not long after sunrise, Cinolth and a young woman arrived in the valley. Some of the older dragons recognized him immediately, and others, like me, knew the stories about what had happened to him long before the Great War. Several of the dragons confronted him and told him he wasn't welcome in the valley, but he'd already thrown a boulder down."

"That means he challenged the throne," Screech said.

"Thank you, Screech." Elros continued, "Once a boulder has been thrown down, the challenge must be met. Quldrai rose from the depths and fought Cinolth with dignity and honor. Once she gained the advantage, and she did, she offered Cinolth the chance to surrender and leave the valley. If he refused, she threatened to rip his wings off."

Nardus couldn't believe what he'd just heard. "Quldrai bested Cinolth?"

Elros nodded. "Yes, but then Cinolth did the unthinkable. He called upon mezhik derk and summoned a deadly fog."

Peorvem stood. "You're certain of this?"

"Without doubt. He commanded the fog to attack Quldrai, and it killed her."

"He has violated everything we hold sacred." Peorvem slammed his fist against the table, cracking it.

"Agreed," Elros said. "Once she died, Cinolth declared himself king. A battle ensued between those who follow tradition blindly and those like me who saw Cinolth for what he was. Pure evil."

Peorvem sat back down. "You're certain it wasn't the young woman who performed the mezhik?"

"Positive," Elros said. "I watched him draw runes on the ground just before he unleashed the fog."

Nardus pulled on his beard. "You're telling me that Cinolth can wield mezhik?"

Peorvem dipped his head. "Although rare, there have been dragons throughout history who have had the ability to wield mezhik."

"If this is true, our future is far more grim than I'd imagined." Nardus sighed as he looked to Elros. "You're absolutely certain about this?"

Elros looked toward the ceiling. "Aria did nothing during the entire battle, but then she collapsed after Cinolth unleashed the fog. Three of the dragons loyal to Cinolth took her and flew off. I believe he commanded them to take her back to Galondu Castle."

"Isn't it obvious?" Wrik said. "He's using her mezhik, and she doesn't even realize he's doing it."

Elros eyed Wrik. "You were there?"

"Yes, but we were trapped in one of the caverns beneath the valley.

Screech helped us escape."

"Correct," Peorvem said. "It took quite some time before we could flag down a ride out of the valley. While we waited for an opportunity, Cinolth had two of the dragons go retrieve two wizards. They weren't gone long, so the wizards must've been close."

Nardus groaned. The more he heard, the worse it seemed to get. "What did he want with them?"

Peorvem continued, "After they expelled every bit of their mezhik into healing his injured wings, they dropped dead. Then, he ate them."

Wrik nodded. "After that, a dragon named Tharos helped us escape from the valley. We hid in the Procerus Mountains for a few days before heading here."

Lanara leaned over the table. "And you're certain you weren't followed?"

"We made sure of it," Wrik said. "As I said earlier, the dragons are patrolling the skies, but there is far more sky than half a dozen of them can cover."

Peorvem hung his head. "Many dragons lost their lives that day."

Nardus stood. "We must stop Cinolth, no matter the cost."

"Agreed, but what's the plan?" Zerenity tapped her fingers on the table. "How do we stop him and save the lives of those he controls?"

"There is a way."

Everyone at the table looked at Peorvem.

Nardus sat back down. "What do you know of it?"

"All this time, you've been looking at the situation with the wrong information."

"How so?"

"Given what we all know of Cinolth and his legendary strength, how is it that Quldrai took him to the edge of defeat?"

It was a good question. With time, Nardus would likely stumble upon an answer, but he never seemed to have enough time to waste. "Luck?"

Savric stood and paced. "Luck has nothing to do with it. As my brother happily pointed out, we have approached this problem with the idea that Cinolth cursed the world at the end of the Great War."

"He did," Nardus said. "I was right there."

"In words, yes. But if you think about the way he poisoned the minds of so many, you will come to a different conclusion."

Zerenity smacked the table. "He used mezhik."

"Precisely," Peorvem said. "And what does that tell you?"

"He must maintain it," Lanara said.

"Yes!" Savric exclaimed.

Berggren raised his hand. "Anyone here besides me that's lost?"

Niesha's hand shot in the air. "Right there with you, big man."

"Eshtak not lost. Eshtak in King's Palace."

Screech snorted. "Love this man!"

"Enough," Nardus said. "Let me make it simple. Mezhik always has a cost. If I create a fireball—" A flaming ball formed over Nardus's outstretched palm. "—using mezhik, I must continually add mezhik to it in order to keep it lit, much like adding wood to a fire. If I don't it will eventually fizzle out." He let the fireball fizzle. "If what Peorvem says is true, and I believe he's right, this same principle can be applied to Cinolth and his hold over those infected with his mezhik. Given the size of his army, it must take a good portion of his strength to continually feed mezhik into the spell that holds them captive. This is the reason that Quldrai almost bested him."

"Yes," Wrik said, "and she would have if Aria hadn't been there for him to drain mezhik from."

Alderan smoothed back his hair. "If I understand what you're saying, we need to figure out a way to keep Aria away from him."

Theyn looked down the table. "Rakzar, you said that no one gave you or Urza a second look, right?"

Rakzar growled, "Right. We blend in."

"What are you thinking?" Nardus said.

Theyn continued, "It would be easy for Rakzar and Urza to infiltrate Aria's army."

Nardus frowned. "To what end?"

Wrik grinned. "To capture her."

Theyn nodded. "Right. Cinolth would come for her." She looked over at Zerenity. "I'm sure you could come up with some sort of concoction to subdue her, right? Perhaps some *níezhäíd ballū*?"

Zerenity tapped her chin with a fingernail. "It would be simple enough.

Along with shackles and a *zäbräzär*, she could be controlled."

Urza twirled one of her blades in her hand. "And how would we get her out of the castle?"

"There's a mirror," Theyn said.

Rakzar growled. "We can't go through it."

"There's no need," Wrik said. "Pravus has a room deep within Galondu Castle with holding chambers designed specifically for those with mezhik. Along with the collar, shackles, and something to keep her in a weakened state, she would have no way of escape."

"You would risk holding her captive in her own castle?" Nardus shook his head. "That's not an option. Cinolth would know where she was. Then, he would summon one of his mind-controlled wizards to free her."

"The mirrors would still work," Alderan said. "We could use them to buy us time and drive Cinolth mad."

Savric chuckled. "That, my boy, is a clever idea. Make him chase her all across the realm."

"As much as I like the idea, it would put far too many lives at risk," Nardus said. "However, I think I might have another solution. Perhaps we can capture her, utilize one of the containment chambers, and move her to where she can't be reached."

Wrik grinned. "Nasduron. I like this idea, but how would we get her there? I'll be risking my life setting foot inside Galondu Castle, and I'm willing to do it, but how can anything be transported to Nasduron?"

Rakzar stood and unstrapped a pack from his back. He set it on the table and rummaged through it. "I have something that will help minimize your risk." He withdrew a black cloak and a silver ring and slid them down the table toward Wrik.

Wrik picked up the ring and examined it. "From what I can tell, this ring is similar to the one Peorvem is wearing."

"Yes, but that one will turn you into a saurian," Rakzar said.

"A saurian..." Wrik held up the cloak. "And this?"

"It will make you invisible," Urza said.

Wrik nodded. "These will definitely mitigate my risk, but there's still the issue with the containment chamber."

"As with anything, you need only touch it as you enter Nasduron," Nardus said.

"Then it's settled." Wrik looked down the table in Rakzar and Urza's direction. "The three of us will infiltrate Galondu Castle and capture Aria."

Nardus rubbed the back of his neck. "It would definitely give us an advantage. With Aria captured, we could control the location of the battle. Cinolth would have no choice but to come to us."

Lanara stood. "Not here."

"No," Nardus said. "I was thinking somewhere far more appropriate. A place even Cinolth would find fitting."

"Summitto Valley," Peorvem said.

"Exactly." Nardus smiled. "We will face him six months from now."

Theyn frowned. "Why wait?"

"Several reasons." Nardus held up a finger. "First, Rakzar and Urza will need time to gain access to Aria and build trust. Second, Calen will return from the Shadow World right about the same time. I don't know about the rest of you, but I'd rather Cinolth's heart be destroyed as quickly as possible once we've ripped it from his chest. Otherwise, we risk it infecting someone else."

"He's right," Wrik said. "Aria is an intelligent woman and would never let anyone get close to her who isn't vetted. Last I checked, she keeps a gnoll at her side. I believe his name is Karraar."

"I know him," Urza said. "I believe we can use it to our advantage."

"Good." Nardus looked around the table. "What else?"

"We still have the issue of Cinolth's army," Zerenity said.

"With Aria subdued, you must do everything possible to wear Cinolth down," Peorvem said. "Bring him to the brink of death, and he will release his control over them. As you know, he will do everything in his power to win the war."

Nardus scratched his head. "I'm not so sure about that. As much as he hates humans, he might take them all down with him."

"It's a risk we must take," Lanara said. "More lives will be lost if he continues to live."

Nardus stood. "Then it's settled. In six months' time, we end this war for good."

"I have a question," Ridan said.

Nardus looked at her. "Speak your mind."

"There are few of us and many of them. How can we possibly win a battle, let alone the war against such a vast army?"

"That's a good question, and I have two answers," Nardus said. "First, we give Cinolth as little time as possible to meet us in the valley. He's arrogant and will likely meet us there whether or not his army has time to reach it."

"This is true," Peorvem said. "However, he will have other dragons with him. The odds will still favor him."

"Correct." Nardus leaned over the table. "And that brings me to my second answer. We need all the allies we can get."

"Agreed." Morcinda stood. "I will go and speak with my father."

Nardus eyed her. "Not to sound bitter, but isn't your father King Forlin?"

"He is."

"As I thought." Nardus sighed. "He refused to lift a finger during the Great War. I fear your journey will prove fruitless."

"If you were to try and persuade him, I'd agree. Even I would have a difficult time if I approached him alone. However, my sister Noella has his ear whether he'd ever admit it or not. If I can convince her of the threat Cinolth poses to us all, she will in turn convince our father. Given his legendary stubbornness, it will take time."

"It's worth a shot," Nardus said. "I pray that five months will be enough time to convince him."

"We shall see. No matter his final answer, I will meet you all in Summitto Valley in six months' time."

"Thank you," Nardus said.

"I will set sail in the morning. Now, I must get some sleep." She turned and left the hall.

Ridan said, "I'll leave in the morning, too. I have little hope of convincing my uncle to help, but I must try."

Nardus nodded at Ridan, then looked to Peorvem. "And the dragons who deny Cinolth's claim to the throne?"

Peorvem twisted the hairs on his chin between his fingers for several seconds, then turned his attention on Elros. "Elros, can I count on you to rally the other dragons?"

"Yes, Ancient One. What message should I take to them?"

"Tell them to defend the cities against the dragons loyal to Cinolth. Stress the importance of wounding but not killing them. Most follow Cinolth because they are bound to the ways of our kind and not because their loyalty lies with him. For those that are too young, small, or scared, guide them to Vallah. Here, they will find refuge."

Elros bowed her head. "It will be as you've commanded, Ancient One. I will leave at once, for the night favors us during these tumultuous times."

"Very well." Peorvem closed his eyes for a moment and said, "May ᒄäʈūr direct your wings."

After Elros left, Nardus looked to those who remained around the table. "Does anyone else have news, suggestions, or concerns?"

Alderan stood. "I do."

"Let's hear it, then," Nardus said.

† † †

Alderan paced behind his chair and ran his fingers through his hair. "I've been thinking about the issue we're going to have even if we capture Aria and defeat Cinolth."

Nardus sat back in his chair. "Which is what?"

"I love my sister more than anything, but I'm also far less foolish than I once was. Cinolth's influence aside, power has gone to her head. She can't be trusted."

"I agree." Nardus sighed. "I've been contemplating what to do with her once we defeat Cinolth, too. The only solutions I've come up with are to either banish her to *Räallm Kenzhärd Dhä* or to banish her to the Shadow World. I'm fond of neither."

"Both are less than desirable, especially given that she's pregnant."

"Agreed."

Lanara stood abruptly and scowled. "The girl is pregnant?"

"She is," Nardus said.

Ridan groaned. "Gods help us."

Alderan looked at each face around the table. "Am I missing something?"

"Pregnancy tends to change the way a woman thinks and reacts to situations," Lanara said. "Everything she does will be driven by instinct to protect her child, rational or not. We must consider this when dealing with her."

"Agreed," Zerenity said.

Alderan stopped pacing and raised his arms. "Fine, she'll be unpredictable. Just like she already is because of Cinolth's influence." He shook his head. "Anyway, after learning about Master Qotan being trapped between here and the between, my mind keeps returning to Intus and what happened there. I've read a lot about the subject, and I believe there is a way that scourge can be stopped."

"So, this is why Qotan can't be seen by us?" Nardus said.

"Correct," Master Savric said.

Nardus frowned. "Then why can you see your brother, and how does Eshtak fit into all this?"

Master Savric stroked his beard. "I reached through a mirror and pulled Qotan out of Intus before scourge fully consumed him. I believe doing so kept part of him in our world and a small part of me in the between. Because of this, I can always see him." He turned to his left and smiled. "Yes, brother. I believe this explains your predicament with perfection."

Nardus eyed Alderan. "And Eshtak?"

Alderan shrugged. "Eshtak is impervious to mezhik."

Zerenity watched him pace. "You think the people of Intus can still be saved?"

Alderan shook his head. "No, I'm certain all of them are dead, except Master Qotan."

"Is that true, Eshtak?" Rayah said.

Eshtak nodded, his eyes brimming with tears. "Eshtak wakes alone. Father gone. Brother gone. City empty. Eshtak waits long time. No one returns. Eshtak alone forever."

Niesha got out of her chair and went over and hugged Eshtak. "You're not alone anymore, and neither am I."

Alderan smiled. "None of us are."

Nardus frowned. "I suppose all of this makes sense, but what do Intus and scourge have to do with Aria?"

"The aethershard crystal." Alderan stopped pacing. "I believe it's the only thing that will solve our Aria problem."

"How so?" Lanara said.

Alderan pulled his hair behind his ears. "Once we end scourge, we can use the aethershard crystal to create a containment barrier that can hold Aria. One large enough to surround a house and perhaps a bit more."

Nardus nodded. "Something like that could definitely work, but I'm unaware as to how scourge can be stopped."

Zerenity smiled. "Eshtak is the key. I'm certain of it." She leaned back in her chair. "He can enter Intus without risk."

"And you think holding his hand will protect you?" Rayah said.

"Huh." Alderan scratched the back of his neck. "Honestly, I hadn't considered that, but it's something we could test."

Nardus slammed his fist against the table, knocking over an empty cup. He glared at Alderan. "I won't allow anyone, especially you, to take such a risk."

Alderan leaned over the back of his chair. "We don't need to test it with scourge. Any mezhik would suffice."

"Absolutely not," Nardus growled. "Even if it did work, the risk would be too great that you or anyone else would fail to keep physical contact with Eshtak while in Intus."

"Fine. I won't argue with you about that because it wasn't my idea anyway. I believe that Master Qotan can enter Intus without being consumed by scourge. From what I read, Intus has a defense barrier that was erected to protect the city, but Magus used it to try and contain scourge."

"I was told the same thing from an old friend," Nardus said.

"Right, so my thought is that Master Qotan and Eshtak could enter Intus and turn off the defense barrier, allowing scourge to disperse and die off."

Eshtak shook his head. "Barrier not turn off. Eshtak tried."

Alderan sat back down and laid his head on the table. "Then I have no plan at all."

"A long time ago, Normak was talking to me about gems and crystals and the difference between them." Everyone at the table turned their attention to Ridan. "According to him, gems are just shiny rocks, but crystals are alive.

He said that they were unique because of their memories, and that this attribute was one of the many reasons wizards and sorceresses coveted them. Once a spell was cast on a crystal it would remember it, keeping the spell alive indefinitely." She looked around the table. "Silly, right?"

Master Savric leaned toward the empty chair to his left. The one Master Qotan occupied. "Yes, brother. You are indeed familiar with crystals." He stroked his beard. "Indeed." He glanced over at Nardus. "Qotan says the girl is correct."

"If what you're saying is true…" Zelanora bit her lip and frowned, then she looked over at Master Savric. "Would it be possible to alter the memory of a crystal or create a new one, like you showed me how to do when we fought the seahounds?"

"Or erase its memory," Rayah said.

Theyn smiled at Rayah. "Exactly."

Nardus leaned forward. "If what Ridan has told us about the crystals holds true, we might be able to save the lives of your sister and Qotan." He turned to Master Savric again. "Is Qotan willing to take the risk?"

"Feathers! Absolutely no—" Master Savric closed his mouth and turned to his left, his face flushed with red. After several seconds, he turned back and said, "Apparently, my brother does not adhere to the same convictions as I do." He huffed. "The old fool says he will do it."

Nardus frowned. "I've yet to explain the plan."

"Qotan says that the importance of saving her life far outweighs any risks involved with him returning to Intus. I disagree vehemently. However, I am not the one trapped between this life and the between. As such, the decision is his alone."

"And yours, Zelanora." Nardus eyed her. "We have no idea what to expect once we get to Intus, but I'm certain your abilities will help us find a way to break the spell. Are you willing to help us?"

"No," Lanara said. "I will not allow it."

Zelanora stood and faced her mother. "This decision isn't yours to make." She nodded at Nardus. "I'm in."

"It is settled, then," Nardus said. "We will travel to Intus tomorrow and end scourge."

CHAPTER FORTY-FOUR

Aria lay in bed, her head throbbing. Every muscle ached, including ones she'd never felt before. Simply breathing exhausted her, and swallowing anything proved far more difficult than it should've. Brisk water with mint pooled in the back of her mouth and slowly trickled down her throat. Although it soothed her throat, it also sent her into coughing fits several times. Brema didn't seem fazed by the coughing, forcing spoonful after spoonful of creamed wheat into Aria's mouth until it had nowhere to go but down or out. Much of it drooled down her chin.

The wretched girl.

Brema wiped Aria's mouth with a cloth. "I'm sorry, my queen, but Master Credan said he would beat me within an inch of my life if I didn't get something solid into your stomach."

"Then I shall kill *him*, too," Aria choked out.

"If you don't eat, you will not recover, and you'll lose your baby. None of us want that."

Aria touched her bare stomach beneath the covers and grimaced. If anything bad happened to her baby, she'd never forgive herself. Even so, she didn't appreciate her servant alluding to her not keeping her baby's health a main priority.

She glared at Brema. "Why do you care what happens to me or my baby?"

"You are my queen, and I…" The girl looked down at the spoonful of mush she held. "I love you."

Anger rose within Aria. "What could someone like you possibly know of love?"

Tears welled in Brema's eyes, and she turned away. "Nothing."

Aria spoke through gritted teeth. "And yet you talk of it as though you do." Had she the strength, she would've slapped the girl.

"Forgive me." Brema shoved the spoon into the half-empty bowl and stood abruptly. "If there's nothing else you require of me, I'd like to be excused."

Executed would be better.

"Express such perverse thoughts while in my presence again, and I will end your life on the spot. Am I clear?"

"Crystal," Brema whispered. "It's just that I…"

Aria forced herself to sit up on her pillow. "You what?"

"You've shown me more kindness than any other person in my life, and I've come to love you like a sister."

"You and I sisters?" Aria scoffed. "Are you mad?" She pointed at the door. "Get out. Now," she growled.

Brema turned and ran out of the room, not even bothering to bow.

Good riddance.

Aria slid back down and drew the covers to her neck. Admittedly, the creamed wheat had returned strength to her limbs, albeit a minimal amount. Another day's rest, and she'd be as good as new.

She closed her eyes and recounted every detail from Cinolth's battle with Quldrai. No matter how many times she went over it, it still didn't make sense. Quldrai had Cinolth within her grasp. One final blow, and Quldrai would've prevailed. Yet that isn't what happened. Somehow, Cinolth had used some sort of mezhik to defeat Quldrai.

But how?

Aria had done nothing to stop the fight or to save Cinolth. For some reason, she had been powerless. The only other time she'd felt that way was when she wore ʒäbräʒär. Yet even then she still felt the presence of her mezhik. But in the valley, she'd felt insignificant. Normal. The way she had always felt growing up. It frightened her. She never wanted to feel that way again. But what could she do when she didn't understand what brought it on in the first place? With Pravus and Wrik gone, she had no one left to consult about questions concerning mezhik. Yes, Cinolth possessed incomprehensible knowledge, but he couldn't be trusted to tell her the truth, especially if he was the one behind it.

But how could he be?

He himself had said that only one living dragon possessed the ability to wield mezhik. If he meant himself, why hadn't he said so? One single reason came to mind.

He didn't want me to know.

Once his wing healed and he returned, she would confront him about it. She pushed the matter out of her mind, but two others replaced it. First, she remembered seeing Wrik in the Valley of Dragons just before passing out. Not a single answer came to mind as to why he would've been there. Moreover, why had the dragons allowed him to be there? Most if not all of them hated humans. The only explanation she could think of revolved around prophecy. Wrik loved prophecy more than anything, so maybe he knew Cinolth would challenge Quldrai for the throne and wanted to see the battle firsthand. It made enough sense to be plausible, but he'd risked his life doing so.

You won't escape me forever, Wrik.

Rayah was the other matter that pestered her. The winged girl had been spotted outside the ruins of Vallah with a wizard several days ago. Where had she been headed? The more she thought about it, the more certain she became of the girl's destination.

The stronghold.

Aria grabbed fistfuls of sheets and roared. As long as her father, Rayah, and Zelanora lived, she'd never rest easy. Soon, the three of them would die.

† † †

Credan found the beast named Karraar outside the castle gates getting ready to string up a substantial number of people who continued to oppose Queen Rosai and stir up trouble. A large crowd gathered, some eager to watch what they deemed a show, and others who pleaded for the lives of their family members or friends bound in chains. The first set would soon be satiated, and the second would mourn their losses.

Karraar scared Credan almost as much as Cinolth did, so he hung back in the courtyard and waited for the spectacle to end. When the soldiers dunked the first man into a vat of pitch and then hoisted him into a massive iron sconce atop a fifteen-foot-tall wooden pole, most of the twenty-seven others began begging for their lives. They would be denied.

A single spark set the first man ablaze, and his screams sent chills racing through Credan's body. The horrific sound would forever haunt him. The rest of the traitors either wailed, cried for mercy, or spouted obscenities and curses toward the queen.

Thank the gods Queen Rosai isn't here.

Soon, all the traitors were set aflame in massive sconces of their own. The human torches lit up the front of the castle and lined the wide road leading up to its gates. They would serve as a warning to all who opposed Queen Rosai's rule. The crowd would make sure of it.

A nauseating mix of burning flesh and pitch wafted into the courtyard. Credan coughed, then held a cloth over his nose and mouth, but the damage had already been dealt. His stomach churned violently, then ejected its contents across the stones. A moment sooner, and the cloth would've been soaked in bile.

Karraar growled with laughter as he entered the courtyard. "Not fond of burned, human flesh, I see."

Credan wiped his lips with the cloth, then patted them dry. He beckoned Karraar to follow him inside. "There's a matter that needs your attention."

Karraar snarled. "Since when do you command me?"

Credan wiped his brow and pulled on his collar, the air growing thicker with smoke by the second. "Only when it concerns the queen."

"Fine."

The beast followed Credan through a handful of corridors and up several flights of stairs before they finally escaped the reach of the wretched stench. Credan opened a set of doors and walked into one of the many halls within the castle. Once Karraar entered, Credan closed the doors behind him. He didn't enjoy being in the room alone with the gnoll, but he had no choice. The matter that needed discussed was of a sensitive nature and unfit for the ears of others.

"Speak before I lose my temper," Karraar said.

"Yes." Credan crossed his arms. "As I'm sure you're aware, the queen's condition is dire, and it couldn't come at a worse time."

"How so?"

"She's been attacked in her bedchambers on two different occasions—"

"What!" Karraar grabbed Credan by his collar, lifted him off the ground, and slammed him against the door. His hot, putrid breath stung Credan's nose and eyes. "You're telling me that Queen Rosai's life has been threatened twice, and you've just now decided to divulge it to me?"

Credan nodded. "Queen Rosai demanded no one be told, and the two soldiers who witnessed it were… silenced."

Karraar slammed Credan against the door again, then let him drop to the floor. He roared and punched the wall. "Point me at this threat, and I will eliminate it."

"It won't be so easy. The man's skills in deception and subterfuge are exceptional, and he fights like no other."

"I'll rip his spine right out of his chest." Karraar growled. "Just give me his name?"

"Reubane."

Karraar came at Credan again and pinned him against the door. "Is this some kind of sick jest?"

Credan shook his head. "No, of course not. Why would you think that?"

"A vile man named Reubane killed my mother." He seethed. "My father told us he'd killed him."

"If it turns out to be the same man, you might get a chance to avenge your mother soon."

"What must I do?"

"Go to the queen's bedchambers and wait."

"That's it?"

"If I know Reubane at all, he'll be back tonight."

"How can you be certain?"

"He's tasted her blood. He'll be unable to resist for much longer."

Karraar growled. "That bastard must be the same one who killed my mother." He pushed Credan aside, threw the door open, and stormed down the corridor.

Credan exhaled and smiled. "I'd hate to be Reubane right now." He straightened his collar, cleaned off his spectacles, then exited the hall. With any luck, the Reubane issue would resolve itself within the next few hours.

† † †

Reubane stood on the balcony outside Aria's bedchambers. She was inside. He smelled her blood. Could almost taste it. However, he smelled something else, too. Nidorous and putrid. The scent reminded him of a time long in the past and almost forgotten. He licked his lips.

Interesting.

No doubt a gnoll would complicate matters, but Reubane thrived in the face of adversity. Once, he'd taken on a pack of the gangly beasts and lived to tell of it. Sure, he'd been bitten by one of them, but it quickly became a blessing once he fended off the infection. It's how he obtained his ability to see in the dark.

As quiet as a mouse, he slipped through the crack at the side of the curtains and hovered in the darkness while his eyes adjusted. It took mere moments.

Across the room, on the opposite side of the bed, lantern-yellow eyes glowed. They stared right at him. Through him. He smiled as he slipped two daggers from his belt and boldly stepped into the room.

The beast stood. Seven feet tall. Perhaps taller. Muscles rippled beneath leather armor. A worthy foe if ever he had one.

Reubane drew closer. Breathed in Aria's scent. Her blood begged to be let, and he would soon acquiesce.

The beast spoke first. "You've made a mistake coming here again, Reubane."

He knows my name.

Excitement drove Reubane's pulse faster. "I fear I'm at a disadvantage, friend."

"You are, and we're not friends." The beast drew an axe. Brandished it. The dim firelight reflected off it.

Reubane chuckled. "Ah, but you misunderstand me. The disadvantage lies in you knowing my name and me having no clue as to yours. Nothing more."

The beast stalked forward. "I am Karraar, son of Brishaar."

"You say that name as though it's supposed to mean something to me, but it doesn't."

"It should. Brishaar was my mother, and you took her life."

Reubane cocked his head, then grinned. "Ah, yes, I remember now." He held up one of his daggers. "Used this very blade to rob her of her heart. It will be an honor to do the same for yours. That is, unless you'd rather step aside."

"You'll touch the queen over my dead body."

Reubane shrugged. "I suppose that will work as my end goal."

The two of them circled. Predators protecting their prey. At least Reubane was.

Karraar snarled. "Why are you here?"

"To take what's mine."

Karraar glanced toward the bed where Aria lay. "She's no one's possession."

"You see, that's where our opinions differ." He pointed a blade at the beast. "I struck a deal with the dragon a few days ago, and now she's mine to use."

"Liar!"

Karraar charged Reubane with lightning speed and swung his axe in an upward arc. Reubane batted away the knife Karraar had thrown and dodged his attack. Then, he pressed forward with several attacks of his own, but Karraar blocked each one with ease and came at him again. The beast had a definite reach advantage, but axes weren't the best weapon for confined, close-range skirmishes.

Reubane backed away, scooped up Karraar's knife and tossed it at him. "Think you dropped that."

Karraar snatched the knife out of the air and shoved it back in its scabbard. Then, he dropped his axe and lowered his arms to his sides. "No more playing games."

"Oh, is that what we've been doing? Playing games?" Reubane laughed. "Had I known, I would've used a few tricks of my own." He twirled his blades in his hands. "You've not seen anything yet."

Karraar lunged at Reubane, claws ready to rip into his flesh, but Reubane expected the move and slid into the shadows. Karraar roared as his claws slashed at nothing.

Karraar turned in a circle, his eyes narrowed. "Show yourself, you coward."

Within the shadows, Reubane moved without hindrance. Circled back behind Karraar. In a flash, he stepped out of the darkness and buried one of his blades in Karraar's side. The beast yelped, then roared as Reubane twisted the blade and drove it deeper.

Karraar reached around and swiped at Reubane's head.

Reubane ducked out of the way but hadn't anticipated Karraar's second set of claws. They ripped into his right leg and struck bone. Blinding pain threatened to drive Reubane to his knees, and it would've had he not mastered physical pain long ago. He quickly contained it, forced it into the back of his mind, and locked it away.

Staggering backward, he ripped his blade out of Karraar's side. "Nice trick, but it won't work twice."

The two faced each other, both wheezing.

Karraar held his side, his fur matted with blood.

Warm blood trickled down Reubane's leg, but he refused to give Karraar the satisfaction of drawing attention to it. Instead, he gritted his teeth. "This doesn't end well for you, beast."

"Me?" Karraar eyed Reubane's leg, then pointed at it. "You're the one who's bleeding out."

Reubane shrugged. "An inconvenience at best." The lie fooled neither of them.

The room began to darken around the edges of Reubane's vision. He yelled, then stepped into the shadows.

An instant later, he reappeared in front of Karraar and drove both blades beneath the beast's ribcage.

Karraar grunted. Wheezed. Expelled the air from his lungs.

It took a few seconds for Reubane to realize he stared directly into Karraar's eyes despite being several inches shorter. His feet dangled in the air.

He latched onto the beast's muscular arm that kept him suspended in the air. Sticky, warm blood covered it.

"It's not mine," Karraar growled.

A coppery taste filled Reubane's mouth, and blood trickled out the sides of it and down his chin.

He tried to say something, but his words just gurgled in the back of his throat.

Karraar roared, then ripped Reubane's head from his neck.

For a split second, the room tumbled around Reubane, and then the shadows devoured him.

† † †

Aria's heart pounded as she watched Karraar drop to the floor. She called out to him several times, but he didn't answer. It took strength she didn't have just to slide herself off the side of the bed. The floor rose and hit her hard, knocking the wind out of her.

Still too weak to stand, she dragged herself around the front of the bed and toward Karraar. Twice, she smacked her chin hard when her hands slipped from beneath her on the blood-slicked floor. She would've stayed where she fell, but Karraar lay in a pool of his own blood and wheezed with each labored breath.

Once she reached him, she took his bloody hand and held it against her chest. "You saved my life in the wastelands, and now your debt has been paid."

"Then I will enter death with peace." He closed his eyes.

"Perhaps you will survive," she said.

The excessive amount of blood said otherwise, even if a good portion of it was the other man's.

"No."

"I told you once that you'd die by my hand, but this isn't my work."

"Take my knife and end my life so that I will die with honor and not by the hand of the man who killed my mother."

Aria reached down and freed Karraar's knife from its scabbard. She remembered all the times she thought about slitting his throat with it but never imagined it would come to pass.

Karraar groaned. "Hurry. Death approaches."

Aria gathered what remained of her strength and pulled herself on top of him. "I will miss you, my friend."

Karraar nodded, then she drew the blade across his throat with as much force as she could muster. Blood oozed from the new wound. Exhausted, she collapsed on top of him and lay there as he expelled the last breath from his lungs.

† † †

Credan knocked on Queen Rosai's bedchamber door several times and called her name but received no response. At first, he thought about returning later in the morning to check on her, but something just didn't feel right. If nothing else, Karraar should've answered the door.

He knocked again and eased the door open. The room smelled of the beast, but there was something more to it. Something vile.

Darkness carried through the room, the fireplace unlit and no candles aflame. Credan dared not enter without light and retreated back into the corridor. He summoned two soldiers and commanded them to bring him a candleholder.

Once they returned, he took the candleholder and stared at the open door. "Wait here."

Credan entered Queen Rosai's bedchambers. The candlelight didn't extend very far ahead of him and hardly made a dent in the darkness of the massive room. Eyes wide and pulse racing, he crept through the receiving area and into the main part of the chamber. Aria's bed sat empty, as did the chair at its side. Nothing lay at the foot of the bed, either. A few steps toward the sitting area and fireplace, the candlelight reflected off the floor. Credan drew near. Crimson stained the floor and rugs. Two more steps, and his eyes found Queen Rosai's body piled atop Karraar. Blood covered them both. Neither moved.

Credan dropped the candleholder and grabbed the sides of his head.

Gods… gods… gods…

Within moments, flames rose next to Credan's leg. Snapped him out of his daze. He yelled for the guards and worked frantically to stamp out the flames before they reached Queen Rosai's body.

† † †

Aria woke to the sound of flowing water and an unexplainable ache in her jaw. Once she forced her eyelids open, she found herself lying on top of an unfamiliar bed in an unfamiliar room. To her right, sunlight filtered through sheer green curtains and bathed her with warmth. Far to her left stood Brema, the girl's back to her. Brema worked feverishly to empty several buckets of steaming water into a copper tub.

Aria tried to sit up, but her body refused to cooperate. Aches abounded in places she'd never experienced before. Her mind raced to find an answer, and then the events of the night came rushing back to her. She gasped.

Brema turned around and faced her. "Queen Rosai!" She rushed over to the bed.

Aria worked her jaw several times before trying to speak. "Where am I?" Each word came with a painful cost and made her wince.

"The fire spread so quickly. Nothing could be done about it, but Master Credan saved your life."

Fire?

The girl made no sense. The only fire in her bedchambers had been the one in the fireplace. She would've told the girl as much, but speaking took too much effort and shot pain into her cheeks and around the back of her neck.

Brema circled the bed. "May I help you into the tub, my queen?"

Aria nodded, and the girl gently scooped her up and carried her over to the tub. The hot water met her naked flesh and soothed her aching bones and muscles. After a time, she managed a single word. "Karraar?"

The girl slowly shook her head. "Fire consumed everything in the room, including both bodies."

Aria nodded and slid farther down into the water where her tears of anger would go unnoticed. She hadn't heard much of what Karraar and Reubane discussed before the fighting ensued, but one thing had stuck in her mind, and it had everything to do with Cinolth.

Why did you send Reubane?

CHAPTER FORTY-FIVE

Rakzar, Urza, and Wrik crouched atop a grassy knoll in the middle of The Plains. Six tents made of animal hides lay several hundred yards to the south. Upwind from the small camp, Rakzar had no doubts as to who occupied them.

Filthy orcs.

Based on the number of tents, there could've been as few as six orcs or as many as twelve. Luckily for them, orcs had poor eyesight at night, and their sense of smell was even worse. Likely one of the reasons they smelled so bad and didn't seem to notice or care. Either way, their best option would be to wait until nightfall and then skirt around the camp. The three of them agreed on the plan, but the plan changed the moment Rakzar spotted Murtag.

That pig needs to die.

Rakzar growled. "New plan. We go in hard and fast. Hit them before they realize what's happening."

Wrik shook his head. "I have no wish for death. There are at least ten of them and only three of us. I'm sure even you understand that the odds do not favor us. Besides, your mission is to infiltrate Aria's army, not get yourself killed engaging them unnecessarily."

Click! Click!

Urza palmed her blades. "As long as Murtag and his two captains live, our chances of discovery will be great. I agree with Rakzar. We take them out while we have the chance."

Wrik huffed. "The two of you are mad."

"Stay here if you want," Rakzar said. "The battle will be quick."

"At least wait until dusk," Wrik said.

Urza chuckled. "I think he's worried about us."

Rakzar licked his snout. "We'll wait until dusk, but not a moment longer."

† † †

Wrik watched the last sunrays fade in the east. The night would take its hold soon, and the moon wouldn't be up for at least a few more hours. The cloudless sky favored them, too. Everything played in their favor. Right up until the night settled in and shifted the wind toward the orcs' camp. Even the shifting wind wouldn't have been an issue, but the orcs weren't alone.

A cloaked figure stood against the firelight of the camp and peered in the direction of Wrik, Rakzar, and Urza. The three of them lay low, but perhaps not low enough. The cloaked figure whistled, and a circular perimeter made of fire lit up the night sky moments later, surrounding the camp.

Wrik cursed. "So much for our advantage."

Rakzar rose on all fours, and Urza did the same.

"Time to slaughter some pigs," Rakzar said. He and Urza took off toward the camp.

Gods, what's wrong with them?

Wrik sighed. Fireballs aside, he had no weapon with which to fight, nor did he have the desire to do so. "I'll just sit here and wait it out."

He removed his spectacles and began wiping them on his robes. The fire ring surged, and its light brightened, but just in a single spot. Its intensity continued to grow, and he could almost hear the air crackling. He slid his spectacles back on.

"Gods!"

Wrik rolled to the side.

A fireball streaked right past him, leaving a burning trail right through the grass where he'd been lying.

"That's it," he growled. "No one tries to burn me to death and gets away with it."

Wrik pushed himself to his feet, set his sights on the cloaked figure, and charged forward.

† † †

Urza's first thought was to stop when she reached the fire ring but doing so would've made her a squatting bird. Plus, she'd built up too much forward momentum to stop in time. She had no choice but to go over or through it, and that single moment of indecision singed some of her fur as she made the deciding leap. A hideous creature stood on the opposite side of the fire ring, its face contorted with rage and a curved blade poised to strike.

Blades in hand, she adjusted midair, forcing herself sideways.

The orc's blade met hers, and its tip scraped along her leather breastplate but didn't have the strength or angle to penetrate. She hit the ground hard and rolled back to her feet in one fluid motion, but the jarring impact knocked the air from her lungs.

The beast swung at her again. She sidestepped the blow and barely got her blade up in time to block a glancing blow from another orc.

Urza ducked beneath the blade of a third attacker and drove one of her blades right through its kneecap. The beast howled, dropped its blade, and fell to its knees. She spun on her knees and slit its throat with her other blade. The orc fell dead in a pool of its own blood, burying her first blade beneath it.

She scooped up the abandoned curve blade just in time to block a deadly blow from the first orc. The move saved her life, but the jarring impact sent the blade flying from her hand.

The second orc swung wildly, missing her completely.

Urza retreated, and the two orcs stalked toward her. A third headed her way, too.

A single blade would make it difficult to fend off all three at once. She had to go on the offensive. Use them to her advantage.

With a loud roar, Urza charged the two closest orcs.

† † †

Rakzar glanced over his shoulder when he heard Urza roar. She charged two orcs and dove to the ground just before reaching them. Their swings missed her completely, but not each other. The two raged and turned their blades against each other. He growled with laughter, then sidestepped an attack and buried one of his axes in the side of the orc's head with a sickening *thud-crunch*. The orc fell in a heap on the ground. Rakzar stepped on the side of its head and yanked his axe free.

Four orcs lay dead from his axes, but none of them were Murtag. Once he laid the fifth to rest, an orc named Kharag and Murtag's second in command, Murtag rose from his perch on a large rock.

Wielding a five-bladed mace, Murtag walked toward Rakzar. "Kharag never had what it took to fight, but you won't be laughing long, dog."

Rakzar growled deep in his throat. "This will be our last fight, and I will avenge my mother."

"That's the difference between you and me. I care for nothing but myself. That's how I stay alive."

"Enough talk!" Rakzar lunged toward Murtag, axes poised to strike.

† † †

Wrik lost count of the number of fireballs he'd dodged while traversing the mid-thigh high grass, and his body ached from hitting the ground several times. His lungs burned, too, not used to such physical maneuvering. His plan had been to preserve his energy and get close before attacking, not realizing how far several hundred yards really was. Now, his plan involved just one thing: survival.

Another fifty yards separated him from the fire ring and the cloaked figure who stood within it. The closer he came, the harder it would be to dodge another fireball. Another dive to the ground would likely seal his fate, too. In his mind, only one choice remained, but it would take perfect timing and placement, neither of which he was confident he could achieve.

Wrik halted. His chest heaved with every breath, and his heart ached from knocking against his chest. His eyes narrowed as he squinted to see through the fire.

The cloaked figure conjured another fireball. Loosed it.

Wrik conjured one of his own and waited.

Three.

Two.

One.

† † †

Urza felled the orc named Zulgha and turned just in time to see a fireball rip right through Wrik. She blinked, stunned, but the fireball sailed onward.

Wrik must've fallen.

Her gaze fell on the cloaked figure. She bolted toward them. Legs pumping and lungs burning.

No more than six feet away from her target, Wrik appeared two steps behind the cloaked figure, a flaming ball in his hands. She slid on the grass. Stumbled forward.

The cloaked figure turned, a fireball rising out of their palm.

Wrik loosed his fireball.

The heat singed her fur as she contorted her body to avoid colliding with it.

The close-range shot struck the cloaked figure's head, incinerating it.

Urza hit the ground. Grunted as it forced the air from her lungs.

The headless body dropped to its knees, then fell forward and into the fire ring.

Urza rolled to the side and Wrik stepped back as flames engulfed the body.

Urza came to a rest on her back. Wrik peered down at her.

"Thought you were dead," she said.

He grinned. "So did I." He proffered his hand, and she took it.

Back on her feet, Urza turned her attention to the other side of the camp. Just one orc remained standing.

Murtag.

She couldn't see Rakzar, but a tent blocked most of her view, its flaps bellowing in the wind. She and Wrik rushed toward the tent.

Then, the tent flap blew the other direction, revealing what it previously hid. Rakzar lay on the ground at Murtag's feet in a pool of blood.

"Rakzar!"

† † †

Rakzar lay there, his neck pulsing with blood. Somehow, the blow from Murtag's mace failed to remove his head from his shoulders, but its razor-sharp spikes bit into his neck and rattled his brain, taking him to the ground.

Murtag stood over him, eyes wide. One hand still clutched his mace, and the other covered a nasty gash across his midsection. Each breath wheezed from his lips and spread the gash wider. Blood poured from the wound, and his intestines draped around his hand.

Rakzar held his neck and growled. "Die already."

Murtag's gaze focused on Rakzar. "You fir—" He coughed blood, and his eyes rolled back in his head. Then, he fell backward and hit the ground with a *thud*.

The light faded, and the darkness moved in, pulling Rakzar into its open arms.

† † †

Wrik worked feverishly for an hour to mend the artery in Rakzar's neck, but the beast had already lost so much blood. Urza didn't help matters, pacing and making threats against his life if he failed to save Rakzar. Part of him doubted she would make good on them, but a little voice reminded him of who she truly was: The Butcher.

He laid back and stared up at the sky, exhausted. "The artery has been repaired, but it's all I can do for now. If he's strong enough, he'll live."

Urza twirled her blades and growled. "As I said, your fates are intertwined."

"Understood." Wrik closed his eyes.

Gods, you better live.

CHAPTER FORTY-SIX

Morcinda watched the Aether Mountains rise above the horizon on the port side of the ship as she sailed south, toward Alcedonia. How many years had it been since she'd been home? Far too many to count. And the longer she stayed away, the easier it became to find excuses not to return.

At the time, her older sister Noella understood the reasons as to why she had to leave Alcedonia, but would Noella still remember? Memory tends to fade with distance and time, even for an elf, but Morcinda would never let it go, nor would she ever forgive her father for what he tried to do to her.

A strong woman, she needed no companion. Loathed the idea of it. He knew this, yet he tried to force her into an arranged marriage to form an alliance with a rival clan. Had she not run, she likely would've died at the hand of her betrothed. All who married the vile man either wound up dead or beaten within an inch of their lives just months into their marriage.

And yet Father still blames me for running.

Anger yet to be reconciled bubbled to the surface of Morcinda's mind. She closed her eyes for a moment and took a deep breath.

I return for the realm, not him.

As she rounded the southern end of the Alcedonia Forest, she slid the ends of her boots into the metal straps attached to the ship's deck and held onto the ship's wheel. Not only would the next turn be tight, but the secret entrance to the kingdom lay at the bottom of the ocean.

With just a thought given to the waters, *The River Maiden* turned belly up and began sinking into the deep waters. She held fast to the wheel as the darkness rose to meet her. The ship twisted around and flipped back over as the undercurrent grabbed hold and shot her into a hidden tunnel entrance.

Moments later, the tunnel opened into the bottom of Alcedonia Lake.

Sunlight penetrated the crystal blue waters, lighting the partially sunken city that loomed ahead.

I'm home.

Morcinda's chest tightened as she pulled up to the submerged dock. A dozen warriors awaited her, their deep blue, watersteel weapons drawn. None of them looked familiar, but she knew which of them was the leader because of the patches of black hair in front of his ears. She met his gaze as she glided through the water and settled on the dock.

The young man sneered as he spoke in the base elvish tongue, "You are not of this clan. Return to your ship, or meet the end of my blade."

She responded in kind. "Are you so young that you do not recognize me?"

"Should I?"

"I am Morcinda Forlin, daughter of King Forlin and second heir to the throne. Lower your weapons or face death."

"Your lips lie." He raised his blade. "I am Tuular, warrior leader of the Crystal Lake clan. I know all, and Princess Noella is the only heir to the throne of King Forlin."

"Stand down, Tuular." A path opened between the warriors, and the slender woman walked forward.

Tuular turned and bowed, sheathing his blade in the process. "Princess Noella."

Morcinda smiled. "Hello, sister."

Noella, her face expressionless, circled Morcinda. Her gaze traveled up and down Morcinda's form, scrutinizing every inch. "The years have not scathed you, your beauty evident, yet I wonder why you still choose to dress like a man."

Morcinda glanced around Noella. "And I wonder why you still choose to hang around a group of shirtless men."

The corners of Noella's lips quavered, then turned upward. She pulled Morcinda into an embrace. "Gods, it's good to see you, sister."

"And you."

"King Forlin will be elated when the news of your return reaches his ears."

"I'm not so sure of that."

"Do not fear his wrath. He forgave you long ago."

"Forgave me?" Morcinda fumed. "*He's* the one who should be seeking *my* forgiveness."

Noella waved her hand. "It matters not. Leave your anger in the past where it belongs."

I will never forget.

Morcinda set her jaw. "Take me to him at once."

"You cannot expect to show up unannounced and gain audience with the king."

"Listen to yourself, Noella. You speak of him as though he's some unreachable god who sits on a pedestal of gold. He's your father. *Our* father. The ways of our kind do not apply to us."

"You've forgotten much, and much has changed." Noella took her hand. "Come, I will show you the kingdom you abandoned."

Morcinda jerked her hand away. "This isn't a social visit, Noella. You and the others live in a bubble untouched by reality while the realm wars against tyranny all around you. Wake up and see the world for what it is."

"We aren't ignorant of the affairs of the realm."

"No? Then explain to me what you've been doing to prepare for the war that will soon be on your doorstep?"

Noella straightened, clearly stunned by the news of a war, but quickly recovered. "We survived the Great War by remaining neutral. I'm certain this new war will pass, too."

"You're more foolish than I thought."

"Prophecy is never wrong. War will never touch us."

"Do you actually believe what you're saying, or are you just regurgitating the words of others?"

Noella turned toward Tuular. "Leave us." Tuular and the others bowed and then retreated from the dock. Once out of earshot, she turned and said, "I have a mind of my own."

"And yet you choose not to use it."

"What do you expect of me?"

"I expect you to be the sister I remember. The one who cares about more than just what happens within her city walls."

"I *am* her."

"You say that, but I see no evidence of it."

"You forget what it's like to live beneath father's heavy thumb." She looked around, fear in her eyes. "He has eyes and ears everywhere. I must always watch what I say, especially around the warriors."

Perhaps she had misjudged her sister after all. "Take me somewhere that we can talk without fear."

Noella nodded and took her hand. "I know just the place."

† † †

Morcinda sat on a stone bench next to Noella inside a dungeon cell. It was the last place she would've thought to go for privacy, but it made perfect sense. Few citizens ever committed crimes, and outsiders were rarely allowed inside Alcedonia's walls, so most of the dungeon cells sat empty. This particular section of dungeon hadn't been used in centuries, evidenced by the dust, mildew, spiderwebs, and rats that infested it. Thankfully, she was used to dank smells. It reminded her of the sea.

Noella played with the end of her braid as she stared at the stone floor. "Father keeps us all in the dark when it comes to news of the world, forcing us to rely on the word of prophets who speak only what he's told them to say. I used to have my own sources, but he saw to it that they disappeared or met untimely deaths. Eventually, I stopped trying to gain knowledge, my conscience unable to handle further deaths attributed to my curiosity."

Morcinda took Noella's hand and intertwined her fingers with Noella's. "It's not your fault. Father is a tyrant."

"He can be, but it doesn't matter if it's his fault or mine. I still feel guilty."

"And he never will."

Noella sighed. "Why did you come back after all these years?"

"We're fighting a war to free the people of the Ancient Realm, but the odds are against us."

"Free them from what?"

"Do you remember the tales Mother used to tell us about the Great War and the evil dragon named Cinolth?"

"Yeah, they used to keep me up at night. I was afraid he would come for me if I fell asleep."

Morcinda squeezed Noella's hand. "I remember. You would come crawling into my bed in the middle of the night."

"I'm the older one, but nothing ever scared you."

"That's not true. I got scared all the time."

"You hid it well, then."

"Maybe so, but I'll tell you right now that I'm scared."

"Of Mother's tales?"

"Those were no tales at all. She spoke of history."

"I don't understand. How could they have been historical when dragons don't exist?"

"Dragons do exist. I've seen several of them with my own eyes. The world waged war twelve-hundred years ago, during the time Mother spoke of, just as it does now. What's worse is that the same evil dragon seeks to destroy it."

"Cinolth?"

"Yes."

"Now I really don't understand. Cinolth died in Mother's tale. Father vanquished him."

"Cinolth did die, but Father had nothing to do with it. None of our people did. We sat here and pretended that nothing beyond our walls existed, just like we're doing today. Father's not a hero but a spineless coward."

"Why would he lie to us, and how is Cinolth alive today if he died in the Great War?"

"I don't know why Father lied, but Cinolth's reemergence is simple to explain. His heart was never destroyed, and someone used mezhik to bring him back from the dead."

"That's horrible." She chewed on her lip. "What can we do? What can I do?"

"You must help me convince Father to join the war."

"What you ask is impossible."

"Why?"

"He's not the same man you once knew."

"No, you mean he *is* the same man I knew."

"No. His heart grew cold the day you left. For a while, he blamed me. Said I helped you escape."

"You did."

"Yes, but that's beside the point. I lost favor with him because of you. In public, I am a princess, but he's made it quite clear that he'll never relinquish the throne to me. He plans to wed again and create new heirs."

"How could he? Mother's not dead."

"I thought that same thing at first, but apparently she was stripped of all titles after having that affair with one of her servants."

"I didn't realize he'd gone so far."

"Father locked her away so that the people would forget her name, and I believe they have."

"Even so, we must try and get through to him."

Noella rested her head on Morcinda's shoulder. "Together, we can accomplish anything."

"I pray that's true."

"It will be. We just need to ease him into the idea over time."

"We live on borrowed time as is."

"I understand, but if we barge into his courts and demand he joins a war he cares nothing about, we will wind up in the same place as Mother."

Morcinda sighed and nodded. "You are right. However, you must keep in mind that we only have a little more than five months to convince him. Pray it's enough time."

Noella stood and pulled Morcinda to her feet. "It will be." She smiled, then hugged Morcinda. "It's so good to have you home."

"It's good to be home."

Even though it might be for the last time.

CHAPTER FORTY-SEVEN

Ridan stood at the gateway to the seventh level of Tectus with a mug of ale in her hand. It'd been more than a decade since she'd set foot inside. Even now, her eyes filled with tears as she thought of her father and mother. Like her, their skills with weapons were legendary, but no skills, no matter how great, could save a person from a collapsing mine. It took two months to unbury their remains.

She walked into the catacombs and right past the ornate marble sarcophagi of her parents. In time, they would likely get a visit from her, but today she came to pay her respects to Normak.

The plain white sarcophagus lay next to two others, each marked with the Stonebreaker name. Had she not known its location, she never would've found it amongst the thousands just like it. It sickened her to think that her uncle had treated Normak like a commoner. Perhaps he was, but what did that make her given that she loved him fiercely and missed him with all her heart?

I am nothing.

Ridan brooded. "Ya deserved better, Normak Stonebreaker." She took the mug of ale and held it over his sarcophagus. "One last drink, my friend."

"No need to waste perfectly good ale on his account."

Ridan turned and watched Torbrek stroll toward her. "Why are ya down here?"

"Heard there was a beautiful young blonde searching for a Stonebreaker." He grinned. "Thought she might be looking for me."

"Guess ya was wrong." She dumped the ale over the top of Normak's sarcophagus and placed the mug on top of it.

Torbrek embraced her. "I'm glad you came back."

She pushed him away. "Wasn't for ya and won't be here long."

"No? Well, that's a shame." Torbrek scanned the area, then frowned. "Where's that mangy mutt of yours?"

Ridan set her jaw and dug her nails into her palms. "Dead."

Torbrek's gaze softened, and he nodded. "I am sorry the gods have failed you in this life."

And they'll fail me in the next.

"As am I." Ridan gave Normak's sarcophagus one last look, then started walking away. Torbrek caught up with her and walked alongside her in silence until they reached the fifth level of Tectus.

"This is me," he said. "Wish you'd stick around awhile."

"To what end?"

He scratched his head and sighed. "I don't know. With Normak gone, my heart feels out of sorts. I serve our king, as I always have, yet it feels as though he serves nothing but his own self-interests. Does my work here truly mean nothing?"

Torbrek's honesty surprised her. In the past, he buried every emotion deep within himself except for his overwhelming charm and legendary temper. Now, he reminded her of Normak just a little.

"Speaking of our king, I plan to pay him a visit once I've worked up the courage."

He raised an eyebrow. "A word with the king? You think it wise even though he favors you?"

"I have no choice." She drew a deep breath and forced it from her lips. "We dwarves live as though the world beyond Tectus doesn't exist."

Torbrek chuckled. "Are you saying it does?"

Ridan thrust her arms in the air. "Yes!"

"I'm not saying that I disagree with you, but I'm uncertain as to how any of it matters. Kingdoms rise and fall in the Ancient Realm all the time, yet we continue to thrive. Does that not prove the outer world means nothing to us?"

"If it means nothing, then that also means that Normak and Bakkan died for nothing."

"I see. And how do you plan to give their deaths meaning?"

"We finish the fight."

"Finish what never should've started to begin with?"

"What's that supposed to mean?"

"You and Normak didn't set out to fight in a war that doesn't concern us."

"Perhaps not, but we were drawn into it."

"And look where it has led. Two deaths and nothing to show for it."

"Ya are a bastard, Torbrek."

Torbrek raised his arms. "Whoa, you're way off base and misunderstand what I'm trying to do here."

"And what's that? Make me feel foolish for caring about something beyond this wretched city?"

"No."

"Then what? Why must ya try and hurt me?"

"I care about you, Ridan, same as Normak did. I'd rather die than hurt you." He pulled on his beard and groaned. "Look, I don't expect you to understand everything I say or why I say it, but know this. I will do anything in my power to help you. Whatever you need. Anything, Ridan. You understand?"

"No, Torbrek, I don't! Normak didn't just care about me. He *loved* me, and I loved him." She balled her fists. "Ugh! Just leave me alone."

Ridan turned to leave, but Torbrek grabbed her arm. She turned around and punched him in the jaw. The blow jerked his head to the side and stunned him. His fingers slipped from her arm.

"Ouch!" He reached up and massaged his jaw.

"Touch me again, and it won't just be yar pretty face I hit."

"I deserved that."

"Ya earned it." She turned away.

How will I convince a king when I can't even convince Normak's brother?

"Wait."

She crossed her arms but didn't look back. "Why should I?"

"Because I owe you an explanation."

"Make it quick. I've got a king to convince."

Torbrek walked around and faced her. "What I said about Tectus and the world isn't what I believe."

"Then why did ya say it?"

"To prepare you for what King Morlek will say." Torbrek stepped closer, then stooped down and picked up a small grayish-black pebble. "What do you think will happen to this pebble if I squeeze it as hard as I can?"

"Nothing."

"Correct, and do you think it will turn into a sapphire if I ask it to?"

Ridan huffed. "That's absurd."

"Exactly." He tossed the pebble on the ground. "King Morlek is that pebble. No matter how hard you squeeze him, he will remain unchanged. Give him all the facts as to why we must enter the war, and he will laugh at you. As long as he thinks we are safe from outside threats, he will never risk the lives of Tectans."

Ridan closed her eyes. She wanted to tell Torbrek that he was wrong about King Morlek, but she knew the man better than most. If pushed, he would likely throw her in the dungeons or banish her for fear of her creating an uprising. Many Tectans prided themselves on bravery, but the king was not among them. Had her father been king, he would've marched the entire army to the battlefield.

Gods, what was I thinking?

Torbrek's breath warmed her ear when he embraced her. She didn't push him away. Couldn't push him away. Like it or not, he was all she had left.

"How much time do we have?" he whispered.

Ridan went rigid as her eyes snapped open. She pulled back and met his gray-eyed gaze. "What do ya mean?"

He scowled at her. "Relax, Ridan. I'm not propositioning you."

The tension in her shoulders fell away. "Then what?"

"King Morlek won't lift a finger for your cause, but I know a handful of others who will." He grimaced. "However, they are a tad green and lack proper training."

Ridan wouldn't allow herself to bring a group of untrained dwarves into battle just to see them slaughtered. It would serve no purpose but to add the weight of more deaths to her shoulders. She already carried as much as she could handle. Perhaps too much.

She shook her head. "We're in need of warriors, not bodies."

"Give them time to train with the two of us, and we'd have ourselves a dozen warriors."

Ridan brooded. Given the size of Cinolth's army and the few who stood against him, how would twelve more bodies help turn the tide? She snorted.

If I think like that, why fight at all?

"Well?" Torbrek said.

"Five months is all we have."

Torbrek clapped his hands together and grinned. "That's four more than I thought you'd give me."

"Then we're in agreement?"

"We are."

"Thanks, Torbrek." Ridan hugged him, then kissed him. Regret followed close behind.

Gods, why did I just do that?

Torbrek cleared his throat. "Uh, not that I'm complaining or anything, but you seem to be sending me mixed signals. Just to be clear, are we on or off?"

"Off," Ridan confirmed. "At least for now."

Torbrek nodded. "I'll be here when you need me."

"I know."

"Right." Torbrek looked around. "Well… guess I'll pull together the troops. Five months will be gone before we know it."

"Tomorrow night, then?"

"Normak's secret spot. No one will bother us there."

After one last awkward hug, Ridan and Torbrek went their separate ways. She needed a drink. Desperately.

We will finish this, Normak.

CHAPTER FORTY-EIGHT

Nardus, Theyn, Alderan, Rayah, Eshtak, Screech, Zelanora, and Qotan stood outside what remained of the entrance into Intus. None of them knew what to expect beyond the wall of rock. From what Nardus remembered, Magus sealed the entrance for fear scourge would continue to spread and infect the entire world. He knew that to be a lie, though. Magus didn't give a damn for anyone else and feared only for his own life.

Not even Emorith's.

Nardus's understanding of spells differed from that of Magus's, yet he understood the man's concern. According to Emorith Darkridge, the scourge spell was like some sort of deadly fog. Under normal circumstances, the spell would've run its course and died out shortly after being cast, but the aethershard crystal amplified the spell and kept it powered. And because of its power, the containment field around the city expanded. Rock, stone, and dirt would do nothing to prevent a spell from spreading if it breeched the containment field altogether.

Nardus addressed the small group. "Once Screech clears the entrance, only Alderan, Eshtak, Qotan, and I will enter. Understood?"

"Not even a little," Theyn said. "You know I go where you go."

"Same with me," Rayah said. "If we don't go, you don't go."

Nardus sighed. "Fine, but the two of you will stay behind the rest of us. Am I clear?"

"As a crystal," they said in unison.

Nardus nodded at Screech. "Time for you to get to work."

The little dragon frowned. "Eating is never work."

"Eshtak loves eating." He bounced from one foot to the other, somehow never lacking energy.

How has my life come to this?

Nardus scowled at Screech. "Just clear a path."

"You got it, boss."

A few hours later, Screech emerged from the newly formed tunnel entrance. "I believe I've reached the cavern." A massive dust cloud followed him out.

Alderan waved his hand in front of his face. "Ugh! There's nothing worse than the smell of dragon waste to start your morning."

Rayah snorted.

Screech scowled at Alderan. "Funny. Real funny. I'll have you know that the smell inside the cavern is far worse than any odor I've ever produced."

"No more joking around once we enter the tunnel," Nardus said. "One misjudged step inside could cost you or someone else their life."

Alderan said, "Yes, sir."

"Got it," Screech added.

"Eshtak not joke."

Nardus, Alderan, and Zelanora conjured orbs of light, then led the others into the tunnel. By the time they made it to the switchback trail that led down to the cavern floor, the wretched stench was strong enough to curdle milk. Something had certainly died in there. Many somethings. Nardus covered his nose and mouth with a scarf, but it only helped a little.

About three miles down the road, a black fog became visible. Poor lighting made it impossible to see just how far it spread, so Nardus brought them to a stop.

Theyn coughed and squeezed her nose. "Who would want to live down here?"

Nardus set his pack down and pulled out a bag full of gypsum. "Believe it or not, this place was once a beautiful oasis."

"Eshtak loved home." Tears streaked his face.

Alderan knelt next to Eshtak. "I can't imagine how difficult this must be for you to return here."

Eshtak nodded, then sucked up a string of snot that hung from his bulbous nose. "Eshtak misses family."

Nardus hadn't even contemplated how it might make Eshtak feel to return home. Sure, it'd been more than 1,200 years since Magus unleashed scourge, but Nardus knew firsthand what loss could do to someone and how the feeling never went away. He rubbed the scars on his left bicep.

I'll never forget you and will always love you, Vitara. And you, Savannah.

He took the gypsum and made a line all the way across the rock road, from the jagged cavern wall to the drop-off into the putrid lake. "For now, no one goes beyond this point except Eshtak and Qotan, understood?"

Once everyone agreed, they began setting up camp. With few supplies, it didn't take long. The air, though rank with odor, didn't feel too cold, but they'd brought firewood with them anyway. A fire would serve both as a beacon in the dim light and as a source of security during their stay. With luck, their stay would be short.

Ƨäṭūr, make it so.

† † †

Qotan clutched his staff in his left hand, its twisted top aglow with pure white light. Savric had insisted he take it with him, and it already proved invaluable both for walking and lighting their path. He followed Eshtak along the road toward Intus until they came upon a distinct delineation between where they stood and where scourge began. It was impossible not to see as the light from his staff quickly diminished against its darkness.

The entire way down into the cavern, he'd wrestled with the method they would utilize to proceed into scourge. Would it be better for him to go it alone, or should he take hold of Eshtak's hand? Given the uncertainty of his current physical state, he wondered if the method would make a lick of difference. In all likelihood, scourge would finish the job of separating his soul from his body the moment he entered its black fog. If death was to be his fate, had he said everything that needed to be said?

Could one ever know the answer to such a question?

He doubted it. In fact, he doubted many things. Indecision overwhelmed him.

"Old friend holds Eshtak's hand?"

You are always listening, Ƨäṭūr. Thank you.

Qotan peered down at Eshtak and smiled. The little man not only had a way with people but with words. Though he used few, their meaning was always clear and without question. "I would appreciate that. Very much, in fact."

Hand in hand, the two of them faced the black fog of scourge ahead and headed straight toward it. Qotan cringed as he stepped into the dense fog, expecting it to attack his lungs and choke him to death, but he detected no change upon his first inhalation. The second and third inhalations proved non-lethal as well.

Do not be such a fool. Ɂäṭūr has a plan.

"Wait!" Nardus yelled.

Qotan and Eshtak turned around as Nardus, Alderan, and Zelanora cautiously approached.

Nardus pointed at them. "Eshtak's tattoos are glowing."

Qotan eyed Eshtak. Each of the tattoos glowed with a different color. "Indeed."

Alderan knelt. "Those aren't tattoos but ancient runes."

"Are you certain?" Nardus said. "I don't recognize any of them."

"Positive. They represent each type of mezhik."

Nardus squinted at Eshtak. "How do you know that? All I see are jumbled lines and shapes."

"One of my abilities is language. I can decipher almost anything."

"It explains why Eshtak is immune to mezhik," Qotan said. "He wears a protection web." When no one reacted to his revelation, he remembered they still couldn't see or hear him. "Tell them what I said, Eshtak."

Eshtak nodded. "Old friend says protection web. Makes Eshtak immune."

"How does this help us?" Zelanora said.

Eshtak reached out of the fog and grabbed Nardus's hand.

Nardus gasped. "Qotan's skin has a slight glow to it, too." He smiled. "Alderan, you were right. Eshtak's protection extends to anything he touches."

Alderan stood. "Technically, it was Rayah's idea, not mine."

Nardus patted Alderan on the back. "No matter whose idea it was, this knowledge will help us."

Qotan and Eshtak stepped back out of the fog and Eshtak's tattoos stopped glowing.

"The fog must activate the runes," Zelanora said.

Qotan looked to Nardus. "How should we proceed?"

Nardus rubbed the back of his neck. "Given what we now know, it makes the most sense for Zelanora to go with Eshtak."

"I'll go, too." Alderan nodded toward Zelanora. "Just in case something needs to be read."

Zelanora looked like she might pass out. "How strong do you think Eshtak's protection web is, and does it extend to someone touching someone else who's touching Eshtak, or must you be touching him directly?"

Qotan stroked his chin. "That is a fine question." He cleared his throat. "As the eldest member of our group, I volunteer myself to test this."

"Qotan will test this," Nardus said. "And I will be the first to enter the fog with Eshtak." He looked at Qotan and smiled. "The first of us fully alive, that is."

"Eshtak scared."

Nardus rubbed Eshtak's bald head. "We all are, my friend."

Each still grasping one of Eshtak's hands, Qotan, Nardus, and Eshtak stepped into the fog. Eshtak's tattoos glowed again, and Nardus and Qotan remained intact.

"One theory tested." Qotan moved around Eshtak while still holding his hand and then took Nardus's free hand with his other, creating a circle. The three of them glowed brighter.

"Interesting," Nardus said. "Closing the loop seems to make the protection spell stronger." He looked at Qotan. "Now, we test the second theory."

Qotan had never felt so nervous in his life, but he didn't understand why. Worst case, he would die and live for eternity with Ɂäţūr.

Unless my soul gets trapped in the between forever.

That was it. The source of his fear. He looked it head-on, sneered at it, then let go of Eshtak's hand. He waited for something to happen, expected the worst, but remained intact. It was a decent test, but it still didn't prove whether or not it would protect more than one of them. After all, scourge might not affect him at all. He must be certain before allowing the others to step into the fog.

Let go.

Qotan exhaled and released Nardus's hand.

"Qotan!" Nardus yelled.

The black fog churned around him and began to take shape. Thick arms. Black claws. It reached for him. Pulled at his very soul.

Eshtak grabbed his hand. Qotan gasped and clutched his chest as the creature faded back into the fog.

"You old fool!" Nardus said. "What were you thinking?"

Qotan scowled. "It had to be tested."

"If Eshtak hadn't grabbed your hand, you'd be dead right now."

"Better to test it now than when we are caught up in the midst of it all."

"You could've warned us."

"If I had, it would not have been a true test, now would it?"

"You're more reckless than my son."

Qotan grinned. "I will take that as a complement."

"You shouldn't," Nardus said.

"It's strange hearing only half of a conversation," Alderan said.

"We must all go together." Zelanora frowned. "Something tells me it's the only way."

Qotan set his staff on the ground and then he and Nardus reached out of the fog. "Take our hands," Nardus said.

Zelanora grabbed Alderan's hand and then Nardus's. Then, Alderan reached over and took Qotan's hand before letting go of Zelanora's.

"This is not right," Qotan said. "You must take Eshtak's hand, and I will take yours. This way, you will not risk me losing my grasp and leaving you to be swallowed by the fog." Alderan agreed, and the two of them made the switch while constantly keeping contact with Eshtak and each other.

"Are we ready now?" Nardus said.

Qotan reached out with his free hand and his staff flew into it. "Indeed, we are."

Ꝟätūr, protect us.

† † †

It took several hours for the five of them to reach the other side of Intus where the bridge crossed over the giant moat and connected the surrounding road to the island city. Despite Master Qotan's glowing staff and the three orbs of light that he, Nardus, and Zelanora had conjured when they'd entered the cavern, Alderan saw little of Intus and relied on Eshtak to guide him and the others. They stopped at the far edge of the bridge, and Master Qotan waved his staff in front of himself. Alderan noticed a slight shimmer.

The defense barrier.

So far, the fog of scourge hadn't taken their lives, but the defense barrier was a whole different beast. Based on his recent readings of the subject and knowledge bestowed upon him by Nardus and others, Alderan had a basic understanding of how it worked.

"Do you think it's safe to cross the defense barrier?" he said.

Zelanora gasped. "What do you mean is it safe?"

"Not hurt Eshtak."

"It prevents anyone from crossing through it, including via teleportation," Nardus said.

"By prevents, my father means it will disintegrate us. Not sure I'm in the mood to be disintegrated."

"I believe that Eshtak's persistent physical touch will safeguard us against it," Master Qotan said.

One surefire way to find out.

Alderan took a deep breath and prayed that Eshtak's touch would keep them intact. "We proceed, then?"

"We do," Nardus said.

The hairs on Alderan's arms stood on end as the five of them passed through the defense barrier, but it did nothing more. He breathed easier as they gained distance from it. Eshtak described the city gates and several other features as they headed toward the center of Intus, but Alderan's focus remained on the task ahead and the ground in front of him. The one thing he did notice—or rather feel—was the way Eshtak hesitated with each step. It concerned him.

Alderan said, "What is it, Eshtak?"

"Eshtak feels sad."

"Can you feel the people? Your people?"

"Family gone. People gone. City alone."

Alderan's heart ached for Eshtak. Losing someone close was difficult enough, but he couldn't fathom losing everyone he ever knew all in a single moment. "I am deeply sorry."

"Eshtak sorry too."

Once they reached what Eshtak called the city square, Alderan spotted their destination. The dense fog cloaked the city, but it couldn't contain the beacon of purple light emanating from the second aethershard. Master Qotan saw it, too, and pointed toward it with his staff. Eshtak nodded and led them toward it.

The slender crystal stood about four feet tall and hovered just above a square, stone platform. A small gap no more than a few inches wide surrounded the entire platform. The fog and darkness skewed his vision, making it difficult to see beneath the platform. From what he could tell, it was suspended over a void.

Perfect.

The five of them stepped onto the platform. Alderan expected it to dip or shift or plunge into the void, but it didn't budge. He exhaled, as did the others.

Alderan could feel the crystal's presence and the mezhik that flowed through it. The air crackled around it.

"We should close the circle," Nardus said.

Zelanora looked up at him. "Around the crystal?"

"Yes."

Master Qotan and Zelanora circled either side of the crystal, and Zelanora took hold of Master Qotan's wrist. The five of them glowed brighter.

Alderan stared at the crystal. Something about it made him want to reach out and touch it. It was as if the crystal called to him.

"No one touches the crystal," Nardus said.

Is he reading my mind?

Alderan knew the answer. It called to each of them. Wanted to feed on their mezhik and consume them.

"What now?" Alderan said, fear in his voice.

Nardus looked to Zelanora. "Reach out with your mind and see if you can connect with it."

Alderan watched Zelanora as she closed her eyes. Her brow furrowed and her nose wrinkled. She remained that way for almost a minute before exhaling.

"It's not working," she said.

Alderan's pulse raced as he inched toward the crystal. "I have an idea."

"Stay back," Nardus growled.

"Listen to me." He looked across at Zelanora. "When you touch an object, you can see its past, right?" She nodded. "I can too, but I only see the last events of whoever touched it. I believe that what we see might be what Normak meant about them having memories. If you touch the crystal, perhaps it will allow you access to its memories."

"Wait," Nardus said. "Because we are all touching each other now, we can combine our mezhik. Qotan and I will contribute pure mezhik while you and Zelanora concentrate on accessing the crystal's memories. Given its power and the fact that its activated, none of us will touch the crystal." He looked down at Eshtak. "Except Eshtak. I believe the protection web will keep him safe."

Eshtak's lips trembled. "Eshtak not touch."

"You must, Eshtak. I believe it's the only way."

"You can do it, Eshtak," Alderan said. "I have faith in you."

"As do I," Master Qotan said.

Zelanora nodded. "Me, too."

Eshtak scowled at the crystal and exhaled. "For old friend." He stepped forward and pressed his forehead against the side of the crystal.

Alderan tensed as an overwhelming force of power coursed through his veins, lighting them on fire. He'd never felt mezhik so strong. The veins in his arms lit up. The others around the circle did the same, and their eyes and mouths pierced the darkness with beams of light.

"I can feel it," Zelanora said. "It indeed has memories and even a voice. It hates what it has done, but it can't stop itself, and I don't know how to erase its memory."

"You said you added new memories before. Take what you see from the crystal and begin removing elements from it. Replace them with nothing."

"I'll try that."

Zelanora's lips moved, and her eyes shifted side-to-side beneath her eyelids. The air shook. Became violent. A great pressure pushed against Alderan's chest. He stood his ground, but then his feet began to inch backward.

"Scourge is trying to rip us apart," Master Qotan said.

The ground quaked, and a massive wind kicked up, howling through the city square. The fog swirled. Began taking shape.

Zelanora's lips continued to move.

Inch by inch, their circle spread, each of them growing closer to losing touch with each other.

Alderan growled as he strained to keep contact with Eshtak and Master Qotan.

His thoughts continued to circle around and land back on Eshtak. He stared at the glowing runes.

What am I supposed to do, ʕäʈūr?

A word formed on his tongue. He knew it. The yellow rune.

"*Əllíʈ,*" he said.

The fog shook. Roared like some ferocious beast.

The yellow rune pulled away from Eshtak's skin and got sucked into the stream of light connecting the two aethershards.

He called out the names of the green one, the blue one, and the red one. Each lifted from Eshtak's skin and melded into the stream of light.

His fingers slipped from Master Qotan's hand, breaking the circle.

He and Master Qotan both staggered backward but remained in contact with the others.

The platform they stood on shifted. Cracked. Began to buckle.

Zelanora's lips still moved.

Alderan called out several more runes. The orange one. Purple. Black. Brown. White.

One rune remained when the entire platform crashed into the hollow space beneath it.

Black claws reached out of the fog as the five of them fell.

No, four!

Somehow, Eshtak managed to grab onto the crystal with one arm, and he hung on its side.

Pain like nothing Alderan had ever felt before ripped at his flesh and tore at his soul.

A silver rune he hadn't seen before shone from beneath Eshtak's shirt. He knew it. Called out its name.

Thunder rocked the entire city with a loud *boom!*

The light from the aethershard pulsed, then faded, casting Alderan into perfect darkness.

The pain ebbed. He remembered the feeling well. It always faded upon death.

So why do I still feel the platform beneath me?

A brilliant blue light filled the air and burned away what remained of the black fog.

Eshtak fell to the ground, the crystal still in his grasp.

Alderan sat up. Nardus groaned. Zelanora lay still, but he could see her breathing.

To his left lay Master Qotan, still as a statue.

He looked down at himself. No part of him touched Eshtak, nor did Eshtak touch Master Qotan.

I can see him.

Eshtak rolled onto his side, then crawled toward Master Qotan, the aethershard still firmly grasped with one hand.

Nardus sat up and rubbed the back of his head. "Did it work?"

Alderan stared at Master Qotan, his heart filled with agony. "We ended scourge, but I'm not sure Master Qotan survived the fall."

Eshtak touched Master Qotan's chest. "Old friend lives?"

"I don't think—"

Alderan's mouth gaped as the crystal began glowing with red light. The red light surged, passing through Eshtak and into Master Qotan.

Master Qotan bolted upright and gasped, his green eyes wide.

"Master Qotan?"

Alderan had been so fixated on Eshtak and Master Qotan that he hadn't noticed Zelanora come to.

"Zätūr's light!" Master Qotan rolled his head and stretched his neck. "I have not felt this much in decades." He cocked his head. "What happened?"

Alderan scratched his head. "I think Eshtak saved your life."

Eshtak frowned and shook his head. "Eshtak not save."

"The crystal did something to you," Nardus said.

Zelanora crawled over to Eshtak and touched the crystal. She closed her eyes. "From what I understand, the crystal pulled the last of scourge out of Master Qotan and returned his soul from the between."

Master Qotan reached out, and his staff flew into his hand. He used it to pull himself to his feet. He looked at each of them in turn and smiled. "I am whole again, am I not?"

"That you are," Nardus said.

"Eshtak has crystal." He held it up.

"Indeed, you do."

Alderan sighed and lay back down. Tears wet his cheeks.

Thank you for protecting us and bringing Master Qotan back, Ɛätūr.

CHAPTER FORTY-NINE

Aria glared at the old man. Once, she trusted Credan with her life, but she'd begun to wonder if his loyalty remained with her. More and more, she found it difficult to locate him. What agenda did he have, and to whom did he serve if not her? The single answer she always returned to was Cinolth. Everything, good or bad, revolved around the wretched beast.

"Where were you this time?"

Credan averted her glare. "Your safety remains my highest concern. As such, I am constantly looking into and thwarting threats on your life."

"Threats on my life?" Aria scoffed. "Who would dare come after me now, given my reputation?"

"Your reputation does give you an advantage, but not all foes fear you or death. Reubane proved that. You must also keep in mind that threats are not exclusively outside."

"Outside of what?"

"Outside these walls. Men cannot be trusted when it comes to power."

"You are a man, are you not?"

Credan swallowed hard. "Physically speaking, I am, but I've never desired power. It corrupts the mind like few other things of this world."

"More than money?"

"It's difficult to say. Money tends to come with power. Therefore, it's hard to separate the two."

"I suppose you're right." She slowly paced, her belly and ankles swollen and her lower back aching. "And what is your solution to eliminate these threats on my life?"

Credan stared at her for several seconds before answering, an obvious attempt to choose his words wisely. "Given your current... condition, you need an escort with you at all times."

Aria's eyes narrowed. "My current condition?"

He pulled on his shirt collar. "As you know, your child will arrive in two-and-a-half fortnights. Given this unchangeable timeline, undue stress could further complicate matters."

Further complicate matters?

Aria trembled, her very soul begging to smite the man where he stood. If she were to eliminate him, matters would far exceed the realm of complicated. The entire castle relied on him to keep everything running. Plus, like it or not, he was all she had left.

She loathed her situation. The last few months left her bedridden more days than not and fueled her rage. It seeped from her pores and lashed out without warning, often with deadly consequence for those within her range. To top it off, Nardus and the others remained elusive despite Cinolth's dragons patrolling the skies and his mind-controlled army scouring the realm for any signs of them.

How do they remain hidden?

Aria swallowed her rage and sighed. "Double my guards if you must, but keep them out of my bedchambers."

"As I said, I fear the men cannot be trusted."

She couldn't be certain, but the way Credan said it made her think he had at least a few men in mind that he didn't trust. If so, they would be dealt with. "What then?"

Credan folded his arms behind his back. "There are two I've come to trust. Ones still loyal to Lord Rosai. You might find their presence... comforting."

Rage twisted Aria, her mezhik crackling at her fingertips. "Look at me! I'm swollen like a fattened calf, and you suggest I take on not one but *two* lovers?"

Credan's face turned crimson. His arms shot up, and he cowered. "Gods, no! Never would I suggest anything of the sort, my queen." He shook his head, terror still in his eyes. "I merely meant to say that they are gnolls."

Aria huffed. "And what makes you think that would comfort me?"

"One of them is a female. She's known as The Butcher. Everyone fears her. The other, a mercenary for hire, worked for Lord Rosai. He kept tabs on your brother and saved his life on multiple occasions, including from the fire that burned Castle Portador Tempestade to the ground."

Gnolls…

Love-hate relationships defined her life. What difference would two more make? "Very well. Send them to me, and I'll see where their loyalties lie."

Credan bowed. "Yes, my queen." He turned to leave.

"One more thing," she said.

He looked back, his eyebrows raised above the rims of his spectacles. "Yes?"

"Bring one of those men you say cannot be trusted as well."

Credan nodded, then exited her bedchambers. Aria waddled over to the couch in front of the fireplace and settled onto it. It took a good deal of effort to lift her legs high enough to get them on the couch with the rest of her. Later, she would summon Brema to come and massage her feet.

She laid back and closed her eyes. The fire crackled, and the scent of cedar livened the air and settled her rage. Darius stirred in her womb, and his tiny little feet kicked her. She stroked her belly and calmed him.

Soon, you will arrive, and then I'll find and kill your grandfather.

† † †

Of all the men Credan knew, there was one in particular that he not only didn't trust but that he also loathed. For whatever reason, Captain Erik Black had made it his mission to usurp and embarrass Credan at every opportunity. Just last week, the man walked into the castle kitchens and demanded that the staff prepare a special meal for him and his men despite Credan explicitly telling him no not an hour before. Several weeks before that, Credan commanded Black to increase patrols of the castle perimeter. Black shoved him to the ground in front of the other men and threatened his life if he ever tried to order Black or his men around ever again. To top it off, the bastard called Credan a pathetic worm and spat in his face.

Credan couldn't be certain as to what Queen Rosai had in mind for whomever he brought before her, but he had a good idea. Her wrath was unquenchable as of late, and he prayed she would unleash it on Black. Put the man in his place or send his soul to Ef Demd Dhä. Either would suffice.

You'll never call me a pathetic worm again.

It didn't take long for Credan to locate Captain Black. As usual, the man leaned against one of the castle walls inside the courtyard, conversing with a local woman who frequented the castle. Known only as Trixa, she had a knack for separating men from their coin, Captain Black a frequent target for several months.

Serves the man right.

Credan approached the pair. "Captain Black."

Black turned, and his smile morphed into a scowl. "Yeh here to eat dirt, worm?" Trixa laughed.

Credan kept calm, his thoughts and hopes set on the man's imminent demise. "Queen Rosai has commanded your presence."

"Has she now?" The man's eyebrow rose, and he glanced at Trixa. "I told yeh it'd be a matter of time before the queen'd be lying on her back and beggin' fer me the way yeh do."

Anger crawled beneath Credan's skin.

If the queen doesn't kill you, I will.

Trixa wrinkled her nose. "S'pose I find me another man, then?"

Black grabbed her arm and twisted it. "Yeh do, an I'll slit yer throat." He jerked her toward him, smashed his lips against hers, then shoved her against the wall. "Stick around, and yeh might earn a bit more coin."

After rounding up Rakzar and Urza, Credan led the three of them through the castle, toward Queen Rosai's bedchambers. His gut churned with trepidation and excitement as his fingers wrapped around the knife hilt within his left pocket.

One way or another, Black.

† † †

After spending more than five months working their way up the ranks of Aria's army and building a relationship with Credan, the sole person responsible for Aria's safety, Rakzar and Urza had finally gained access to the queen herself. According to Credan, she trusted no one, especially after the incident that took Karraar's life. Rakzar didn't blame her for being cautious. Anyone who overthrows a king is bound to create many enemies. In her shoes, he wouldn't trust anyone, either.

The timing of their meeting with Aria couldn't have come at a better juncture, their six-month timeline all but diminished. Many would chalk it up to pure luck, and Rakzar would have too not long ago, but now he couldn't help but feel a higher power intervened on their behalf. Urza would disagree and call him foolish for such beliefs, but he'd witnessed too many events over the last year to deny what he now felt in his heart.

You exist, Ʒäṭūr.

Another sign came from the lips of Wizard Wrik the previous day. He'd heard from Nardus, and everything was in place. A few days from now, they would face Cinolth on the battlefield and fight to the death.

Unless we die tonight.

"She awaits you inside," Credan said, opening the double doors into the expansive bedchambers.

Captain Black, a despicable man, pushed past Rakzar and Urza. "She asked fer me by name, yeh dirty dogs, so watch yerselfs."

Rakzar and Urza followed Captain Black through a lush receiving room and into the main area of the bedchambers. Aria sat on a gray couch in front of a blazing fire, a book propped open atop her bulging stomach. She didn't rise when they entered but tossed the book aside and commanded the three of them to stand before her. Even in her current state, she exuded an air of superiority and instilled a tinge of fear in Rakzar's heart. Black, a man who suffered from diarrhea of the mouth relentlessly, kept his trap shut.

Aria looked to the three of them in turn, her gaze ever calculating. "Are you aware as to the reason I summoned the three of you?"

"Yes, my queen," Rakzar and Urza said.

Black grinned. "I know my worth."

"Do you?" A smile curled Aria's lip. "Then you come willing to die?"

"Yeh—" Black's grin vanished. "Wait, what?"

"You heard what I asked. Now answer the question."

Black fidgeted with the hilt of the sword hanging at his waist, his eyes shifty. "I don't understand."

Click!

Urza's arm moved so fast that Black didn't even flinch until after she buried her blade in the side of his neck. He whimpered as she retracted the blade. Blood sprayed from the wound, peppering Urza, the floor, and the table that sat between them and the couch.

Black clutched his neck, but the damage had been dealt. Face pale, he dropped to his knees, then fell face-first into the side of the table with a sickening *thud-crunch*. He slid to the side and collapsed on the floor in a pool of his own blood.

During the entire event, Aria didn't so much as flinch. Her gaze moved from the floor to Urza. Urza licked her blade clean, then returned it to its holder on her forearm.

Rakzar's pulse raced. This hadn't been part of any plan they'd discussed. He hated Black, too, but to kill him in front of Aria made no sense.

What is she trying to do, get us killed?

Aria's gaze steeled. "Tell me your name, and explain your action."

"My name is Urza, and I serve the crown. Captain Black served only himself. A man like him cannot be trusted, especially when opportunity arises as it did today. I am trained to eliminate threats without need for direction, and I sensed that he posed a direct threat to you, my queen. Therefore, I acted." She dipped her head. "I assure you that he will not be mourned, nor will he be honored."

"You're not what I expected." She turned her gaze on Rakzar, but it had already softened. "And you?"

"I'm Rakzar, my queen."

"Credan told me that you saved my brother's life on several occasions. Is this true?"

"Yes, and he saved mine twice, too."

"I see." She stroked her belly. "Calm yourself, Darius. All is well." After a time, she said, "Did you protect my brother on my behalf, or were the two of you friends?"

She's probing, but to what end?

"We did not start out as friends, but his death devastated me."

"So, you fought at his side and against me?"

How am I supposed to answer that without getting us killed?

Rakzar swallowed, then nodded. "Yes, my queen."

"And you stand in front of me now, proclaiming your loyalty to the crown and to me. I wonder, are your loyalties always so fluid? Perhaps you serve the coin and not the crown." She held up a finger, silencing him. "Give me one good reason I shouldn't kill you."

"Even though you stood in opposition, the White Knight—err Alderan—sacrificed his life to save yours. I dedicated my life to him, and it stood to reason that if he deemed your life worth preserving, even unto death, then I should, too. That is the reason I joined your army. Admittedly, I do not serve the crown but the one who wears it. As such, my loyalty lies with you, Aria Rosai, queen of the Ancient Realm."

Aria raised a finger toward Urza. "And her?"

Rakzar eyed Urza. "She is my sister and goes wherever I do."

With seemingly great effort, Aria rose from the couch. She moved around the table and stood before Urza. Rising on her tippytoes, Aria reached up and wiped blood spatter from Urza's cheek.

"Moving forward, the two of you will serve as my personal guard. One or both of you will accompany me at all times and guard my bedchambers with your lives." She touched her belly. "Nothing—not even the death of my father—matter more to me than my child. Protect us."

"With our lives," Rakzar said. Urza nodded.

"Good." She looked down at Captain Black. "Tell Credan to send someone in to remove this traitor and clean up the mess."

"Right away," Urza said.

"And Urza, get yourself cleaned up, too. I can't have my personal guards walking around with dried blood in their fur."

Urza dipped her head. "Yes, my queen."

† † †

Far below Galondu Castle, Wrik located the tapestry depicting a scene of savagery and slavery from the Great War and stepped through the black stone wall to its right. The hidden passage led to a stairway with thirty-three steps. He descended them and entered the place Pravus called the transformation chamber.

Wrik, cloaked with invisibility and wearing the saurian ring, slithered across the sixty-foot-long white marble walkway and to the center of the room. The octagonal-shaped platform matched the walkway. Seven glass-walled containment chambers, ten feet wide, tall, and deep hung in the darkness, each suspended three feet away from the central platform.

Gods, those are larger than I remember.

After lowering the hood of his cloak, he removed the ring. The transformation from a lizard-like saurian body back to his own human form took just seconds, but the pain associated with it lasted an eternity within his mind. Unlike the dragon ring, the saurian one left him aching with pain every time he returned back to normal. The only explanation for the pain that made sense to him was the fact that his body size decreased tremendously when in saurian form but remained fairly consistent when transformed into a dragon.

A few more hours, and I'll never have need for this wretched ring again.

He reached out toward the closest containment chamber to his left. It slid toward the platform, closing the three-foot gap and coming to a rest. If Nardus was correct, it wouldn't take much to move the containment chamber from where it sat to Nasduron. But how would he hold it and take the necessary step while doing so?

"Perhaps I need only touch it."

Wrik set his mind on Nasduron, reached out and touched the containment chamber's glass wall, then stepped forward. He and the containment chamber phased into the Great Library. The containment chamber wound up perched atop one of the tables.

"Not an ideal placement."

Craaaaack!

The containment chamber's weight fissured the table.

"Gods!" Wrik dove to the floor.

Boom!

The table exploded and the containment chamber crashed to the floor, sending slivers of splintered wood shooting in every direction. The deadly projectiles skewered everything they hit, including Wrik's exposed legs.

"Oh, my!" Gnaud slid to a stop next to Wrik. "What have you done to yourself?" He helped Wrik sit up.

Wrik began pulling slivers out of his legs, wincing with each one. "Gods, that was unexpected."

Gnaud harrumphed. "Perhaps you should've come here and cleared a space for your—" He glanced back at the glass containment chamber and frowned. "—whatever that glass contraption is."

Wrik wiped blood from a few of the deeper wounds, then used mezhik to heal them. He admired the mess he made and chuckled. "Hindsight, right?"

"Dear Ƨäţūr! This is no laughing matter." He scowled at Wrik, and his whiskers twitched. "What if I had been on that table when you appeared? It would have crushed me to death!"

Wrik sighed, then nodded. "You are absolutely right."

"What is it, and why did you bring it here?"

"Tonight, we will capture Aria. Then, once we've lured Cinolth into position, we will bring Aria here for safe keeping."

Gnaud eyed the glass containment chamber and cocked his head. "It is some sort of holding cell?"

"Precisely."

"I've read almost every book in Centauria, yet the mezhik of this world still finds ways to astound me."

"May it always be so." Wrik pulled himself up and dusted off his robes. "I would stay and help clean this mess up, but time is pressing."

"Oh, I'm certain it is. Guess I'll go get a broom." Gnaud muttered something to himself as he walked away.

Wrik smiled, then stepped out of the Great Library and back onto the octagonal platform in the transformation chamber. The sleeve of his robe kept snagging as he crossed the long walkway and traversed the stairs. Finally fed up with it, he stopped at the end of the hidden passage and rolled up his sleeve. A two-inch sliver of wood hung from his forearm. He ripped it out and tossed it on the floor.

"Worthless little—" He gasped, realizing the sliver's worth. If he'd emerged from the hidden passage before donning the saurian ring and invisibility cloak, it could've cost him his life. The little sliver had granted him the time he needed to remember he wasn't welcome in Galondu Castle.

Two guards traversed the corridor not three seconds after he stepped through the wall and into it. He held his breath as they walked by, the nearest of them almost stepping on his foot.

"Hold up," one said. He sniffed the air. "Man, it smells like something died in here."

The other one crossed his arms. "For the last time, it wasn't me."

"Oh, it was you before alright, but this is different." He turned and started walking right toward Wrik, sniffing the air along the way.

Wrik skirted around the man, keeping his distance, but the man followed him around.

"The smell's moving around."

"Maybe it's you," the other said. "Come on, our shift is almost over, and I'm ready for a pint."

The first man huffed. "All you think about is ale."

"And women."

The first man gave the air one final sniff and shook his head, then the two of them walked off.

Gods, that was close.

† † †

After Urza washed the blood from her fur and leather armor, she tied a green string to her necklace and stuffed it back into the hidden pouch behind her leather breastplate. Although she no longer wore it, she still used it to keep track of her kills. One day, perhaps soon, she would answer for each of them.

Rakzar waited for her in the corridor, the fear in his eyes belying his calm exterior. It concerned her.

She grabbed his arm. "Keep it up, and she will know."

He eyed her claws dug into his hide. "Know what?"

She took a long sniff of him. "Ugh. You reek of fear."

"Do not." He sniffed himself. "I'm fine."

"You got the stuff?"

He patted his breastplate. "Right here."

Urza nodded. "Good. Come on."

She led the two of them back to the corridor where Aria's chambers were located. Credan stood in the middle of the corridor with a small squad of soldiers.

"What's going on?" Urza said.

"Three dead soldiers in the atrium."

She glanced at Rakzar. His eyes told her it wasn't him. "Dead from what?"

"Knife wounds to the throat, same as Captain Black."

Damn! This isn't part of the plan.

Urza growled. "From the sound of your tone, I'd say you're blaming one of us."

Credan swallowed hard. "You do understand *how* it looks, right?"

"Looks like a setup," Rakzar said.

Understanding hit Urza. These were Captain Black's men. They must've killed the other three.

A coup.

Urza touched Rakzar's arm. "I believe it's a simple misunderstanding."

"No misunderstanding," said one of the soldiers. He drew his sword. "Saw you do it."

"He's a liar," Urza said. "You need to *drop* it, Credan."

Credan smiled.

I think he understands.

He held up two fingers. "*Two* reasons I cannot. *One!*"

Credan dropped to the floor.

Click! Click!

Urza lunged forward, stabbing at the two closest soldiers. The first managed to block her strike with his forearm, but the second one fumbled to free his sword from its scabbard and paid with his life, her blade buried in his right eye.

Rakzar drove his shoulder into the third soldier, knocking him back into two other soldiers. Two of the three crashed to the floor, and the last one took the handle of Rakzar's axe right underneath his chin. Bone cracked, and blood ran from the man's lips as he fell backward.

Urza ducked beneath the first soldier's swing and sliced his forearm just above his leather gauntlet. He cried out and dropped his sword, leaving himself open. She sliced through his throat with her other blade and moved toward the next soldier.

Having realized the difficulty in using a sword in such close quarters, the man dropped his sword and drew a curved dagger. His marred face gave her pause, his smile split by a knotty scar. A man with so many scars would likely be a formidable foe. She liked a challenge.

Thunk!

The man's eyes bulged, and he dropped to his knees. His curved dagger clattered to the floor. Rakzar worked his axe from the back of the man's skull, then kicked him to the ground.

All seven soldiers lay dead, each in a pool of their own blood.

Rakzar growled. "Five to your two. What does that tell you about the way I smell?"

"Not sure, but your arm's bleeding."

A servant girl stood just down the corridor, right in front of the doors to Aria's bedchambers. Her mouth gaped and eyes bulged. She held a silver serving tray in her hands.

Our opening.

Urza stalked toward the girl. "Set the tray on the floor and back away."

"Do as she says, Brema," Credan said. "Everything will be okay."

The girl nodded and set the tray down, but she didn't back away. "I-I won't let y-you hurt her."

"We're not here to hurt the queen," Urza said. "You can trust me."

The girl trembled but held her ground. Such bravery in the midst of fear. "I trust no one."

Credan stepped past Urza and cradled her in his arm. "Urza and Rakzar just saved my life and that of Queen Rosai. They are on our side." She nodded, and Credan escorted her farther down the corridor.

Urza picked up the serving tray. Rakzar already had the pouch with the nízzhäíd bəllū in his hand. He removed the lid and tossed a handful into the bowl of soup and the glass of wine. Zerenity hadn't specified how much to use, so she hoped it was enough to knock Aria out.

Rakzar returned the lid to the tray and the pouch back behind his breastplate just as Credan walked back over to them.

"Brema will be fine," Credan said. "Given her role as Queen Rosai's handmaid, she's seen her fair share of death." He reached for the serving tray. "May I?" Urza handed it to him.

The three of them entered the bedchambers. Aria sat in her bed, propped up by a mountain of pillows. A scowl covered her face when she looked at Urza.

"Didn't I ask you to clean yourself up?"

Credan set the tray on Aria's legs. "You must forgive her, my queen."

"Must I?"

"Seven more men, all loyal to Captain Black, were bent on revenge," Credan said. "Urza and Rakzar eliminated the threat minutes before we entered your bedchambers. She did not have time to clean herself up again."

"I see." The way Aria said it made Urza nervous, but then she smiled. "A single day, and the two of you have already earned your keep."

Urza bowed. "My queen."

Aria removed the lid from the tray and set it next to herself on the bed. "This again?" She moaned. "Do we have no other food in this entire castle?"

Credan adjusted his collar. "I assure you that we are working diligently with our suppliers to procure the goods necessary to satisfy the queen's cravings."

"And what is wrong with the suppliers?"

Terror flashed across Credan's face. "If I may be as direct as possible, the issue stems from the fact that our main supplier of goods, West Hotah, was burned to the ground. It will likely take years for them to recover, if ever."

Aria glared at Credan. "I see. Perhaps they've learned their lesson about defying my orders."

She's ruthless. I'll give her that.

Credan nodded and stared at her tray. "In light of today's events, would it be pertinent to have someone taste your food for you?"

Urza's heart thumped harder.

Say no, damn you!

Aria sneered. "Are you volunteering, Credan?"

Rakzar said, "I will, if it pleases my queen."

"Traitors to the crown lurk in every shadow, do they not, Credan?" She lifted the glass of wine to her lips, then hesitated. "Am I to fear everything?"

Credan lowered his head. "No, my queen."

"Indeed, not." She tilted her head back and drained the entire glass of wine in a single swallow.

Urza glanced at Rakzar. He nodded ever so slightly.

Now, we wait.

† † †

Minutes after consuming her soup, Aria knew something wasn't right. The room spun around her, and it wasn't because of the wine. Someone had poisoned her.

"Credan." She waited for him to spin back around. "Fetch the herbalist. The alchemist. Whatever it takes."

"She's been poisoned!" Rakzar said.

Credan turned pale as a sheep. "Gods…"

"Now," Aria shouted.

Credan ran out of the bedchambers.

"You," Aria said, pointing at Urza. "You did this to me." Her words slurred from her lips.

She reached for her mezhik. Conjured a fireball and set the bed on fire.

"Gods!" Urza yelled. "What are you doing?"

Rakzar scooped Aria up just before the entire bed became engulfed in flames.

"You think I don't know, but I do," Aria said. Her head lulled to the side, and she couldn't lift it back up. "Alderan sent you from the dead. Saw him in a fire." Mezhik crackled at her fingertips. Tiny bolts of lightning shot from them, narrowly missing Urza. Aria laughed.

"Wrik!" Rakzar yelled.

Wrik?

Why would the beast call for him? Her mind could hardly grasp the concept of breathing, let alone anything else.

A smell beyond death entered the room. Aria retched, unable to control herself.

A scaly beast slithered out of the night and shoved something silver at her.

"No!" She swatted the air. Darkness crept around her, and her mezhik faded. "What's hap—" Her eyelids drooped. Closed. Too heavy to lift again. Drool slid down the side of her cheek.

Hands of darkness grabbed hold of her and pulled her into the depths of sleep.

† † †

Wrik led Rakzar and Urza through the castle corridors, and toward the mirror. Rakzar carried Aria, and Urza trailed them to make sure no one tried to stop them. At the mirror, Wrik quickly removed the cloak and saurian ring and threw them on the floor. He set his mind on Tyrosha, just like Nardus told him to do, and touched the mirror's surface. Its reflection swirled, then turned black. A faint light shone in the distance through the mirror.

Wrik turned around, and Rakzar handed Aria to him.

Urza joined them. "We'll meet you in Summitto Valley."

Wrik nodded.

"Stop!" Credan yelled. Rakzar and Urza turned around.

Like a fool, the man had come alone.

Click! Click!

Urza's blades dropped into her hands. "Stay out of this, and you'll live."

"Do whatever's necessary," Wrik said. He turned and stepped through the mirror.

† † †

Credan stood there, stunned. He didn't understand why Rakzar and Urza would be working with Wizard Wrik. The man had tried to kill Queen Rosai.

"You've ended your lives," Credan said. "And mine."

"You seem to genuinely care about Aria," Urza said. "Am I wrong?"

Credan fidgeted with his spectacles. "I swore an oath on my life to protect her."

"As did we. If what you say is true, then you'll let us leave."

"How can I?"

"Cinolth controls her," Rakzar said. "As long as she remains at his side, he will continue to use her until nothing remains of the girl you first met."

Credan remembered the night she arrived at the castle well. She'd been such a young, innocent girl. How things had changed in such a short time. No matter how much he wanted to deny it, he knew Rakzar was right.

"What do you want me to do?"

Urza said, "Misdirect the soldiers so that we can escape through the gateway."

Credan nodded. "I can do that."

"Good." Urza sheathed her blades. "Will you also deliver a message to Cinolth?"

Gods... must I?

One way or another, he'd eventually have to face the scaly beast. "What's the message?"

"Tell him that he'll never see Aria again," Urza said.

He scratched the back of his neck. "I will, but it won't matter where you take her. He can sense her presence anywhere."

Urza grinned. "That's what we're counting on."

Thirty minutes later, after misdirecting the entire castle to the western side and assuring Rakzar and Urza a safe escape, he headed up to the southern ramparts. Cinolth awaited him. Snatched him up right as he exited the stairwell.

"Tell me what happened!" Cinolth roared.

Credan had no doubt as to the fate he would face and took a deep breath. "Queen Rosai is better off without you."

Cinolth's grip tightened around Credan, and his claws bit into his flesh. Smoke billowed from his nostrils. "Answer me."

Credan could scarcely draw a breath, both lungs punctured by razor-sharp claws. "They said to give you a message," he managed to choke out.

Cinolth's presence filled his head. *"And what is this message?"*

Credan closed his eyes, his spark of life quickly fading. He answered the wicked beast through mindspeak. *"You'll never see her again, you bas—"*

Cinolth squeezed Credan until the wind faded, the smell of Cinolth's sulfuric breath dissipated, and the darkness faded into light. Then, Credan slipped into death.

CHAPTER FIFTY

Nardus stood on the western edge of Summitto Valley's rim, marveling at just how far the valley stretched to the north and south. A thick blanket of snow covered its grass fields, a rare sight for early fall weather.

He rubbed his hands together, but the chill in them remained. Had he known what the weather would be like ahead of time, he might've chosen a different day. Then again, fire-breathing dragons loathed the cold because it took so much more energy for them to produce their flames than it did in warmer weather.

Ƨätūr, allow this to work in our favor.

Theyn stood at his side. A plume of vapor escaped from her lips as she exhaled. Although from a warmer climate than him, she preferred the cold weather. He didn't understand her at all.

"The snow changes everything," she said.

"No matter the conditions, this battle will be hard fought."

"I agree, but that's not what I meant." Theyn gazed into his eyes and smiled. "The vision we shared did not take place in the snow, therefore we will not die today."

"Perhaps not, but that doesn't mean we should take unnecessary risks, either." He eyed a small group approaching from the north. "And, not to ruin your bright mood, but if our vision comes to pass, that means this will not be the last battle we face."

"I care only about this day."

"As do I." Nardus retrieved a spyglass from his pack and used it to identify the approaching group. "Ridan's returned."

Rayah joined them at the edge of the rim. "I knew she would."

"Torbrek's with her, plus about a dozen others," Urza said.

Theyn smiled. "Then our odds have increased."

"Ever increasing," Savric said. "Morcinda and her clan docked in Calx Acta several hours ago. They should arrive soon."

Nardus turned and eyed Savric. "Are you saying what I think you are?"

"Indeed. King Forlin has come with them."

This is your doing, Ɂäṭūr.

† † †

An hour later, Nardus and all their allies stood in the middle of the valley, toward its northern end. Including the dwarves, elves, and dragons, there were eighty-nine of them. Nardus prayed it would be enough.

Tharos landed close to Nardus. "Elros spotted Cinolth and three other dragons heading directly for us. They're coming from the southeast."

Nardus rubbed his hands together. "Then our plan is working." He turned toward Savric. "As soon as they enter the designated area, conjure the light shield so that his army can't interfere when they arrive."

Savric stroked his beard and touched the triad Lanara gave him. "I am ready."

King Forlin stepped out of the crowd. His pale skin blended well with the surrounding snow. "What kind of dragons are they?"

"With him are an ice dragon named Aquis, a nature dragon named Zemeral, and an earth dragon named Slag," Tharos said.

King Forlin nodded. "Leave Aquis to us."

"We'll take on Zemeral," Ridan said.

"A wise choice, and a formidable foe," Tharos said. "I will join you."

Urza nodded. "As will I and Rakzar."

"That leaves Cinolth and Slag to the rest of us," Lanara said.

Elros came in fast and slid through the snow. "They're here!"

Fifty yards to the south, Wrik stood in the middle of the valley, Aria in his arms. Nízhäíd bəllū coursed through her veins and kept her sedated.

A minute later, Cinolth and the three dragons dropped from the sky, landing just south of Wrik's position.

"Ɂzhäəlld əllíṭ!" Savric yelled, slamming the butt-end of the staff he held into the ground. Just as it had done over Vallah, a brilliant, yellow light shot up from the staff's orb, about a hundred yards in the air, and began spreading outward in an ever-expanding circle.

As the light shield continued growing, Nardus began wondering just how good of a plan it actually was. For better or worse, they'd trapped themselves inside an impenetrable bubble with the most vicious and evil being to ever have lived, save Diᴢäfär.

No going back, now.

† † †

Wrik faced Cinolth and the other three dragons. "Heard you've been flying all over the realm. Tired yet?"

"You think this is a game?" Cinolth roared.

Wrik grinned. "I like to call it where's Aria."

Smoke billowed from Cinolth's nostrils. "Release her, and I will make your death quick."

Wrik backed up a step. "Do us all a favor and die."

Cinolth's eyes narrowed. "Aria, it is time."

Aria's palm caught Wrik right under his jaw. She drove it up so hard that his teeth snapped together. Blood filled his mouth as pain erupted from the left side of his tongue. He staggered backward, dropping Aria in the process.

Gods, that hurt!

He spat a mouthful of blood, then looked down to grab Aria, but she'd already taken off running toward Cinolth. In her place roared a stream of fire. Wrik dove to the ground just as the column of fire whizzed past his head. He scrambled to his feet and teleported closer to Nardus and the others.

Nardus was on him in seconds. "What in *Ef Demd Dhä* did you just do?"

"Me?" Wrik pointed at Zerenity. "Her concoction failed." He spat and peppered the snow with crimson.

"Impossible," Zerenity said.

Nardus swiped his hand in front of himself. "Forget that. What did Cinolth say to you?"

"He said, 'Aria, it is time.'"

"Damn!" Nardus kicked the snow. "I think we played right into his hands."

"Stick to the plan," Wrik said. "I will make this right."

Or die trying.

† † †

As soon as King Forlin gave the command, Morcinda and the other äǝllf äkfeţik charged toward Aquis, a white dragon with blue-tipped wings. As they closed the distance, the beast grew in size, his girth matching that of Cinolth's.

Aquis crouched, then pummeled them with razor-sharp ice projectiles.

Morcinda squeezed the bracelet on her left wrist, activating her water shield. Swirling, translucent blue water created a barrier between her and the incoming projectiles, its extreme heat melting the ice before it reached her.

One of her clan hadn't been as quick as her, taking three projectiles in the chest. The forceful impact ripped him off his feet and threw him to the ground, and the freezing ice froze him in place before his blood had a chance to run.

The first of many deaths today.

She offered up a prayer for him and surged forward, her watersteel blade dragging in the snow at her side. Without a water source, the blade would act like ordinary steel, but the snow was enough to activate it, turning it from silver to a glowing, crystal blue.

A battle cry rose from deep within her chest and exploded from her lips as she deactivated her shield and lunged toward Aquis.

† † †

Ridan missed Bakkan with all her heart, but Normak's winged boots provided her with far greater agility. Unfortunately, they also came with a cost. She wore her usual armor and carried a spear without issue, but when she'd tried to carry a dwarven shield, it'd proved too heavy.

Torbrek had begged her to leave the boots behind and acquire another familiar, but it hadn't been an option. At some point she might think about it, but she wasn't ready to move on. Maybe she never would be.

She and the other dwarves surged forward, those with the best armor at the front. Zemeral, a green and brown nature dragon with leafy wings and vine-like appendages, stomped her foot and ushered a shrill roar, a sound Ridan would be okay never hearing again. The dragon reared her head back, then thrust it forward, her mouth agape.

Hundreds of needle-like thorns ripped through the air and thumped against the dwarven armor and shields.

None of her dwarven kin went down, but Torbrek's cousin Bremlok pulled one of the thorns from his neck.

"I'm fine," Bremlok shouted. "Hardly left a scratch." A moment later, he fell off the side of his mastiff familiar.

Ridan rushed over to him. The tiny puncture wound in his neck had already ballooned to the size of a cabbage. A greenish-yellow pus seeped from the wound and caused his skin to bubble. It smelled worse than raw sewage.

"Don't touch it!" Tharos shouted. "The poison becomes acidic the moment it comes into contact with blood. It will eat through everything."

Bremlok peered up at Ridan. "Please help me."

Torbrek snatched Ridan's spear out of her hand and drove it through the side of Bremlok's head. A final breath wheezed from Bremlok's lips, then his eyes turned to glass. Torbrek dislodged the spearhead and handed the spear back to Ridan.

He slapped her on the back. "Come on, let's make that leafy lizard pay."

† † †

For some reason, Aria couldn't remove the collar. She'd easily removed ones like it twice in the past. Because of it, she wasn't able to use her mezhik, and it concerned her. Although she'd grown up with a bow in her hand, and Karraar had taught her how to use melee weapons while they were in the wastelands, she hadn't been so pregnant. Or rather pregnant at all. Fighting around her large belly would be difficult at best. Nevertheless, she appropriated a curved weapon from one of the dead elves.

Aria reached out to Cinolth with her mind. *"Why can't I remove this collar?"*

Rage filled her head. *"Do not be such a foolish girl. Just stay alive, and I'll do the rest."*

Her collar glowed red, and she sensed a depletion of energy, but she hadn't tried to use her mezhik. Her mind returned to the Valley of Dragons. She'd been helpless that day, too.

Anger drove her through the snow and toward the beast. *"You're using me."*

"Stay back, and do what you're told, or we're both dead." Cinolth spewed

a column of fire at a blue dragon, charring its hide.

Aria set her jaw and headed straight for her father.

No one tells me what to do.

† † †

The heart locket dismantled Calen at a cellular level and pulled him into itself, the Shadow World fading from his vision. As the darkness settled in, his thoughts turned toward Centauria. Would the war still be raging, or had it ended months before? If it ended, who won? Would anyone be waiting for him in Summitto Valley? When he reassembled, would it be into a world he no longer recognized? In a few seconds, it would all be made known.

A faint light returned his vision as Centauria began to materialize before him. More clarity came with each moment, and it became obvious that the war hadn't ended. In fact, a battle ensued all around him.

A black, spiked tail whipped across the snow-covered ground and struck him. He screamed, but his mouth had yet to be formed. Bits of himself scattered.

ʔätūr, no!

Like an elastic band, his bits reached a certain distance, then came shooting back. The tail whipped around again, this time aimed at his torso. The transfer complete, he dropped to the ground. The air blew back his hair, narrowly missing his head.

He grabbed the hammer and rolled to his left, avoiding another strike. When he poked his head up, he saw that the dragon had its back to him, unaware of his presence. He crawled out of striking distance and pulled himself to his feet.

Calen looked around. "When did this become a war of dragons?"

"Who the gods are you?"

Calen turned and faced a hairless, large man with ebony skin. "Calen. Who are you?"

"The name's Wrik. I thought you were a lot younger."

"I was, right up until I wasn't."

"You mind helping me? I'm trying to recapture Aria." He pointed at an extremely pregnant woman with blonde hair. The blood-red streaks through it were unique.

Calen grabbed Wrik's arm and yanked him out of the way of a rogue ice ball. "Watch yourself."

Wrik nodded, then adjusted his spectacles. "Aria is the most dangerous foe on the battlefield, so be careful."

Calen eyed her. He'd heard her name mentioned many times. Nardus's daughter and Alderan's sister. He turned back to Wrik. "You said capture, right?"

"Yes."

Calen knelt and motioned Wrik to join him. "I have a plan."

† † †

Not ten yards in front of Alderan, the snow began to crack in a circular pattern. He took several steps back and nocked an arrow. Seven other spots did the same thing.

He turned to Rayah. "You seeing this?"

She nodded and zoomed into the air, two silver blades in her hands.

The patches of snow flipped up, and dozens of zhebəllin began crawling out of them.

Alderan shot six arrows in quick succession, each hitting their mark with deadly precision, but two more zhebəllin appeared for each of those he killed.

Rayah's blades flew through the air, each avoiding the zhebəllin blades and slicing into their throats.

"There are too many of them," Rayah shouted. Her blades returned to her hands.

Large dirt hands rose out of the ground and clapped together, crushing half a dozen of the zhebəllin. Alderan risked a backward glance and confirmed Master Qotan had joined them. Theyn tore through the middle of the group in a flash of tan fur, leaving a path of black ichor in her wake.

"Now, that's more like it!" Alderan conjured a fireball and blasted a hole right through the chests of three zhebəllin.

While Rayah's blades continued to carve through the zhebəllin, Master Qotan conjured an earth golem and set it loose. Zhebəllin bodies piled up quickly, but they kept coming, seemingly unfazed by their fallen brethren.

Ɂäṭūr, how many of them are there?

† † †

Zerenity's lips ceased to stop moving as she, Lanara, and Zelanora ran to face Slag, a massive earth dragon. Clods of mud covered his body like plates of armor and dripped from his outstretched wings. As they neared, she released her mezhik. Vines sprang up around the beast, ensnaring his legs and tying down his pancake-shaped tail.

Hopefully, that will hold him.

Slag roared. Globs of saliva dripped from his jowls and splattered on the ground, melting the snow and saturating the ground. He scooped up a large mouthful of earth and spewed it at her and the others.

Clumps of thick, sticky mud splattered Zerenity, weighing her down.

A large clump sent Zelanora to her knees.

Slag bit into the earth again.

Elros flew overhead and breathed lightning at Slag.

The strike didn't faze Slag, and he spewed gelatinous mud at Elros. The shot missed Elros's torso completely, but Zerenity quickly realized that wasn't what the beast had aimed for. Globs of mud coated Elros's wings. She fought to shake it from them, then crashed to the ground seconds later.

Slag busted out of the vines ensnaring him, then roared, "I will bury you all!"

Zelanora struggled to free herself from the mud. Zerenity conjured a vine and instructed it to pull Zelanora to safety.

Lanara looked to Zerenity. "We need another plan."

Zerenity conjured two green fireballs and shot them at Slag. One sailed wide, but the other struck him on his left side. The blast dried out the mud plate, cracking it. The shot seemed to stun him for a moment.

"Nice try," Slag roared. He licked the dried spot with a long, flat tongue, and the area healed itself, reverting back to mud.

Lanara smiled. "I think I know what to do."

Zelanora joined them, the lower half of her body caked with mud. "Elros needs help."

"Use fire to dry out the mud," Zerenity said. "Your mother and I will keep Slag busy."

Zelanora nodded and strode toward Elros.

Zerenity shot several more fireballs at Slag, then said, "What's your plan?"

Lanara set her jaw. "We set the mud on fire and turn him into a clay sculpture."

† † †

Rakzar ducked beneath one vine-like appendage only to be ensnared by two more. He swung his axes wildly, completely missing both of them as they wrapped around his ankles and pulled his feet out from beneath him. He cracked his head hard when he hit the snow-covered ground, and his vision blurred.

The appendages dragged him across the ground, separating him from his axes. Two more grabbed his wrists, and then the four of them began pulling him in four different directions. His strength matched theirs, creating a stalemate, but he feared he would be the one to give in first.

Urza had her hands full, too, her blades sharp but ineffective against the dastardly appendages.

Tharos continued to attack her with fire, but her appendages proved resistant.

If Rakzar managed to break free from Zemeral's clutches, he'd have to implement another strategy.

"Aargh!"

Rakzar looked to his left just as Torbrek severed the appendage wrapped around his left wrist, but then another appendage wrapped around Torbrek's throat and pulled him away.

Ridan flashed by and dropped one of Rakzar's axes in his hand. He hefted it across his body and hacked at the appendage holding his right arm until it released him. He made quick work of the two around his ankles, then charged after the one choking Torbrek.

"He's not dying on my watch!"

† † †

Savric kept an eye on the myriad of battles going on while maintaining the light shield. The triad proved to be quite useful, the drain on his mezhik virtually undetectable. As the battle raged, he began to see dozens of people gather around the outside of the light shield. Based on their pale skin and black veins, they were Cinolth's mind controlled.

He reached out to Nardus with his mind. *"The shield is doing its job, but Cinolth's army has arrived, including two more dragons. I fear they will eventually bring it down."*

Nardus responded, *"If you can keep it up long enough for us to kill Cinolth, then it may not matter."*

"I will do all I can."

Savric severed the link and dug his heels in. "This war will not be lost because of me."

Ƨätūr, make it so.

✝ ✝ ✝

Every time Morcinda and the others gained ground on Aquis, he seemed to find a way to drive them back. The snow powered their weapons, but not long enough to make them effective. What they needed was a bit of fire to melt the snow. Unfortunately, they'd managed to take their battle with Aquis a good distance from the others.

She reached out with her mind and found Savric. *"We need fire."*

"I cannot help you, but I will find someone who can."

Moments later, Nardus appeared in a whirlwind of snow. "You called for fire?"

"Our blades are useless without it," Morcinda said.

Nardus cleared the snow from a patch of grass, then set it on fire. It didn't take long for the surrounding snow to begin melting.

Morcinda dipped her head. "You've evened the field."

"Take advantage of it," he said, then teleported somewhere else.

Aquis fired boulders of ice across the valley floor, bombarding a group of elves, including her sister Noella and her father King Forlin. One boulder smashed into a shield right in front of King Forlin. A large chunk of it sheared off and hit King Forlin in the forehead. He dropped to the ground.

"Father!" Morcinda yelled.

Noella's voice entered her mind. *"Father's unconscious but breathing."*

Aquis roared with laughter. "Give up, you wretched elves. I've felled your king, and your pathetic weapons are useless against me. You'll never defeat me!"

Morcinda could do nothing to help her father, so she faced Aquis and dipped the tip of her watersteel sword into the newly formed pool of water. She stormed toward Aquis.

"You shouldn't have done that!"

† † †

Everywhere Nardus looked, his allies were falling. Something needed to change, or all would be lost. He set his sights on Cinolth and drew Brinzhär Dädh. The mighty sword sang and filled him with energy. He stalked toward Cinolth.

Naaroo, a black fire dragon with red markings across her belly and down the middle of her face, and Sheeva, a dark gray smoke dragon with ethereal wings, continued their coordinated attacks against Cinolth. Sheeva billowed toxic smoke all around Cinolth, and then Naaroo set the smoke on fire. If nothing else, they kept Cinolth distracted and wore him down.

Cinolth rose up on his hind legs and roared. Purple energy gathered between his palms, swirling and crackling. He clapped his hands together.

"Dear Ɂäṯūr!"

Purple lightning ripped across the sky and shot straight down and through Sheeva, using her like a lightning rod. Thunder shook the valley, and the ground split open beneath Sheeva, swallowing her charred body whole.

The entire battlefield fell silent, everyone stunned.

Cinolth beat his chest with his fist. "I am the king of this world! Bow to me, or face death."

Nardus spat, then charged forward.

I choose death.

† † †

"Aria!"

She turned and faced the man wielding a golden hammer. The wind billowed his shoulder-length hair. He wore clothing unlike any she'd ever seen. "Do I know you?"

"No, but you will soon enough. My name is Calen, and I'm here to save you."

Aria scoffed. "Save me?"

He drew closer. Almost within striking distance. "A battlefield is no place for a woman in your condition."

"And what condition is that?"

"You stand without purpose, your weapon dragging at your side. Your legs quake, and not from the cold. Plus, you're with child. One soon bound for this world from the looks of it."

None of his observations were lies. She hardly had the energy to stand, let alone brandish her weapon. Cinolth's demonstration had cost her much.

She circled Calen. "I will not go down easily."

He smiled. "Nor will I."

Aria knew in that moment that she had just one chance to take him down before her strength failed her. Without warning, she kicked her sword up and threw it at him. He batted it away with his hammer, giving her the opportunity she needed. She kicked him between the legs as hard as she could.

Calen gasped, dropped the hammer, and clutched his stomach. Fire blazed across his cheeks as he dropped to his knees.

Aria started to retrieve the sword, but then her eye caught something that couldn't possibly be there. Every muscle in her body went rigid, rooting her to the ground where she stood.

Alderan?

† † †

Wrik smiled to himself. Calen's plan to distract Aria had worked flawlessly. For certain, it hadn't gone quite the way Calen had described it. Nevertheless, Wrik grabbed her arm and stepped out of Summitto Valley and into the Great Library.

Aria didn't fight him. Didn't even look up at him when he shoved her into the glass containment chamber.

What the gods happened to her?

† † †

Morcinda had no idea how many of her clan had fallen and how many lay injured, but just seven of them remained standing, her sister one of them.

Noella grabbed her arm, pulling her to a stop. "Were you able to gather enough water into the blade?"

"There's only one way to know." She looked to the others. "Help me get close enough."

Tuular scowled. "I am the leader of our warriors."

"Then do your job," Morcinda growled. "Distract Aquis."

"Do as she says," Noella snapped.

Aquis pelted them with another round of ice shards. One caught Noella in the shoulder. Morcinda ripped it out before it could do further damage.

Noella winced, the spot already black with frostbite. "I'm alright."

Tuular and the others charged Aquis, striking at him with useless swords.

Aquis grabbed Tuular in his claws, lifted him up, and spewed liquid ice all over him. Then, Aquis threw Tuular to the ground, and Tuular shattered upon impact.

Morcinda sounded her battle cry and charged Aquis.

The dragon swiped at her with his claws, but she dove to the ground and slid underneath his hand.

Morcinda sprang to her feet and lunged at Aquis, her sword raised over her head.

Hitting Aquis square in the chest knocked the wind from Morcinda, but her sword met its mark. Thanks to the water, the sword buried itself all the way to its hilt. She hung on it and rode it to the ground as it flayed Aquis's chest.

Aquis roared. "You may have damaged me, but ice can be reformed."

Morcinda released the hilt and retreated.

Aquis trembled. He looked down at his chest. Water streamed from the gaping wound. "What have you done to me?"

Noella came to Morcinda's side and latched onto her arm. "Watersteel blades, when activated, will dehydrate anything they cut."

Aquis dropped to the ground, his legs reduced to puddles. Soon, the mighty dragon collapsed into his own puddle. The water sizzled. Steamed. Then, the dragon was no more.

† † †

Cinolth charged Nardus and swiped at his head. Nardus teleported beyond his reach.

"What have you done with her?" he roared.

Nardus smirked. "Sounds like you've lost your source of mezhik and energy."

Cinolth streamed a column of fire at Nardus, but it moved harmlessly around him thanks to the necklace Rakzar retrieved for him from the last battlefield.

Naaroo leapt onto Cinolth's back and sank her teeth into his shoulder. Her claws dug into the membranes of his wings. Cinolth tried to shake her off, but Naaroo wouldn't budge. Crimson ran down the front of Cinolth's shoulder, and he dropped to the ground.

Nardus approached the fallen beast. "You've grown weak, and your allies have begun to fall. You lost your life in this valley once before, and you'll do so again today."

"Never!" Cinolth closed his eyes, and smoke billowed from his nostrils.

Savric's voice entered Nardus's head. *"Cinolth must've released his control over his army."*

Cinolth roared as he returned to his feet. He whipped his head back and cracked heads with Naaroo. The blow caused Naaroo to slip off Cinolth's back, but she still hung onto his shoulder with her teeth. Cinolth twisted his body and flung Naaroo to the ground in front of him. He snatched her neck in his jaws and bit down, tearing her head from her body.

He spat her severed head aside. Blood dripped from his maw. "Today, you will meet your maker, Cyrus!"

Naaroo's body turned to ash and scattered in the wind, leaving the ground charred where she died.

"My name is Nardus, not Cyrus, and those of us who trust in Ӡäṭūr look forward to the day we see him face-to-face."

"I am your god!" Cinolth thundered.

"Alderan!"

† † †

No matter what they did, Ridan and the others couldn't get close enough to Zemeral to inflict damage. Her appendages proved formidable, and the poisonous darts deadly. Four of her clan had already died.

Tharos faced off with her, but neither of them could gain an advantage. Her skin resisted fire, and his scales repelled her poisonous darts. What they needed was some sort of distraction, and she had an idea.

Ridan and the others regrouped behind Tharos. "I don't know about the rest of ya, but I'm getting tired. Once she wears us down, we'll all be dead."

Rakzar growled. "What do you suggest we do?"

Ridan laid out her plan. "All of ya will attack her appendages, and I will attack her head."

"Isn't that what we've been doing?" Urza said.

"Yes, but not in a coordinated fashion. Ya must keep all of her appendages away from me for this to work."

"I don't like it," Torbrek said.

"Neither do I, but it's better than nothing," Ridan said.

Torbrek finally conceded, and he and the others moved into position.

"Go!" Ridan shouted.

She faced Zemeral, spear in hand, and waited for the right moment.

It took no time for the others to engage Zemeral's appendages.

Zemeral glared at Ridan. "Toss your spear all you want, but it will do you no good. Sooner or later, you will all die." She reared her head back, and opened her maw.

Ridan shot forward, her winged boots propelling her like the wind. She launched her spear just as Zemeral's head came forward. The spear flew true, burying itself in the back of Zemeral's throat, but it didn't stop her flurry of poisonous thorns. Ridan slid to the ground and covered her head, but she knew the thorns would hit their mark.

Zemeral coughed and choked.

Ridan waited several seconds, expecting the worst, but nothing hit her. She looked up and saw Tharos's wing protecting her.

Rising to her feet, she stood and watched Zemeral fight to dislodge the spear from the back of her throat. Tharos grabbed Zemeral by the throat and spewed fire into her mouth.

Zemeral coughed up black smoke, and then her entire body burst into flames. It took just moments to consume her, the inside of her body like kindling.

Tharos turned his head and winked at her. "Well done, young one."

Ridan dropped to the ground and lay back, exhausted.

† † †

Lanara remembered a picture book from when she was a little girl. The story revolved around a small girl no older than five who thwarted an evil dragon's plan by luring him into a pit of tar and setting it on fire. She had no tar to lure Slag into, but she didn't need it. The only thing she needed was for him to believe it.

Zerenity continued to launch fireballs at Slag, keeping him focused on healing himself instead of attacking. Thankfully, they'd drawn a dragon with far less intelligence than she thought possible.

Not far from her, Zelanora continued to work on healing Elros. She couldn't have been more proud of her daughter.

Lanara reached within herself, touched her mezhik, and began altering the battlefield. The mud pit surrounding Slag darkened to a nice black color, and its consistency would lend itself to the illusion.

"Back off," she said to Zerenity.

Zerenity retreated.

Slag looked down at the ground. "What is this? What have you done?" He tried to lift his front foot, but the thick tar held it in place.

Lanara glanced at Zerenity and smiled. "It's time to light him up and bake him."

"Wait," Slag said. "You can't do this."

"You chose your side, and now you'll pay the price."

She and Zerenity conjured fireballs and shot them into the tar. Smoke rose from the tar, and then the entire area around Slag burst into flames.

Slag roared as the fire climbed up his legs and turned his muddy scales to dirt. The fire quickly spread to his torso and traveled up his neck, turning his head into dirt. His muddy wings dried, then crashed down on top of him, turning him into a pile of dust.

Zerenity cheered, along with many others across the battlefield. Just one foe remained.

Cinolth.

† † †

Alderan stood with the wind at his back and measured the distance between him and Cinolth with his eyes. A quick calculation of wind speed helped him line up his shot.

Cinolth glared at him with defiance. "You fire that arrow, and it will be the last thing you do, boy."

"You're right," Alderan said. "Once I do, this war will be finished, and you'll be dead."

"Like your sister, you learn nothing. Your arrow cannot penetrate my scales, nor can your mezhik harm me. You've fought all day, and weariness grows in your bones, yet I remain strong."

"Take the shot, Alderan!" Nardus said.

Alderan drew in a breath and held it as he drew the string. Rakzar had told him about the target practice in Torbrek's armory, yet he still found it impossible to believe. How could a simple arrow shatter a substance harder than anything he'd ever encountered?

His heart slowed. Gaze focused on the spot where Cinolth's heart should be. He loosed the arrow.

Whoosh!

Six more arrows flew in succession.

Whoosh! Whoosh! Whoosh! Whoosh! Whoosh! Whoosh!

Cinolth snarled as the first arrow struck.

Shick!

"It actually worked."

Cinolth looked down at his chest just as the six other arrows shattered his scales and buried themselves in his hide.

Shick! Shick! Shick! Shick! Shick! Shick!

A perfect circle with one arrow at its center.

Cinolth roared and reached for his chest.

Alderan jerked his hand back, and the seven arrows ripped themselves back out of Cinolth's chest and flew back across the field and into Alderan's outstretched hand. Six of the arrows held nothing, but the seventh grasped a small grayish-white stone.

Blood ran down Cinolth's chest. He shook his head and roared, spewing fire in a wide arc.

Alderan held up the arrow with the stone. "We have it!"

"This must be some sort of illusion," Cinolth growled. He staggered forward and fell.

Nardus approached him. "The only illusion was your false power." He spat in Cinolth's face.

Alderan joined his father. "It is finished."

"I will never truly die." Cinolth exhaled one final breath, then his body caught fire. The flames consumed him in seconds, and his ashes blew into the wind and disintegrated.

Cheers erupted across the battlefield.

Alderan rubbed the back of his head. "I can't believe it's finally over."

Theyn tackled Nardus and kissed his face. "We did it!"

Rayah flew over, too, and fell into Alderan's arms. He held her, kissed her, and thanked Ɂäṱūr they'd made it out alive.

Nardus sat up. "Let me see his heart."

Alderan handed him the arrow that still clutched the stone. Nardus freed the stone and examined it.

"Damn!"

Alderan and the others who had gathered around all gasped. "What's wrong?" Alderan said.

"A piece of it is missing."

"You're certain?" Theyn said.

Nardus held the heart up. The hole at its center wasn't natural.

Alderan checked the other arrows again, but none of them grasped anything. "Where could it be?"

Nardus stood. "There's only one place I know of, and it explains a lot."

Alderan nodded, little doubt his guess would be wrong. "Aria."

"Yes, and you must get it back from her, but whatever you do, don't try to take it by force. She must give it to you willingly."

"I understand." Alderan dropped everything, then stepped out of Summitto Valley.

CHAPTER FIFTY-ONE

Aria lay on her back on a glass bench, her gaze fixed upon a massive crystal chandelier, but her mind focused on the illusion that recaptured her. She never should've fallen for such a cruel and devious trick, yet she had. She harbored no doubts as to Alderan's death, the horrific event forever burned into her memories. The fact that she felt nothing of the bond they once shared should've been enough for her to see through the illusion, but she wanted him alive more than just about anything. Her last conversation with him had ended poorly, yet he still sacrificed himself to save her even though he fought for the opposition. She wished she could have some of those moments back. Retract the harsh things she'd said to him.

It will never be.

Tears slid down her cheeks, some for Alderan and some of self-pity and loathing. Everything she'd accomplished sifted through her fingers, sandcastles destroyed by ocean waves. She closed her eyes and wept.

"He's dead."

Alderan's voice.

Waves of guilt pummeled her. "You think I don't know that?"

"Ah, right. Your bond with him. Is that why you're crying?"

"Why do you say *him* when I know you're referring to yourself?"

"Myself? I think you misunderstand, sister. Cinolth is dead, not me."

Aria's breath caught in her throat. Madness always started with irrational thoughts and delusions. She refused to have a conversation with her dead brother. Besides, what would he know of Cinolth?

She wiped her eyes and sat up. Alderan, or at least an apparition that looked like him, stood on the other side of the glass wall in front of her. "Auh!"

Aria squeezed her eyes shut. "I know you're not really there."

"I am, and I've come for the piece of heart."

Her pulse raced as she opened one eye just enough to see what shouldn't be there. "How do you know about that?"

"Once I removed Cinolth's heart, it was easy to see the missing piece." He held out his hand. "You need to give it to me."

Aria stood. Balled her fists and glared at the apparition. "You're not real," she growled. "Get out of my head."

The false Alderan glanced over his shoulder. "Gnaud, can you come over here for a minute?"

The furry little creature bounded over to Alderan and looked up at him. "Is there a problem?"

"Assure my sister that I'm not a figment of her imagination."

"Oh, my!" He turned and looked up at Aria. "Alderan is most certainly here."

Aria ignored the little creature and stared at Alderan. "You're dead, and that furball is most definitely a creature of my imagination."

"You can go back to whatever it was you were doing, Gnaud." Alderan ran his fingers through his hair and sighed. "How can I convince you that I'm really here?"

"I'm not even sure where *here* is, but the only way what you're saying is possible is if I'm dead, too."

"You're wrong." Alderan removed his cloak and started taking off his shirt.

Aria averted her eyes. "What are you doing?"

"Trying to help you understand how it's possible that I am who I say I am."

"By stripping?"

"I've only removed my shirt. Come over to the glass."

Aria sighed. "Fine, but you'll never convince me." She walked over to where Alderan stood, still uneasy about him being shirtless. The more she thought about it, the more ridiculous she realized it was. She'd seen her brother without a shirt many times in the past, and it had never bothered her, so why would it now? He was still her brother, figment or not.

She looked at him. His arms were covered in feathers from wrist to shoulder. "I don't understand. Why are your arms covered in feathers?"

"My legs are, too, but they're not actually feathers." He pulled his shirt back over his head. "Remember that day you came to see me in Wrik's bedchambers?"

Aria nodded. "It was the first time we'd seen each other for a long time. I thought you were dead."

"Right. We couldn't feel each other because you wore a ƹäbräƹär for a long time and then I did."

"Yes, but neither of us were actually dead. I saw you die and turn to ash on the battlefield after you saved my life from Wrik."

"I agree. That is what you saw, but that isn't what really happened."

Aria's eyes widened. "It was an illusion?"

"Yes, and no." Alderan pulled his shirt back on then slipped his arms into the sleeves of his cloak. "Anyway, before you walked into Wrik's bedchambers, I was thumbing through some stuff on his desk because I was bored. I knocked over some stuff, and a necklace with a feather fell out of one of the books. I slipped it on for a moment, and then couldn't get it back off because it had somehow burned itself into my skin. That feather necklace is what saved my life and what gave me the feathers on my arms and legs. After I got hit by Wrik's fireballs and thought I'd died, I woke up in another realm and walked out of a pit of fire."

Aria jerked upright. "You came to me in my dreams, didn't you?"

"Yeah. I didn't remember who I was until you said my name that night."

In a world controlled by mezhik, Aria couldn't deny that what he said could be true. Although she read as many books as she could, she still knew little about the possibilities of mezhik. Perhaps they were limitless.

Alderan held out his hand again. "You need to give me the piece of heart."

"What if I told you no?"

"I love you, Aria, and would do almost anything for you, but as long as it remains a part of you, you will never leave that containment chamber."

Anger burned within her. "You would do that to me? To my son? Force him to live in a glass cell his entire life?"

"That's not how it would work. He would be taken from you, and you'd never see him again. Is keeping the piece of heart worth that to you?"

"You can't make me choose!"

"It shouldn't be a choice. Cinolth has done nothing but use you. He still is."

The truth struck Aria in the face. How could anything be more important than her son?

It isn't.

She pressed herself against the glass. "Reach inside my chest and take it before I change my mind."

Alderan's hand reached through the glass and plunged into her chest. A part of her died the moment he pulled the piece out of her, and the presence within her mind she'd grown to depend on ceased to exist. After a few minutes, a fog she hadn't known existed began to lift, her thoughts becoming clearer.

Tears spilled down her cheeks as she stared at her brother. "I am sorry for everything."

Alderan frowned, then nodded. "I know you are, and I forgive you." Without another word, he turned, took a step, then vanished.

He forgives me…

† † †

Alderan stood in the valley, his heart pounding. Hatred emanated from the piece of heart he held in his hand. Never had he felt so much evil, nor had he ever felt as far from Ɂäʈūr as he did right then. It nearly overwhelmed him. He couldn't fathom how Aria had managed to live with it for so long without it driving her mad. It was no wonder she did so much evil.

Will she ever find a way to forgive herself?

Nardus held out his hand. "Give it to me."

Despite how wretched it made him feel, Alderan found it difficult to relinquish the piece of heart. How could one small shard of grayish-white stone wield so much power?

Nardus snatched the piece of heart from Alderan's hand. "You saw what this did to your sister. I won't allow it to corrupt your mind, too."

Alderan stepped back, a strong need to distance himself from it. "She cannot be held responsible for her actions."

"I'm sorry, son, but not every bad deed stemmed from the influence of Cinolth. She must be held accountable."

Ӡäṭūr, save her.

Nardus took the piece of heart and inserted it into the larger one. It fit perfectly and sealed itself. "We've got what we needed."

Alderan followed his father over to a large, flat rock. Calen stood next to it with a golden hammer resting on his shoulder. Alderan still couldn't get over how different Calen looked from when he'd left for the Shadow World. The pudgy boy returned a strapping man with bulging muscles and a full beard.

The others gathered around, and Nardus set Cinolth's heart on the flat rock. Calen offered him the hammer.

"You risked your life going to the Shadow World and returned with *Hemär Dhef Əllit.* The honor of destroying the heart is yours."

Alderan stared at the grayish-white stone. "Should we say something first?"

Rakzar spat on the stone. "Good riddance, you scaly bastard."

One by one, they spat on the stone and repeated Rakzar's words. Nardus was the last to spit on it.

"I've waited more than twelve-hundred years for this moment," he said. "My soul can finally rest easy knowing his will suffer forever in *Ef Demd Dhä.*" He spat again. "Good riddance, you scaly bastard."

Nardus stepped back and nodded to Calen. Calen took aim, lifted the hammer over his head, and roared as he slammed it down onto Cinolth's heart.

Boom!

The ground quaked, and a blinding light lit the night. Then, a concussive wave of energy exploded outward from the stone, knocking Alderan and everyone else to the ground, except Calen. He stood strong. When he lifted the hammer, nothing remained of Cinolth's heart. The flat rock cracked and broke into thousands of pieces.

Alderan got back to his feet and dusted off his cloak. "It is finished."

Everyone left in the valley cheered.

Nardus stood and proffered his hand to Calen. Calen took it. "Well done, son. Well done."

"Thanks," Calen said.

Alderan shook his head. "I still can't believe you lived in the Shadow World for ten years even though you were only gone here six months. Now, you're several years older than me. What happened?"

Calen shrugged. "It's a long story and one I'd rather not get into right now. Suffice it to say that it took me a long time to remember my purpose."

"Glad you did." Nardus squeezed Calen's shoulder. "Thanks to you, Cinolth will never threaten Centauria again."

Calen looked around. "This was a group effort, and I'm just glad I was able to contribute."

Alderan admired Calen's modesty. He looked to his father and the others. "What do we do now?"

Nardus eyed the valley and rubbed his left bicep. "We begin picking up the pieces."

CHAPTER FIFTY-TWO

Aria sat on a wide bench inside a transparent containment chamber somewhere deep within Galondu Castle, her belly swollen with pregnancy. Darius, her baby, wouldn't arrive for another two weeks, yet his fate and hers hung in the balance. Seven wizards, mages, and sorceresses, her father and brother among them, stood outside her prison. They would determine her fate. Darius's fate.

Ʒäţūr, don't make him suffer because of me.

Lanara Zaridus stood in the center of the seven, her arms crossed and brow furrowed. "Aria Rosai, you sit before this council to be sentenced for the war crimes and atrocities you committed against the people of the Ancient Realm. Do you understand this?"

Aria nodded, her pulse elevated. "I do."

"Very well." Lanara cleared her throat and continued, "This council has unanimously determined that you are a threat to society, a threat to the Ancient Realm, and a threat to all Centauria."

Aria's heart sank. She'd carried hope in her heart that the council would be lenient with her given that most of what she'd done had been while under the direct influence of Cinolth. Her father of all people should've understood the power Cinolth wielded.

But she said it was unanimous.

She lowered her head and held her belly with one hand. "I understand."

Earlier that day, her father, Nardus, had assured her that Darius would be looked after no matter the decision. At least she still had that to hold onto.

Lanara continued, "We did not come to this decision without thought or heated debate, all of us understanding the strenuous circumstances surrounding your actions. You must understand that we considered every last detail, going as far as to probe your memories in order to help us understand the reason behind many of your poor choices. As this did give us insight into your actions, it also highlighted an element of great concern. Mezhik intoxicates you. Triggers an emotional response unlike any we've seen before. You must also understand that this response, coupled with your mezhik abilities, poses a threat that cannot be overlooked. As such, you cannot be allowed freedom of any measure. Having said that, understanding this threat enabled us to set parameters by which we used to determine a suitable punishment. With this consideration, we came to the decision that you will be given a choice as to the punishment you will face."

A choice?

Based on the woman's inflection each time she mentioned punishment, Aria understood it to be a choice of how she would prefer to die. Her hands began to tremble. "And what choice do I have?"

Lanara glanced at her father. "Although I do not agree with it, you will be given three choices, each with their own positives and negatives. Your first option would be banishment to the Shadow World."

Aria had never heard of the Shadow World, but the name alone conjured fear within her. She held fast to her belly and fought to draw breath.

"The second option would banish you to *Räallm Kenzhärd Dhä*, and the third will keep you in Centauria within a containment field, much like the one you're in now, but on a larger scale."

Aria rose and walked over to the glass or whatever it was that her containment chamber was made of. "How can I make a choice between fates I do not understand?"

Lanara began to speak, but her father raised his hand, silencing her. "I am the only one on this council who has been to both *Räallm Kenzhärd Dhä* and the Shadow World. Therefore, I will explain what each is and the sacrifice you must make for each."

Aria nodded. "I'm listening."

"The Shadow World is just as it sounds. An entirely different world from ours that lies somewhere within the stars of the night sky. If you choose this path, you'll be free to live out your life there, but there are a few things you must consider. First, this other world distorts mezhik and yields unexpected and often harmful or fateful consequences. Second, you'll never be able to return to Centauria if you make this choice. Third, you will not be sent there until you've given birth. Once you have, you will be banished and never see your child again."

The air grew cold, and the walls inched toward Aria. She backed up until the backs of her knees met the bench. She sat down, her heart racing. "And *Räallm Kenzhärd Dhä*?"

Nardus rubbed his left bicep. "*Räallm Kenzhärd Dhä* is a place conjured by ancient mezhik. It was created to hold not just Cinolth's heart but also the bodies of Magus Carac and those who served him during the Great War. It is a harsh and violent place, designed to prevent anyone from ever escaping. If you choose this fate, you will be free to live your life there with your child, but you'll lose your mezhik and will never be able to leave. Nor will your child."

Aria wrapped her arms around herself and perched her feet on the edge of the bench, neither choice appealing. "And the containment field?"

Lanara spoke again, "This choice is not one I approved of. Nevertheless, I was outvoted. However, I demanded a stipulation of my own, so listen closely."

"Lanara is right," Nardus said. "The containment field will provide you with more freedom, but it will also cost you far more if you fail to meet the terms of which I will lay out. First, you will be placed within this containment field for the remainder of your days without hope of freedom. It will prevent you from venturing outside of its bounds. Second, you will be required to wear ɀäbräɀär. If removed, it will trigger not only your death but the death of your child. This requirement is the stipulation Lanara spoke of."

He eyed Lanara. "Let it be known that the remainder of this council did not approve of this decision but acquiesced with the knowledge that the containment field is by far the most lenient option. Third, and this is also very important, if you are caught practicing any form of mezhik, including that of rune or blood mezhik, refer to the punishment for removing ɀäbräɀär. Unlike the first two options, your child will be able to come and go as necessary, as will anyone who might want to visit you."

Lanara stepped forward and glared at Aria. "Your decision must be made now, or one will be made for you."

"Living without my child would be worse than death, so the Shadow World isn't an option. *Räallm Kenzhärd Dhä* would keep us together, but it would also punish him for my mistakes. Therefore, the only viable option you've given me is the containment field."

Lanara's eyes narrowed. "Be happy you've been given a choice at all. If it were up to me, your head would be taken from your shoulders and your child would die in your womb."

"Enough, Lanara." Nardus walked up to the containment cell and smiled. "You've made a wise decision, Aria, but you must never forget the consequences of removing ʑäbräʑär." He retrieved a brass-colored collar from within his robes and stared at it. "It pains me to do this to you."

She stood, walked over to the translucent wall, and placed her hands against it. "You've given me far more than I deserve."

His left hand penetrated the wall and touched her right one. "Are you certain of your decision? It cannot be undone, not even by me."

Tears filled her eyes. "Yes, Father."

He nodded, then slipped the collar around her neck before removing the silver one she wore. "It is finished. You will remain here until we've conjured the containment field."

The others began to walk away, Alderan included. He hadn't said a single word the entire time, nor had he looked at her. After what had happened with the shard of Cinolth's heart, she could hardly blame him. She prayed that ʑäʈūr would heal the wounds she'd caused him.

Nardus turned to leave.

"Father, wait."

He sighed and glanced over his shoulder. "Everything that could be said has been for now. I will return for you."

She leaned her forehead against the containment chamber wall. "And what of Wizard Wrik's fate? What will happen to him?"

"He will remain here at Galondu Castle."

"Imprisoned?"

He turned back, his brow furrowed. "Of course not. He will take over as lord of this castle."

"What?" Aria staggered backward. "I don't understand. I've accepted my fate, but why should he go free? He's the one who orchestrated everything."

Nardus frowned. "What are you talking about?"

"He told Pravus about the prophecy of the twins and how it could be fulfilled. Gave him the location of *Ūrdär Dhef 2äfn Dhä*, where you were in stasis. I thought you knew that."

Nardus shook, his face a shade of red. "I'm going to kill that bastard!"

† † †

Nardus stormed through Galondu Castle, enraged. Once he located Wrik, he would rip him apart with his bare hands. He'd grown to trust the man and considered him a friend, but now he knew the truth. Wrik was the one responsible for all the pain he'd suffered.

How could I not see it?

Alderan jogged toward him. "Father!"

"Not now," he growled.

Alderan came along side Nardus and kept pace with him. "I heard what Aria told you about Wizard Wrik."

"Then you also understand why I must kill him."

"No, I don't."

Nardus halted, his rage simmering just beneath the surface. "He's responsible for both your mother's death and for your little sister's, not to mention the others in *Ūrdär Dhef 2äfn Dhä*."

"Maybe so, but if it wasn't for him, I wouldn't exist. Neither would Aria. In fact, you'd still be asleep in some strange chamber, squandering the life 2äţūr gave you."

"Squandering!" Nardus balled his fists and charged down the corridor. "You know nothing."

† † †

Alderan knew of just a few places Wizard Wrik might be. The first was Wizard Wrik's bedchambers, but he found them empty. Pravus's library and the war room were empty as well, leaving him with two places to check. Technically, he could check just one of them since he had no idea where Wizard Wrik's secret room was located or how to get into it even if he found it.

In a single step, he teleported from the castle corridors up to the northern ramparts, where the nítfinzh were kept. Sure enough, Wizard Wrik was in the middle of feeding them. Alderan would've waited for Wizard Wrik to finish, but he had no idea how long it would be before his father located Wizard Wrik.

"You need to leave," Alderan said.

Wizard Wrik tossed a chunk of raw meat toward Blackwind. She snatched it out of the air and swallowed it whole. He turned around, his broad smile genuine. "And why would I do that?"

"My father knows what you did. He knows everything."

Wizard Wrik's smile faded. "Knows everything about what?"

"Pravus. The prophecy. Everything."

"Gods…"

"Like I said, you need to leave."

Wizard Wrik shook his head. "No."

Stubborn oaf!

"What do you mean, no? Don't you get it? He will kill you."

"It's a risk I must take." He pulled a silver collar out of a pocket within his robes and offered it to Alderan. "Put it on me before I change my mind."

"Your life is in danger, and you want me to cripple you?"

"If your father is adamant about taking my life, he will succeed. Having the use of my mezhik would only prolong the inevitable."

"You're out of your mind." Alderan took the zäbräzär and shoved it onto Wizard Wrik's neck.

Wizard Wrik reached up and tugged on the collar. It remained in place. "Good." He took a deep breath. "Take me to your father."

Slaughter's more like it.

† † †

Nardus stood in the middle of the Hall of Dragons, his rage still unchecked. Given the size of Galondu Castle, Wrik could hide from him indefinitely without ever setting foot outside its walls. Plus, Wrik had the advantage of living there for several decades and understood the secrets of its halls and corridors.

He conjured a fireball and launched it at the nearest dragon sculpture.

The green and brown dragon fizzled and smoked as the fire consumed it. Several more fireballs and felled dragons later, Nardus's rage began to wane.

"There you are," Alderan said.

Nardus turned around to see Wrik standing at Alderan's side. The large man dwarfed Alderan and made him look like a young boy next to him. Anger began to swell in his chest once again.

Nardus stalked forward, his hands crackling with mezhik. "Step aside, son."

Alderan stepped in front of Wrik. "I won't let you kill him."

"You can't stop me."

"You'd hurt me just to end his life?"

Nardus halted. Shook his head. "That's not what I said. I would never do anything to harm you or your sister."

"Don't you understand? Wrik's my friend. Yes, he's made mistakes, and he's willing to face the consequences for them, but those consequences shouldn't include dying."

"Countless lives have been destroyed because of him, and you don't think he deserves to die?"

"We fight to preserve life, Father, not destroy it. Kill him, and you're no different than Pravus, Magus, or anyone else."

"He killed your mother!"

"No, he didn't."

Wrik stepped around Alderan. "Allow me to explain myself. Once I've finished, I'll allow you to determine my fate."

"Talking will only prolong your death."

"So be it." Wrik adjusted his spectacles. "As you know, I'm a man of prophecy and history. Both fascinate and drive me, sometimes beyond rational thought. When I read the prophecy about the twins, I couldn't stop thinking about it. After a few days, it consumed my thoughts as though it were alive. From that moment forward, I spent every waking hour researching everything about the Great War and the unfulfilled prophecies. Then, I met Pravus. He told me about his father and how he dreamed of restoring Galondu Castle and his father's kingdom. Hearing it made me think harder about the prophecy. Eventually, I couldn't contain all the knowledge within my head and needed someone to confide in about what I'd discovered. Pravus was the only one I knew who would understand, so I told him everything. I never thought he would act on the knowledge I gave him, or at least that's what I told myself. But like I said, I'm driven by prophecy. Once I knew his plan, I couldn't stop him. Didn't want to stop him. I wanted to experience the prophecy as it unfolded. How many people would ever have that chance? To watch the paths of prophecy open and be fulfilled?"

Nardus seethed. "So you helped him locate *Ūrdär Dhef 2äfn Dhä* and murdered all but Ilia and me."

"I had nothing to do with that. In fact, I didn't know what he'd done until it was too late. He was supposed to wake you and Ilia and leave the others alone, but the power went to his head. He threatened to kill me if I interfered with his plans. Knew things about me that kept me from doing anything but watch."

"What could he possibly hold over you?"

"Noella."

"King Forlin's daughter?"

"Yes." Wrik sighed. "He threatened to expose our relationship. If he had, King Forlin would've killed me and banished her."

"Why should I believe you? Why should I believe any of it?" Nardus sliced the air with his hands.

"Because it's the truth." He pointed to the silver collar around his neck. "I had Alderan put this on me and asked him to bring me to you even though he warned me that you wanted to kill me. I could've run, but I didn't."

"You should have."

"I'm tired of hiding behind lies and refuse to live my life with one eye always at my back." Wrik stepped forward and knelt in front of Nardus. "My life is in your hands. Do with it as you choose."

Alderan crossed his arms. "Kill him, and I will never speak to you again, nor will Aria."

Why does he still defend the man?

Nardus scowled at Alderan. "Why would Aria care? She's the one who gave him up."

"Yes, but not for the reason you think."

Nardus left Wrik on his knees and approached Alderan. "Enlighten me."

† † †

Qotan stood in front of the small cottage and sized it up. He'd never been asked to move an object of its size before and didn't know if it would even be possible, but his brother stood next to him, exuding enough confidence for them both.

"You need only think about moving the dirt and not the house," Savric said.

"Yes, of course. A simple task for someone of exceptional skill." Qotan scratched his head. "So, how did my name come up?"

Savric chuckled. "Brother, you are the most exceptional of the exceptional. After all, you once moved an entire cave. A small house should be no feat at all."

"I fear your faculties have indeed begun to slip. As I remember it, it was you who misplaced the cave. I merely located it."

"I assure you that my faculties are still intact. I checked up on them earlier this morning. In truth, you are far too modest."

"Untrue." Qotan grinned. "I rarely stay clothed when I visit the bathhouse in Tyrosha."

The two of them chuckled.

Zerenity sighed. "Listening to the two of you banter as though you sit in the comfort of your own home in front of a blazing fire truly warms my soul, but it does nothing to fight off the biting wind. In light of this fact and the fact that the two of you will stand there forever, I say we begin the process before we run out of daylight."

Qotan ribbed Savric. "I have become privy to the fact that you and she fail to practice modesty, even when children are present."

Savric's cheeks turned several shades redder than they already were. "She is a seductress and refuses to keep her hands where they belong."

"Guilty as charged." She reached over and squeezed Savric's buttocks. He yelped and staggered forward several steps.

Savric whipped around and glared at her. "Feathers, woman!"

"Keep moving, Savvy, or you'll truly understand the meaning of embarrassment." She winked at Qotan, and he chuckled.

"You will rue the day." Savric stomped off.

"Quite the performance, if I do say so." Qotan cracked his knuckles and rolled his shoulders. Then, he held his arms out in front of himself. "But I reign supreme when it comes to theatrics."

Qotan reached out with his mezhik, pouring it into the ground. At first, nothing happened, but then the ground began to vibrate. The vibrations built into a crescendo and then the ground split open all around Alderan's cottage. Sweat ran down the sides of Qotan's face as he concentrated his mezhik on the soil beneath the cottage. Inch by inch, the cottage began to rise until it sat atop several feet of dirt. The effort left Qotan winded, and it was just the first part of the move.

How will I survive the rest?

Savric appeared next to Qotan and clasped his shoulder. "Valiant effort, brother. Now comes the hard part."

"Indeed."

He handed Qotan's staff to him. "I believe this will come in handy at some juncture during the move."

"Indeed," Qotan said, still winded.

"You will find a sufficient amount of mezhik stored within it to ease the move."

Qotan raised an eyebrow. "Will I? Pray tell."

"Rest assured that it was not I who contributed mezhik to your staff but Alderan and Nardus. I merely offered the suggestion."

"You are wise beyond your years, brother. One day, I hope to attain such wisdom."

Savric stroked his beard. "Alas, it is fleeting."

"Are you ready for the move?" Zerenity said.

Qotan took a deep breath, then nodded. "You move the vegetation out of its path, and I will guide the house to its final resting place."

Green tendrils of mezhik slithered around Zerenity's fingertips. "Ready when you are, old man."

Qotan gruffed, then dug his feet into the ground. "If I am old, what does that make you?"

"Far wiser." She laughed as she rounded the cottage and headed toward the forest.

With the added power of his staff, Qotan poured mezhik into the ground once again. The cottage groaned. Shook. Then jolted backward. Slowly, the cottage began to crawl across the soil. Or at least that's what it looked like. In reality, Qotan continuously shifted the soil beneath the cottage, creating a wave for the cottage to surf across. Once the house neared the dense forest, Zerenity did her part, coaxing the trees and bushes to pull up root and make way for the cottage to pass through. The process worked without a hitch, the cottage arriving at the cliff edge about four hours later.

Qotan made a few final adjustments, orienting the front of the house toward the Gelu Ocean. Once finished, he plopped down on the ground, exhausted.

Savric knelt next to him. "Brother, you have outdone yourself once again."

Qotan nodded, unable to form words between heaves of ragged breath.

Zerenity plopped down next to Qotan. "And I?"

Savric smiled. "You as well, Reni."

Zerenity leaned against Qotan. "She will love it here."

"Indeed," Qotan managed.

Savric stroked his beard. "And what shall be done with the basement entrance that we just left exposed?"

Zerenity tapped her chin. "I believe a large stone with an inscription recognizing what once used to be Viscus D'Silva would serve as a proper cap."

"Indeed." Savric rubbed his hands together. "Let us go and make it so."

† † †

Rayah, Alderan, Nardus, and Theyn stood on the beach at the bottom of the cliff, all admiring the beautiful aethershard crystal. It sparkled in the sunlight, sending out prisms of red light across the beach. Soon, it would be buried forty feet beneath the sand.

Nardus rubbed his left bicep. "You're certain you can handle this?"

Rayah rolled her eyes. "I'm a soil dryte. It's kinda what I do."

"I know, but forty feet is a long way down, especially given the proximity to the ocean. Plus, the crystal is almost as big as you are."

Alderan took her hand. "He's right, Rayah. The soil will be extremely wet."

What did she need to say to convince them? Yeah, she appreciated their concern, but it was just sand. Nothing more.

"I promise I'll be okay." She kissed Alderan's cheek, then wrapped her arms around the crystal. "Be back in five."

Rayah beat her wings, took to the air with the crystal, then dove straight into the sandy beach. Several feet down, the sand became wet. At twenty feet, she realized just how heavy it had become. By the time she reached the forty-foot mark, the pressure of the sand had become insufferable. She placed the crystal where it needed to go, then turned around, but the water-saturated sand held onto her like tar.

The water created another issue she hadn't anticipated. It made breathing difficult, each breath allowing a small amount of water into her lungs. If she didn't work her way out of the sand soon, she'd wind up drowning.

Ƨäṭūr, grant me the strength to free myself.

† † †

Alderan kept an eye on the sun and tracked the time in his mind. With every passing minute, he became more concerned for Rayah.

He held his head. "She should've been back ten minutes ago."

"She'll be alright," Theyn said. "She can breathe just fine in the dirt, right?"

"Yeah. No. I mean I don't know. Most of the dirt she travels through is far above sea level." He sank to his knees and grabbed fistfuls of sand. "I shouldn't have let her go."

"Have faith in her, son." His voice betrayed the confidence of his words.

"I—"

"Alderan!"

Alderan's heart stopped the moment he heard Rayah cry out his name in his mind.

"Something's wrong!" He frantically clawed at the sand.

"Qotan!" Nardus shouted.

Sand spiraled into the air as Qotan, Savric, and Zerenity all appeared on the beach at once.

"I can't breathe."

Tears filled Alderan's eyes as he continued to shovel sand with his hands. "She's calling to me."

Nardus grabbed Alderan and pulled him back. Alderan struggled to break free.

"What are you doing!"

"Talk to her. Reassure her. Qotan and I will do the rest."

Alderan relaxed and nodded. He closed his eyes and reached out to Rayah with his mind. *"I'm here, my love. We're working as fast as we can to dig you out, but you need to hold on just a bit longer, understand?"*

"I'm so sorry. I should've listened to you and your father. I'm sorry."

"It's okay. Just keep talking, alright?"

Rayah dldn't respond.

"Rayah? Answer me!" Alderan beat the ground with his fists. *"Rayah!"*

† † †

Sand and water sprayed everywhere as Nardus and Qotan worked to tunnel down into the ground. Nardus created a vortex of wind to hold back the walls of sand while Qotan drilled ever deeper. Just past twenty feet, Qotan collapsed.

Nardus struggled against the weight of the sand, the effort to keep it from filling the hole back in far more taxing than he'd ever imagined.

Zerenity knelt close to the hole. Tendrils of green mezhik seeped into the sand. At first, Nardus didn't understand what she was attempting, but then he saw the entanglement of vines crawling down the sides of the hole. The farther they reached, the less effort it took for him to hold the sand back.

"Alderan!" Nardus said.

"She isn't responding!"

"Forget about that right now. I need your help."

"To do what?"

"You're an extraordinary young man. I've seen it firsthand and have also heard tales of what you can do."

"None of that matters. My mind refuses to think of anything but her."

"Use it to your advantage. We've managed to dig down twenty feet. You need to do the rest."

"How?"

"I don't know, but I believe in you."

"So do I," Theyn said. "Rayah does, too."

"You can do it," Zerenity said.

Savric added, "Save her, my boy."

† † †

Alderan stood. Raised his head toward the sky and spread his arms wide. *Ɂätūr, guide me.*

He closed his eyes and reached within himself, to the core of his mezhik, and poured everything he had into the sand as he reached out to Rayah with his mind. *"You are my life, Rayah. I will not live it without you."*

Within the confines of his mind, Alderan pictured Rayah deep in the sand. He directed his mezhik to that spot and could feel her as though his hands touched her. He reached out and wrapped her tight in his arms, and then lifted her toward him.

Alderan grunted and dropped to his knees as he struggled against the overwhelming weight.

Ɂätūr, give me strength.

He pulled so hard that his head began to spin, but he couldn't give up. He would never give up on her. Would rather die on the beach.

"I see something!" Theyn said.

The weight suddenly fell away, and Alderan flew onto his back. It knocked the wind from his lungs. Or rather something had. When he opened his eyes, he saw her there in his arms. She didn't move. Didn't breathe.

Alderan wept.

† † †

Savric pulled Rayah from Alderan's arms and lay her on the sand. He turned her head to the side and began compressing her chest. As he did, memories of her flooded his mind. He'd always thought of her as his granddaughter and wondered if she'd thought of him as her grandfather. It was a strange thought, given the circumstances, but it kept circling his mind as he worked to revive her.

"You need to start her heart, brother. Give her the familiar old zap."

Qotan was right. Why hadn't he thought of it himself?

He touched his mezhik, called it to his fingertips, and pressed his hands against Rayah's chest. He pulsed her with light energy, but not enough to kill her. The jolt did nothing.

A little more, perhaps?

He did it several more times, each time increasing the amount of mezhik he used, but she remained still.

"Give her everything," Qotan said.

Again, Qotan was right. He'd been afraid of harming her, but the alternative would be to let her die or stay dead. Either way, it was her only hope of revival.

Ɂäʈūr, bring her back to us.

Savric touched Rayah once more and gave it his full power. Rayah arched up, then lay still.

He looked up at Qotan and shook his head, but then Rayah stirred and coughed up water.

Praise you, Ɂäʈūr!

† † †

A week later, Nardus stood on the edge of the cliff outside the small cottage, admiring the majestic view of the Gelu Ocean as the sun began to rise in the west. Aria would arrive that afternoon, and every last detail both inside the cottage and of the surrounding area had been meticulously planned out and executed. No doubt remained in his mind as to whether or not she would feel at home here. From the placement of the cottage to the garden Zerenity started behind it to the stairway carved into the side of the cliff that led down to the beach, it was perfect.

He gazed toward the sky. At just the right angle and with proper lighting, the containment field's transparent surface glistened with a rainbow of colors. It reminded him of a soap bubble, not just because of its rainbow effect but also because of its spherical shape. The field stretched three-quarters of a mile in every direction, the cottage its center and anchor point. The red aethershard crystal Rayah buried beneath the beach would keep the containment field active indefinitely, its power limitless.

Unlike a solid barrier, the containment field would allow the elements and nature to pass through it as though it didn't exist, whether it be the ocean waves, rain, snow, wind, or the occasional animals and birds. Only those names written into the aethershard's memory would be confined within the field. Aria's name had already been added. Once she stepped inside the containment field that afternoon, she would never be able to leave.

It is the only way.

† † †

Aria held her belly as she waddled down one of many corridors in Galondu Castle. She lacked the gift of prophecy, yet she knew in her heart that she carried a son in her womb. She expected him to arrive in another week and couldn't wait to finally meet him and hold him. Doing so would help keep her strong, both mentally and physically.

She couldn't help but smile as Alderan escorted her down a final flight of stairs before heading toward the courtyard and castle gates. No matter how many times she heard the tale and mulled it over in her mind, she still didn't understand how he literally rose from the ashes of death. He certainly wasn't the timid young man she remembered seeing in Wrik's bedchambers the previous winter. Somehow, his death had awakened a lion within him and put him in touch with his mezhik in a miraculous way.

"I'm proud of you," she said.

He ushered her through the castle gates. "For what?"

"Becoming the man that Gretchen and Red always knew you'd be."

"Well, I'm proud of you, too."

A lump rose in Aria's throat. "You shouldn't be. I killed many people and nearly destroyed the realm."

"I know, but you owned up to it and repented. Many never would have."

"I'm not sure I had a choice."

He took her arm as they walked. "Everyone has a choice."

Alderan led them around the north side of the castle and over toward the massive gateway. Seeing it again reminded her of all the evil acts she committed during its construction. In a way, that part of her life felt like it had been lived by someone else. She'd been so innocent growing up and trusted Ʒaţūr with all her heart, but the night Karraar beheaded Red right in front of her changed her. It wasn't an immediate change, but the events that followed led her down a path that made her susceptible to Pravus's charms and a lust for power. Looking back, it sickened her.

I became the villain of the story.

Tears filled her eyes, and she let them run their course, blurring her vision. Once the guilt passed, or at least returned from a flareup to a simmer, she wiped her eyes.

Forgive me, Ɂät̪ūr.

On the other side of the gateway stood a majestic beast. Silver with black splotches and beautiful wings. Unlike Cinolth, she stood just eight feet tall at the peak of her back and wasn't covered in hardened scales but smooth reptilian skin. Her eyes were unlike any Aria had ever seen, black holes ringed in sapphire. They exuded kindness.

"This Is Elros The Thunderer," Alderan said. "She will take us to our destination."

My prison.

Aria chided herself. If she thought of her new home as a prison, she'd never be happy. Her son deserved better from her.

"I am Aria Rosai. It's a pleasure to meet you."

Elros dipped her head. "The pleasure is mine." She eyed Aria's swollen belly. "He will come soon. We must hurry."

Aria looked down at herself and smiled. "He is ready."

Alderan helped Aria climb onto Elros's back, and then he climbed on in front of her. He glanced over his shoulder and grinned. "Hold on to my waist, and don't let go."

Aria scoffed. "I know how to ride a dragon, little brother."

He shook his head. "You've never ridden a dragon like Elros. Plus, you've no mezhik to help balance yourself."

Aria sighed and wrapped her arms around his waist as best she could. The boulder in her belly made the reach difficult. "How far do we have to go?"

"About three hours."

Aria's mind immediately began calculating all the possible destinations, but there were far too many given their centralized location outside Duos

Flumen. Once Elros took to the sky, she would have a better idea.

"I'm ready," she said.

Elros crouched down, spread her wings wide, and leapt into the air as she beat her wings furiously. The strange sensation sent Aria's stomach into her throat. She held Alderan tighter, the experience nothing like any she had with Cinolth.

Within seconds, Aria knew their destination, and it scared her. How would she be able to live in a house where she would constantly be reminded of Red's death every time she looked out the window?

Alderan must've sensed her apprehension, his hand reaching back and touching her leg. "Trust me. It's not what you think."

She took a deep breath and nodded. "I do."

Trivers Lake, Vallah, The King's Palace, and the Orbis Mountains came and went as they continued north. For a while, she could see nothing below them but the Reis'Duron Grasslands and what looked like a small stream. She knew the stream to be that of the Hotah River, a mile wide for a good portion of its length.

"This is—" A sharp pain in her stomach paralyzed her. Then, she felt like she peed herself, a warmth spreading down her legs.

Ʒäțūr, this can't be happening right now!

Pain pulsed through her abdomen with increasing intensity and frequency.

A foreign presence entered her mind. *"Hang on, Aria. It won't be much longer now."*

"Elros?"

"Yes. I'm flying as fast as my wings will allow."

Alderan glanced over his shoulder. "Did—did you just pee on me?"

"No, you oaf! My water broke."

The blood drained from Alderan's face. "I mean... you can't... we're not..." he stammered.

"I don't have a choice in this." Pain wracked her. "The baby's coming!"

"Elros, we need to land!" Alderan said.

Aria screamed. She tried not to push, but it just happened.

"I will fly as steady as I can, but there's no place for me to land."

"She can't land," Aria said in between horrific pangs. "You're going to have to turn around and deliver your nephew."

"I know nothing about delivering babies!"

Aria groaned. "Neither do I, but we have no choice."

Aria slid back a foot, and Alderan turned himself around. His pale face had a green tint to it. If they survived this, it would be a family tale for generations.

Aria leaned back and braced herself on Elros's sides. Pain stabbed her again and again.

Alderan just sat there, his eyes bulging. "What do I do?"

Aria gathered up her dress with one hand. "You need to remove my underwear."

Alderan closed his eyes. "Okay, but I can't watch."

† † †

Nardus pointed toward the southern sky. "I see Elros." He cocked his head, his mind confused by what his eyes saw. "Why is Alderan riding backward?"

Qotan stroked his chin. "A peculiar sight, indeed."

Savric joined them. "What is all the fuss about?"

Qotan eyed Savric and shook his head. "The sky. The dragon. Alderan riding backward. Honestly, brother, you must get yourself new spectacles."

Elros circled the cottage, gradually descending with each pass.

"Why doesn't she just land like usual?" Theyn said.

"Something must be wrong!" Rayah shot into the sky, her wings fluttering at her back.

"Or something's just right." All of them glanced over at Zerenity.

Savric huffed. "And what do you know of it, woman?"

Nardus watched Rayah fly alongside Elros as they circled for a final landing. Alderan handed Rayah a wadded-up cloak, and then Elros landed with a thud ten yards from the cottage and lay on the ground. Blood ran down her sides, and Aria lay atop her as Alderan slid off her back and to the ground.

Ɂäṭūr, no!

Nardus ran toward them, his heart pounding and stomach in his throat.

"What happened?" he shouted.

Alderan reached up and pulled Aria into his arms. Blood covered them both. Nardus saw Aria's chest rise and fall when Alderan turned around.

She's still alive.

Alderan smiled. "She was right, you know."

The strange comment confused Nardus. "Right about what?"

"It's a boy."

Nardus look up to see Rayah hovering in the air, her face beaming as she stared at the wadded-up cloak in her arms. Realization hit, and Nardus breathed a sigh of relief. "It's a boy."

Rayah fluttered to the ground and handed the bundle to Nardus. "Meet Darius, your grandson."

CHAPTER FIFTY-THREE

Lanara stood atop the King's Palace, Zelanora at her side. With the illusion spell removed, much of the palace and most of Vallah still lay in ruins. The streets and roads had been cleared of debris and the demolished buildings hauled off, but the road ahead would be long and arduous, especially if the people refused to accept a ruler born with mezhik.

Fifty days had passed since Cinolth breathed his final breath, yet the scars he inflicted upon the realm would last years. Some would never fade. It saddened Lanara to think about it.

"Where do we begin in order to bring the people back together?" Zelanora said.

Lanara took in the majestic view of the Orbis Mountains and Trivers Lake. Although content, she still found it difficult to accept the way she'd come to reside in the Three Kingdoms once again. The loss of Pius moved her very little, but knowing she'd never see Rictar again pained her without end. How she wished she'd had one more day with him.

She turned toward her daughter. A talented, beautiful, young woman. Many of the people adored her. But how many still would if they knew the power she wielded? Eventually, the entire realm would know the truth. Zelanora was her daughter in every way.

Lanara said, "First, we must reach the people. Connect with them. I believe celebrating freedom will help start the process of healing. I've arranged for several carts to traverse the main street and hand out free bread and ale."

"It's a start, but I was thinking more about the fissure between us and the people. Thanks to my father, most of them have grown to hate mezhik and those who wield it."

Lanara placed her hand over Zelanora's and smiled. "Only time and good deeds will change their minds about us and those like us."

"Agreed, so where do we begin?"

Lanara led them over to two chairs, and they sat down. "With the assistance of Zerenity, Savric, Qotan, and others like them, we help rebuild their homes, restore their lands, and establish a system of rule once more."

Zelanora sighed. "All good ideas, but I fear they will never bow to a queen who wields mezhik."

"A queen?" Lanara laughed. "I shall not rule this kingdom, nor shall you."

Zelanora frowned. "I don't understand. You are their queen."

"No, my dear. I was once." She pulled her hair back into a ponytail and tied it together with a length of blue ribbon she fished from her pocket. "When your father and brother died, the throne passed down to you. However, you are not the true heir."

Zelanora gasped. "I have another brother?"

Lanara laughed again. "Certainly not. At least not unless your father had a bastard son."

"I'm positive father never moved on after your death—or rather your false death."

"Despite his shortcomings and unwavering rules against those with mezhik, I still believe he loved me."

"He always spoke well of you."

Lanara smiled. "It makes me happy to hear you say that."

"So, if I'm not the true heir of the Three Kingdoms, then who is?"

"Cyrus Nithik. He is the last remaining heir of King Ordin's family."

"He doesn't go by that name anymore."

"Perhaps not, but that has little to do with the fact of him being the true heir."

Zelanora chewed on her lower lip. "Remind me of who King Ordin was."

"He ruled the Three Kingdoms and the Ancient Realm before the Great War and stood opposed to Magus Carac. His family was the first to rule over the realm, and by blood and birthright should've continued to rule through the ages. Cyrus is the last of the bloodline."

"I may not know much about Nardus, but I'm certain he will never accept."

"I agree, but I've set a plan in motion that might change his mind. Sway him toward our way of thinking. While you've been away, I've met with several leaders of the mid and upper races. Come, and you will understand everything."

Lanara led Zelanora over to the railing. Several small crowds of people had already gathered below, and many more were making their way toward the twisted and broken city gates. Within the hour, the streets churned with people and the air carried with it many conversations.

Upon her signal, a man who stood outside the King's Palace below blew a ram's horn. The sound blasted the Three Kingdoms for more than a minute, echoing off the lake and the surrounding mountains. The people fell silent, their attention drawn toward the King's Palace.

It begins.

Lanara gathered her voice and addressed the crowd. "Citizens of the Three Kingdoms, the Ancient Realm, and all of Centauria, welcome to the celebration of freedom!"

Far below, on the northern shore of Trivers Lake stood a wooden replica of Cinolth The Dark, nearly forty feet tall. A fireball arced over the lake from the south, where Elatos once stood. Another came from the east and the ruins of Borza. A third arced down from the lower level of the King's Palace. The three fireballs converged on the replica, setting it ablaze.

The crowd cheered as the dragon burned, and thunderous drums shook the air. By the time the sun began to slide behind the eastern slope of the Orbis Mountains, the streets were full of cheer, food, and fun.

Lanara returned to the balcony railing and addressed the crowds again. "Some of you know who I am, but many of you do not. My name is Lanara Zaridus, and I am the former wife and queen to King Pius Zaridus. First and foremost, I want you to understand that I am not your queen. Nor is my daughter, Princess Zelanora."

"Then why are we listening to you?" one man shouted.

A woman shouted, "We don't need anyone to rule over us!" Several others agreed with her.

An old man shook his fist. "Mezhik be damned!"

Nardus joined Lanara and Zelanora at the railing. "Not long ago, I would have agreed with you, my friend."

"He's one of them that slayed the dragon!" shouted a boy.

Lanara gestured toward Nardus and smiled. "Yes, this man helped defeat the fiercest enemy this realm has ever faced, and he also just happens to be the last heir of King Ordin, the original and true ruler of the Ancient Realm. As such, he is the true heir of the Three Kingdoms and the Ancient Realm!"

The crowd erupted with both cheers and boos. Nardus held up his hand until the crowd finally settled.

He cleared his throat. "I cannot and will not deny the blood which runs through my veins. I am indeed the last heir of King Ordin. However, I must also inform you of the fact that I have no desire to rule over this mighty kingdom. Although faulted, as we all are, King Zaridus reigned over this realm with peace. I know the heart of this woman who stands next to me. She loves each and every one of you and has your best interests at heart. As the true heir of the Three Kingdoms and the Ancient Realm, I make my first and final ruling, renouncing my claim to the throne. Instead, I offer you, the people, a joint council comprised of all the high races. This new council will be headed up by Lanara Zaridus, your new queen."

How does he know of the council?

Again, the crowd split between cheers and boos. It was impossible for Lanara to determine which of them won out.

Well, that didn't quite go according to plan.

Nardus hadn't given her the chance to convince him to be king, and now it didn't matter. Once renounced, Nardus would never be able to rule. She had no choice but to accept the position.

Like Nardus, she held up her hand and waited for the crowd to calm. This time, it took far longer. She wondered if it had anything to do with her being a woman but quickly dismissed it.

"I accept the crown, heavy as it may be. As your new queen, I shall make my first decree. Unlike my husband before me, I hold no biases toward individuals regardless of their race or nature. As such, I decree that mezhik will no longer be banished in the Three Kingdoms or the Ancient Realm."

At the rate to which the citizens cheered and booed, it would likely take all night for her to get through everything she needed to say, but none of it could wait.

After several minutes, she addressed the crowd again. "One cannot call an area the Three Kingdoms if only one kingdom stands. However, I have no intention of changing the name. Therefore, the restorations of Elatos and Borza will begin tomorrow. You will have your cities back!"

Finally, something she said elicited more cheers than boos.

"Tomorrow, my daughter and I will begin interviewing any who wish to serve in my courts as counselors and also those who wish to represent the people of our great cities and towns. Now, please give it up for some of your new council members." She turned and motioned her two guests forward. "Tharos The Cunning will represent the dragons, and King Forlin will represent the äəllf äkfeţik. Others will soon join, making our kingdom and the realm stronger than ever before."

† † †

Later that night, Nardus stood inside the main dining hall within the King's Palace. Many gathered to celebrate the new queen and her joint council. Among them was King Forlin of the Äəllf Äkfeţik. He never thought the elven king would join the war, but he'd been wrong. Not only had they come in full force, but they'd helped turn the tide.

Ridan, Torbrek, and almost a dozen other dwarves hovered around the barrels of ale, drinking, singing, and dancing without a care in the world. Nardus would forever be indebted to Ridan for gathering such a fierce band of warriors. Their heart and strength helped turn the tides of the battle. The band of them would head back to Tectus in the morning and face the wrath of King Morlek. Luckily, they held an important bargaining chip, thanks to Lanara. If King Morlek agreed to honor Ridan, Torbrek, and the others as Tectan heroes, he would be given a seat in the joint council. If not, he would suffer the consequences of his actions via trade embargoes.

Nardus walked over to Tharos. The mighty dragon stood next to Peorvem and Screech. "Well, what do you think of the modifications to the King's Palace so far?"

Tharos grinned. "We are the first three dragons to ever set foot in this palace."

Screech shrugged and took a bite out of a large boulder. "You didn't need to make modifications for me."

"You will grow, my young friend," Peorvem said.

Nardus eyed Tharos. "I hear no one challenged you for the dragon throne."

Tharos blew smoke from his nostrils. "Nor would they."

"Every dragon knows he's friends with the greatest mage to ever live," Screech said. "We all live in fear." A puff of dirt rose from behind him. He shrugged and grinned. "Oops."

Nardus chuckled. "I look forward to seeing each of you in the future." He winked at Screech. "Even you."

Morcinda and Noella, her sister, approached King Forlin. It was the first time he'd ever witnessed Morcinda apprehensive about anything. He thought about moving closer to eavesdrop on their conversation, but there was no need to do so. King Forlin made it known to everyone.

King Forlin glared at Morcinda. "You think I will stand here and allow you to take your sister away from me?"

Noella's hands flew onto her hips. "She's not taking me away, Father. It will only be for a few years."

"A few years!"

"Sailing the world takes time," Morcinda said. "Besides, it's time I get to know my sister better."

"I agree," Noella said. "You won't be ready to give up your throne for another five hundred years, anyway, so what's the big deal?"

King Forlin huffed. "I rely on your council, Noella."

Noella touched her father's face. "And you will receive it once I return."

He raised his arms. "Very well."

Theyn's arm slipped around Nardus's. "If you've had your fill of this party, I thought we might slip away."

Nardus smiled. "Never thought you'd ask."

CHAPTER FIFTY-FOUR

Jagger stood at the bow of the ship, her legs spread wide to keep herself balanced as they sailed across the jarring, rough waters. Eis lay at her feet, surprisingly at home on the waters. Miles behind Jagger, nestled deep within the Zmaj Mountains of Reothadh, lay Zimska Vala. Her childhood home. Her past.

She'd never called anywhere else home before, and the thought of doing so left Ice in her veins, yet she knew she'd never return to Reothadh. After everything that'd happened, how could she? Her people were calloused. Unforgiving. Downright evil at times. The past eight months proved it and solidified it in her mind.

The pack she carried on her back, a small one at that, contained every possession she'd ever owned. Plus a sealed clay jar with her mother's remains. Grimbold, her father, once told her about her mother's desire to travel the seas. It stemmed from her mother's own father and his tales as a fisherman for the clan. Jagger never met her grandfather, his life ended in a skirmish years before hers began.

She removed the clay jar from her pack and held it in her hands. Her mother's spirit never resided in the jar, yet she couldn't deny a sense of closeness to it. Every time she touched it, the jar brought her comfort and conjured memories of her mother.

Jagger removed the lid and smiled. After spending decades couped up inside a jar, her mother would get her wish and be set free to roam the seas. The jangle of copper coins brought a smile to her lips.

"It's time, then?" She turned and watched Grimbold approach, Rauch at his side.

"Yes."

Grimbold joined her at the bow, and the two of them stared out at the tumultuous sea. "Tis a beautiful place."

Jagger smiled. "She would've loved it."

"Would've?" He scoffed.

Still of the old world and its ways, Grimbold clung to his gods and to the idea that a soul never leaves its body. She once held the same beliefs, but that was before she met the flamewalker. Although she spent just a week with him, the experience changed her life forever. Now, she saw the world through his eyes. Recognized the beauty and evidence of his creator. Alderan, the flamewalker, called him ʕäṭūr, and perhaps it really was his true name, but she suspected he answered to many names. For now, she would call him ʕäṭūr, too.

"You know what I mean." She proffered him the jar. "I believe the honor is yours, father."

Grimbold grunted, then took the jar. The two of them leaned over the railing and watched as he poured her mother's ashes out of the jar and into the deep blue waters. Tears streaked her cheeks.

Grimbold wiped away tears of his own. "Goodbye, my love. We will see each other again, soon." He chucked the empty jar into the sea. Jagger elbowed Grimbold in his ribs. He eyed her with a frown. "What?"

"Maybe I wanted to keep the jar."

"Why? Once I emptied your mother's ashes, the jar reached the end of its usefulness."

"For you, perhaps, but it was the only thing I had left to remind me of her."

"I see." He scratched his chin for a few seconds. "Well, the deed is done. However, I think I have just the thing to remedy this." He reached behind his neck with both hands and grunted several times before producing the ends of a leather necklace. The rest flopped over the top of his shirt, revealing its treasure.

Jagger swallowed hard as she watched the sunlight refract off the sapphire and onto Grimbold's shirt. "Mother's ring."

"Yes, and her mother's before her. Seven generations, if memory serves me." He held it out to her. "Take it."

She shook her head. "I can't do that."

"You can, and you will." He took her hand, forced it open, and laid the ring and leather necklace in her palm.

"But this is yours, Father."

"No, it belongs to you. I should've given it to you when she died, but I just couldn't bring myself to do so."

The ship lurched and dipped forward as the waves grew stronger. Jagger clenched her fist around the ring for fear of losing it. "And what's changed?"

Grimbold held up his arms and turned in a circle. "Everything."

Jagger took a deep breath. Her father had never been more right. She knelt, pulled the ring off the necklace, then slid it onto her finger. The snug fit couldn't have been better if the ring had been made for her. She stood and wrapped her arms around Grimbold's waist. "Thank you, Father."

"You're welcome."

After a final squeeze, she released him and turned back toward the sea, her gaze locked on the ring. An image of a crown flashed in her mind. She looked down at Eis and smiled. "Royalty or not, I feel like a queen."

Grimbold placed his hands on the railing. "Eis is right, Jagger. You are a queen."

"How did you know—oh, never mind. You'll never tell me your secret."

He winked at her. "And where are we headed now, your majesty?"

Jagger stared into the blue beyond and smiled. "To see an old friend."

CHAPTER FIFTY-FIVE

Alderan sat atop the rocky cliffs overlooking the Gelu Ocean. Far below, the ocean's early morning waves rolled up the sandy beach then rescinded in a mesmerizing fashion. Later that evening, he would stand on that same beach and proclaim his love for Rayah in front of ʕäṭūr, his family, and a handful of friends.

In the past, such a momentous occasion would've terrified him to the point of paralyzation, but today, a sense of peace enveloped him. The love of his life would finally be his to hold and keep forever. He could hardly wait.

Rayah sat next to him, her eyes closed as tears streaked down the sides of her face and nose. In an instant, his perfect world came crashing down around him, his peaceful mood evaporated. Pulse spiked, he took her hand in his. She didn't recoil, but she didn't open her eyes, either.

He rubbed the top of her hand with his thumb. "What's wrong? Do you not want to get married in this spot because you almost died here?"

"No, it's not that at all." Tears dripped from her chin and splattered on the rock she sat upon. "I've kept something from you."

A tinge of anger flared in his chest. "What do you mean?"

"Would you…" Her lips quivered. She drew a deep breath, then looked him in the eye. "Would you still love me if I were… normal?"

Alderan just sat there, unable to process the strange question. He could think of a thousand words to describe her, but normal would never be one of them. Extraordinary, remarkable, and beautiful would be just a few, but never normal. Never had he met anyone else like her, and not just because of her race. Her beauty, her heart, and her love for ʕäṭūr set her far above all others. The fact that she had beautiful wings and could do extraordinary things just made her more desirable. But normal?

Never.

"I'm not sure I understand the question. How could you ever be what one might consider normal?"

"Growing up, Shalaidah told me that I would… I would lose my wings if I ever gave myself to someone I loved, even another dryte."

Alderan released Rayah's hand and clutched his stomach. How could something so vile and sinister be true? Why would Ɂätūr do that to her? To him? He fell in love with and loved everything about her, wings included. They were as much a part of her as his mezhik was a part of him. More so, perhaps. No, he couldn't accept something so preposterous.

"That's ridiculous," he said.

Rayah touched his leg and peered into his eyes when he looked at her. "Is it?"

"How could it not be? You're a dryte, and drytes have wings. Right?"

"Yes, but that doesn't mean I get to keep them forever. Look at caterpillars. They start off grounded and later morph into butterflies. Why would it be so difficult to believe a similar process couldn't happen to me?"

"I've already changed." He pulled up one of his sleeves and pointed at his feathered arm. "Do you love me less because of these markings?"

She scowled. "Of course not."

"Exactly. Besides, caterpillars change into something more, not less. Not only do they become more beautiful, but they also *gain* the ability to fly, not *lose* it."

Tears began running down Rayah's cheeks again. "So, you'd think less of me."

Alderan huffed. "I never said that."

"Yes, you did." Rayah wiped her face. "Perhaps this whole wedding is a bad idea."

Alderan turned toward her. "No, Rayah. We're destined to be together. I came back from the dead to be with you, remember? How many others could ever say that?"

"You're not just saying that?"

"Wings or not, I will love you until I breathe my last breath." He pulled her against his chest and held her. "Even beyond the veil of death."

The two of them sat there for a while, but then Rayah pulled away and rose to her feet. "There's something I must do." Urgency laced her voice.

Alderan stood, his chest suddenly tight. "Right now?" Rayah nodded. "Is it something I can help you with?"

"No, but I'll be back in time for the wedding." She kissed him on the lips. "I promise."

"I trust you," he said.

She nodded, fluttered her wings, and took to the sky. He watched her until she disappeared above the cliff edge. His heart ached. Not because of her absence, but because of what would soon come. He harbored no doubts as to whether he would still love her without her wings, but would she love herself?

Ɛätūr, are we doing the right thing? I pray for your wisdom.

† † †

A multitude of feelings wrestled within Rayah's heart as she stared up at the massive chestnut oak tree. Doubts arose in her mind as to the purpose of her visit. No words would ever draw Shalaidah from her grove. Her home.

But she deserves to know.

Rayah pressed her palm against the tree's massive trunk and recited the words she'd committed to memory ages ago. "Shalaidah, tree spirit of the mighty oak, hear me now and awaken." She stepped back and waited several seconds, but the tree failed to come alive. A second try yielded the same result.

Rayah sighed as she settled on the ground in front of the tree. "Today, I am to be married to the love of my life. I just wanted you to know."

"And so you have."

Rayah looked up. Shalaidah stood next to the oak tree, a rare smile upon her brown lips.

"You're not in your tree," Rayah said.

"Not this day."

Rayah rose. "I don't understand."

Shalaidah tapped her side, then said, "Walk with me."

At first, Rayah held onto the tension in her chest, expecting the worst of Shalaidah, but with each step she allowed a bit of it to slip away until none of it remained.

Shalaidah spoke as they weaved their way through the trees of the oak grove. "You must answer one question before I will bless this marriage of yours."

Bless my marriage?

Rayah hadn't come to receive Shalaidah's blessing, nor had she ever thought it would be possible. Now that the idea existed, she couldn't stop thinking about it. Now, she yearned for the woman's blessing. Not receiving it would change nothing, but having it would change everything.

"What is your question?"

Shalaidah stopped beneath one of the trees and plucked a small, brown chestnut from one of its lower limbs. "This man you intend to marry. Are you willing to give up everything for him? Do you love him that much?"

"I assume when you say give up everything, you're referring to my wings and my ability to burrow beneath the dirt and soil. Am I correct?"

"Wings and mezhik mean nothing." She grunted as she smashed the chestnut between her fingers. After a few seconds, it cracked open. She ripped off the shell and offered the savory nut to Rayah.

Rayah took the nut and rolled it around in her hand. "Then what?"

Shalaidah plucked another chestnut from the tree and worked it with her fingers. "Would you sacrifice your life to save his?"

"Without hesitation." Rayah popped the nut into her mouth and chewed it up. Although primarily nutty, its taste also contained a sweet note of honey.

"And you're certain he's the one for you?"

"I am a dryte, and I'm bonded to him forever."

Shalaidah scowled at her. "Hogwash."

"Why would you say that? When we connect, he can see and feel the things I do. We are bonded."

"You may be bound to him for now, but all things can be broken." She tossed the shelled nut into her mouth.

Rayah frowned. "I don't understand. You told me before that the bond of a dryte lasts forever."

Shalaidah shook her head. "Have you no understanding of my ways?"

"Understanding?" Anger swelled in Rayah's chest. "I took your words as truth. Should I not have?"

"You're still a foolish girl." She exhaled forcefully. "Truth lies in my words, but one must sift them like wheat in order to remove the chaff."

Rayah balled her fists. "Why can't you just speak plainly to me?"

"It is not in my nature to do so."

"Then take a step out of your nature and tell me what you mean."

Shalaidah's green eyes flashed with rage. "I could do so with as much difficulty as you would have shedding your wings."

"Ugh! I shouldn't have come here." Rayah turned and stormed away.

"Wait."

That single word stopped Rayah in her tracks. Not because Shalaidah held sway over her and compelled her to do so but because of the way she said it. It sounded almost like a plea for help.

Rayah turned around and faced Shalaidah but didn't approach her. "Why should I?"

Shalaidah frowned, then stared at the ground. "I'm… sorry."

Rayah gasped and braced herself for the world to implode, yet somehow it didn't. Instead, it triggered just a single change, and that change took place within her heart. She rushed over to Shalaidah and wrapped her arms around the woman.

"I forgive you," Rayah said, tears in her eyes.

Those three words brought the entire world to a standstill. Faded the sounds of the forest and the wind through the trees until nothing remained but the shallow breaths and beating hearts of her and Shalaidah.

Shalaidah pulled back and wiped the tears from Rayah's cheeks with her thumbs. "Don't be so quick to change your heart."

Rayah stared into her eyes. Drank in the sorrow that poured out of them. "No matter what you've done, I forgive you."

"The beliefs you hold regarding yourself and your nature are less than true. The day Rakzar dropped you off at my doorstep, I made a decision for you that wasn't mine to make. Everything I taught you about yourself and the world revolved around keeping you close to me forever. I realize now how selfish that was, but until you arrived that day, I had been alone for centuries."

"What are you saying?"

"First, your bond to this man is real. However, it will only last until his death. At that point, you will be free to love another."

Rayah nodded. "Fine, but that changes nothing."

"I understand, and I am glad it does not, but the real lie revolves around you losing your wings and your abilities." Shalaidah stepped back and leaned against the tree. "I thought if I were to tell you something like that it would keep you from ever wanting to leave me. That it would prevent you from opening your heart to someone else. I peddled fear, yet I find you're fearless."

Rayah dropped to her knees and touched the ground. The soil slithered across the tops of her knuckles as though it were alive. She'd spent so many months anguishing over the thought of losing the ability, not because it was a part of her but because of the fear it instilled in her. The world proved itself to be full of evil, and without her wings or her abilities with soil, she would be helpless to defend Alderan as she'd sworn to do. Now, that burden lifted from her shoulders. An enormous weight she'd carried too long.

She lifted her eyes to the heavens. "Thank you, ʕäṭūr."

Shalaidah sighed. "I'll understand if you never want to see me again."

Rayah stood and approached the woman who raised her. "As I said, I forgive you."

Shalaidah cocked her head. "You do?"

"Yes… However, there's one thing you must do for me."

"Name your price, and I will gladly pay it."

Rayah took Shalaidah's hand and smiled. "Come to my wedding. Meet the man of my dreams."

Shalaidah looked around the grove, then smiled. "It would be an honor."

† † †

Alderan watched Eshtak and Niesha play in the sand, each taking turns being buried neck deep. It reminded him of building sandcastles with Aria long ago. He imagined that one day his children would play on the beach with hers. That is if he and Rayah had children. He'd never discussed the subject with Rayah, and it made him wonder if it was something she wanted. If not, he would be content.

To be honest, children scared him. Not in the sense of their proximity to him or anything they might do or say but in the sense of how children of his own might turn out. To his knowledge, a wizard and a dryte had never had children before, and he couldn't imagine a wizard or sorceress with wings. Nevertheless, the thought intrigued him.

Zerenity, Zelanora, Theyn, Berggren, and a few others worked feverishly as they prepped a nice spot for the wedding on the beach. Thanks to Qotan and his earth magic, the sand lay perfectly flat. It would likely remain that way as long as the ceremony and celebration commenced before high tide rolled in. Then again, Morcinda had a way with water.

Everything will work out perfectly.

By the time Rayah returned, more than half the day had passed. He tried getting her alone for one final conversation about the wedding, but Aria insisted he not see her again until the ceremony. No one could outargue her.

An hour later, Nardus walked over to Alderan, his face beaming. "You ready, son?"

Alderan looked down at himself and admired his new robes. They matched his father's robes with the exception of his being silver rather than blue. "I believe I am."

"Good. It's time you take your place on the beach."

"What about you?"

"I'll be right in front of you and will guide you through everything."

"No, I mean what about you and Theyn? Will the two of you ever get married?"

Nardus chuckled. "Our hearts have been bound for some time. Therefore, a few words will change nothing."

"And Theyn feels the same way?"

"Those were her words, not mine."

"So, you're okay with it?"

"I was married once before. Or at least that's what I was made to believe. Either way, it doesn't matter. As you know, these events are strictly for the woman."

Alderan didn't agree, but there was no point in him saying so. Once the two of them took their places on the beach, family and guests formed makeshift rows on either side of a central aisle lined with twelve torches atop golden poles. Yellow and white flowers spiraled up each pole, and white petals covered the ground. It was far more beautiful that anything Alderan could've ever imagined.

As the anticipation of seeing Rayah began to build, his nerves crept up. How would he ever be everything she deserved? Although older and in control of his mezhik, he still found himself to be the same oaf who met her just two years before.

The beach eroded, the torches faded, and the sound of the waves crashing on the beach fell from his ears as Rayah stepped into the center aisle. Never had he seen her more radiant. Her dress hugged the contour of her body, leaving little to the imagination. Its yellow hue matched the flowers in her hair and set off a magnificent rainbow of colors on her translucent wings.

His heart, full of longing and love, ached in his chest as her wings fluttered behind her and carried her forward. Every last doubt cleared from his mind, save one. As she approached, he couldn't shake it from his mind. He had no right to take her wings from her no matter how much they loved each other.

She settled next to him, and his father began to speak, but the words fell short of his ears. Hands trembling, he took hers. She turned to him, and the beach fell silent. Rayah represented everything he ever wanted, yet he would never be able to have her.

I must be crazy.

She stared into his eyes. "What is it, Alderan?"

His heart had crawled into his throat, so he forced it back down. "We can't do this."

She squeezed his hands. "We can, and we will."

Tears stung his eyes. He fought them back, but they were relentless. "Your wings are part of what makes you so special, and I cannot allow you to sacrifice them for me."

She smiled. "Nor shall you."

"I—what?" Perhaps he hadn't heard her right.

"I will explain everything later. You need to trust me."

Trust her?

At several points in their relationship, she'd lied to him and kept information from him, but it was all in the past. "I do."

Nardus cleared his throat. "Perhaps we should move straight to the vows." Rayah nodded.

Alderan looked to his family and friends for a few moments, then focused on his beautiful bride. "I give you my heart and love in perpetuity and vow to defend your life as though it were my own, even unto death."

Rayah dipped her head. "And I, yours."

The rest of the ceremony blurred together, right up until his father smacked him on the back of the head.

"Ouch!" Alderan rubbed his head as he glared at his father, and everyone laughed, including Rayah.

Nardus chuckled. "I said you may kiss your bride."

Despite the fear of everyone watching, Alderan embraced Rayah and kissed her. Everyone cheered as they turned and bowed.

Hours later, the night settled in. Conversation filled the beach. So many had come, and Alderan couldn't help but feel blessed. As he looked around, he remembered the few who hadn't made it. From all the tales of the fearless dwarf, it would've been a far grander affair if Normak had been there. He wished he had known him. Of the living, the one he missed most was Jagger.

I pray you found your father.

Rakzar sat down next to Alderan. "Just had to have the wedding on the beach, didn't you?"

Alderan laughed. "It's always good to have a reminder that even the mighty Rakzar fears something."

Rakzar clasped Alderan's shoulder. "Well, thanks to you, I no longer fear death or what comes after."

Alderan knew that tone. "You're leaving, aren't you?"

"For now, but fear not, White Knight, I shall return."

"Where are you headed?"

"Urza and I have agreed to help the council eradicate those who remain loyal to Pravus and chaos." He stood. "Earlier, I received word of a threat in

Calx Acta."

Alderan stood. "Need assistance?"

Rakzar growled and pointed a claw at Alderan's chest. "You take care of my girl, or you'll be the one in need of assistance. Clear?"

Alderan eyed Rayah and smiled when she looked over at him. "Crystal."

Alderan watched Rakzar and Urza fade into the night, then joined in for a bit of dancing and a lot of food. In the distance, beneath the pale moonlight, Alderan spotted a small ship approaching the beach. Ten minutes later, a smaller boat rowed to shore.

"Expecting someone else?" Nardus said.

Alderan squinted down the beach. "No."

Four figures piled out of the boat. Two large beasts on all fours, and two large humanoids. Alderan's heart raced as he took off down the beach.

"Jagger!"

CHAPTER FIFTY-SIX

Nerves consumed Calen as he stood at the front door of Aunt Tahmara's house. The door needed a good sanding, its green paint chipped, scratched, and faded with age. Although he'd walked through it hundreds if not thousands of times before, today was unlike any other before it. Master Savric called it a momentous day, and Calen was inclined to agree.

In Aunt Tahmara's mind, it'd been about three months since she'd last seen him. Add in the time she'd spent under Cinolth's control, and it rounded out to about a year. From what Mistress Zerenity and others had told him, she would remember none of her time while controlled by the evil dragon.

For Calen, it'd been almost ten-and-a-half years since he last saw her. He couldn't help but wonder how she would react when he walked through the door. Would she recognize the man he'd become, or would she think a stranger entered her house? Would she be the same as he remembered? How had she weathered the war? So many questions floated through his mind it paralyzed him.

I should've asked Master Savric to prepare her for our reunion.

Even if he had, could anything prepare a person for the events that had transpired? How often does someone travel to another world and return a decade older? Other than him, perhaps no one.

The longer he stood at the door, the more the thought of turning around and leaving grew within his mind. Traveling to the Shadow World had taken great courage, yet he wondered if it had been easier to do. No chance in the world existed for him to actually walk away but knowing so didn't make the idea less enticing.

She still loves me, and I love her.

After exhaling a deep breath, he turned the knob and entered the small house. The aromas of fresh bread and rabbit stew hit his nostrils immediately.

Even with the millions of thoughts running through his head, not one of them had been about food or how much he'd missed Aunt Tahmara's cooking. If discovered, Master Savric would chide him for it for the rest of his life. After all, nothing was more sacred to Master Savric than food. Well, except for Ɂätür.

Calen looked around. "Aunt Tahmara?"

"In the kitchen, dear. Make sure you clean your boots and wash your hands before coming into my sanctuary."

Calen chuckled. Some things would never change. "Yes, ma'am."

After a quick wash in the basin next to the door, Calen stepped into the kitchen. Aunt Tamarah stood with her back to him, tending a large pot of stew with a wooden spoon. With each passing moment, Calen's pulse increased. After just a few seconds, his heart thundered in his ears.

Aunt Tahmara turned. "Did you—" The wooden spoon clattered to the floor, and she grabbed at her chest, her face as white as a sheet. "God almighty!"

Calen knew better than to approach her, given her reaction, so he just stood in the doorway. "It's me, Aunt Tahmara."

"C-Calen?"

"Yeah." He stuffed his hands in his pockets and smiled. "It's really good to see you."

Aunt Tahmara stared at him for a good thirty seconds before she shook her head. "If I didn't recognize those beautiful eyes of yours, I wouldn't believe it." She held out her arms. "Well, don't just stand there. Come give your aunt a hug and kiss."

Two hours later and at least a dozen times through the story of how he'd gone to another world and lived there for ten years, she finally accepted it. The timing was perfect, too, Master Savric, Master Qotan, and Mistress Zerenity all arriving just minutes later. The five of them talked long into the afternoon, and Calen enjoyed the camaraderie and conversation immensely, yet he couldn't help but feel out of place.

Master Savric must've sensed it, too. "My dear boy, it is obvious that something immense weighs on your shoulders. Fear not, for you are among family and friends. Unburden yourself."

No matter how Calen arranged the words in his mind, they felt inadequate as to explain himself and his feelings. He'd called Daltura home for fourteen years and loved much about Centauria and the Ancient Realm, yet the Shadow World called to him. Beckoned him to return.

"It's just that…" He sighed. "I don't think you'd…" Words failed him.

"It's simple, darling," Mistress Zerenity said. "I see it in your eyes just as plain as the sun in the sky. You feel like you don't belong here anymore. Am I right?"

Calen frowned then nodded. "It's complicated."

"It doesn't need to be." Aunt Tahmara reached across the table and touched his hand. "You're a man now, Calen. As such, I'm sure you need to make your own way in this world. I've loved you like a son, and it will sadden me to see you go, but believe me when I tell you that I understand. My love for you isn't contingent on you living with me. I'll always love you no matter what."

Master Qotan removed the pipe from his mouth and held it up. "Ah, yes. I see it now. Quite clear in fact." Everyone at the table, including Calen, turned toward Qotan. He chuckled. "Zerenity was partially correct in her initial analysis of Calen's eyes, but she failed to take into consideration all the facts presented. It is an absolute fact that Calen feels untethered to this present life, but not in the way she inferred. No, to be certain, this is not the world in which Calen wishes to live."

Master Savric's eyebrows dipped over the bridge of his nose. "Is this true, my boy?"

Calen couldn't deny the truth, nor did he want to, but he also didn't want to upset Aunt Tahmara, either. Even so, what difference did it make? He no longer possessed the heart locket, nor could he retrieve it on his own.

"Yes, sir." He stared at his hands. At the calluses on his fingers. Remembered the hard work it took to build them up.

Aunt Tahmara moved around the table and sat next to Calen. She put her arm around his shoulders and pulled him close. "If this Shadow World is where you will be most happy, then you must return."

Calen sighed and shook his head. "Even if I had the means to return, I couldn't just leave you here all alone."

"Bugger bees," Master Savric said. "Your aunt will never be alone as long as these old lungs continue to produce oxygen and my heart beats in my chest."

"Agreed," Master Qotan said. "Her cooking and my appetite make a fine pair." Aunt Tahmara blushed, creating a chain reaction around the table.

"Or… I could go with you," Aunt Tahmara said.

"Your life is here, Aunt Tahmara. I could never ask you to leave it all behind."

"No matter where I am, my life is complete as long as you're in it somehow." She glanced over at Master Qotan. "No offense."

"He is far more handsome than I," Master Qotan said.

Master Savric chuckled. "Indeed."

"Stop." Calen shrugged away Aunt Tahmara's arm. "Alderan returned the heart locket to Gnaud, so it doesn't matter."

Mistress Zerenity tapped her chin. "Perhaps there's still a way, darling." She looked over at Master Savric. "You do still have the book, right?"

Master Savric reached into the folds of his robes and produced a leather-bound book. Mistress Zerenity reached over and snatched it from his hands.

Master Savric glared at her. "Feathers, woman!"

"Pipe down, old man." Mistress Zerenity placed her palm over the book's cover and said, "*In əllít Hiz.*" The golden clasp popped open, and she opened the book to its first page. She held her hand out toward Master Savric. "Hand over the fountain pen." He complied, along with muttering a string of unrecognizable sounds and grunts.

She jotted down a few lines of text, tapped the page, and the words faded. "There we go. Now, we'll just have to wait for a response."

Fifteen minutes later, the symbol on the front of the book began to pulse with light. Mistress Zerenity opened the book and read the message aloud: "Calen helped rid the world of Cinolth and the evil he conjured. Therefore, Calen has my blessing. Nardus." She smiled at Calen. "Now that was simple, right?"

After retrieving the heart locket from Gnaud, Savric stood in front of Calen and Aunt Tahmara with it. He eyed Calen. "You know the way this works."

"I do."

"Make sure this locket stays in the right hands." He handed it to Calen.

"Yes, sir. If needed, I will return it to Gazsi."

Qotan smiled at Aunt Tahmara. "And we will be waiting in Summitto Valley six months from now to see who returns."

"I have just one question before we leave, Master Savric."

"Anything, my boy."

"Will you miss me?"

Tears filled Master Savric's eyes. "A piece of my heart travels with you."

"And a piece of mine stays with you." He embraced Master Savric. "I will never forget you, and I will strive to be the kind of father you always were to me. I love you."

"And I you, my boy."

Calen stepped back, wiped the tears from his face, and took Aunt Tahmara's hand. It trembled. He smiled and kissed her cheek. "Next stop, the Shadow World." He placed the necklace around his neck, and the world began to quake.

CHAPTER FIFTY-SEVEN

As soon as Berggren opened the pale green door and stepped across its threshold, a hand struck the side of his face. Although he'd expected as much, he still hadn't seen it coming. Dhaldra stood there, her other hand on her hip and fire in her gray eyes. The years had favored her, adding a bit of silver to her raven locks and a few wrinkles in the corners of her eyes and lips. She was everything and more than he remembered.

Gods, I've missed her.

"That's for not writing," Dhaldra said. She struck his other cheek, perhaps a bit harder, but he didn't flinch or raise an arm to block her. "That's for staying away years longer than you promised me." After a third strike, her eyes filled with tears. "And that's for making me think you were dead."

Berggren ignored the sting in his cheeks and pulled Dhaldra into his arms. "Missed you too, my love."

When their lips met, the years and distance that had separated them for so long melted away. He would've stayed right there in that moment forever, but too many thoughts weighed him down. Also, they weren't alone. He picked Dhaldra up and carried her farther into the room before setting her back down.

Theyn entered the house and pulled Nardus inside with her. "Hello, Mother."

Dhaldra's face brightened, and she pushed Berggren aside. "My beautiful daughter!" The two of them embraced.

Berggren gruffed, "See some things haven't changed."

Dhaldra threw Berggren a scowl over her shoulder. "She's not the one who abandoned me."

Theyn gestured toward Nardus. "This is…"

Nardus proffered his hand toward Dhaldra. "Nardus. Theyn's told me so much about you."

Dhaldra hesitated before taking Nardus's hand. "Yes…" Her hand fell to her side as she turned toward Berggren. Sorrow filled her eyes. "Shaul?"

Berggren lowered his head and shook it. "He didn't—" Berggren trembled as tears fell from his eyes and splattered on the wooden floor. Dhaldra came over to him and embraced him.

"It wasn't—"

"No," Berggren said, knowing what Dhaldra was about to ask. "Believe me when I say she had nothing to do with it."

Dhaldra pulled away. "Does Keerie know?"

Berggren shook his head. "No, and I'm not sure how to tell her, either."

"He was her son, Berggren. She must know."

"Like a son," he said.

"*Like* a son?" Theyn joined them. "What do you mean?"

Berggren located a chair and collapsed into it. "Shaul was mine, not Keerie's. My first wife, Noreen, died in childbirth."

Theyn and Dhaldra gasped. Dhaldra said, "Why didn't you ever tell me?"

"It was long before you came into my life. By then, he'd become Keerie's son." He wiped his eyes and gazed at Dhaldra. "Look, there's more I need to tell you."

The blood drained from Dhaldra's face. "You've found another woman, haven't you?"

"Never," Berggren barked. "At least not in the way you're implying." He looked past Dhaldra and toward the open door. "Niesha, come in here."

Niesha strolled through the door. "What's going on, big man?"

Dhaldra glanced back and forth between Berggren and Niesha several times. "I don't understand."

Berggren opened his mouth to explain, but Niesha beat him to it. "My mother's dead or might as well be for all I know. Berggren's been taking care of me. Well, that's what he'd tell you, anyway, but it's really the other way around. Without me, he'd be long dead already. I talk a lot and speak my mind more than I should, and I'm hungry all the time. It's okay if you don't want me to live with you. I've lived alone for quite some time and could do so again if needed. So, don't worry—"

"Niesha." Berggren stood and met Dhaldra's gaze. "Love you more than words, Dhaldra, but I love Niesha, too." He smiled. "We're a package deal, like it or not."

Niesha began trembling, then collapsed on the floor and sobbed. Berggren rushed over to her and scooped her into his arms. "What's wrong, Niesha?"

She buried her face in his neck and sobbed harder. After a few minutes, she calmed down and took a deep breath. Tendrils of snot hung from her nose and attached to Berggren's neck. Niesha used her sleeve to wipe her face and Berggren's neck. "Sorry about that, big man."

Berggren brushed his fingers through Niesha's stringy hair, pulling it away from her face. "Are you okay?"

Niesha nodded. "It's just... I've never... No one's ever loved me before."

Berggren fought back tears of his own. "You'll never have to say that again."

"Eshtak loves friend too." He hugged Berggren's leg. Lost in the moment, Berggren had forgotten about him.

Berggren rubbed Eshtak's head as he eyed Dhaldra. A smile crept upon his lips. "A package of three?"

Dhaldra sighed. "A ship's no place to raise children."

"Eshtak not child."

Everyone laughed.

"He's older than all of us," Nardus said.

"Still, you can't expect to sail off again with another child."

Berggren nodded. "You're right, Dhaldra." He kissed the top of Niesha's head, then set her down. "If you're willing to put up with the lot of us, I'm willing to hang up my sailing hat."

"You've never worn a hat in your life," Theyn said.

"Eshtak loves hats!" He spun in a circle, then grabbed Niesha's hands and spun her around with him.

A few hours later, Keerie and Lancing dropped by. The news of Shaul's death devastated them, especially Keerie. Time would lessen their pain, but Berggren knew it would never fully pass.

The eight of them retired to the back porch and talked long into the night before Theyn and Nardus bid them farewell. Hours later, Keerie and Lancing left, leaving Berggren and Dhaldra alone with Eshtak and Niesha. The moon shone like a beacon from the heavens, blanketing Niesha and Eshtak in its light as they lay fast asleep on the grass, arm in arm.

Berggren smiled as he held Dhaldra in his arms, determined to never let her go again.

CHAPTER FIFTY-EIGHT

Nardus stood atop the King's Palace with Theyn at his side. A cool breeze prickled his neck as the morning sun made its first appearance over the western range of the Orbis Mountains. Soon, the entire valley including Trivers Lake would shine like Ɂäʈūr's light. Far to the south, reconstruction of Elatos continued. This time, the ancient city would not be made of timber. In a year's time and aided by a small army of wizards and sorceresses, the Three Kingdoms and the other cities of the Ancient Realm would breathe new life once again.

With Alderan and Rayah's wedding behind them and Berggren reunited with his family, Nardus determined in his mind to return to Nasduron. The only question that remained was how to accomplish it after exiting Nasduron through the archway. Blood mezhik was binding in a far more fundamental way than any given spell of pure mezhik. One could not simply exchange their blood with someone else to escape the bond. Had it been possible, he would've contemplated it further.

But I'm the rule breaker.

Theyn held his arm. "You're awfully quiet this morning, my love. What are you thinking about?"

"Nasduron."

"You miss your little friend, don't you?"

"There are many things about Nasduron that I miss, but Gnaud is the biggest part of it. What bothers me more is the fact that Gnaud lives there all alone."

"He has Alderan and a few others that can visit him."

"Yes, but they're all busy."

Far below, a blue dragon burst out of the waters of Trivers Lake and flew straight toward Nardus and Theyn.

Peorvem.

The old dragon took up residence in the lake after his home in the Valley of Dragons was destroyed by Quldrai.

"He's coming to see you?" Theyn said.

"Yes. Together, we've been formulating a plan."

"Oh, I see. Does this plan happen to include me?"

Nardus pulled Theyn close and kissed her deep. "A plan is no plan at all if you're not involved."

"Good. Just checking."

A minute later, Peorvem landed on the rooftop. A small leather pouch hung from his neck. He reached into it, pulled out a ring, and slipped it onto the tip of his claw. The transformation into a human form took just a few seconds. Thankfully, he'd figured out that he didn't need to strip off his clothes before transforming between human and dragon forms. The clothing integrated into his scales and skin while a dragon, much like Theyn's clothes when she shifted into a cat.

"Good morning, Peorvem," Nardus said.

Peorvem stretched his arms wide and yawned. "Yes, I believe it is."

Nardus eyed Peorvem and his flowing blue cloak. "You've thought of something, haven't you?"

"As we've discussed before, blood mezhik can be a bit tricky to overcome. However, loose translations and vague wording play big roles, too."

"How so?" Theyn said.

"Think of it like this. If you come across a line in the road and there's a sign that tells you not to cross the line or you'll be ripped to shreds, what would you do?"

"I wouldn't cross the line."

"Precisely." Peorvem held up a finger. "Now, the real question that presents itself is where does that line begin and end? If it stopped at a boulder and didn't continue past it, could you go around the end, or would you perish?"

"I'm not sure. The sign didn't specify."

"Exactly." He turned to Nardus. "I believe the same logic can be applied to your predicament regarding Nasduron."

"Explain," Nardus said.

"Well, did you know how to get to Nasduron the first time you went there? Did you know where it was?"

"Depends on how you look at it. Obviously, I must've known about it on some sort of subconscious level."

"Yes, but isn't that how the mezhik works?"

"You're saying that the blood mezhik doesn't actually prevent me from going to Nasduron but blocks my memory of its location." Nardus scratched his head. "Because of that block, I cannot tell someone else where it's located."

Peorvem nodded. "As you said. Based on what you've told me of Nasduron and your ability to 'step into it,' as you say, there's no need for you to know its physical location."

"Huh." The dragon made perfect sense. "You're saying I've had access all this time and didn't know it."

"In a way, yes. As I said, mezhik is a funny thing. If you believe it to be capable of preventing you from doing something, then it will."

Nardus smiled. "Well, there's a simple way to test your theory."

Theyn grabbed Nardus's arm, then Peorvem's. "I'm ready."

The three of them stepped forward and into the Great Library.

"Oh, my! Nardus!" Gnaud launched himself off the table and hit Nardus square in the chest. Theyn's arm saved them from hitting the floor.

Nardus laughed. "It's so good to see you, my furry little friend." After prying Gnaud's arms from around his neck, he set the little gordak back on the table. He gestured toward Peorvem. "This is our friend, Peorvem."

Peorvem bowed. "It is a pleasure to finally meet you, Gnaudius L'Dorak. I've heard a great deal about you and how you helped save the realm from utter destruction."

Gnaud bowed his head. "The way you put things make them sound far grander than they really are. However, I fear I'm at a loss as to who you are. I've read many books in my lifetime, and I've ever only come across one individual named Peorvem. Peorvem The Ancient, to be exact."

"He's one and the same," Theyn said.

Gnaud stepped back and eyed Peorvem. After a few seconds, he cocked his head. "You look nothing like any dragon I've ever met."

Nardus, Theyn, and Peorvem laughed.

Gnaud scowled at Nardus. "Did I miss the punchline of the joke?"

"Come with us, and you'll see."

Nardus led the others out of the Great Library and around its side. They traversed two hidden paths through thick trees and overgrowth before popping out in front of a large clearing with a massive pond. Crystal blue water filled the pond, along with a wide range of fish and other creatures.

Gnaud crossed his arms and frowned. "This is my private oasis. Why have we come out here?"

Nardus chuckled. "This pond will soon be home to an intelligent water dragon who's older than even you."

"I'm still not buying the dragon line," Gnaud said.

Smack!

Water splashed Nardus and Theyn and soaked Gnaud.

"Oh, my! What was that?" Gnaud stared at the pond.

Peorvem, now in dragon form, raised his head out of the water and smiled. "Ah, it's nice to return to a properly-sized body of water."

Gnaud gasped and fell onto his backside. "Dear Ʒät̪ūr!"

Theyn shrugged. "I told you he was a dragon."

After several hours filled with unbelievable stories, Nardus and Theyn bid Gnaud and Peorvem goodbye, then stepped out of Nasduron and back to the rooftop of the King's Palace. The sun hung straight overhead, its reflection off the lake blinding. Satisfied with himself and the fact that Gnaud would never be alone again, Nardus led Theyn back into the palace. There was still much work to do.

CHAPTER FIFTY-NINE

Savric settled into his rocking chair in front of the fireplace for the first time in almost two years. Qotan sat to his left in his own rocking chair, and they'd added a third rocking chair for Zerenity to his right. After helping with the reconstruction of Vallah, Borza, Elatos, West Hotah, and portions of several other cities and towns, they were all weary and worn.

A small table separated his chair from Qotan's. A large book lay atop it, the end of a green feather protruding from it. Savric picked up the book and opened it to the page marked by the green feather. No matter how much he squinted or how close he held the book to his face, the words refused to stay in focus.

Savric sighed heavily and set the book back down.

Qotan lowered the book he held and looked over at Savric. "A problem, brother?"

"Indeed." He stared at the fire and frowned. "As it turns out, time has bested me yet again."

Zerenity reached over and patted the top of Savric's hand. "How so?"

"As previously stated years ago, the writing in every book I attempt to read shrinks beyond recognition."

Qotan chuckled. "Curious that this strange phenomenon continues to affect *your* books but never *mine*."

"Curious, indeed."

Qotan stroked his bald chin. "If memory serves me, and I do believe it does, I offered you an explanation as to the cause of this phenomenon."

Zerenity winked at Qotan. "Old age?"

Savric scowled at her. "Feathers, woman! You are older than I."

"Age is but a number, Savvy." She stroked several strands of her sliver hair, then shrugged. "Perhaps you should embrace it instead of using it as a crutch."

"Bugger bees," Savric muttered. "If I desired to have a cart filled with manure dropped at my door, I would have summoned one of the Dalturan stable boys." He glared at each of them for several seconds, then said, "Trust me when I say I have no such desire."

Qotan held his book back up to his nose. "For what it is worth, my analysis stands. It is most certainly your eyesight that worsens and not the size of the writing that continues to shrink."

"His attitude as well," Zerenity added. "Perhaps we all need a change of pace."

"A change of pace?" Savric stroked his beard as he stared at the flames. "Is this not the change of pace we sought?"

Qotan leaned forward in his chair and eyed Zerenity. "And what change of pace might you have in mind, sorceress?"

Zerenity tapped her chin and smiled. "Admittedly, I have a devious plan. But before we get to it, I believe there are certain issues that need addressing."

Savric cocked his head. "Issues?"

"First and foremost, you will give Qotan's staff back to him."

"Feathers, woman!" Savric huffed. "I assure you that I am far frailer than he is."

"Do not be so sure, brother." Qotan shook the book he held. "I struggle to keep this book aloft."

"Both of you are beyond ridiculous." Zerenity stood. "Both of you wait right here." She left the room.

Savric scowled. "And where would we go at this hour?"

Qotan chuckled. "I dare say, it is after eleven in the morning. The world lies at our feet. All we need do is stand and take a few steps."

Savric's stomach rumbled. He patted it and smiled. "You are right, brother. We will need sustenance soon. Perhaps a quick trip to Orna's Café is in order."

Zerenity returned carrying two large boxes. She handed one to each of them. "Go ahead and open them."

Savric tore off the ribbon securing the box and pulled off the lid. Buried within layers of colored paper lay new robes of yellow and a white cloak. He pulled them out of the box and held them up. Each looked to be sized just for him. He looked over and saw Qotan's box contained the same items, except the robes were brown and the cloak a dark tan color.

Zerenity smiled. "I thought those colors would be more fitting for each of you."

"Yellow and white?" Savric frowned.

"You are Fizärd Əllíṯ, are you not?" Zerenity said.

Logically, it made perfect sense. Bright robes for a light wizard. However, Savric had a hard enough time keeping his brown robes looking clean. Objection clung to the tip of his tongue, and he forced it back down. Instead, he smiled. "Thank you, Reni. They are perfect."

"As are mine," Qotan said. "Thank you."

She smiled. "There is one last thing."

Zerenity reached out to her side, and a grayish-white staff flew into it. A blue crystal in the shape of a six-pointed star sat atop the staff. Four prongs held the crystal in place, and the staff itself tapered to a point at its end. Striations ran the length of the shaft, creating the illusion of it being the tail of a comet or shooting star. In truth, Savric had never seen a staff more beautiful.

"In case you're wondering, it's a water crystal," Zerenity said. "It's capable of storing ten times the mezhik of your previous crystal."

Savric eyed the staff and its crystal. "Where did you find such a beautiful staff?"

"Morcinda talked her father into having it made for you. At my request, of course."

Savric nodded. "Naturally."

Zerenity held it out. "This is yours as well, Savvy."

Tears filled Savric's eyes, and his open mouth could find no words to express how he felt. He sat the box with his new robes and cloak on the floor in front of himself and pulled himself to his feet. He took the staff, handed it to Qotan, then took Zerenity into his arms. Their lips met for the first time in decades, and the rest of the world faded.

At some point, Qotan cleared his throat loud enough to break through the enchantment. He stood at the fire, Savric's new staff in his grasp.

Savric and Zerenity pulled away from each other but held onto each other's hands, their gazes locked. Savric's heart hammered in his chest, his palms became sweaty, and his lips trembled. "You complete me, Reni."

She smiled at him. "Always have, Savvy."

Qotan grimaced. "I fear I am but a third wheel."

Savric and Zerenity pulled Qotan into an embrace.

"Our cart has always had three wheels," Zerenity said.

Savric chuckled. "Indeed."

A few hours later and after a delectable lunch courtesy of Orna, the three of them stood in the warm afternoon sun. Daltura hadn't changed much over the years, but there were a few vendor carts missing from the main thoroughfare, and several buildings boarded up. The war had indeed taken its toll on the citizens, but never had there been so much hope for the future.

Praise be to you, Ɂäṭūr.

Qotan peered up and down the road, then stroked his chin. He turned toward Zerenity. "Now that our bellies are full, perhaps you can enlighten us on this devious plan of yours."

A wicked, awful, beautiful grin spread across Zerenity's lips. "Now that everything is returning to normal, I thought we might take a stroll down memory lane."

Qotan rubbed his hands together. "Are you suggesting we do some travel, or am I mistaken?"

"Travel?" Savric shook his head. "There is no sense—"

Zerenity eyed Qotan and cut Savric off. "Given the past, are you sure you're up for mirror-jumping?"

"Feathers, woman!" Savric couldn't believe his ears. "Have you already forgotten the past? The pain we endured?"

"I never will," Qotan said, "but I refuse to allow it to hinder my future."

"Well said." Zerenity smiled. "What's it going to be, Savvy? You in or out?"

Savric shook his head and sighed. Given everything they'd lost because of the mirrors, he'd never contemplated them being so foolish again. The thought of losing one of them for good didn't sit well with him, yet he couldn't deny the spark of adventure the mere mentioning of mirror-jumping had caused within him. That aside, he also must consider the fact that nothing would persuade either of them to reconsider once their minds were set. And, based on the mischief lurking within their eyes, he had his answer as to the setting of their hearts and minds.

He stroked his beard and frowned. "I have but one condition."

Qotan clasped Savric's shoulder. "Pray tell, brother."

"I'm first through the mirror this time."

"Deal." Qotan raised his hand. "To the cave!" He slammed the butt-end of his staff against the ground and disappeared.

Zerenity grabbed the sides of Savric's face and kissed his lips. She drew back and smiled. "Last one there's a rotten fish!" She spun around and disappeared in a whirlwind of dust.

Savric chuckled to himself. "Good thing I am the one who hid the cave this time." After setting his mind to the south and the cave hidden within the hills, he slammed his staff into the ground and disappeared, leaving the road in front of Orna's Café deserted.

CHAPTER SIXTY

Berggren sat on a stump in the yard, whittling away at a piece of wood. Despite him saying he was about done with it, Nardus still had no clue as to what it was supposed to be. Either way, he was happy to have the big man around after nearly two years, even if it was just for a few weeks.

Niesha and Eshtak ran around with slings, shooting rocks at everything no matter if it moved or not. Surprisingly, they hadn't turned the slings on each other.

Zerenity exited the house and stood on the porch for a minute. "It won't be long now."

Nardus nodded, and Zerenity returned inside. As much as he wanted to be at Theyn's side right then, it wasn't his place. Besides, she had Rayah, Zerenity, Keerie, and Dhaldra with her. What could he possibly add besides tension?

Nothing.

Savric and Qotan sat on a bench on the porch, Savric with a book in his face and Qotan with his lips wrapped around the end of a pipe. To that day, Nardus had yet to see Qotan actually smoke anything in it.

Alderan sat on the lowest step, his fingers tracing runes in the dirt.

Nardus sat down next to him. "Something on your mind?"

"Is it that obvious?"

"You've been tracing the same three runes for the last two hours."

Alderan scraped the ground with his boot, erasing the runes. "It just doesn't feel right without Aria and Darius here."

"I understand, but her actions could not go without consequences."

He pushed his hair out of his face. "Yeah, I know."

"Are you ready for this? To be a big bro—"

A cry echoed from the house. Nardus and the others rose to their feet.

Zerenity came to the door, a grin upon her lips. "It's a boy!"

Everyone began congratulating Nardus, but halted when another cry sounded.

Nardus scowled. "What was that?"

Zerenity disappeared for half a minute before returning with another announcement. "It's also a girl!"

Nardus shook his head and smiled. "Twins."

Alderan hugged him. "You are blessed, Father."

"As will you be one day."

After another round of congratulations, Nardus went inside and straight into the bedroom. Theyn lay there, a beautiful baby in each arm.

Tears blurred his vision as he knelt next to the bed. After enduring so much pain, Ɂätūr finally made good on his promise.

"We will have our hands full," he said.

"Take your son," Theyn said. "Show him the world."

Nardus took the beautiful little boy from her arm. "And what of our precious daughter?"

"Atheyna." She wrapped her arms around the girl. "For now, she's all mine."

"Atheyna." Nardus smiled. "I like it."

"And what will you name our son?"

Nardus held him up. "We shall call him Shauldan."

Berggren stepped into the room. "Shauldan?"

"In honor of your son."

Berggren wiped a tear from his eye. "Yeah, got that."

"To Shauldan and Atheyna," Zerenity said.

CHAPTER SIXTY-ONE

Aria set the candle holder down on the small table next to Darius's bed and knelt. She peered into his golden eyes and smiled. Somehow, he'd been blessed with all the features she loved about Pravus and none of the traits of his she'd despised.

My precious, perfect angel.

The speed at which the passing of time occurred astounded her, and the older she became, the quicker it went. In the morning, they would celebrate Darius's fourth name day. Her throat tightened a little. Soon, her precious little boy would grow into a man. She often dreamt of who he might become one day and, like any good mother did, prayed that Ɂäṭūr would help him grow up to be a strong, good man.

She smoothed back his blonde hair and kissed his forehead. "Did you say your prayers, Darius?"

He yawned and nodded. "When will I get my puppy?"

Aria frowned. "What do you mean?"

He touched the side of her face. "Silly Mama. That's what I prayed for."

"Oh, I see." She tousled his dark hair and pretended to steal his nose. He giggled, as he always did. She relished the sound of his laughter and hoped he would always be so joyous. After pulling the covers up to his neck, she kissed him on the forehead again. "Perhaps you'll get a dog one day, but you must remember that prayer doesn't always work the way you might think it should."

Darius scowled, his perfect little lips pursed. "Why not?"

She thought of her father and all the horrific things he endured, some by her hand. Although he struggled at times with it, his faith in Ɂäṭūr never truly died. Years of darkness would've ruined most people, but he not only survived them but thrived, Theyn and their precious twins evidence of it.

Give me his strength, Ɂäṭūr.

Aria wrinkled her nose, then grinned. "We see but a single piece of the puzzle we call life, but Ɂäṭūr sees it all. Because of this, we sometimes ask for things that aren't always what we need."

Darius groaned. "But I *need* a puppy!"

"Maybe. Maybe not." Aria leaned forward and rested her forehead against his. Her eyes crossed when she looked at him. "Everything I need is right in front of me."

"But what if you turn around?"

"Then it will all be right behind me." She smoothed his hair and moved it away from his face. "Now, go to sleep. We've got a long day ahead of us."

"Okay." He yawned again, then closed his eyes. "Love you, Mama."

"And I love you, my precious boy."

Aria rose, then blew out the candle, casting the room into darkness. She stood there for several minutes with her hand on her chest as she watched Darius struggle to fight off the need for sleep. Life could be no better.

As she moved to slip through the cracked bedroom door, a strange feeling swept through her. Her pulse rose as she struggled to recall when she'd experienced such a feeling before. Weakness crept into her legs as beads of sweat formed on her brow and nape and cascaded the length of her back. She grabbed onto the door and held fast to it, afraid to turn around. Nausea tore at her stomach and clawed its way up into her throat.

Get a hold of yourself, Aria. You have nothing to fear.

"It's okay, Mama. Sometimes, I'm afraid of the dark, too. But there's no need to be."

Aria slowly turned and faced the corner of the room where Darius lay. Her nails dug into the flesh of her palms, and her heart hammered in her chest.

In the darkness, Darius's eyes glowed red. "He's always with me."

She staggered backward and pulled the door shut as she exited the room. The wall behind her pushed the breath from her lungs when she ran into it. Her legs weak, she slid to the floor. Tears welled in her eyes and spilled onto her cheeks.

"Aria?" Chair legs screeched across the kitchen floor. "Is everything okay?"

Aria quickly wiped her face with her sleeve and pulled herself up from the floor just as Wrik came around the corner. Remnants of tears clung to her eyelashes. She tried to blink them away, but he'd already noticed them.

He wrapped his arm around her shoulders and drew her into his arms. "You can tell me anything."

"I know." She clung to Wrik, but her gaze remained on Darius's bedroom door. At some point, Wrik would discover the truth, but for now she fed him a lie. "Sometimes, it's hard to accept all the blessings Ɂäʈūr has bestowed upon me."

"We are both uniquely blessed." He pulled back and gazed down at her. His perfect, white teeth gleamed in the candlelight when he smiled. "Come. There's something I want to show you."

Wrik led her into the kitchen. Three candles burned bright in their holders, lighting the room. Several rolled-up pieces of parchment lay on the wooden table next to an ink bottle and a feather pen.

Aria looked up at him and searched his eyes. "What is all this?"

He gestured toward the parchment. "Just take a look."

She unrolled one of the parchments on the table and held it open with her palms as she leaned over it. At first, she didn't grasp the meaning of the words scrawled on it, but then it hit her. Nearly floored her. "Auh!" She stepped back from the table, and the parchment rolled itself back up. "You've…"

"Written a prophecy?" Wrik grinned. "Indeed."

"You're wearing *ɂäbräɂär*. It shouldn't be possible."

He shrugged. "I may have exaggerated… many of the finer details. It's just a story for the boy."

Wrik clearly didn't understand the context or gravity of his prophecy, false or otherwise, but Aria held no doubts as to its true meaning. She pulled out a chair and sat down. Her hands trembled as she returned to Darius's bedroom within her mind.

My precious boy.

THE END

PLEASE TELL OTHERS WHAT YOU THOUGHT

Thank you for taking this journey with me. If you'd like to show your support for my work, please leave a review wherever you purchased this book. It's free to do so, and it'll only take you a minute to write a quick sentence expressing your thoughts about the book.

Your review is especially important to independent, self-published authors like me. Internet and online bookstore algorithms favor books with reviews. They display in search results and at the top of search results more often than books without reviews.

Did you know that there's a minimum number of reviews needed to purchase certain advertising? It's true. Help me reach that threshold by leaving a review. Doing so will help more people find this book and will in turn help me sell more books, which means I can keep authoring more books for you.

Go to danielkuhnley.com/reviews if you need a link to where you can leave a review.

Thank you!

READ *SCOURGE* FOR FREE

Do Eshtak's tattoos hold the key to the between?

danielkuhnley.com/become-a-conqueror

Sign up and read *Scourge*, A World Of Centauria Novella. Be the **FIRST** to get sneak peeks at my upcoming novels and the chance to win **FREE** stuff, like signed books.

Never use persuasion magic on a powerful wizard.

That was Emorith's hardest lesson to learn. Right from that fateful moment, Magus forced her to use her manipulative sorcery to further his evil purposes. She regretted everything he put her through with one exception: their son Illian. Him, she loved with all her heart.

Magus demanded she cast an apocalyptic curse and destroy an unsuspecting city. She steeled herself to refuse him... but then he threatened the life of her beloved child.

With Illian's life on the line, what choice did she have? She wanted to protect the city and its citizens, but her son would always come first. No, there must be another way. Will she be able to thwart Magus and save them all in time? Or is their fate already sealed?

Scourge is a prequel novella to *The Dragon's Stone*, the first book in *The Dark Heart Chronicles* epic dragon fantasy series. If you like thrilling adventures and terrifying magic, then you'll love Daniel Kuhnley's enthralling tale.

ABOUT THE AUTHOR

Daniel Kuhnley is an American author of Epic Dragon Fantasy, Supernatural Serial Killer, and Christian YA Sci-Fi/Fantasy stories. Some of his novels include *Reborn*, *The Braille Killer*, and *Kiara Kole And The Key Of Truth*. He enjoys watching movies, reading novels, and programming. He lives in Albuquerque, NM with his wife who also writes.

CONNECT WITH DANIEL

danielkuhnley.com/connect

www.ingramcontent.com/pod-product-compliance
Lightning Source LLC
Chambersburg PA
CBHW030656190726
48286CB00001B/41